P

Gini Grossenbacher

M000318015

This year's exciting addition to historical fiction

"Readers were effusive in their praise of Gini Grossenbacher's dynamic debut novel *Madam of My Heart*, based on the life of the infamous brothel owner Belle Cora. This, the prequel to her American Madams Series, is inspired by the life of a beautiful young Chinese woman of high birth brought to California against her will. She was able—and willing—to do whatever it took to find security, love and fortune in Gold Rush San Francisco. *Madam in Silk* is this year's exciting addition to historical fiction."

—Cheryl Anne Stapp, Author of *Disaster & Triumph:*
Sacramento Women, Gold Rush Through the Civil War

Madam of My Heart: For everyone who likes
well-deployed language and intense stories

"A debut historical novel that chronicles the struggles, loves, and joys of an exceptional madam in 19th-century America. Grossenbacher's book, the first in a planned series, dramatizes the early life and busy career of a woman named Brianna Baird. Raised in Baltimore in the decades before the Civil War, Brianna dreams of one day growing up to own a seamstress shop and marry a sweet man of virtue. But her plans unravel after she meets young Spenser Brown, a sweet-talking violinist who leaves her pregnant and betrays the promises he made. Alone and knowing little of the world, she travels to New Orleans and finds work at the notorious parlor house of Madam DeSalle. There, she earns her keep first as a seamstress and later as the exclusive courtesan of gambler Edward Spina.

"Grossenbacher's prose is both graceful and inventive. She absorbingly limns the various cities Brianna inhabits, from New Orleans and its 'web of Creole cottages, chaotic marketplaces, and secretive balconies, simmering outside her window,' to the rowdy atmosphere of frontier-era San Francisco. The occasional marvelous metaphor will surprise readers, as when 'the truth hit Brianna like a badly aimed bowling pin.'

"This isn't just a novel for lovers of history's more prurient corners; it's for everyone who likes well-deployed language and intense stories. A seamier side of American history, engagingly told through one woman's unexpected adventures."

—*Kirkus Reviews, A "Recommended" Book*

Brilliantly written novel of love and loss

"Every now and then you come across a new author who was born to write historical romantic fiction. Her talents include exquisite prose, exceptional historical research, and marvelous storytelling. I was immediately pulled into Brianna Baird's character, her father's alcoholic abuse and her life in Baltimore, Maryland in 1849, and subsequently in New Orleans in early 1850. If you ever wondered what life was like in those historical periods, Gini details every interaction and observation so acutely that the reader lives and breathes the sights, aromas and sounds as if one were peering through a window glass watching the story unfold. Often, I read paragraphs and then went back and re-read them because they were poignant and touching.

"Everything about this novel is excellent: the cover design depicts Brianna so well that you read the story with her visually in your mind; the headings for each chapter carry a caption you find in the story (and look for it). With Brianna's dreams of being a seamstress, you applaud her for making the best of a difficult situation. It accurately reflects society's underbelly, life in a brothel and her eventual salvation at the hand of a gambler she comes to respect as a person she can trust, Edward, who cherishes her and helps free a family from slavery before heading to San Francisco. There are surprises and tension, fear and frustration you don't expect to keep you reading long into the night. I read the last chapters holding my breath!"

—Sherry Joyce, Author of *Dangerous Duplicity* and
The Dordogne Deception

Grabbed my attention on the first page and kept me mesmerized to the end

"The book was mystical story-telling from Page One through the Epilogue. Between 1849 and 1861, I time- traveled from Baltimore, through New Orleans, San Francisco, and a quick moment in Paris. Through the exquisite detail, I experienced the sounds, sights, smells, tastes, and the feel of each scene. I knew how Brianna and Edward looked, and felt, their strengths and weaknesses. It was an enthralling story from beginning to end. Looking forward to Gini Grossenbacher's next book."

—Loy Holder, Author of *Dancing Up the Ladder*

Finely-crafted

"Such a fascinating story, which is made even more intriguing by the fact that the characters are loosely based on a true historical couple who lived in the 1800s. I loved the settings of New Orleans filled with French, Creole and Southern culture with its hints of voodoo, plus bawdy San

Francisco with its saloons, gambling and sporting parlors. It was evident the author did a considerable amount of research to make these settings alive and vital. The writing is finely crafted and the descriptions are worth slowing down to savor. This book kept me turning pages, wondering how the main character, Brianna, and her lover, Edward Spina, would resolve their ongoing situations. The ending is so powerful, it gave me goose bumps.

—Carolyn Radmanovich, Author of *The Shape-Shifter's Wife*

ALSO BY GINI GROSSENBACHER

Madam of My Heart:
A Novel of Love, Loss, and Redemption

MADAM IN SILK

GINI GROSSENBACHER

JGKS
Press
the past comes to life

JGKS Press
the past comes to life
WWW.JKGS PRESS.COM

Madam in Silk is a work of historical fiction. All incidents and dialogue, and all characters, with the exception of some well-known historical figures, are products of the author's imagination and are not to be construed as real. Where real-life historical persons appear, the situations, incidents, and dialogues concerning those persons are entirely fictional and are not intended to depict actual events or to change the entirely fictional nature of the work. In all other respects, any resemblance to persons living or dead is entirely coincidental.

Cover design by Clarissa Yeo at Yocla Designs
Book design by Maureen Cutajar at Go Published

**Publisher's Cataloging-in-Publication Data
Provided by Five Rainbows Cataloging Services**

Names: Grossenbacher, Gini, author.
Title: Madam in silk : a novel / Gini Grossenbacher.
Description: Elk Grove, CA : JGKS Press, 2019.
Identifiers: LCCN 2019907332 | ISBN 978-0-9983806-5-0 (paperback) | ISBN 978-0-9983806-6-7 (epub ebook) | ISBN 978-0-9983806-7-4 (mobi ebook) | ISBN 978-0-9983806-8-1 (PDF) | ISBN 978-0-9983806-9-8 (RTF ebook)
Subjects: LCSH: Brothels--Fiction. | Chinese--United States--Fiction. | Immigrants--United States--Fiction. | San Francisco (Calif.)--History--19th century--Fiction. | Historical fiction, American. | Romance fiction. | BISAC: FICTION / Historical. | FICTION / Romance / Historical / American. | FICTION / Romance / Multicultural & Interracial. | GSAFD: Historical fiction. | Love stories.
Classification: LCC PS3607.R66 M32 2019 (print) | LCC PS3607.R66 (ebook) | DDC 813/.6--dc23..

To Karl.
His unflagging devotion and wonderful meal preparation ensured this book would see the light of day.

To my grandson Marco.
I pray he will grow up in a world where truth, justice and dignity exist for all people, no matter their race or national origin.

DRAMATIS PERSONAE
(NOT IN ORDER OF APPEARANCE)

Captain *The Eagle*
Captain & First Mate *The Oregon*
Captain *The Surprise*
Doctor *The Oregon*
Judge Almond Judge, Recorder's Court, San Francisco
Sam Brannan California's first millionaire, first president, San Francisco Committee of Vigilance
Tung Chee Ah Toy's husband, dies on ship to San Francisco
Tung Chao Ah Toy's brother-in-law, wishes to marry Ah Toy
Chen Ah Toy's servant and bodyguard
John Clark San Francisco policeman, befriends Ah Toy
Susannah Clark John Clark's wife
William Coleman Businessman, leading figure, San Francisco's Committee of Vigilance
Henry Conrad Importer-Exporter, friend of Larkins and Daileys
Reverend Dailey American missionary, befriends Ah Toy
Elizabeth Dailey Missionary's wife, teaches English to Ah Toy
Li Fan Rival madam in Little Canton
Flannery Irish wagon driver, owns Swinney the mule
Freddie & James Dailey children
Hortencia The Daileys' Californio maid
Jade Ah Toy's cat, Little Canton
Lee Shau Kee Tung Chao's agent and emissary
Kuang Runs opium parlor, Little Canton
Thomas Larkin American merchant and diplomat
Rachel Larkin Thomas Larkin's wife
Lee Lai San (called San) Prostitute
Joe Ludding Illustrator, Alta California newspaper
Toy Lee Lung Ah Toy's brother, Guangdong
Wong Sau Man (Man-Man) Prostitute
Harold Painter Detective, San Francisco Police Department
Harold Snow Reporter, *Alta California* newspaper
Mr. Tom Owner, vegetable market, Little Canton
Ah Toy First Cantonese woman, San Francisco
Officer Wong Official, Kong Chow Company, Little Canton
Ma Ka Yee (called Yee) Prostitute

Part One

ACROSS THE BLUE HORIZON

See those containers painted gold?
White porcelain plates costing more than my life
I throw the chopsticks overboard
Yesterday's food and wine have no taste
I must unsheathe my magic sword
Prepare for the battle to come

Minds confused stare around me
See the ice floes blocking the eastern way?
Will I ever feel the snowfall again in the T'ai-hang Mountain?
Quiet I look into the dark Pacific waters
I fear our fragile boat might drift off-course
So many side-tracks between us and land
Wave after wave and, where am I?
New breezes fill our sails
Across the Blue Horizon

IN THE MANNER OF LI PO

One

❦ OVERBOARD ❧

San Francisco
U.S. Military Territory
February 1849

*A*h Toy's husband Tung Chee told perfect lies, but for once he told a perfect truth. San Francisco Bay was a canvas of wondrous blue sky, mirroring placid water that lay like a sheet of glass. As soon as the brig *Eagle* entered the massive inlet, Ah headed to starboard, her lotus shoes pinching her bound feet. She grasped the railing as the trading ship rolled toward the dock, avoiding ships at anchor.

The *Eagle's* timbers creaked as sailors scrambled up and down ratlines, pulled down flapping sails, and fed rope out to the longshoremen who waited, their arms outstretched. The pungent aroma of rotting fish stung her eyes. Her mystical inner dragon awoke, its nostrils flared, its eyes wide.

For a moment she pictured Tung Chee's body, gray and still. Only a week under sail and consumption claimed the angry man. Gone was his nest of perfect lies about San Francisco: the weather would cure his coughs; they would escape his grasping brother Tung Chao, they would start their business anew and grow rich. When she objected, he back-handed her, leaving her cheek raw and sore. Even now, three weeks later, she saw the sailors tighten the canvas shroud around his body, and heard the few words of the Captain. "May God rest his soul."

She had stood next to Chen on the *Eagle's* weather deck, the wild winds whipping around them. The black water of the deep Pacific opened its jaws to receive the plunging body disappearing under the waves. The Captain asked, "Do you wish to say a prayer, Mrs. Toy?" She shook her head. She had no sensation of grief then, nor now. Maybe she was numb—maybe she was relieved. So many times in Guangdong, called Canton by the British, she had wished him dead.

But now behind her the blue waters churned in the Bay, swells that pushed back through the Golden Gate straits. Out beyond, the Pacific Ocean expanded endlessly until it stopped, China standing in its way. Had she really crossed the largest body of water on earth? She swallowed hard, her inner butterflies rising and falling with each breath. *Thank you, Goddess Mazu, patron of the seas. You delivered me and Chen safely to shore.*

Erratic shouts in different languages from sailors and brown-skinned dock workers rang up and down the wharf. Ah watched horses draw away stacks of crates in open wagons. Some drivers arrived with empty drays, waiting to load barrels of porcelain, silks, and dry goods. Symbols for fish, tea, and rice marked crates on the dock. Men loaded heavy equipment onto other large drays.

Guangzhou's wharf sounds were a mere hum compared to the bustle of this place. San Franciscans must be building houses, churches, and businesses. People who lived here would be hungry; people would want fine clothing and furniture for new homes.

Round-eyed men moved everywhere; many workers were tanned like the shoes people wore in Hong Kong. Where were the women? In Guangdong one would see them padding about in their bright *qipao*, children dancing by their side. Here? Maybe men kept them kept indoors like dolls. She sucked in a breath. Women of the rich, the wealthy, the highborn.

The Captain joined her for a moment, puffing on a ball clay pipe.

She looked up at his full beard and even brown teeth. "You told us to watch the bustle at Long Wharf, but I had not expected this." She pointed at two wagons colliding on the dock.

He let the smoke stream out of his mouth. "My shipping company says the first loads of American miners are on their way to the gold mines. The city is preparing to house them." He pointed over at the next wharf. "Look there."

Following his direction, she saw *The California*, a US mail ship. "What is going on there? Who are all those men and where are they headed?"

The Captain ran his pipe stem lazily across his lower lip. "My company says *The California* carried dozens of prospectors who boarded her at Panama City—east coast men crossing the Isthmus to save time."

The California's passengers and crew scuttled off the ship as fast as ants toward a sugar mound. Around her, in what the Captain called Yerba Buena Cove, the harbor filled up with deserted ships left on the tidal flats. She said, "How can they leave their valuable ships? Aren't they worried someone will steal them?"

The Captain puffed a breath. "I think not, Mrs. Toy. My purser says the treasure they seek lies in California's golden hills. They will be richer than Midas, according to reports."

She waved her fan, clearing the pipe smoke between them. "You are not joining them?"

"If you know the story of Midas, you understand why I do not abandon my ship."

"No, I did not learn about your Midas in Guangdong. Mrs. Dailey taught me the Bible."

He puffed thoughtfully. "According to the Greek legend, King Midas quested after gold. No matter the amount, he was never satisfied."

"So, he wanted more and more?"

The Captain nodded. "In the end, he was overcome with his obsession. He died of starvation."

She cringed. "I saw people starving to death in Guangdong."

He lifted his pipe stem and pointed it at it *The California.* "Watch and wait, Mrs. Toy. Gold will do funny things to these men." He glanced toward the foredeck. "But now, I must leave you and wish you godspeed. We are soon to disembark." He strode away toward the sailors awaiting further orders.

Smack! The gangplank hit its mark, and dust rose on the dock. Scruffy, ill-shaven men in an array of brown coats and hats waited there. They stepped back, greeting the passengers leaving the gangplank. "Smith! Over here!" Some men in top hats and frock coats pressed others out of the way and pushed ahead down the line. "O'Leary! Your driver is waiting!" They tugged their friends off the ship, clapping them on the back; they waved down a trio of Cantonese merchants in silk jackets whom they piled into a waiting wagon.

Ah shambled over to portside and scanned the Bay. Brown hills lay to the north side, dotted with trees. A curl of white smoke spiraled up from what might have been a campfire. Clusters of gray fog draped over the tops of hills and rested there as if someone had flung coats over the backs of chairs.

She glanced over her shoulder. What happened to Chen? He had been below decks as they entered the straits of the Golden Gate. A heaviness drew her into the ship's white planking. What would she do all alone? This new land would be unbearable. Besides, he had her suitcase.

She headed toward the passenger line amidst other people shuffling down the gangway. The minister and his family surrounded her. The tall Reverend Dailey and his thin wife Elizabeth, along with their boys Freddie and James, came all the way with her from Guangdong.

Elizabeth drew near. "The boys are wondering about that set of flags." They pointed at tall buildings with signal flags that sat atop a hill facing the shore. "I do not know what they represent," she said, then returned to the view. Such a strange intimacy about this bay, like the Zhujiang, what the British called the Pearl River Delta in Guangzhou. The same dotted islands.

Little five-year-old Freddie broke into her thoughts. "What do the flags say, Mrs. Toy?"

Ah peered down into his brown eyes. "I am not sure, but I think flags tell the ships what to do. Like the flags on the *Eagle*. See?" She pointed up at the red, white and blue flag hoisted on the mast.

"What does that flag say?" James wedged in between Ah and Freddie.

"America." Her word traveled upward in the air.

The children's voices echoed her own excitement, but soon the Daileys would go to Monterey. If only they did not have to go. Elizabeth taught her English grammar and pronunciation since she was ten years old—English was the language of America. But the whole family spoke Cantonese, since they spent the last ten years at their Baptist mission in the river city of Guangzhou.

Ah turned to Elizabeth. "Have you seen Chen?" His name conjured pictures—his queue, a long braid winding down his back; his black jacket resting neatly on his broad shoulders.

Elizabeth's eyes narrowed. The orange feather on her bonnet swayed in the breeze. "Maybe he is gathering all your bags. He should join us soon."

Reverend Dailey patted her arm. "Our driver is leaving now. The ship's purser arranged a local man to take us south." He tipped his hat. "We hope to see both you and Chen again soon, Mrs.—er—Toy. Will you still be going by 'Mrs.' now, even though you are a widow?"

"Certainly." Ah absorbed the stark realization that she was no longer married. Goose bumps rose under her thin silk cloak. "Is it always this cold in California? I miss the warm breeze that followed our ship from Hong Kong."

"You are forgetting." Elizabeth continued in a soft tone. "We are from Boston, so the weather in San Francisco is new to us, too. We hope it will be warmer in Monterey, where we are headed to the Reverend's new mission church." "Yes, of course." A sharp needle of loss dug into Ah's chest. Elizabeth allowed Ah to master English alongside her brother at the mission school in Guangzhou, even though girls were not usually taught there. In China girls were never allowed to learn English, let alone in a school with boys. What would she do without her teacher in this town of so many men?

Elizabeth pressed a paper into Ah's hands. "Our address in Monterey. We will send for you to come for a visit. After you are settled here, of course." Her voice radiated a familiar warmth. She had never abandoned Ah, even during her most desperate moments.

"I will miss you," Ah whispered. She brought a shaky hand to her forehead.

"As soon as I arrive, I will write you." Elizabeth's arm encircled her shoulders.

Ah mumbled into Elizabeth's cloak. "Do not forget to send the word sheets you always make for me. I like to practice my English vocabulary."

Elizabeth's hand tapped hers. "You are fluent in English now like a proper Bostonian. Any further study will be refinement. But do not forget to look up words you do not know. Remember the Cantonese-English dictionary I gave you." Elizabeth squeezed her shoulders, then took long steps to rejoin her family.

"Thank you, dear friend." Ah waved as Elizabeth rejoined her husband.

The Daileys made their way down the plank, the boys scampering ahead, then waiting down below with upturned faces. Ah grinned at them, yet a niggling thought persisted. The last page of this book was now read, so it was time for her to close the volume and submit it to memory. *What would happen to her now?*

Two

◆ MR. BROWN ◆

After the Daileys vanished down the wharf, Ah could wait for Chen no longer. Where was he? She took a series of tiny steps down the plank. "Curses!" Her toes curled under in an inconvenient distortion, her lotus feet a Chinese emblem of nobility and bondage.

Since the lotus came as an honor during childhood, she had known no difference. Though she could usually take small, quick steps on flat surfaces, the uneven surface of the deck posed a challenge. She stifled a rough sob. Would she ever get used to this?

Long ago, her parents said that marriage, wealth, and dignity were her future. She shook her head. Now at twenty, she looked back at that childhood fable. Sure, there had been a fancy wedding to Tung Chee; sure, there had been wealth, but never dignity. Meanwhile, she held on to the side ropes of the gangway, pitching forward, then back as she made her way down to the wharf.

Chen's familiar iron grip caught her wrist. Though a wave of relief washed over her, she poured out her Cantonese words against the wind.

"Where have you been? I thought you had fallen overboard. You missed the Daileys' departure." The refracted light from the water glistened on his striking feataures.

His smooth skin pulled taut over the elegant ridge of his cheekbones. "I have been ill, *si tau po,* my mistress. The waves entering the bay spun my stomach around like the moon. I did not want you to see me that way—especially after Tung Chee's passing." Drops of sweat clung to his forehead. He spoke Cantonese with a Mandarin accent, having been raised north in Beijing.

"I see." She stepped forward onto the dock, Chen's arm at her elbow. "And—" she put a dragon's energy into her words "—you scared me. Don't do that again or I will gnaw your eyebrows." She cast an eye over their luggage at his feet. "Good—you have brought Tung Chee's suitcase."

"What will you do with his things?"

"Save them for now. They are of the finest quality."

"Very well." He offered her a bemused grin. "I-I am sorry to have frightened you; I beg forgiveness."

She could never stay mad at him for long. "I must know where you are at all times." Her tone softened. "We are alone, you see, without Tung Chee, and—"

A white man wearing shabby light blue pants and a careworn grey military jacket shuffled toward them, all the while doffing his greasy-looking low-billed cap. A badge clung for life on his left lapel.

"Who is that?" Chen's expressive face turned somber.

The stranger's voice rang out. "Mrs. Toy!" The breeze ruffled the shafts of gray hair rising from his head.

"I am." Her feet throbbed. After the uneven plank walk, her ankles radiated shooting pains. Besides, a chill wind whipped her sleeves.

"Good." A full salt-and-pepper beard covered his mouth and his blue eyes crinkled.

She pointed at his jacket." Are you in the army?"

He raised a hand to his forehead in a sharp salute. "Dragoon in the Mexican War. In '46 I served alongside General Kearny at Santa Fe." He shook his head, a faraway look in his eyes. "Lost too many men from New York where I come from."

Stopped by his word "dragoon," she wondered. That was a word worth looking up in Elizabeth's dictionary. She stole a look at him. How did he manage to eat underneath all that fur? All sorts of scabs and ticks sprang to mind. Besides that, he carried the foul stench of rough living. She He held his cap against the top roll of his stomach. "You are the first Celestial woman to arrive in San Francisco." His eyes followed the arc of her fan as it fluttered back and forth.

"Oh—. No other Chinese women?" She waved the realization aside, like brushing yellow paint on a scroll of chrysanthemums.

He leaned down to her and extended a hand which she did not shake. "Name's Harold Painter, part time with San Francisco Police Department, part time with the Thompson Agency. Exchanged letters with you and your husband in Canton."

She aimed the tip of her fan. "My servant, Chen."

He exchanged nods with Chen and moved back a step. "Uh, your husband?"

"Died—buried at sea." She steadied her gaze on his wide-eyed expression.

"Please accept my deepest sympathies. But you traveled the rest of the way alone with your servant?"

She nodded. "We had other companions aboard ship."

"Your people have strange customs." He scratched his ear. "On these shores, we do not let our womenfolk travel with men, unless they have a chaperone. But then—of course—I am sorry for your loss." Awe tinged his voice. "Sure didn't think you could speak English—guess I forgot about the British in Canton."

Ignoring his comment, she set her hand on her waist. "What about positions you promised me and my husband in the business of a rich man named Sylvester Brown? My husband was to build a porcelain factory here in San Francisco with this man, and I was to help with Chinese translations. Though my husband is no longer with us, I would like to work in that capacity for Mr. Brown."

"Of course. Your English is well—very good." He rubbed the back of his hand against his mouth.

Now was the time for him to take her suitcase, her arm, and help her and Chen to awaiting transport. If not a rickshaw, at least a wagon. Why was he hesitating?

His jaw muscle quivered. "I hate to tote this news, Mrs. Toy, Mr. Chen, after your sea journey and all, but—"

She broke in. "I have many bags to carry. Do you not have a donkey? A wagon?" She drew open a pouch dangling from the belt on her waist, and lifted out a Hong Kong silver coin.

"Well, yes—but there is a problem." Painter glanced at the money.

Her dragon's warning whispered in her head, but she ignored it, holding out the coin. "Here. Take me to Mr. Brown."

"Keep your money." His beard shifted and his focus strayed away toward the Bay.

"What?" She took a moment. Maybe Mr. Brown's house was burning down, or he was sick with plague, or his children were threatening to kill him. Something terrible must be wrong. She placed a hand on Chen's arm—his muscles were flexed and taut.

Painter shook his head. "Brown, the man I told you about—well, he lost everything, gambled away at faro. Wouldn't listen to anyone. Not even his wife. Lost her, too. She up and left him. Sailed back to New Orleans to her parents."

Her former sympathy drained into the bay. "Where is Mr. Brown?" She dropped the coin back into her pouch; if he did not want the money, she could use it. She had several more secreted from her husband before they left Guangzhou for Hong Kong that night, but who knew how fast she would spend it in this new land? Tung Chee never let her handle money; with his death, the family's wealth would be managed by his brother, Tung Chao.

Painter shrugged. "Dead. Found out at Washerwoman's Lagoon last week. Musta got into a bad fix. Throat slit. Brigands or gamblers probably trying to collect their dues off him. Nobody knows for sure."

"What about other jobs? My husband died. I want to work." Emptiness hollowed the pit of her stomach. "I can translate from Chinese to English."

"I could not interest anyone else." He crossed his arms.

"Why not?"

He raked his fingers through his beard. "Your letter said you had bad feet and were limited in walking. I can see for myself you are not fit for strong labor. A servant has to walk miles toting baskets of heavy items."

"I have never been a servant." She eyed her lotus shoes. Curses. If only she had unbound feet like Manchurian women.

Painter leaned closer. "Now—your partner Chen here—might be able to get him a laboring job up in the gold hills. Word is Celestials are working in mines there. 'Course I would have to separate you." He gave her a hard smile, the dry skin cracking on his lips.

She heard the quick intake of Chen's breath. "No—we stay together," he said.

After she swallowed what seemed like a rock, she found her voice. "If you knew this, Mr. Painter, why did you not contact us in Guangdong?" If only her dragon would reach out its fangs to bite him.

"I tried, but even when I sent your husband the letter, I knew you would not receive it by the time you sailed. News came too late." He twisted the brim of his cap.

"Now what do I do?" Those dragon fangs would tear off that hair on his face. Then she would feed it to the chickens.

He reached into his inner coat pocket, drew out an envelope, and held it out to her. "Here is money to get by for a month. Lodging, room and board."

"Only a month?" She took the envelope, her hands trembling.

Painter's patient tone grew curt. "I got you a room in Little Canton until you can get another ship's passage home. You better leave on the next sail. Believe me, without a job you are a gone circumstance amidst all these varmints."

"What are varmints?" she asked.

He tapped the badge clinging to his lapel. "Men with no good intent. You'll see men who call themselves Hounds from New York who parade around town with fife and drum. Stay away from that lot. They prey on immigrants, such as your fellow Celestials and Mexicans.

Then there's men called Sydney Ducks. Prison mates from Australia. These gangs are flooding our city, carrying their thieving, arsonist ways direct from down under. They pick on unsuspecting folks like you. Especially because, well, you are—different."

She took a half-step toward him. "I am strong. Willing to work." Maybe if she said the words, they would come true. Was her dragon listening?

He gave a nervous laugh. "Mind my words, Mrs. Toy. This town ain't no quilting bee. You are so fragile, dainty. You cannot mind for yourself. Why, look at your tiny hands, your feet." He stepped back, his gaze flickering over her. "Such a fine figure." He flattened his right palm over his heart.

"Why should I believe your story?" She bit her lip so it would not quiver.

He blew out a noisy breath "Why? 'Cause there is a miserable few women here—mostly none. Not only the Ducks and Hounds will give you suspicion. Add to them all sorts of dusty miners up to tarnation. They come to the city from the gold hills to get a drink, a bath and a snatch. God's truth." His held his mouth in a tight, grim line.

She gave a sigh and spoke her undeniable truth. "I cannot go home to China."

"Why ever not? No family there?" He cocked his head.

15

"Not anymore." The words burned her throat. "My daughters are dead, my mother and father's bones lie crumbling in our family plot, and my husband is food for the sea turtles."

"Darn shame," Painter said. "Would hate to see the end of you here." He whistled out to the road across from the pier, and a red-haired driver and a mule wagon carrying whiskey crates drew up alongside him. "Flannery, can you give these folks here a ride to the usual boarding house?"

Flannery nodded, then Painter eased her into the wagon and placed her baggage next to her on the seat next to a crate labeled "whiskey." A whiff of alcohol rose from the bottles and she blinked.

Chen settled next to her, holding his baggage on his lap. Was that a determined look crossing his face, same as that second-to-last evening in Guangzhou?

The night before their escape, Mrs. Dailey advised the three of them about their trip to California, and she had flashed the three extra tickets, then told them it the ship would sail the next night and they must leave by midnight. Tung Chee had kept the San Francisco voyage a secret from his grasping brother, Tung Chao. He wanted to separate the businesses and start fresh in California. She had no choice but to follow her husband. But now she was here, what was to become of her—and Chen?

Painter reached up and palmed her arm. "Now, Mrs. Toy, best be on your way to your rooms near Little Canton. Then get you both to the harbormaster tomorrow and book your passage back home. Do as I say, y'hear?"

Ah withdrew her arm very slowly from his grasp. "I shall consider your advice." Though she spoke those words, she knew better. She would make a life here or die trying.

Flannery clucked to the mule, "Swinney, let's go!" The mule nickered, Flannery slapped the reins, and the wagon rolled away from the wharf, bumping across the uneven pilings.

After she watched Painter saunter away down the docks, she shifted in her seat, then turned to survey the wharf. Sailors, shipwrights, and boatmen scurried past, headed toward the docks on her right and left. Where were the women? Her question floated in the salty breeze..

All passengers now departed, the *Eagle's* crew were coiling the ropes and swabbing the decks. Further down the wharf, something large and round rolled out of a crate as a laborer in overalls hoisted it aboard a cargo vessel. A melon gained momentum, then dropped with a splash into the bay.

Three

❧ RIPPLES ❧

March 1849

One morning Ah looked up from the accounts at her writing desk in her shanty on Pike Street, and fingered the closed fan resting on her lap. She placed it next to a seagull feather on the desk. For the first time in awhile, she gave a catlike stretch. After wetting her lips, she remembered. A month had passed since their arrival in San Francisco.

For some reason, their money slipped through their fingers like sand, and they could no longer pay for the boarding house. Some days they faced near-starvation, and some nights they slept curled under canvas sails at the wharf. But—to her credit—Ah listened carefully to Chen and all the voices around her. Her dragon had given her counsel.

She lifted her fan and ran it back and forth across her lips Funny that she could not seem to shake these scarring memories. Back then, as soon as white shipowners saw her small stature and bound feet, they shook their heads and doors closed against her. Word about her got around. Who would hire the little Celestial lady who walked funny? Yet their doors would open wide when she had money to spend.

During those tearful days, she acknowledged Painter's truth—no one wanted a little woman who could not carry heavy laundry baskets for washing in Yerba Buena Cove. But through all the rejection, Chen stayed by her side.

Then, after hearing a group of sailors talking about their favorite parlor where girls posed or paraded naked before them, she had the idea of starting her own Lookee Shop. Pooling her remaining coins, she rented a ramshackle shanty for her and Chen on Pike Street which led from Washington to Sacramento Street. Situated between the busy Dupont and Stockton thoroughfares, the shanty soon became home.

At the time, Pike Street was home to a rickety collection of shacks, shanties, and two-story buildings, all thrown up in haste. Considered an alley, it was a one lane street, narrower than the grander DuPont Street which accommodated two wagons passing at once.

Their one-story place stood cheek-by-jowl with other decrepit structures and consisted of only two rooms. One held the kitchen, the other featured an open room with space for her well-loved belongings: a Buddhist altar, her statue of Goddess Mazu, her high chair, two long scrolls, and a screen borrowed from a Cantonese merchant on DuPont Street.

She and Chen found a cast-off table on the wharf, and Flannery, the wagon-driver, agreed to help them lug it to the shanty, along with four chairs. Another small table served as her business desk. For the most part, she and Chen slept on pallets spread out in the open room, glad to warm themselves by the fire at night.

At the mercantile, she exchanged a pair of apple-green jade earrings for lanterns, kitchen supplies, pots and pans, and simple chinaware. Since the shanty already had a small Ben Franklin stove with a pipe through the roof, she stood back satisfied. At least they would be warm;

the bay breezes penetrated her skin. On the other hand, on warm days she was glad to prop open the mullioned window facing Pike Street, letting in fresh air and sunshine into the otherwise shadowy chamber.

Each day she noticed more Chinese men on the streets. In Little Canton, story said over landers were on their way from Missouri, but already, in the fall of 1848, several hundred Americans had come from Oregon, a whole caravan led south by Peter Burnett

The news sheets mentioned that those residents who rushed off to Coloma last May for gold had returned to town, realizing they could get rich quicker by becoming merchants and saloon owners

She and Chen saw a dozen other services pop up: hostlers, livery keepers, and more mercantile. The new miners who came by sea needed food, equipment, clothing and mules.

Story said that mining camps were sprouting up all over the place—hundreds of them along distant inland streams and ravines—from far in the northern realms of California and across the now-famous Mother Lode that stretched 120 miles through the Sierra Nevada.

Streets filled with young men returning to San Francisco where they sought women, refreshment, and repose, usually in that order.

She and Chen did very little advertising: once word of mouth got around the wharf, men began to line up on Pike Street in front of the Lookee Shop, word spreading of the gorgeous Chinese beauty within.

Some men would visit her once, then go back to the end of the line to see her one more time before heading to the gold hills. She became a sensation. In no time at all, her coffers lined with gold dust and nuggets. Bankers opened their hands to her, and men tipped their hats as she took tiny, swaying steps with Chen on the streets.

Footsteps broke into her waking dreams. Chen's shadow darkened the open doorway to the shanty, an envelope clutched in his hand. From outside, men's shouts echoed from over at the gambling den down on Clay Street. Their racket mixed with cries of vegetable vendors and fortunetellers hawking their wares to the unsuspecting miners who customarily gathered outside Ah's Lookee Shop.

Sailors and miners assembled in noisy clumps, awaiting their turn to view the wondrous, naked Ah Toy. Chen made sure they knew her policy: watch, do not touch.

"Chen. Come in." After closing the ledger and putting down her fan, Ah gave him a sideways glance. She had always admired his tall and muscular physique, having watched him grow up by her side. When she turned thirteen, her father had given her a boy-servant as a gift. A eunuch from Beijing, Chen was one of many youths who did not pass the test for servant to the Emperor. Though subservient, he had become closer to her than Toy Lee Lung, her brother, who was three years older than she.

Chen learned Cantonese quickly, and she taught him from the English books Mrs. Dailey gave her when she first started learning the language. Last year he came away with her in haste from China, and she was in his debt. Though they each spoke English well, Cantonese became their sacred language when they were away from Little Canton. This allowed them a secret communication among the many round-eyed faces in San Francisco.

Last week Chen's powerful hands squeezed a man's throat in order to ward him off her premises. The ruffian came back with a cudgel and pounded out some of the boards lining the front of her shanty. Without Chen she would not have been able to put up rice paper to block the wind, then nail new siding onto the house. And every day he would arrange the men in straight rows as they waited for a glimpse of her.

Chen bent over her and his long queue, or pigtail, dangled over his shoulder. He passed her the small brown envelope. His gaze lingered on the red Chinese stamp for moment, and Ah held the envelope near the candle and read the postmark "Guangdong."

She said, "My personal business, Chen. Remember our talk—you know nothing. Better that way."

His crescent eyes glimmered like burning embers. "I only wish your welfare." He started to back away, but she held out her hand. "Please stay. These letters make me tired."

She grabbed a small knife and ran it under the lip of the envelope. Her brother-in-law Tung Chao's calligraphy was much like her deceased husband's script, but some of the brushstrokes were formed differently. How many letters had he sent since she left Guangdong? She had lost count, though the pile in her drawer was growing larger.

A bitter loneliness dug its claws into her chest. After unfolding the paper, she scanned the columns of Cantonese script, reading from top to bottom, right to left.

Ah,

It is time you stopped this ridiculous charade. As your brother-in-law, I order you to come home. By staying in San Francisco, you are being disloyal to your family. I wish to take you as my wife and produce the male heirs my brother never did. My mother says the house is not the same without you, and she favors our marriage.

A good Chinese woman returns to serve her husband's family. You must come back now. The journey is long. They tell me it is several weeks by ship. I am contacting the Kong Chow Company, and I will send my emissary to bring you home from San Francisco.

Your faithful brother-in-law,
Tung Chao

"Pah!" she spat, saliva blurring the inscriptions on the paper. "Tung Chao? My faithful brother-in-law? A marvelous charade? He should know." She clutched the paper. "So much like my husband, Tung Chee.

What lies he tells, yet his eyes are clear, his voice sincere. Stripes on my back still hurt from Tung Chee's whipping all those years. Like bad burns. I cannot sleep on my back anymore. And his brother is worse. One time I saw Tung Chao beat a donkey to death on the docks near the factories."

She cast a fevered glanced at Chen.

He said, "Many were the nights I put herbal compresses on your back to soothe your sores, si tau po." His voice broke.

She pressed her index fingers against the bridge of her nose. She would not cry. "Tung Chao does not wish to lose face with his employees, with his business partners, with his family. Tung Chee prided himself on having me, the subservient wife. Now Tung Chao wants to carry on the tradition. Selfish imposter. His mother misses me. Ridiculous!" Her pulse quickened. "The woman only wants me to wait on her and massage her feet."

"But Tung Chao will send Lee Shau Kee to bring you back?" Chen asked.

"That is what he says. But what kind of a threat is Lee Shau Kee?" She ran her fingers over the water-smeared calligraphy on the page. "I remember that boy growing up in Guangzhou. He must be the same age as you."

"I well remember," Chen said. "His father was in the porcelain trade, and Lee Shau Kee was a courier between the artisans who made the famous Guang Cai pottery and the merchants at the port of Guangzhou. I used to think he was full of himself, strutting around."

"I always thought his relationship with my husband was a bit suspicious. It was in working for his father that Lee Shau Kee got to know the Toy family's large factory which packed and shipped pottery on the ships to distant shores." She stuffed the letter back in the envelope.

"Suspicious? That well may be. Lee Shau Kee was bright, but a bit too devilish for his own good, finding it easier to sluff off and lie about it than go ahead and do the assigned work."

Ah clucked her tongue. "But he was not all bad. Lee Shau Kee loved his little sister Lily and would fawn over her endlessly. At times she would come for dinner at the house. She was only eight years old, and he treated her like a little doll."

Chen's eyes narrowed. "There was something twisted in him, though. He told many lies. One could never be sure."

"I kind of feel sorry for him, especially now if Tung Chao has taken advantage of his loyalty."

"Do you think that Lee Shau Kee and Tung Chao could have some kind of—you know—underhanded relationship?"

"I saw my husband and his brother with all kinds . . . it is possible."

"Anything more, si tau po?" Chen's eyebrows drew together.

Ah said, "I must think on this news."

Chen backed out of the shanty and closed the door behind him. He would be filling in his customary post outside on the front step facing Pike Street.

Should she destroy the letter or keep it? She extracted the letter from the envelope. Holding the envelope over the candle flame, she watched it curl, turning from yellow to red to black.

She gathered the ashes in a teacup and tossed them onto her fireplace hearth, much as Tung Chee used to throw hot water in her face when she disagreed with him. The letter she would keep, along with the rest Tung Chao had sent before this. So, she folded the letter and put it next to the bags of gold dust in her drawer.

After that moment's turmoil had passed, Ah breathed in, stood up straight, and balanced on her lotus shoes. She had work to do. Grabbing a white chrysanthemum from the vase on her desk, she tucked it behind her ear.

She peeked out the window in the wall; Chen stood guard at the door. Many clipper ships were in port today, and sailors were home from the sea.

The crowd outside their shanty was large —maybe twenty. Men of all heights milled about, picked their teeth, and looked uncomfortable in city shoes. A recent rain muddied the alley, but the men did not seem to care.

She opened the door and stepped around Chen into the narrow alleyway, only eighteen feet across. On each side, the street was lined with wooden shanties, some double-storied with a balcony above. Other houses were mere one-story lean-to's, thrown together after the latest fire. At the sight of her, the crowd sent up a cheer.

Chen side-stepped beside her, braving the muddy street. He formed the men into a line that snaked down the road.

One man with long brown hair stared at her. "Such a beauty! I dream of her naked body."

Another blew out a puff of cigar smoke and cheered, "I thought of her all night."

Chen held her arm as Ah picked her way up and down the line, holding up her pantaloons so they would not be soiled from the mud. She surveyed the men, gesturing here and there with a feathered fan.

Only kind faces could be with her. Better yet, no face with a bush. A face must be clean, clear-eyed, without drink or opium.

She chose five from the line of thirty, then Chen ordered the others to go away.

Those five men were subject to her closer inspection—she sniffed their breath, examined their teeth, and studied the expressions on their leather-tanned faces.

The first jaunty lad had jet black eyes. Though he was clean shaven, she sent him away. A youth with jet black eyes like those had stolen a Chinese vase from her last month.

The second was an older man, maybe a dock worker with big muscles bulging through his shirt. Muscular men could hold a woman against her will—that had happened last year, and Chen had to summon the policeman who clubbed the man off her, leaving her broken and sobbing.

"Take him away!" she ordered.

Chen hustled the man away down the block, ignoring his threats.

The third man was of medium build, clean-shaven, blond with star-tling blue eyes. He tipped the brim of his tan hat. His teeth were white and even, and to her astonishment, he had all of them.

She waved at him to stand aside for consideration.

She examined the fourth and fifth men together like yin and yang. One was short, the other tall. One held out a hand, clutching a bag of gold dust. The other looked up at Chen, pressing his lips together. Innocent enough. Perhaps they could come in later.

She looked back at the white even teeth of the clean-shaven, blond man. He pleased her in a way none of the others did. "This one," she said.

Chen gestured the blond man inside the shanty, told some to wait, and moved others down the alley in the direction of Portsmouth Plaza

She went back inside the shanty. After Chen followed in accompanied by the man with the white teeth. After Chen and closed the shanty door, she led the man to her desk. A strong smell of tobacco lingered in the air around him.

She opened her ledger while he pulled out his bag of gold dust from a jacket pocket. She held up her palm towards him. Your name?" She picked up her pencil.

After removing his squash hat, the man flushed. "John Clark, but most folks just call me Clark."

"Fine," she said. She wrote his name down in English lettering on the ledger page, then held it up. "Did I spell it correctly?"

"Yes." His tone was solemn. On the other side of the desk, the plink of gold filings dropped from Clark's bag onto Chen's scales.

Chen stood adjusting the weights, his eyes mere arrow slits as he measured the troy ounces of the gold's weight. Clark's bag of gold rested on the table.

She glanced at Chen. "I can take care of this payment."

"Would you like me to stay?" Chen's thin brows rose high above his eyes.

"No. See to the door outside. The line continues to grow."

"Yes, si tau po." He cast a stern look toward Clark.

After returning Clark's bag to him, she pointed. "You sit over there." Clark complied, settling on a small, rickety chair. Looking up, she double-checked Chen's presence at the open door. She threw a log on the Ben Franklin stove to warm the quarters.

With soft steps, she slipped behind a curtained divider and removed her clothing. She hung her silk jacket and pants, called *qipao*, on carefully placed hooks. Her fine red and white silks were easily damaged by saltwater or grease. She touched the white chrysanthemum behind her ear, then adjusted it. She breathed deeply to center her next steps.

With light tread, her lotus feet whispered on the pine boards. Naked as a babe, she sat before the man, all the while keeping an eye on his expression. With practice she had learned to measure the intake of a man's breath, the movements of his shoulders, the dilation of the eyes, nose, and mouth.

The man smiled. "You are so very lovely, Mrs. Toy. Your skin is like alabaster, your hair like spun silk."

She put a finger to her lips. She would never talk to the customers. Talk would excite them further, and then the worst would happen. The less said the better.

She steadied her breathing, gazing at the Buddha placed in the corner shrine, next to the sticks of incense. She was keenly aware of this man's unabashed staring while he plainly absorbed every nook and cranny of her flesh.

"I reckon I must be the luckiest man alive." His longing spoke of fresh spring grasses, the trickle of water over river rock, and the deep sound of a temple bell.

Sitting before John Clark, great nostalgia took hold of her. Thoughts of her village on the Zhujiang Delta came flying to her like daggers. Ah Toy saw the long yellow fingernail Tung Chee used to cultivate on his pinky. As a rich merchant, he meted out punishment to the slaves who labored in his porcelain factories; he governed his family from the narrow authority passed down from his elders—his was the only voice that mattered.

Her mind's eye centered on the fingernail, an extension of her husband's voice, like an oar to a sampan. When she had failed to stand up straight at a ceremony introducing a new line of pottery to other merchants in the trade, Ah would feel a sharp stab of her husband's nail in her rib. Later, her backtalk would result in a scrape across her face.

Her brother Toy Lee Lung, who ran the ceramic ovens, bore a lattice of scars on each cheek, a testament to transgressions he committed doing business for Tung Chee. Each fresh scar reminded her of Toy Lee Lung's paradoxical fortune. Tung Chee had taken Toy Lee Lung into the company, somewhat reluctantly. Later, he treated him like a useless piece of baggage attached to her meagre dowry.

She shifted her attention back to Clark. Was that a tinge of sadness in his face? Somehow she did not mind his obvious examination and approval. When Clark stepped forward in response to Chen's invitation into to her shanty, she expected the worst. In her view, a man was usually good for one thing—a bodyguard. Yet the air around Clark carried the heat of a warm candle on a cool night.

In a little while, the sun angled lower on the window ledge. Her time with Clark was over. She rose, stepped behind the divider, and changed back into a green jacket and her silk pantaloons. With hurried movements, she pinned her shiny hair up in a knot to keep it clean.

With quick steps, Ah stood across the table from this man's kind face with the blue eyes, the shock of blond hair falling over his brows. She gazed at him in silence, her heart pounding. Seldom had she seen such a handsome white man.

He held an additional pouch with gold dust toward her. "Here—for you."

She measured the shavings and the scales, but then thought better of taking his money. Seldom did she have such a kind customer. She handed the unnecessary amount back to him and stammered. "Y-You have already paid. This is too much."

He pushed it back toward her. "No, please. I want you to have it. I had good luck in the mines last year, and although I've abandoned the effort, I am well fixed." What an oddly considerate gesture.

"Fixed?" she asked. "That is not a word I learned from my teacher, Mrs. Dailey."

"In California, that means "set." You see, I have plenty of money now. My position allows me to—that is—I am able to spend the money I make and even give some to my friends." His chin dipped down. "Friends like you."

She struggled not to like this man. Best be wary. "I am not your friend, Mr. Clark, but you may come back again if you like another look."

"I certainly will." He turned toward the door.

Maybe she had been too cold. She tried a warmer tone. "What job do you do in San Francisco?"

He made a half-turn and gave her an earnest smile. "When the call of "Gold!" spread to New York from California, I could not resist. So, I joined other men in the quest for instant riches. After sailing west through Panama, I found myself in the Placer mines, pan and shovel in hand."

She had heard this story before—his was not the first one. "So why are you back here in San Francisco, rather than continuing your search for riches?"

"Well, ma'am, the answer is quite simple really. Though I did find several grand nuggets which helped me pay the bills, I soon realized mining was a risky business. All around me were men whose lives hinged on quick-rich schemes that ended up in bare dirt."

She nodded. "I see them lying on the streets every day. They think to relieve their sorrows in the mines, but they end up drowning themselves in drink."

"Sure enough, I soon came to realize there was more security in applying my law and order background to San Francisco." He frowned. "What a disorderly, uncivilized air this place has."

Bile rose in her throat. "I will not argue. Not long ago a man was murdered on Stockton Street. Left to rot for several days before anyone came to take him away." She shivered.

"When men and women first came to the city, it was a mere encampment by the Bay. Gradually, as shanties and tents began staking their claims to the already designated streets, I began to see my place among its citizenry. You know, my father Josiah was with the New York Police Department. So was I before coming West."

"So, you come from a tradition." She tilted her head. Now that he mentioned it, she could see an air of dedication about him. Such men had sworn to guard the communities around them. But such men could also take advantage of those they protected.

He continued. "I am off duty right now. But there is talk of trouble caused by Australian ships, their holds filled with gangs of men from Sydney they call 'Ducks.' And I am a good shot with a revolver."

"Our people tell stories about the Ducks," she said. "You are a policeman, so you know our streets?"

He shrugged. "I am assigned to District Three, Little Canton, but I also patrol the wharf."

She leaned forward. "Would you be able to come to my shanty and say hello every day for safety?"

"But you already have a bodyguard, and by the likes of him, he can handle the situation."

"Yes, Chen is good, but lately I have another menace."

He raised his eyebrows. "What kind of trouble? Ducks again?"

"No—from my people. Trouble inside Little Canton."

"I do not understand. Your Kong Chow Company will take charge to protect you in those affairs." He tilted his head, regarding her.

She chewed her lower lip. "I need another kind of shield, too. Maybe the Kong Chow Company and Chen are not enough." She stepped toward him across the sunbeam cutting through the small-paned window.

His face softened. "Well, I think you are quite capable to taking care of yourself, Mrs. Toy, but I would be glad to come by to say hello each day on my way down to the harbor." He thrust out his hand.

She let him fold her hand in his grasp. "I am most grateful, Mr. Clark." His palm was surprisingly warm.

Shouts of the men outside filtered in through the thin walls. Time to drop his hand and see the next customer. She liked talking to John Clark, his face tan with small wrinkles around his blue eyes. But words wasted time; actions made money.

She picked up an ivory walking stick and rapped at the door. Chen opened the door from the outside. Instead of moving ahead, Clark followed behind her.

His presence unnerved her a bit. On one hand, he was a policeman who had the power to shut down Ah's Lookee Shop; on the other hand, his gentle nature and soft voice gave her pause. Had she done right by asking for his guard? She would offer an orange to Buddha and contemplate this man's intentions.

She turned and he gave a slight bow. "Farewell, Mrs. Toy." He stepped into the alley and adjusted the brim of his hat against the sun.

Chen moved into the doorway. "Should I bring in the next customer?"

"A moment, please." She padded out to the edge of the step, and stared down the muddy street, littered with paper and empty bottles. Clark's long-legged shape faded into the harbor haze. If only she were as close as the air around him.

The next day Ah stood with Chen in reverential silence before the three officers of the Kong Chow Company, a merchant guild overseeing affairs in Little Canton. If businesses like hers paid their taxes, the Company would stand up for them. The officers sat in regal fashion, their smooth faces gleaming above her on a high dais. Behind the men stood a gold ornate screen covered with green peacocks and blue peonies; to their right and left, large candles flickered inside tall, wooden-screened lanterns.

"Please, you may sit." A voice said in Cantonese.

Blinking her eyes against the bright gold halo, Ah Toy clutched her letter from Tung Chao. She took in the leaders arrayed in black riding jackets and black hats, worn over the traditional *changshan,* a long silk embroidered garment appropriate for government officials. Their faces were wizened; their chins reclined on layers of soft flesh.

"Thank you," she said, sitting on a bench before them, Chen beside her. A cockroach would have greater stature in the officers' presence. Lowly and small, she was subject to the whims of male authority. She chewed her lower lip, mulling over her concerns before they invited her to speak.

Would they hear her cause, or dismiss her? Goddess Mazu would surely guide her to convince these leaders to see the letter and know her concerns. Maybe they would take pity and side with her before Lee Shau Kee arrived on the *Eagle* from Hong Kong.

The middle officer led the introductions in Cantonese. "I am Officer Lam, and this is Yuen and Wong. You are most welcome here, Mrs. Toy, and we are happy to give you a short hearing on this matter." Though his smile was broad, his eyes were cold. In his role he had probably heard every kind of problem. A kind of indifference permeated his semi-regal pose.

Ah rose to her feet. "Thank you, officers for hearing my case. I am most honored." She held up the letter from Tung Chao. "I wish to discuss a matter of great importance contained in this correspondence. Would the officers desire to read the letter in question?"

Officer Lam gave a faint smile. "But you must know we have also received a copy of your letter from your brother-in-law, and we are familiar with its contents."

Sweat pearled under her arms. "You have?" That filthy bastard Tung Chao had gone behind her back. She shook her head. This should not surprise her.

"Mrs. Toy, the letter states you are to return to China." His Cantonese was clipped and formal. As if she were a package, already wrapped to send back to Guangdong.

Inside her dragon's claws tingled. No—they must stay retracted and at bay. This was not the time to use them.

Lam continued, his eyelids fluttering. "The *Eagle* will be due back in port next month to take on passengers for the westward voyage to Hong Kong."

She swallowed the urge to scream. "I am not able to return home to China. I now have my own business here in San Francisco."

"Tung Chao has sent a man known as Lee Shau Kee who is en route to find you in San Francisco and collect you for your deceased husband's family. Tung Chao wishes to take you as his wife, and he has every right to do so." He narrowed his eyes and lowered his voice. "You should be grateful."

"With respect, Officer Lam, I earn a sizeable income. I do not wish to go back to the Tung family who treated me like a donkey." Her voice amplified, and the officers exchanged glances and shifted in their seats.

She swallowed the dragon's fire in her stomach. "The economic tide is turning now in Guangdong province, with famine and hardship affecting all business, including the Tung family's porcelain company. Tung Chao only wants me back to bear him sons. He used to leer at me in the most disrespectful manner."

Officer Yuen glared. "A man has a right to determine which wife he wants and how many children he desires to raise as his own. It is his household."

Her fire could no longer be controlled, and she shrieked. "Gone! Killed—do you hear me? The Tung family stood by while my husband Tung Chee threw three of my girl babies over a cliff. He insisted they were stillborn, but that is not true. I held them in my arms, and they were full-term and alive."

Officer Lam blinked a couple of times but said nothing.

She lowered her voice. "His brother Chao was present when Tung Chee told me that if we had boy children, he would send them to his mother's house to be raised. Tung Chao gave his opinion that I would have no say in their upbringing. If I marry him, I will be nothing but a senseless sow who bears his children."

She leaned back in her chair, then glanced at Chen who stiffened in silence.

Had she gone too far?

Hard smiles lined the officers' faces.

Her heart sank. Did that mean they thought her ridiculous? No, that could not be. Here she was free, in America, the San Francisco of blue sky and placid water. Surely, they would understand. But then again, they were bound by ancient custom and law.

Officer Lam got up from his seat, and the others rose as well. Lam said, "We shall discuss your case, Mrs. Toy. Please wait here for our decision."

The other leaders followed Lam out the door into the antechamber. A door closed, and Ah could hear the men's words rising and falling on the other side of the wall. Yet, she could not make out what they said. Did their discussion mean they were deciding in her favor? Did she dare to hope?

The aroma of fried dumplings and roast duck filtered in from the behind the door. She knew they had paused for lunch. Maybe after a meal and plum wine they would be kinder to her.

Some minutes passed, and Chen opened the pouch fastened to his belt and passed her a rice cake. They each nibbled and waited in silence, exchanging sidelong glances.

She had no escape plan should Lee Shau Kee disembark in San Francisco and find her. Worse than that, she wanted to stay in San Francisco. She liked it here, independent and free. Clark's gentle blue eyes and soft smile glimmered in her memory. This was her land now, new and vibrant, and she would be wealthy here.

But was she overly optimistic? Her daily life in the Lookee Shop was no delight. Every day brought the frightening possibility that with one step across her floor, a man could assault and rape her. Sure, Chen was strong, and knew how to use his knife, but what good was that against the force of a several well-aimed revolvers?

Ah's back began to ache from long sitting when suddenly the door opened, and in strode the men in their embroidered jackets, their chins greasy with duck droppings and dumpling spatter.

Rather than easing into the gentle stream of sympathy toward her, the men's faces were as stony as the faces of temple gods. There they sat, their chests as broad as the scholar warriors in the Cantonese opera, their faces as stiff as Tung Chee's after death. Where was the soft, motherly face of Goddess Mazu whose radiant glow guided her over the waves to California?

Officer Lam said, "We have discussed your case. It is no matter, Mrs. Toy." He tucked Tung Chao's letter into a portfolio on the dais.

"No matter?" she asked. His words burned into her like a brand on bare flesh. She seethed with the fire of anger all mothers recognize, a fire of justice, of salvation. *It is no matter.* She would not go back to China. Even if she had to claw their eyes out and have her dragon breathe flame onto their faces. *It is no matter.* She would fly up and lash them with her dragon's tail until their armor was cracked and splintered like a shipwreck's hull floating in the bay.

Officer Lam raised his chin and cleared his throat.

Ah Toy braced herself, straightening her spine. Her dragon's scales would deflect the bad news, and its wings would grasp the good news and hold it tightly against her body.

Lam pronounced. "A woman should look on her husband's family as if they were Heaven itself, and never weary of thinking how she may yield to them. For these principles and all we hold dear, we cannot allow your request, and we shall honor your brother-in-law's letter."

She sucked in her breath; Chen stiffened at her side.

Lam gave her a pointed look. "We shall advise the emissary named Lee Shau Kee that he may come and seize your property and bring you home to Hong Kong when the *Eagle* returns. You and all your earthly goods belong to your husband's family." His face hardened into chiseled rock.

She rose up on her lotus shoes, but all the officers stood, turned their backs, and filed out of the room in silence, much as soundless waves draw away from the shoreline at low tide.

No matter how she might run along the beach and summon back the waters, she was powerless to bring back the waves. By the same token she was helpless to summon the Kong Chow Company to her side.

Yet she would not surrender, even if she must die defending her freedom to remain in San Francisco. *That was the matter.*

Four

❧ TEA AND BURLAP ❧

Ah watched the rest of March pass into April without news of either Tung Chao or Lee Shau Kee. Though she and Chen discussed the possibility of fleeing to the gold hills if Lee Shau Kee were to arrive in San Francisco, they decided it best to stay in place and continue earning their wealth in gold nuggets. Their best weapon was the money they made. If bad news came, they could always ask John Clark to bring more policemen to guard them.

That morning's fog nestled on the tops of the hills like drifts of sea foam, at times pulled apart by the wind, at others hugging the shores of San Francisco, gripping the darkened bay with fierce determination. Ah held onto Chen's arm to avoid tipping her lotus shoes and twisting her ankles as she had done many times before.

She looked up at him—the long braid of his queue swung back and forth while he navigated the twists and turns of muddy roads that lay in all directions. Some new structures had been built from hulls of ships; others had used the timbers of the masts, plugging spaces between boards with newsprint. Others had canvas sides, and through the open flaps, she could see miners resting on cots or writing at desks. Outside some lean-to's, men were stirring pots of stew over open flames.

The smell of sweet tobacco mixed with mildew and perspiration. And everywhere hammers pounded nails as buildings were being put up as fast as men poured off ships, their minds filled with visions of gold. She spread her fan over her mouth and nose against whiffs of offal and sewage that people threw out of windows and doors into the street.

Since San Francisco was a small town, and most permanent residents knew each other, her former customers often leered as they passed her, even while she selected tomatoes at the marketplace. The few white, black, or brown women she saw would either gawk at her exotic appearance or cross the street in order to avoid being seen in her company.

Though Ah glimpsed Clark on his daily rounds and heard his friendly knock and hello, she yearned to know more about him. It had been awhile since they had spoken at length, and from time to time she reflected on his life and what he was about. People came from many nations to seek their fortunes. What had his life been like in the gold mines? Or in New York? Where was his family?

To her relief, Portsmouth Plaza with its central flagpole loomed ahead. Ah let Chen guide her arm, and they crossed the bumpy surface. A pair of miners in work boots and dusty hats walked across the Plaza in front of them. All around was the stink of rotting carcasses mixed with the sharp smell of wood shavings.

After crossing the Plaza, she glanced at the Book and Job Printing office, then over at the California Restaurant where a cook stood in the door, legs akimbo, his white apron streaked with grease. Paper trash littered the ground as Ah and Chen passed, and a horse and wagon stopped to let them by. Above them, the long, dry grasses of the steep hills swished as the wind swept in from the Bay.

"Mrs. Toy," someone said.

She squinted into the sunlight made diffuse by the strands of fog now emerging like small rain drops. The fog was growing thicker, beginning its descent over the streets and the Bay, shrouding the windmill on the hill and the masts of ships in the far harbor.

Chen thrust his hand into his jacket pocket, probably fingering the handle of his knife.

Clark's tall figure came into view. She returned his greeting, surprised at the joy in her own voice. "Mr. Clark, hello, that is, good afternoon. I was wondering when I would talk with you again."

"Delighted to see you." He doffed his hat and he gave her a nod, then flashed a smile at Chen. "Headed to the market?"

"I am going to an incense shop with remarkable spices one can only find in China," Ah Toy said.

"I have a few moments, may I go?" He turned to Chen. "Is that acceptable?"

Chen nodded, stepping aside.

Clark grinned. "You're a considerable man."

Chen beamed a response.

The flow of passersby swept around them in the street; theirs was an island of three. Ah Toy wrapped her arm under Clark's elbow. He smelled of garlic and something fried. A whiff of whiskey floated on his breath, but then all the men drank as a habit, so she relaxed, drifting into a pleasant stream of conversation.

"I have not had time to talk at your shanty, but there is a reason," he said.

"Oh?" She tilted her head, fighting the urge to stare at his blue eyes.

His cheeks reddened. "I have a new position now, you see."

"And that is . . . ."

He pulled open his jacket where a silver star with seven points gleamed on his vest. He tapped it with his fingernail. "They have changed my assignment away from the wharf. I am now a policeman assigned to control the cavortin' miners who prowl the gambling dens and prostitutes, especially in your Little Canton alleys."

She brushed a strand of hair from her eye. "I am not sure whether that is a good or bad idea, Mr. Clark." She slowed her step and peered up at him, searching his angular face for a grain of truth, a rarity in the gold rush town. Miners preferred to exaggerate their take, though it took little time at the faro tables to reveal the extent of their financial worth.

Clark continued. "Why not good? Many in your own trade could seek to harm you, especially since you are the only Cantonese woman here, other than a servant who remains indoors all the time."

"Chen guards me." She anchored a hand on her hip.

"Wait a minute—you asked me to stop at your shanty every day, didn't you? When first you asked, I thought it was a good idea. After all, you are in the—er—delicate trade." He tugged at his jacket collar.

She tightened her fists. "Ah's Lookee Shop does not let in just *any* man."

A blush crept across his cheeks. "That may be true, but with the town expanding, you may need even more fortification under the law."

She flinched at the truth he spoke. Especially since the Kong Chow Company did not offer her much in the way of support.

"How will this be different now?" she asked.

"I will not only stop to say hello each day, but I will be nearby when you need my assistance. All you have to do is call out or send Chen to find me on DuPont, Washington, or Stockton Streets."

She paused. Had he read the yearning in her eyes?

A strong breeze whipped up from the direction of the bay, and a lock of hair unraveled from her hairpin and glided across her face. She struggled to secure it behind an ear. "I am going to the incense shop, then we will go home before dark. I am not safe on our streets at night, even with Chen."

"Let me take you to the shop and home," he said.

"Small steps please." She pointed to her tiny feet.

"I have time today," he said.

A gold ring decorated the fourth finger of his left hand. Why had she not noticed it before? Was he married? For a moment, her heart debated with her head. If he belonged to another, had given his heart to another, would he deserve her interest, or even more, her trust? Not that it mattered, since she had already wrangled with one husband. Besides, trust was fleeting, often an illusion. Why add another wrinkle to the material of her current life? She enjoyed his company, and he made her laugh.

She extended her left arm to Clark and her right to Chen. They guided her path to the shop on Stockton Street. How lucky she was to have two friends in the fog shadowing the roads. She led the way to the counter, and soon the clerk had filled some silk bags with the chosen incense sticks.

Clark looked down into her eyes. "What are those for? I am not familiar with these odd things."

She held one up to him. "Smell this."

He sniffed. "Hmmm—smells like pine, cedar—and maybe camphor?"

She nodded. "We use incense sticks to keep time during our meditations. As a girl, I was told that the ancient poet Yu Jianwu said, 'By burning incense we know the o'clock of the night; With graduated candles we confirm the tally of the watches.' They began to be used in Buddhist monasteries, but now we use them in our own humble shrines."

"We have many traditions going back generations," Chen said.

After a series of sweet-smelling purchases, Ah pointed her toes back home.

Clark worried their prior conversation like a dog would gnaw a bone. "I will be guarding your Pike Street address as part of my new post with the police."

Her heart beat faster. Should she be happy?

Clark turned and whispered something to Chen who nodded, then fell back, leaving the two of them alone. Clark leaned in and his arm tucked under her elbow. They continued onto DuPont Street, past the groups of smoking men reading broadsides tacked to the sides of buildings.

She swallowed hard. "I am not available to lookee this afternoon." He reddened, but instead of pulling away, he kept his arm laced with hers. "I am not interested in lookee business, Mrs. Toy. I am interested in you." He gave her a sidelong glance whose intensity would melt iron.

What should she say? No man had ever said those things to her before in English. "Interested" must mean something more than lust, deeper than looking at her flesh.

She had no idea what to say, but a lightness replaced her former hesitation.

The turn of his mouth, the tilt of his chin, the merriment at play on his face. There was no mistaking it. He was drawing her to him with invisible strings.

And the funny thing was—she liked it more than she could say.

He said, "I would like to make a deal with you—as a friend of course." A grin played across his mouth.

She followed that uneven smile, then her gaze traveled to his shock of blond hair. "Deal? Like gambling?"

"Sort of, but more like business. Let us make a contract that I will continue to visit your shanty every day to make sure you are safe, as well as Chen of course."

He had managed to break through the walls of hesitation that surrounded her; now he was plowing the fertile ground inside her heart.

"I would like that." Despite the cool wind whipping her sleeves, her skin flushed warm.

He gave her forearm a gentle squeeze. "Me, too. And, what is more, I must be on your block each day on patrol. You and Chen will be safe harbor in the midst of the dark business I must do every day."

Someone came up behind them. She glanced over her shoulder. Chen stood behind her, chewing his bottom lip. He said, "Si tau po, we must get home. The line of men will start to form at the Lookee Shop, and we are late."

"I am sorry to have kept you." Clark pulled his hat off and held it over his heart. "Maybe someday I will not have to share you with other men." Though his voice was gentle, his meaning rang clear. "Tomorrow I will call on you to check the house."

"I will be visiting the tea shop tomorrow. Chen and I already planned this outing."

"May I accompany you both? What time should I arrive?"

"Ten o'clock," she said.

He tipped his hat, and soon disappeared into the fog.

For the first time she knew the feeling of wanting a man more than he wanted her. Yet confusion tiptoed behind her desire. She hardly knew him. What did that gold ring signify? Who was this man? What magic did he use to silence her dragon and offer his own sheltering wing so that she would go soft as jelly in his presence?

The fog burned away early the next day. Shafts of sunlight burst onto the muddy roads between the rows of shanties. Once inside with Clark and Chen, Ah surveyed the interior of the tea shop, jammed with wooden drawers, various blends lining each wall. In the corners, small shipping crates were stacked one on another. A rush of customers entered through the tinkling door behind them, and Ah was pressed next to three large Cantonese men in black jackets, pants and shoes.

She edged around them over to the counter where three joyful porcelain Buddhas sat side-by-side, beaming out at the customers. Clark took up her left side, and Chen stood to her right.

Clark paused, then said, "I have never been in here before." His words blew into the clamor of the crowd.

"What say?" Chen cupped his ear.

Ah shouted. "The best tea shop in Little Canton."

Clark nodded, clearly in awe of his surroundings.

Beside him, Ah Toy regarded the tiny drawers with interest, pointing with her index finger at the top row. "Jasmine Pearl," she read first in Cantonese, then translated into English.

Clark spoke over the din of voices. "Never drank it. Course, I'm partial to my two fingers of whiskey to calm the nerves."

"Jasmine tea makes the breath smell of flowers; whiskey makes the breath smell of rat poison." Ah made a frown.

Clark said, "To each his own. Me, I like my whiskey." Clark eyed Chen. "You seem loyal to your Mrs. Toy" he said.

"I stay by her side, Mr. Clark." Chen stepped closer to Ah, his hand ever ready on his knife handle. "I guard her since childhood days."

Meanwhile, Ah addressed the robust clerk in the Manchurian black jacket. A stream of Cantonese flowed between her and the tea seller.

Chen turned to Clark. "Money is precious. With her salary, I buy and send home large packages of unusual goods, such as cotton and wheat, to my family in Beijing. She has also been kind to me, and I am loyal in return."

Meanwhile, Ah Toy haggled with the shopkeeper, keeping a sharp eye on their mutual mounds of gold dust and tea leaves pouring into and out of small bags. The voices around them rose and fell in soft drumbeats, harmonizing with the clack of wooden drawers opening and shutting.

The front door hinges squealed as someone entered the tea shop, but Ah paid no mind since the shop was filling with even more customers. She even ignored the sound of footsteps and the hush that fell over the customers behind her in line.

It was only when the calm turned to complete silence that an odd, primitive chill enveloped her. A large burlap bag was being cast over her head as someone blinded her, knotted it tightly around her shoulders, and skillfully trapped her arms behind her. She cried, "Help!"

Instead of surrender, the thug hoisted her into his arms; her feet flailed out in all directions. One of her lotus shoes fell off and thudded to the floor with a clang. Now all would see one of her disfigured feet, toes curved under, bones twisted in a knot.

"Oooh." That was the sound people made when they saw the impossible happen in front of them.

She pictured the crowd of onlookers in the shop falling back into an invisible mass of black shirts. When all else failed, be invisible—that seemed to be their means of avoiding trouble. Maddening, but true.

This was Tung Chao's way. Back in Guangzhou he was known to get rid of disfavored concubines, forcing them into sacks and hurling them into the Pearl River Delta. He was behind this. She tried to scream, but the burlap clung to her face, and when she moved her lips, a scratch burned across her mouth.

Someone was throwing her and the bag over his shoulder. She kicked, but his arms were strong, tightening around her calves when she moved. Where was Chen? Was he rooted to the wooden floor, his shoes unmoving, his open mouth a Plaza of disbelief? For her sake, why didn't he do something? Better yet, where was Clark? He had sworn to guard her.

She heard a shuffling, the cocking of a trigger, but meantime her captor was walking fast, and her face was bouncing against his back. She turned her cheek to avoid bashing her nose.

Someone jerked him, and she heard Clark's voice call out. "Let her go, fellow."

More shuffling. Probably she was yet inside the store, but her captor seemed to be taking ragged steps through the crowd of buyers, most likely toward the door. Her frame continued to bang against him like a bag of rice. She screamed and bumped back and forth with her head and feet. If only she could unbalance the scoundrel.

What was going on? Probably the crowd of buyers was backing away, their mouths gaping. She had seen this many times in Canton. An eerie silence resumed its grip on the tea seller's shop and its inhabitants.

More jouncing. The brigand continued moving forward through space. He must have ignored Clark's demand and pushed past him toward the door.

She considered. If he took her outside and ran somewhere with her, Clark and Chen might never find her again. What then?

Since Clark was the only white-skinned man in the shop, she may not get help from the throng of reluctant men. If Clark shot the man, the crowd could grab his weapon, then set upon him. "Come on, Chen! Help me!" Clark's sharp cries rang through the shop. More scraping of feet. Clark must be pushing through the crowd, aiming his gun at the kidnapper.

She kept up a forceful wave of cries. "Please, Clark, Chen, don't let him take me."

"Halt or I'll shoot, son!" Clark's voice bristled.

Suddenly she sensed a sudden push, and her captor wobbled side to side. Someone was springing into action. Chen yelled in Cantonese, and the marauder stopped. Maybe Clark would have time to approach, since now her captor was outmanned.

Clark's words rang out. "I am the police, and I demand to know what this is about."

"This man speaks no English," Chen said.

Clark's voice filtered through the bag. "Well, find out what the blazes he wants, and hurry up about it.

From inside the bag, Ah Toy could see little through the burlap's tight weave. It scraped her face, and a fine powder filled the crevices around her eyes and mouth. The kidnapper gripped her wrists, and his rope dug into her flesh. The pain worsened with each bit of struggle. Her skin felt rubbed by razors, and although the pains of childbirth had been terrible, this was almost as bad.

Heat flashed through her. This had to be Lee Shau Kee, sent to bring her back to China. She had no recourse, since the Kong Chow Company would side with Tung Chao, seize her assets, and set her on the *Eagle* back to China. If she returned to a slave's life, she would serve little use but the childbirth bed.

Her duty would be to produce male heirs, little boys she would see maybe once a year. If she had girls, how many more would be killed? She shuddered like the ground during the small but jarring earthquakes that hit San Francisco from time to time. If only the earth would open right now so she could vanish into the crevice.

Clark's tone hardened. "Show me the letter from her brother-in-law."

Chen murmured the translation to her captor, and a paper crackled outside her burlap. It must be the letter, maybe a copy of the one she had, or worse, one more directly addressing the Kong Chow Company. This would leave her out of the equation, like a horse being traded, or a crate of teacups. *How dare he.*

Clark's voice resumed. "I will vouch for Mrs. Toy, and I will see that she appears in the Recorder's Court to argue her case. You may not take her now against her will. That is kidnapping, against the law of the land."

She recognized Lee Shau Kee's words resonating like a bear's low growl. "What is it worth to you?"

Chen murmured the English translation to Clark.

A moment later she heard something like coins clinking—someone was paying someone off. Her mind raced. Had it been Clark or Chen who bought her freedom?

The rope loosened, and the cord relaxed around her wrists. Her shoeless foot ached, and her hip twisted. She fell forward, and someone caught her, pulling the burlap off her head, scraping the skin on her arms and face, and snagging swatches of her hair as the rope and twine was removed.

She blinked into hazy men's faces. A tall, burly Cantonese, his mug layered with disgust, dropped the burlap, then turned and slammed out of the tea shop. Though she had not seen him in a long time, she was sure—he was none other than Lee Shau Kee.

As though the entertainment had reached its conclusion, the tea seller and his assistants ignored her, then raised their voices again, summoning the buyers to resume their orders at the counter.

"Let us get you home again in short meter." Clark reached out an arm to her, and she collapsed against it. Chen gave a worried frown and stood back. They stepped out of the tea shop into Stockton Street.

Ah looked up at Clark, then over at Chen. "Which of you paid off Lee Shau Kee? I owe you my gratitude." She held onto Clark for balance.

Chen inclined his head toward Clark. "We each gave money for your freedom."

"Thank you both." She looked down so they would not see her pleasure-filled grin. "How did Lee Shau Kee know where to find me?"

A Chinese man carrying a pole with two full baskets of laundry on either shoulder stepped around them.

"Every man in San Francisco knows your whereabouts. You are famous," Clark said.

Her skin tingled.

Chen stepped forward. "I would have stabbed him with my knife, but then I would be in trouble with the Kong Chow Company who supports Tung Chao. The only way to escape him would be to go away from here." He waved in the direction of the harbor.

Clark said, "You could always go to New York. I know people there."

She set her jaw. "No. I will not leave. San Francisco is my home now."

Clark looked into her eyes. "Some stubborn gal you are."

Adrift in his blue crystalline gaze, she said, "I have waited all my life to be free—I would rather die than give this up."

Chen said, "I feel the same way."

Clark said, "In that case, let us get you home." He led her through the crowds of black-jacketed Cantonese on the way toward Pike Street. They ducked around a man throwing night refuse out a second story window, then skirted the body of a dead man, flies buzzing around him. She would leave that for someone else to take care of—she had more than enough problems.

Five

◀ DRAW MY MAGIC SWORD ▶

May 1849

The San Francisco Recorder's Court was tucked into the little schoolhouse at Portsmouth Plaza and Clay Street. The court shared quarters with the nascent San Francisco Police Department. Next door, the burned hulk of a building smoked from a fire the previous evening. Ah looked around at the geographical maps and charts that hung on the walls. A central aisle separated two long rows of student benches, and a pot-belly stove in the center served to warm the room even in the city's cool summer months. Judge Almond's hulking figure presided at a teacher's desk five feet away.

As Ah sat down on a student bench in the second row, she swept up her embroidered apricot-colored sleeves, remembering that day long ago in Guangzhou when she had first worn this jacket and the delight she had found in its white flower designs. She remained in the memory, fastening her regrets from the past to the unwieldy present.

In fact, Ah had worn this silk jacket and skirt the first time when she was sixteen. She attended a merchant fair where Tung Chee was being celebrated; she was standing back, watching him through transparent silk drapery where he sat up on the dais along with his brother Tung Chao and the other merchants of Guangzhou's Six Factories.

The present sliced into her past dream. What if the judge did not understand her case? Or worse, what if he was corrupt? What would she do then? She glanced down at the contours of her yellow and white paneled skirt. Since her arrival in the Bay City, she had kept this precious qipao wrapped in tight bundles underneath other garments so the colors would not fade. Smoke, dust and mildew would ruin the fabric.

"In the matter of Ah Toy. You may approach the bench." The deep tones of Judge Almond's voice reverberated through the one-room schoolhouse.

Chen's jacket rustled next to her. She took his arm and he guided her steps over to the table where she sat down and faced the judge. The magistrate's gray-red beard and knotted brows gave him a fierce look and she shivered. Oh—he was disfigured.

Ugly faces in Canton flickered in her memory: the judge's pock-marked cheeks were scarcely hidden under his beard. Could that mean he had suffered from smallpox? Had the Judge been ill in his youth? Would he show compassion? She could only hope.

A cheer rose from the observer's gallery. Men who lounged mere seconds before now rose from their seats and cried out their heart's desires.

"Mrs. Toy? Won't you be mine?"

"Mrs. Toy, I love you!"

"Mrs. Toy, take me, gorgeous!"

She recognized some faces: one swarthy sailor who frequented her Lookee Shop, and another drunken miner who was always turned away. Her inner dragon recoiled. She valued the Lookee Shop's reputation as a source of income, but she could never get used to the catcalls.

She gripped Chen's arm, yet maintained her composure. If she could only tear their tongues out and make paste of it for the sharks.

The Judge narrowed his eyes upon hearing the uproar. Facing the crowd, he rose and pounded his gavel. "Order! Bailiff, please remove anyone who continues to shout!" After further murmurs, the Judge sat down and commandeered the makeshift bench. He snarled. "Anyone who disrupts this court proceeding today will answer to my authority."

The former chants died down, followed by an occasional cough or the moving of a chair. Ah relaxed her hold on Chen and arranged her long silk sleeves.

Chen sighed, then withdrew his arm and settled onto the creaking seat adjoining hers. She glanced behind her at the gallery where the gaggle of disheveled white men lounged, their gaze boring into her. Her dragon pricked his ears.

Clark waved from the fourth row on the right side, where his blue jacket set him apart from the other men. She lifted a finger, but when the judge exhaled sharply, she turned back to face him.

The judge leaned forward. "I would prefer to send your case to the Kong Chow Company, Mrs. Toy. They take care of their own country-men hereabouts. Why aren't you seeking a hearing in their district?"

"The Chinese fathers are not protecting me, and I fear I will not receive justice at their hands." She spoke quickly, wringing her hands.

His frown settled into a straight line. "And what is the exact nature of your case, Mrs. Toy?"

"My complaint is against Lee Shau Kee who attempted to kidnap me. I fear he will stay here in San Francisco and try again. I am in fear of my life." She fought back stinging tears, but one escaped and rolled down her cheek.

"Mrs. Toy, I see the accusation you have brought against Mr. Lee, but I need you to understand that a charge of assault, battery, and attempted kidnapping can only be made in the presence of the defendant." He looked down at some papers. "I see here that our Detective Painter was unable to find Mr. Lee anywhere in this jurisdiction.

"In order to issue a restraining order, we must be able to find and serve him with a summons to appear before this court. Are you aware of an address or a residence where we might locate Mr. Lee?" He wrinkled his brow.

"No, but did you search all the ships leaving for China?"

"Mr. Painter checked all the rosters, but no Lee Shau Kee sailed to China." Judge Almond ran a hand through his wiry hair. "Do you have a witness who can vouch for your standing? After all, you are not a citizen of these parts, and your presence in court is highly unusual." His half-open lips revealed a top row of uneven yellow teeth.

She sat in silence, absorbing the judge's legal language; words like "rosters," "witness," and "vouch" became a puzzle without her dictionary. Her dragon curled up in a corner of its dark cave. What was she to do? She glanced back at Clark in the gallery and mouthed, "Please help me." She held up the letter from Tung Chao.

Clark nodded in her direction, crossed the courtroom, and stopped next to her at her table. He snatched the letter from her outstretched hand and faced the bench.

Judge Almond rasped. "Mrs. Toy? What are you attempting? Bailiff?"

The bailiff popped out of his chair beside the judge. He held up a hand facing Clark as he stepped from Ah's table toward the judge's bench. "Just a minute, there, sir," he said, his fist resting on his holster.

Ah said, "Your Honor, this is my friend Officer Clark who has some evidence to show you."

The judge poked a pair of spectacles onto the bridge of his nose, and said, "Hmmm." He shifted toward the bailiff. "Allow him to approach."

The bailiff withdrew and Clark anchored his feet before the bench.

Her hands grew clammy, and she exchanged a glance with Chen who sat in silence. Her dragon's ears unfolded, listening intently.

The judge cleared his throat and peered at Clark. "Your badge indicates you are a lawman, but I do not recollect seeing you in my court before this."

"John Clark. Your Honor, I am a deputized policeman with knowledge of Mrs. Toy and her case."

"Indeed. Please proceed." The judge nodded.

Clark passed the letter to the bailiff who handed it to the judge. He said, "This will explain the reason behind Lee Shau Kee's actions. He is an agent from Mrs. Toy's brother-in-law in China who demands she return to marry him against her will."

Despite her sense of caution, Ah Toy rose up on her lotus shoes. Chen's hand brushed her arm, but she swept it away. "May I speak, Your Honor?" she called out.

"Go ahead." The judge removed his glasses and grew silent a moment while he plucked a gray handkerchief from his pocket and rubbed the lenses. Then his stubby fingers poked his glasses back on the bridge of his nose.

Ah's voice rose and fell with each small step toward the bench where she took her place next to Clark. "Please protect me, dear Judge. I have come to San Francisco for a better life. I can support myself. The Chinese fathers will not shelter me; in fact, they wish to send me home."

"She is afraid for her safety in the hands of her brother-in-law; in fact, for her life." Clark said. His shoulder bumped hers, and she grasped the edge of the bench for balance. All she needed now was to tumble over in front of the spectators. Clark's arm slipped around her shoulders, bringing her closer.

The judge moved his nose from side to side as he read the letter. Any moment he might flick his tongue in and out as he considered the words on the page.

She settled against Clark's arm and tingled from the contact.

Judge Almond said, "I like your spirit, Mrs. Toy. And please remind this court how you intend to support yourself?

For a moment, she heard only the sound of someone, maybe a miner, cracking his knuckles behind her. "I own a Lookee Shop, Your Honor."

His eyes widened. "And what do your customers 'look' at?"

The gallery rippled with laughter.

"Well—um—they look at me." Her tone was fierce; sweat gathered under her arms.

"I see. That is, I think I understand." He cleared his throat. "And do you pay your taxes as required on these—er—transactions?"

Someone snickered behind her.

"Yes, Your Honor. Would you like to see my receipts? I keep a careful ledger."

His lizard face took on a kindly air. "No, not at this time. For some reason I do not think you would lie about that. Not when tax violators could be deported."

"I am part of San Francisco, and I wish to contribute to my community." Her voice rang steady and true.

"Very well, Mrs. Toy. Come back tomorrow when I will render a decision." His tongue flicked in and out, wetting his lips. "This session is adjourned." His robes flashed and the schoolhouse door slammed behind him.

The loungers in the gallery rose to their feet, some cheering, many clapping.

"I am confused." She whispered into Clark's ear. "Why do they cheer?"

"Judge Almond is known to be against Celestial immigration, but at least he will consider your point. That is what you must remember. The men like your Lookee Shop. That is why they congratulate you."

She turned around and nodded her head toward the men in the courtroom. Even the seediest miner had a grin spread across his face. The men leaped to their feet, cheering, "Mrs. Toy! Mrs. Toy!"

Her eyes brimmed with tears. Where was Chen? She found him standing tall in the sea of white men. But instead of a smile, was that a sad expression creeping across his face? She tucked the impression away, much like stuffing new lotus shoes into a trunk to be opened later.

On her way out, Ah exchanged Clark's arm for Chen's. She made her way down the schoolhouse steps, nearly tripping over the timbers fallen from the fire. The hulky remnants of a burned out livery next door sent up trails of smoke. Something or other was always on fire in San Francisco. The hasty construction, flimsy wood products, and cook stoves lit by drunken miners made for a tinder box of a town.

"What is that stink in the air, I mean besides the smoke?" She reached into the silk pouch on her belt, eased out her fan, then spread it over her nose and mouth to block out the air filled with cinders.

Chen said, "You smell horseflesh. Two ponies died in that fire and the owner suffered severe burns."

"Do they know who or what caused the fire?" She waved the fan back and forth while she walked.

"The *Alta* paper says the Sydney Ducks set the fire." He cocked his head to one side, regarding her.

She gave him her most quizzical look.

Clark's silver badge reflected the midday light. "A bunch of hooligans. These Australians failed in our gold country, so they came back to a part of our city they called Sydney Town. Having nothing better to do, they loosed their anger and frustration on our Bay City. Stealing, raping, pillaging—they are a gang to fear."

He set his hat further back on his head and tugged his ear. "'Minds me of New York. I cut my teeth on the Bowery Boys who thought nothing of chopping off ears and slitting throats to get what they wanted."

Ah nodded. "Many of those kind in Guangdong." She shifted her thoughts to Cantonese ways. Those riverfront thugs usually disappeared as fast as they emerged. In Guangdong, the penalties for mayhem were severe: bodies were quartered and left to ripen in the sun as public examples of what happened to people who broke the law.

Clark observed a group of men in top hats lingering on the corner. Maybe they were assessing the extent of the fire damage to the building. One man in shabby attire drew a picture of the ruins, perhaps to sell to newcomers at the wharf. One short stocky fellow, a pencil behind his ear and a satchel over his shoulder, stared at her, and she pressed Chen's hand. He took her arm and firmly guided her down to the end of the steps.

"Care for a refreshment, Mrs. Toy?" Clark's cheerful voice filled the air behind her. The sound took her breath away.

Chen's arm stiffened around her forearm, but she patted his hand, "It is all well."

He said, "I hope you are right this time."

Clark said, "Mrs. Toy, you did well in court today. Judge Almond usually rages at those providing testimony. He listened to you. And—he did agree to consider your case." He tilted his head. "Good sign."

She nodded. "I am happy for the moment. You mentioned refreshments, Mr. Clark? The judge said you were an officer of the court. Since you are my witness, are you allowed to dine with me?" She exchanged glances with Chen.

Clark squared his shoulders. "As a policeman, they call me an officer of the court. Even though I am your witness, I am free to dine with you. The California Restaurant is not far."

"Please lead the way." She fluttered her fan back and forth. Why did the idea of dining with Clark give her butterflies?

After a few minutes' walk, skirting stray cats and drunken men sleeping in doorways, Clark led the way into the California Restaurant. The host, wearing an apron covered with smatterings of blood and syrup, guided them to a table in the corner.

She sat down next to the lace curtain facing a window with a missing pane. Clark and Chen settled in across the table. Chen's red and watery eyes peered back at her. Clearly, he had not expected this turn of events.

A cool bay breeze ruffled the curtain, and Ah inhaled the aromas of roasting meats.

Clark glanced out the window and gave a short cough. "Will these San Francisco fires never end? The city fathers keep building with toothpicks rather than bricks and mortar." He shook his head. "Hear tell some have shanties with nothing more than tarpaper for walls. Buildings are being thrown up in haste in order to house the miners, bankers, and merchants. Still no time for much else—all it takes is an overturned candle, and *wup!* The whole block goes up like hellfire."

She said, "My shanty would go up in a second, such a flimsy set of boards that make its four walls."

"Now do you see why I insist on keeping a pail of water near the shanty door, just in case?" Chen fingered the queue draping over his shoulder.

Ah shook her head. "You will more likely trip on it than use it to put out a fire."

"Chen has the right idea, but unfortunately I have seen the worst." Clark drew his brows closer together. "Flames rage across entire blocks in minutes, destroying everything in the way. A pail of water can do nothing to stop them."

The three sat in momentary silence. Their city was helpless against those who did not respect the power that could kill them all.

The host returned and slapped down three plates with shredded meat, beans, and rice in a mélange of brown gravy, a creamy froth bubbling around the edges.

Clark posed with his fork and knife in each hand. He gazed up at the host. "My good man, whatever shall we call this excrescence?"

The host's cheeks went from pink to scarlet. "Ah, some kinda hang town hash or t'other. They say it come down from Placer diggins, and the miners call fer it so often, I just make it fer all now. If I tries to serve roast beef and potatoes, they just push it away and calls for hash."

Ah rested back against her chair. She would give anything for chopsticks and a tasty cabbage roll.

The host lifted his sauce-stained apron, then wiped his drippy nose on it.

She lifted her fork and dipped it into the hash, hardly daring to disturb the plate. She gave a sigh. Where was the roast duck from the merchant's fair in Guangdong?

Her taste of a small bit of the hash revealed mush, goo, and salt, the taste reminding her of the Pearl River's stinky shores at low tide. How could anyone eat this? She had hardly taken a swallow when voices rang out in the distance, first at the doorway, then followed by stamping boots traveling toward her across the plank flooring.

Chen nudged her shoulder. "What is it?" she whispered. He tilted his head toward the doorway.

Clark was staring at two men approaching their table.

Ah turned. This was the same stocky fellow with the squashed hat from the scene outside the courthouse. With rapid movements, he tugged a pencil from behind his ear and pulled out a sheaf of paper from his satchel.

She clenched her jaw and tugged at Chen's forearm. Her dragon awoke in the presence of this stranger.

The stocky fellow stopped abruptly at her table, then rested his hands on his protruding stomach. He extended a hand toward her, his fingers soft and white. The taller man lingered behind; he yanked out a piece of butcher's paper and a black crayon. Dirt encrusted his fingernails.

Where on earth had their filthy hands been? Ah did not shake their outstretched hands; instead, she tucked her own hands into the folds of her jacket where her fan lay in comforting stillness. The stocky fellow's fist fell onto the table, punctuating the awkward silence.

A tense moment passed. Chen rose to his feet, the chair creaking where he must have gripped the back of it. Maybe he was curious, but also worried for her welfare.

She met Clark's glance. "I do not want to speak to these men."

Clark straightened his back, the crinkles deepening around his blue eyes. He turned to the men. "What do you wish with the lady?" he asked. "And, by the way, who are you?"

"I am a reporter from the *Alta California*. And this here is my sketch artist. He follows me from story to story, capturing the scenes. That way I can remember what I saw."

The newsman gave a crackling laugh. "This town and even the whole El Dorado buzzes with the story of this gorgeous Mrs. Toy with her silk white skin, lotus-bound feet, and hair like black satin. A few words with the lady is all I seek."

"Name?" Chen growled.

"Harold Snow. And this here artist is Joe Ludding." Snow doffed his squashed hat and smashed it into his bag.

"Careful, Snow." Clark reddened, and he clenched his fists resting on the tabletop.

Clark seemed to care about her welfare. She offered a wave of thanks to Goddess Mazu.

Their voices went silent.

Chen slipped into back his chair, two worry lines flashing between his eyes.

As if on command, Ludding sat down at the end of the table, then flattened out his drawing paper. He laid out an array of colored pencils and began to sketch Ah's portrait. Beneath his black pencil, her delicate nose, mouth, and chin emerged onto the page. First one ear appeared, then the other.

He crowned her head with black hair, topped by the Manchurian style chignon she wore today, with a ruby, gold, and pearl pendant hanging from a comb where she tucked it into the side. He managed to capture the angle and sparkle in her eyes, and the skeptical look with which she regarded everyone and everything in America.

Something about the sketch enthralled her. The face he drew was wistful but filled with hope. Quivering, she gazed not only into the black satin of her own eyes, but also into the mirror of her own past in Guangdong. That remembrance greeted her at sunrise every morning and bedded her at moonrise each night.

He finished off her portrait with the Manchurian style jacket, its strips of white silk crossing her breasts. He reached into his bag and brought out an orange and white crayon which he mixed together on the jacket, coloring it to match the same apricot sheen as in real life.

Harold Snow exclaimed, "See what an exceptional beauty you are, Mrs. Toy? No wonder the miners dream about you at night, and race to your shanty from the dock, wishing only for a glimpse of you?"

Chen looked from Snow to Ah, clearly waiting for her response.

She grew warm. "Thank you, Mr. Snow. It is much like the picture I see in the looking glass each morning."

Clark looked down at the portrait, then over at her. "If I owned such a considerable likeness, I might want to stare at it every day, forgetting everything else." She detected a slight tremor in his voice. Did he truly mean what he said?

"If you like, I can ask Mr. Ludding to make another one for you." She turned and asked, "You would not mind, would you? For Mr. Clark?"

Ludding glowed. Maybe he was not used to this level of appreciation. "Might as well. Now that I have one for Snow, I can make a copy to cap the climax." Within a few minutes, he completed another version of Ah's portrait, this time coloring her apricot silk with an even more vibrant hue. "There." He rolled up her second portrait with a length of black grosgrain ribbon from his pocket. With a flourish, he set it in Clark's open palm.

Clark fingered the scroll. His gaze was steady. "I'll treasure this portrait, but I still have a hankering for the real woman." His glance traveled from her eyes, to her apricot silk, taking in the length of her yellow and white paneled skirt. Was he remembering her naked body?

She cleared her throat, tamping down the rising flames tickling her.

At that moment, the host reappeared with tumblers of whiskey for them. As he bent over to pass the drinks to her companions, the man's rope belt loosened, and Ah saw his pants sag below his waistline in back, revealing a line of freckly skin playing tag with the strings of his greasy apron.

She stifled a chuckle.

Snow and Ludding took their tumblers, downing the contents in one sip.

When the host held out her tumbler, she shook her head.

"None for the lady?" he asked.

She patted her stomach. "Already enough in here."

"Only the finest likker served here." He sighed and downed the tumbler himself, before shuffling back to the kitchen.

She glanced around her table. What kind of men were these? Oh, well—they may be simple, but they were not Lee Shau Kee or Tung Chao, and they did not want to hurt her.

Clark's voice urged, "Chen, take a swig."

At first Chen shrank from his tumbler, but then he lifted it to his lips. "Strong," he said, "like *Baijiu* in Canton." He took another sip, then coughed.

Clark clapped him on the back. "Good man." He grinned.

Chen pounded his chest but followed with a crooked smile. "Different from Baijiu, not as fragrant."

Clark leaned toward Chen. "Takes some getting used to, they tell me. Me, I've drunk it all my life. Where I grew up in New York, my Daddy said it would make me a strong man. Guess he was right!" He lifted the glass, and the amber liquid vanished into his mouth.

She warmed to see Clark and Chen on friendly terms. Not only did they protect her, but they were also her family in such a strange land filled with rough men who spoke words like "likker" and "varmint." These versions of English sounded as foreign to her as the Mandarin language spoken outside Canton.

Chen had gladly offered to remain her bodyguard; in fact, he had become her island refuge in this odd world of white men with lewd habits and lascivious ways.

The next morning, the sun streamed through the schoolhouse windows, illuminating the previous fire's dust where it carpeted the room. She shook her head. Fires were breaking out continually around the town, and on every block a half-burned building sat, its empty windows yawning like dark, hungry mouths.

Ah wrote in Chinese lettering with her index finger on the grimy table. A sunbeam flowed across Chen's slender hands resting on the table. Why was Judge Almond taking forever today?

This time the bailiff allowed Clark to sit alongside her and Chen, and the three waited, growing increasingly restless. The room was quiet save for street sounds: the pounding of nails and clopping of horses' hooves.

Though she could feel Clark's eyes on her, she avoided his gaze. He was like a spark to kindling: the closer she was, the less control she had. This was not the time to lose herself in the landscape of his strength. She must focus on the task at hand.

She cleared her throat made thick from the gritty air. If not heavy with smoke, the atmosphere would fill with the dust of building and rebuilding. Timbers that went up today would be torn down tomorrow, if they hadn't burned down first, or been ripped apart by strong winds. At any time, a major fire might sweep across the entire city, causing millions in damage and many lives lost. Were these small, deadly fires a sign of worse to come?

Then another question occupied her. Where was Lee Shau Kee hiding in the growing town? Clark had checked the ships in port and reported that Lee Shau Kee was not recorded as having a reservation, nor had he been logged in as a passenger returning to Hong Kong.

Her thoughts rolled in like breakers reaching the shore. On one hand, she could sympathize with Lee Shau Kee. He loved his little sister Lily and would fawn over her endlessly. Yet she had watched Tung Chao take Lee Shau Kee's brotherly affection as a sign of weakness. She never saw proof, but she always wondered if Tung Chao threatened to harm Lily if Lee Shau Kee did not do his bidding. Tung Chao recognized Lee Shau

Kee's crafty mind when he used him, and so from time to time, he employed him to creep aboard another rival's ship and steal the contents. This was a common practice on the wharf at Guangzhou, but the Cantonese authorities exacted harsh penalties for those who got caught. The risk sharpened the wits of someone like Lee Shau Kee, who became stealthy and clever, and who lurked around the deep bowels of ships, avoiding detection.

Tung Chao kept up with the innovations of his competitors by using tools like Lee Shau Kee. Over the years she watched her brother-in-law became more competitive than her husband; in fact, the more money he made, the more ruthless he became. In time, Lee Shau Kee was transformed from a mere instrument into Tung Chao's darker ally.

Petty thievery? Bank fraud? Blackmail? Story said Lee Shau Kee was getting involved in serious crimes. Of course, any time she had broached the subject with Tung Chee, he would frown and tell her to stay in her place—be silent—an obedient wife.

Around the time that Ah and Tung Chee left Guangdong, rumors flew that Lee Shau Kee had murdered a dockworker on the wharf at Guangzhou. But despite his arrest and accusation, he was never tried in court. Someone had gotten him off, and that someone had to be Tung Chao.

When she heard that Lee Shau Kee had fled to the gold fields, she could hardly blame him. People said there were millions of gold nuggets to be had. Week by week, San Francisco Bay filled with more ships, the vessels abandoned as would-be miners scrambled overboard, swam to shore, and headed to the gold mines to stake their claims.

Her thoughts grew increasingly troubled—doubtless Lee Shau Kee would come back to try kidnapping her again, but when? Was he secreted among the denizens of the dark alleys and byways with the Cantonese louts who frequented opium dens and nefarious gambling haunts? She shrank at the possibility—the only place she knew to go for help would be the Daileys' in Monterey. But if Lee Shau Kee had money and a long reach, even there she would not be safe. Plus, she would be putting the Dailey family in danger.

"All rise!" The bailiff called, breaking her chain of thoughts.

Ah, Chen, and Clark rose to their feet.

Tall, heavyset Judge Almond entered with a flourish of his black gown and took his seat upon the bench. Wearing his rimless glasses at a rakish angle, he resembled an oversized lizard. He struck the gavel and ordered the court in session. "I hereby summon Mrs. Toy, Mr. Chen, and Deputy Clark to my chambers, if you please." He disappeared into a small storeroom adjacent to the school house. This served as a temporary office for the judge, next to the Recorder's Court. Ah and Chen followed Clark through the open door into a small space lit only by a small window. There they met the judge, his glasses askew, who was seated at a student desk. Since he was rocking the inkwell, his large knees must be hitting the underside of the desk. She suppressed a giggle.

After waving the bailiff to wait outside the door, the judge said, "Do sit down." He pointed to some oversized blocks that doubled for children's seats when school was in session. Behind him a set of McGuffey Readers lined a bookshelf .

Ah recognized the blue and yellow books. In Guangzhou Mrs. Dailey had used them to teach her English. She had often sounded out the words on the page. Mrs. Dailey had said the strange word "phonics" over and over, breaking the full words down into their sounds so Ah could hear them. Ah would imitate the syllables until Mrs. Dailey would clap and say she had learned them correctly.

Following the Judge's gesture, Ah sat down first, minding that her silk pantaloons did not catch on the uneven wood surfaces. She watched Chen and Clark perch on the adjacent blocks, their knees to their chests. She swallowed, trying to remain respectful.

Judge Almond pushed his glasses up on his forehead. "I apologize for the state of my chambers, but we must make do until a new courthouse is built. Since this is a matter of some delicacy, I have summoned you into private chambers, away from prying eyes. That crowd of tomfoolery in the courtroom might play mischief in spreading untruths about you, Mrs. Toy. *The Alta* will be printing the news of my decision soon enough."

Ah lowered her head. "I am grateful, Judge Almond." She eased her fan from her pouch and waved it gently back and forth.

Clark said, "Yesterday we were followed into the California Restaurant by a reporter enchanted by Mrs. Toy. He was all words, Your Honor. A nuisance."

The Judge shrugged. "Well, Mrs. Toy is rather—shall we say—unique."

Ah watched Clark clench his fist. Was he being defensive?

The judge continued in a softer tone. "Detectives report that Mr. Lee is not in San Francisco, so for now, Mrs. Toy, you are free to stay in the city, and you should no longer be concerned for your safety."

How did they know Lee Shau Kee was not in the city? She let out a loud breath.

Clark broke in. "With all due respect, Your Honor, Mr. Lee could return from the gold hills at any moment and attempt to accost Mrs. Toy again. He would have a sizeable reward waiting for him in Hong Kong, so it would behoove him to attempt it another time."

Judge Almond ran his tongue across his lower lip. "You have a point, Officer Clark. Yet, should he strike it rich as some are rumored to be doing in the Placer mines, he may wish to stay and prosper on this side of the Pacific rather than return home."

Ah snapped her fan shut. "Your Honor, I wish to speak."

"By all means, do say your part, Mrs. Toy."

"What about my safety? If Lee Shau Kee presses his cause, will you take Tung Chao's side and force me back to China where I will be nothing more than a slave to my brother-in-law?"

Judge Almond reddened. "Mrs. Toy, the occupation you have chosen—this lookee girl business—makes you a target for those unsavory men who would accost you anywhere you go in this town." He set his glasses onto the bridge of his nose and peered at her through the foggy lenses.

Her inner dragon flared. "Are you saying, then, that no matter that Lee Shau Kee attempted to kidnap me in front of Chen and Mr. Clark, these two witnesses, plus many other men in the teashop, that I am not deserving of justice because of what I do?" Her voice rose, her words bouncing off the McGuffey Readers.

"I do not believe you are an American citizen, Mrs. Toy." A greenish-gray cast crept across his cheeks.

A rising tide washed over her, and she did everything she could to avoid screaming at him. "I work hard, I pay my taxes, I do not break most laws."

The judge held up his hands. "Mrs. Toy, do calm yourself. You make an—er—interesting argument. Yet, according to the law of the land, we must have proof of any wrongdoing, and we must have Mr. Lee detained and questioned in order to arrest him for kidnapping. We also have to hear valid witness testimony."

Ah exchanged glances with Chen. Few Cantonese would dare come forward to a court hearing.

The judge paused for a moment, then continued. "As it stands now, I think Mr. Lee was just doing his job for his master in Hong Kong. After all, he was sent as Tung Chao's emissary to find you and bring you back to your lawful husband-to-be. Of course, you are in America now, a legal resident, though not a citizen, and subject to our laws and freedoms. Tung Chao cannot simply force you to go back to China against your will."

"You have proof that Lee Shau Kee assaulted and attempted to kidnap me." She frowned. "In Guangdong, such a man would be taken and torn apart." She stretched the truth a bit and experienced a pang of guilt.

"I have only one valid witness here, and that is Mr. Clark." He tapped his finger on the student desk.

"What about Chen? Other men in the tea shop?"

"Mr. Chen is your employee, and the men in the shop would not speak about it. Besides, I do not count the hearsay of immigrants." The judge shifted and pointed at the bookshelf behind him. "See those McGuffey Readers, Mrs. Toy?" He reached up and pulled down a book. "Since you come from heathen lands, you may not recognize this." He set the book on his desk, the cover facing toward her.

Of course, the poor judge did not know what he was talking about. Her lip trembled slightly. "I do know the McGuffey Reader. Mrs. Dailey taught me to read from one of those back in Guangzhou."

He gave her a dismissive glance. "Well, Mrs. Toy, as child reading McGuffey, I learned the value of the steady firmness of moral force and the strong effect of determination. In our country, we suppress our scenes of carnage and choose instead to exercise fair hearings and apply justice."

She paused, absorbing his lofty words. "Your Honor, all I ask is for fairness from the court." The air in the chamber grew thick and suffocating; she opened her fan and fluttered it.

His reptilian skin took on a sweaty sheen and he stroked his beard. "Officer Clark walks your precinct, and he will be aware of any future misdeeds. Under his watch, you should be duly surveilled."

Clark tapped his badge. "Indeed, Your Honor."

"Oh—and one more thing, Mrs. Toy." His eyelids flickered.

"What is that, Your Honor?"

"I am only telling you this because I sense you are a good woman." His eyes shifted back and forth. "There is a law-and-order movement arising in this town, a very powerful one. The members of the Know-Nothing Party and other factions. They harbor a dislike for Celestial immigrants. If Lee Shau Kee were to bump up against them, they would slap him on a ship back to China lickety-split. I get lists all the time of men they want us to arrest, Mrs. Toy. The Know-Nothings may have nabbed him first. Wouldn't be surprised. That could happen."

Ah wondered. Could the judge be a Know-Nothing, too? Treacherous waters ran not only in the Bay. Was the judge lenient toward her Lookee Shop in order to curry favor for himself? Or was it because he pitied her? Men like him kept power by talking out of both sides of their mouths.

The judge stood up and placed the McGuffey Reader up on the bookshelf behind him. He pulled his robes about him. "This meeting is adjourned." With that he opened the creaky door, and swept in haste out of the tiny chambers.

The bailiff led them safely out of the side entrance onto the street. On her way out, Ah heard male voices churning in the schoolroom. No doubt Judge Almond had a new trial to hear.

Six

❦ ICE FLOES ❦

*T*hree evenings later in the shanty, Chen's queue fell over his shoulder, almost dipping into the soup he poured into Ah's cup. She gave a lighthearted laugh. One of these times his long braid would fall into the food. "Chen, you must trim back your queue. Would you like me to do it?"

His Manchurian eyes grew hard. She recognized that look, so familiar since childhood. If only she could summon the words back into her mouth. His hair was a sacred, private matter, never discussed with a woman. Whenever she offended him, he would go quiet, and the silence would flow between them like eddies on the Pearl River Delta.

Despite her transgression, he softened. "I will go to *lei faat din* on Stockton Street. The barber there has sharp tools and can straighten the edges for me. But cut the queue? Never. You know that was an ancient edict from the Qing emperor, and we must never disobey."

"Of course." Persistent heavy knocking at the shanty door drowned out her words. "Who is that?" Ever since Lee Shau Kee's attempted kidnapping, her heart would pound when someone came to the door.

She fixed her gaze on the back of Chen's black jacket while he crossed the room, his queue sailing behind him. He lifted the small block of wood in the peephole and peered out into the street.

"Chen," a voice cried. "Officer Clark. I say, please open up."

Although Clark's voice startled her, she did not move. Her feet were heavy as bricks. She grew weary of that day's dressing and undressing for salacious miners, so she sat in her pink satin robe, mixing her chicken and vegetable soup's contents with her chopsticks.

The door opened, casting a fog's grayish light into the shanty. "Mrs. Toy, I must talk to you." Clark's voice was smooth and resonant.

She flushed—if only she were dressed more presentably. She must look a fright. After resting her spoon on the table, she turned toward him. "I do not take gentleman callers at this hour, Mr. Clark. I am sure you must be aware that I meditate in the evenings. I am very tired, you see."

He crossed the room with a long-legged stride. "You do appear buck tired, Mrs. Toy, so let me be brief." He clutched his hat loosely. A smile played about the edges of his mouth.

Clark was being very formal, calling her twice by her name. Was this a serious matter?

Chen kept an eye on his bowl of soup as though memorizing its contents.

Clark's smile disappeared. "Our men captured Lee Shau Kee, and this morning they set him aboard the brig *Correo de Cobija*, bound for Hong Kong. I came as soon as I heard."

She blinked. "I can hardly believe it."

"Sure tell, he is a goner." His eyes widened.

Ah turned to Chen, "Could you please go to the woodpile, get some logs, and light the fire?"

Chen cast a longing glance at his soup bowl and scuttled out the door.

Clark looked about him. "My, it is dark as pit-coal indigo in here."

71

Ah Toy struck a match and lit the candle on the table. "The window lets in light during the day, but at twilight, especially in foggy summer, it is very somber in here."

She paused, watching the candle's fire burst sputter and dance, blending the red, yellow and blue flames, first lightening, then darkening in swirls.

Clark glanced down at the soup.

"Would you like some?" she asked. "Chen made it only now, and there is more."

Clark shook his head. "No, I am on watch and I must return to the Plaza. Another time I think, but now back to the subject of Lee Shau Kee."

"Yes, back to him." She gave an involuntary shudder.

"The story goes like this—one of our wharf-side detectives, Harold Painter, nabbed the scoundrel this morning and took him to the judge who slapped an order of deportation on him. Painter threw him back on the ship this morning. The darned Lee Shau Kee was whipped. That soap lock and rowdy is now headed for home, never to return."

She could not help pondering how Harold Painter was involved. "Did this really happen? I can see where you might want to soothe my fears by telling me this news."

He threw his hands up in the air. "You are indeed a lucky woman that we nabbed him this quick. It is some pumpkins, sure. The search has been called off. All detectives may stand down." He stepped back, regarding her. "But I do not understand—I thought you would be joy-jumpin' at the news."

"I am pleased." Ah Toy lost herself in thought. Even if Lee Shau Kee were sent back to Guangdong, he would return here and keep trying until he caught her for good. Tung Chao was persistent—she had seen him nagging workers on the docks in Guangzhou. A sudden idea came to her: she needed more details. "Mr. Clark, may I speak to Mr. Painter, the detective who found Lee Shau Kee?"

"No need—" He stretched out his hand, his fingertips grazing her arm.

Though she welcomed his gentle touch, she cocked her head to the side. "I want to be sure, though."

A frown crept across his face, and he looked away into a corner of the shanty.

Had she disappointed him? She cleared her throat. "Well, I am sure you are correct. I am most sorry for questioning you." She rose, lingered there for a moment, then took a step closer to him. The candle's glow turned his hair from golden to blond, and his blue eyes reflected the flickering light.

He looked at her and breathed sharply. Was he surprised at her closeness? His mouth opened, and she saw the same wonder on his face as the day she first sat before him, naked as a babe.

And in turn she longed for him, something she had never experienced. Her heart raced, and her breath quickened. A strange heat consumed her. But she needed to step away. Was there hesitation in his eyes? After a moment's lingering, she moved back.

After widening the distance between them, she shuffled to the door and held it open a crack. "Thank you," she turned toward him. "You have been very kind to come and tell me this news." She lowered her head; his footsteps brushed the floorboards.

Again, his nearness made her weak, unfamiliar desire rising in her like a tickling flame.

"Good night," he said, his voice low and throaty. His hand slid down her arm and his fingers lightly entwined her wrist.

Time held them together in a web of spun silk. If only the moment would last.

Someone banged against the door, breaking their precious silence. Clark released her hand.

"Come in." She stepped away, her eyes lingering on Clark's face.

Chen pushed past her through the open door. He carried three pine logs which shifted precariously in his arms. After he skirted Clark, he set them into the Ben Franklin stove.

"Thank you, Mr. Clark." She cleared her throat, resuming a formal tone.

Wordless, Clark put on his policeman's cap, adjusted the brim, and backed away down the street, his eyes leveled on her. Only after tripping on a tin can did he face away toward town.

After a night of sleepless tosses and turns on her mat, Ah Toy met the day already dressed. She wore her hair bound into a knot atop her head, and she carried her lotus shoes in her right hand. After opening her bedroom door, she stepped over Chen where he slept on his mat. She padded over to the window, then raised the cotton shade with her left hand, letting in a ray of sunshine which tumbled across his sleeping form.

He responded through a series of snores.

Laughing, Ah Toy bent down and touched his back.

He murmured, "*Laan hoi,*" and turned onto his other side facing away from her.

She gave his back a push. "I am not going away. Get up!"

He groaned and turned to face her, half-rising, rubbing his hand across his eyes. "Yes, *si tau po,* Lady Boss. I must go out to the back alley to wash first." He rolled out of his bedding fully dressed, and sat on his mat, easing into his shoes.

After he went out through the squeaky door into the rear alley, Ah tiptoed into their makeshift kitchen, and pulled down the tin of rice cakes from a high shelf. She extracted two cakes, then deposited them into a small satin pouch affixed to her belt. Later on they would be hungry.

By the time Chen returned, Ah rocked on her lotus shoes near the door, waiting for him to open it and survey the street outside, ensuring that it was safe enough for them to travel. He ambled toward her, pulling on his black quilted jacket.

Once outside, Chen turned the key in the lock of their door, and Ah aimed toward the wharf. The sun was made its way onto the horizon as the dawn approached, and a strange but lively blend of pink and purple gilded the puffy clouds sailing across the western sky.

Chen's fingertips braced her arm, and he guided her across plank streets. They skirted piles of horse droppings. Around the dung buzzed a swarm of flies, their wings whirring like a small engine. As they neared the harbor, they heard dockworkers shouting as they loaded trunks and barrels. Their cries blended with those of carpenters and provisioners driving wagons about as various clipper ships made ready for departure.

Every so often, she heard a catcall. "Celestial lovely! Visiting you soon!" Or she would hear, "Lookee Girl! Naked—she is mine!" She refused to look at those who called to her and clung resolutely to Chen's arm.

Hundreds of vessels lay abandoned in the bay, their masts tilting back and forth, their hulls bobbing on the waves. Such a mess of rotting real estate. Some of the ships were already being converted to other uses: prisons, hotels, or restaurants. One could see wood from yardarms and hulls jutting out from shanties in the street. Some hotels like the Niantic were named after the stolen parts of the ships embedded in the building. A warm breeze blew into the bay, and Ah held her face up toward the sun to capture the warmth of its rays.

Chen paused before an Italian man roasting chickens on a spit. He tapped her shoulder. "Si tau po, I must ask a question." The breeze loosened a lock of hair from his queue and he brushed it back behind his ear.

"Of course, Chen." A part of her reveled in their friendly exchanges.

"Why are we here at the wharf and not preparing the shanty for to-day's visitors?" His eyes darted over to the chicken roasting." She grinned, watching him savor the aroma of rosemary and garlic that flowed in the air.

Ah said, "I would have you follow me since we must act in haste. I shall tell you as we go. We are looking for Harold Painter, the detective Officer Clark told us about yesterday."

He ran his tongue across his lips. "Why? I am hungry."

"Shhh, Chen, not now...later." She broke away from his arm and aimed toward a ship's captain who stood, legs akimbo, sucking on a pipe, its tobacco streaming into the air.

The sharp, pungent whiff hit her like a fist. She blinked it way, then waved. "Captain, may I have a word?"

To her relief, the captain smiled. Thankfully he did not stare at her the way most of the round eyes did—with a mixture of awe and ridicule. Maybe he was accustomed to the ways of Chinese people on his seafaring voyages. Maybe he would help her.

She met Chen's quick gaze. He could not hide his hunger. And somehow the roast chicken's aroma was stirring her own appetite, so she might eat alongside him.

Chuckling, she reached into her pouch and lifted out a gold coin.

Chen grinned, extended his hand and took the money.

She said, "Buy a half chicken for us. We will eat some now, some later back at the shanty." When he hesitated, she gave his arm a little push. "Go—now. I can ask the captain here a question, then when you return, we can take turns biting on the chicken."

"Yes, si tau po." But as he stepped away from her toward the chicken vendor, he looked back at her. Did he know she was watching? After all these years, she continued to harbor a painful distrust of men. But no time to consider that—he had already reached the chicken vendor and was layering heavenly chicken onto his slice of brown paper.

Ah turned back to the captain.

"Yes, Miss?" Even as he spoke, his teeth gripped his pipe.

"We are looking for a policeman."

"Are you in trouble, Miss?" His eyebrows lifted.

"No, we wish to speak to him on a matter."

"I know most of the policemen on the wharf. His name?" Smoke swirled about his head.

"Harold Painter."

"Hmmm—not a man I know—let me check." The captain stepped over to a dockworker loading a large wagon labeled WOOL. "Joseph, don't forget the lumber, but, say, I have a question." He shouted over the clatter of wagon wheels rolling by.

"Aye, Captain." The dockworker's voice rang out. "Something else?"

Circling back to Ah Toy, the captain asked, "The name again?"

"Painter, Harold." She pressed down fear. What if she could not ever find Painter? Her prayers to the Goddess Mazu might come in handy today.

The captain looked back at the dockworker. "Know a detective on the wharf named Painter?"

"Aye, indeed." The worker pointed east. "Saw him this morning headed that way toward *The Tarominta*. You know the one—the mining company ship. Brought her in this morning from New York. Mighty fine vessel, that one."

The captain nodded, then shifted toward her. "If you hurry, Miss, you've a smart chance of catching him."

"Yes, Captain." She whirled around. Where was Chen? She made ready some keen English words to use on him, such as *laggard* or *wastrel*. He had never disappointed her up to now, but there was always a first time. Though he usually stayed by her side, especially when she was with strange men, she had indulged him this one time. Had she made a mistake? Was that him in the distance, jogging her way? It had better be.

Chen scurried toward her, holding a dripping half-breast of chicken over brown paper, in addition to a greasy bag, and Ah Toy saw him watching the chicken like a cat would eye a dangling mouse. "Want some, si tau po?"

"No, go ahead." She chuckled. How could she be mad at him?

After looping the bag around his wrist, Chen bit into the chicken's soft flesh, and he ate as they veered around wagons, horses, and crates. Then when he had chewed the meat off the second joint, he stopped, casting the bones off the wharf into the Bay. "My wish for good luck today." He regarded the water, a grin spreading across his face.

She basked in this communal joy. "Yes, good luck." The water rippled. It was probably a seal, but it could be the deft movement of a tiger shark whose snap would devour the bones and all its floating remnants. She pictured the chicken roosting in its new, underwater home.

After fifteen minutes' walk along the wharf, Ah's feet throbbed. How fast a moment of joy could disintegrate into misery. Maybe this outing was a failure. Maybe she could not do it alone with Chen.

As if sensing her weakness, the dead Tung Chee's voice reverberated with each step she took. *You are lower than the rock I overturned and found you under. You are only good enough to drown in the river. One baby girl after another? All your fault.*

She shook off the unpleasant haunting. Though she and Chen had passed many men of all colors and nationalities, arriving and departing from parts around the world, they saw no sign of the policeman named Harold Painter. In fact, no one sauntered by wearing a badge.

She drew nearer to Chen. "What use is a policeman if they are not patrolling?" After observing the blob of chicken grease on Chen's chest, she said, "You made a mess."

He frowned, licking the fingers of his right hand and making stabs at the stains. At the sound of men's shouts, Chen raised a greasy finger, then pointed forward. "Look!"

She fixed on a set of pilings some feet away on the dock where two men perched on a huge coil of thick rope. After taking small steps toward the men, she paused, absorbing their scene. One wore a long coat, open to reveal a badge pinned to his vest; the other was a shabby bearded man as young as twenty-five.

On the wharf, a clipper ship made ready to sail. Ah caught a whiff of linseed oil, pitch pine resin, and paint. Smells like those had mixed with vomit and excrement on the *Eagle*. Dull pounding could be heard in the distance. Someone must be repairing the deck of a ship.

The coated man passed a clear bottle of what might be whiskey over to the bearded one who took a healthy swig. Was that Painter? It had been awhile since that first day on the docks.

Her resolve strengthened. "Sir, a word?" She pictured herself small, like a chip in a porcelain teacup.

"Well, who might you be, almond eyes?" The coated man tugged vainly at a black forelock adorning the middle of his brow. "Not too many of yer kind in town." A flicker of recognition passed over his face. "Wait—God's breath, do I know you?"

She ignored his question. "I am looking for Officer Harold Painter—the dockworker on the wharf told me I would find him here." If only she could tamp down the urgent fire in her dragon's chest.

"I am Painter." He stepped down off the rope, and straightened himself. "How may I help, Miss Almond Eyes?"

Ah sidestepped the language, having been called worse. "Mrs. Toy is my name."

"That's it! Now I recognize you. You didn't go back to China when I told you to. But—I got to give you credit—the news sheets call you 'The Girl in the Green Silk Pantaloons.' Officer Clark says you run some 'lookee' place or t'other." He stroked his throat and burped loudly.

She trembled at the memory of their first meeting. Going back to China? What a deadly possibility.

"What can I do for you?" His gaze flickered over Chen, then returned to her.

She peered at him through watery eyes. Holding her fan over her nose and mouth, she continued. "I want to know the whereabouts of a man named Lee Shau Kee. He was supposed to have been put on a brig back to Hong Kong yesterday?"

Painter narrowed his eyes. He assumed a strangely silent pose.

Was he studying her? A coldness crept up her legs and into her spine. If he ordered one man onto a boat back to Hong Kong, he could always put her on the next one, too. Then, what would he do to Chen?

After a moment, he said, "Yes, I did." His eyes shifted left, then right. "That vermin Lee Shau Kee went aboard, kicking like a mule."

"He was kicking?" Clark had Lee he had been whipped, so he would have been too tired to kick. Something strange took over Painter's voice—a certain strain, maybe?

Painter ran a lazy hand over his holster. "Yes, ma'am. My aim is to get rid of those Celestial ruffians any way I can. City needs to cleanse itself of the rotten bastards, no offense, my lady."

She bristled at the words "Celestial ruffians." Chen's arm pressed against hers. Best not to argue with a man like Painter, hardened by the parade of burly characters on the docks and wharves of the Bay City. On the other hand, he probably knew no better. Men like him had to survive the wharf's mean ways.

She said, "I agree that Lee Shau Kee is a bastard, and I feel great relief that you have sent him back to China."

Painter glanced up at his partner, seeming anxious to get back up to his drink. Ah observed him out of the corner of her eye. He had more power than he let on. He knew the docks and their smarmy inhabitants, along with the shipping industry and its corrupt ways. He was in deep with the criminals he had sworn to eliminate.

"Is that all?" he asked. Another trace of crab and whiskey stew floated toward her. "Yes, thank you." Her inner dragon sparked a further realization. Painter was the same sort as Tung Chao, ruthless and self-centered. How frail she was—with a flick of his wrist he could tie her onto a piling, rape, and drown her without a second thought. On the other hand, she might need to get information from him later.

So instead of questions, she fell silent. This time she would not give him trouble. Instead, she turned to Chen and snapped her fan shut, then pointed it eastward, their signal to leave. After taking Chen's arm, she said farewell to Painter, and small-stepped her way up the wharf.

Yet a notion pestered her, so she retrieved her fan once more. She flicked it opened, and waved it near her face. The gentle back and forth, the soft flow of air, relaxed her.

The flow of thoughts resumed. Her male customers spoke freely about the shipping life. Money from all nations and gold changed hands at the docks. And men on the wharves made as much, if not more money, than the gold rushers who abandoned their ships in favor of the mining camps.

She often listened to stories of these dockhands—they pilfered silken goods, drank fine French brandies from cargo, and helped themselves to jade imported from Cantonese merchants.

A man like Painter would offer a safeguard to the shipping companies in return for a wink and a nod should he ever need a favor. And judging from Painter's hard-bitten exterior, Ah suspected that he was a customary part of life on the Bay.

An array of docks stretched out before her and Chen. Long Wharf jutted out into the blue waters. Those coiled ropes reeled in hundreds of ships brimming with men whose hearts traded hope for gold, brass filings for despair. Steamboats passed clipper ships, their crews waving in salute. A black cormorant dove into the water for a fish, leaving a series of widening rings.

She shut her fan and tapped Chen's arm. "I think Painter was lying about Lee Shau Kee."

Chen tightened his grip on her elbow, guiding her steps. "Why do you think so?"

"He would have no reason to get rid of such a man, unless it were for show."

"I do not understand, si tau po." He helped her step over some wood pilings in their path.

She continued. "Such a man might find a Lee Shau Kee useful, maybe for *hauu zaa*."

"Blackmail?"

"Yes, but we must discuss this when we are alone." The big toe on her right foot twinged, and she limped a few steps further. "Please call us a wagon." She leaned against a post. Sometimes her feet were nothing but trouble, especially on days like these.

Chen ran over to a wagon whose driver was loading firewood. The two men were exchanging words, but then her legs numbed and buckled under.

She could do nothing but slowly fall to earth, her legs angled like bent chopsticks.

Chen's voice rang out, filled with panic. "What is wrong?" His footsteps rang out on the plank walk as he ran back to her.

After mumbling an incoherent word, his arms lifted her from where she was kneeling on the wharf. She had always been afraid of a moment like this when her feet failed her. "Take me back," she said.

He cradled her like a child in his strong arms. After setting her onto the wagon seat, he sat next to her. She looked up into his frown-lined face. She sighed, leaning back into the hard wood. Without Chen, how would she survive?

She straightened her skirt, tucked her fan into her pouch, and prepared for the bumpy ride home. But a peculiar torment blended with the numbing pain of her feet. Painter had not put Lee Shau Kee directly on the ship. What if he was still here? Or worse, if he had gone back to Guangzhou, what if he reported his failure to Tung Chao? What would be Lee Shau Kee's next move?

Seven

❧ THIS JAGGED REFLECTION ☙

June 1849

The noonday fog crept into her shanty, wrapping Ah in its blanket. The vapor twisted around her dragon's soul and pinned it down, a vine enfolding a head of cabbage. After she put down her stitching on a torn sleeve of her silk cape, she padded to the mullioned window. She rubbed the glass with the heel of her hand, but it made no difference—the light refused to penetrate the dirty pane, instead remaining as dim at noon as it had been at dawn.

Where was Chen? She had sent him out for some noodles and fresh fish, but since he hadn't returned yet, she would have to get after him. In recent days, he had cast longing glances down the alley known as Pike Street where a gambling den took root the last few months.

Her loneliness reappeared like an unwelcomed friend, and along with her dark thoughts came the sound of cooing and giggling as though children played in the corner of the shanty. She observed the empty stillness while the image focused in her memory. Right there her baby Ling's tiny form hovered in the dim light, bathed in evanescent hues of white, blue, and green.

A slender, delicate thread linked her to the apparition. Ling, her firstborn, had lived the longest of the three daughters, for Tung Chee had gone away while she was in labor, surveying outside factories and territories with his brother. With the firstborn, she had time to hold the babe, to nurse her at the breast, to feel the infant's little fingers grasp her thumb and startle the way a newborn did. And Ah had time to run her fingers through the babe's thatch of black hair, abundant for a newborn, her maid had said.

And even now, floating in the corner of her memory, the child's skin was ivory-colored, like the statue of the Buddha her family had given her the day she had married Tung Chee. Ling was named for dawn, the courage of first light, to embody all those elements of the Dragon King's granddaughter. Yet now, as always, she turned her eyes away from Ling, letting the child's spirit run free to rejoin her another time.

A passing figure drew her eye—this time no apparition. Clark was sauntering past her window. She could hear his whistling, even from inside the shanty. She padded to the door, flung it open, and stepped outside. Maybe Clark's company, along with a breath of cold air, might rid her of the momentary pain of tiny Ling's memory. By then he was two houses away, and she called his name. "Mr. Clark, I am happy to see you." Her voice was freer than usual.

He ambled back in her direction, doffed his hat, and made a half bow.

"I am glad you called to me, Mrs. Toy. I nearly forgot—I have something to share with you. May we step inside?" His gaze traveled over her face and searched her eyes.

Something stirred in the pit of her stomach. "Of course, do come in."

At the small shanty table that also served for business and meals, Clark pulled a news sheet from his coat pocket. He unrolled the paper, then anchored it onto the table with two candlesticks. "Look, an article about you."

Shivers rippled through her small frame. "What to say? A publication for everyone to see?"

Clark frowned. "But surely a wealthy man like Tung Chee would have publicized your beauty the way rich men in America paint portraits of their wives. Gosh, they put them in giant gilt frames and even hang them in their drawing rooms back in New York. They even have parties to celebrate the pictures."

"I do not mind a single portrait. Rather I fear having my doings spread everywhere. Men get news of my shanty through word of mouth. I stay away from the jeers of men in streets and on the docks. But if this news about me is written on walls, everyone will know me."

She read the headline aloud. "CELESTIAL WOMAN, BEAUTY OF SAN FRANCISCO."

"See this." Clark tapped the paper. "The article sings your praises, says your charms are unusual, and your Lookee Shop is not to be missed. He lifted the paper up and read from it. 'Ah Toy, a jewel that sparkles in the sunlight, the girl in apricot silk.'" His voice deepened.

Though moved by the smoldering flame in his eyes, a ribbon unraveled in her bound feet and snaked upward into her core. "I do not wish this. Painter already says they call me the Girl in Green Silk Pantaloons. Now I am in apricot silk? Tell that reporter to take the news back—take it to the Bay and drop it in where the sharks will eat the paper." Her breath came in ragged waves.

Clark's hand grasped her shoulder.

She tried to erect a defensive wall against his gentle grip, but his nearness overwhelmed her.

He leaned down to her ear and whispered. "My dear Mrs. Toy, there is no taking it back. It is like love. Once it is out in the world, it continues . . . I mean, it goes on . . . ." He drew her toward him, a gentle spark lightening the blueness of his eyes.

She trembled, hesitating. There was no denying he held an attraction for her, but this much, so soon? Should she surrender to this surging wave, or wait to find out more about him?

He bent toward her and his lips pressed hers softly. She leaned into his welcoming body. Tung Chee had never held her this way. Should she be afraid? Not only of him, but what her feelings could do? Clark's arms tightened around her, capturing her like a sparrow with a broken wing. In return, she wrapped her arms around his neck. Not only did this feel natural, but for a long moment she could be floating.

Warmth and passion poured from this man like seawater through a broken dike. Crushing her to him, he pressed his mouth to hers. She drank in the lingering sweetness of his kiss. With a certain reluctance, she eased her lips away from his and rested in the shelter of his body, savoring the touch of his fingers on her cheek. His large hand cupped her chin, holding it up to his lips for another kiss. The dim light surrounded them, sheltering them in a sacred moment away from the world's peering eyes.

It had been a long time since a man had kissed her. Tung Chee would mount her as if she were a saddle horse, but he rarely kissed her lips. Clark's tender lips lingered lazily against her cheek. His breathing lulled her into a peaceful sanctuary—she fit into his chest the way a ship finds safe harbor in a rainstorm.

Chen's key clattered in the bolt, and the door swung open.

She inhaled sharply and stepped back from Clark's embrace.

In turn, Clark drew away and gathered up the paper, stuffing it into his jacket pocket. For a moment, a wistfulness crept into his expression. She put aside the mysterious, lovely aching in her limbs.

Ah smoothed her yellow silk qipao. She squared her shoulders and adjusted her smile.

Chen toted in a burlap bag filled with fruit and small bags of goods to the table, where he set it down. A banana fell out of a bag and he reached out and grabbed it before it landed to the floor.

A wordless moment passed, but she filled it with a sharp reprimand. "You have been too long, Chen. Which gambling den?"

He looked down at his feet. "I—I do not really remember."

Ah moved next to him. "Let me smell you?" She sniffed. "Hmmm, lucky no opium on you. If I smell opium, you will eat many hot peppers in my shanty."

Chen's jaw clenched. Was that a shadow crossing his features? Had he been gambling?

Clark's face closed like that of a servant guarding an Emperor's secret. "I must continue on my rounds." He disappeared through the doorway onto the street, followed by the sound of cheerful whistling as he continued along his daily route.

A few moments later, Chen bustled away to the anteroom that also served as a kitchen, and Ah heard knives chopping on wood. The shanty continued to darken, so she crept around, lighting candles with a matchstick, then stoking the fire's oak log

She returned to Clark's mention of her in the news sheets. How would she handle the sudden notoriety that came with her name plastered on posters and news dailies lining walls of the Bay City? She shook her head. The tide of infamy lashed against her small shanty on Pike Street. Was there nothing she could do to stop it? She chewed her thumbnail. Well, she had brought it on herself. Her desperate ploy to make money at the Lookee Shop had paid off, but along with the gold dust came a wasp's sting.

Why were these men so blatant in their admiration of her? This was not the subtle Cantonese way. And they were not kind in their attentions—these public men wanted something from her. Their gold dust gave her security, but at the same time it robbed her of what she wanted most in San Francisco—her dignity.

She could still smell the aroma of Clark's tobacco, and when she ran her tongue across her lips, she tasted the salt lingering from his kiss. An invisible web was building between them; each time she saw him, the filaments grew stronger, drawing her toward his warmth and his vitality.

Yet something else rose within the yellow-blue flame of the candle she had lit at the table. The image of Tung Chee's face, his mouth in a snarl of rage. Her skin prickled. That was how he looked on her worst day with him. The last of the many times when he had stripped her naked and raked her back with his long fingernail, etching crisscross patterns into her skin as he rammed himself into her, over and over until she thought her head would never stop pounding.

His brutality would rise and fall with the fortunes of his business, and the wars and famines that plagued the Empire would affect the Cantonese economy. And times were hard and getting worse. She could expect no better at the hands of Tung Chao.

What was that? A knock at the door jarred her, breaking into these jagged reflections. Who could it be at this hour? She called out. "Chen! Someone at the door."

He marched out of the anteroom and across the floor. The aroma of tobacco smoke and loose tea wafted around him. She watched him open the block of wood in the tiny window of the door and jerk his head around, his queue curling onto his chest. He mouthed, "Officer Wong from the Kong Chow Company."

"One moment, Chen." Her pulse quickened, but she restrained her dragon's impulse to flee to the alleyway, stumble down the street, and take refuge under a half-burned tree. No, that would not be right. She must sit tall and proud. If others did not accord her dignity, she would at least claim it for herself.

Ah backed away, and took a seat on the higher chair where she usually sat in naked beauty before her gentlemen callers. Yet this time she was dressed, and she arranged herself in a regal manner, pulling down the sleeves of her peach-silk jacket, then placing the folds of her long yellow skirt in careful pleats around her. She steadied her hands on the arms of the chair and waited among the flickering candles.

A pale slice of light from the open door illuminated the dark corners of the shanty. A short, chunky man strode in behind Chen. She recognized Officer Wong's unmistakable bulk and girth as he filled the space. He stepped forward to her chair and reached up a hand of friendship.

She shook his hand. "Officer Wong, what good luck brings you to our house?"

She gazed down at the mustached man whose black Manchurian jacket buoyed out, ill-disguising the many rolls of fat underneath. His skin had a sheen of sweat on it, as though he was not used to walking very far, and his chest heaved slightly. He must be trying to catch his breath.

Wong paused. Was he waiting for her to step down from the chair, to subjugate herself to him, to *kau tau* as all his women did, kneeling, and touching their foreheads to the ground, as he demanded?

Ah Toy sat erect, not unlike a Buddha in meditation. "Officer Wong, what may I offer you?" She turned to Chen's upturned face. "Hot water for tea?"

"I will heat the water, si tau po." Chen shuffled away into the kitchen.

Wong raised his eyes to her, his long stringy beard catching the candlelight. "I have no time for tea, Mrs. Toy."

"What did you come to tell me?" she asked, smoothing her peach silk sleeve and letting it drape across her right arm over the chair.

"I came to deliver a warning. The Kong Chow Company does not know I am here."

"Oh?" She papered over her astonishment with a mild tone.

His mouth formed a half-moon. "In fact, they do not know I intercepted the letter before the Committee could see it."

"What letter?"

"The Company received another letter from Tung Chao. Do you wish to read it?" He cast her a narrowed, glinting glance.

She hesitated. Sure, he may have this letter, but many men lied. And even though the letter may be genuine, what secret transaction between Tung Chao and Wong might have taken place?

Chen padded toward her from the kitchen. He paused in the doorway separating the two rooms. She gave him a sideways glance. "Please, Chen, you may come in. I wish to have you present to hear the contents of the letter."

He lowered his head and stepped to her side.

Ah Toy stretched out her hand. "May I see it?"

Officer Wong lifted the missive from the open envelope, then passed it up to her. She unfolded the document and read the print, her eyes roving up and down the page, following the lines of Cantonese calligraphy.

She paused a moment.

Wong sniffed and cleared his throat.

Her voice was steady. "I shall read to you from the letter, Chen, so you may share my concerns. I shall spare you the beginning of the letter, but here is the most important part."

If the Kong Chow Company does not succeed in returning my brother's wife to me, I shall unleash the power of my economy upon you, and my wealth and influence shall haunt you in San Francisco. I shall refrain from providing my companies access to your city for delivery of all my goods on order, and you will no longer have the fine porcelain which you now enjoy.

She took a halting breath and continued to read.

I am also connected to Guangzhou's many jade and jewelry merchants, and I will advise them to withhold their business as well. San Francisco is not our only trading port. You may be assured that if my future wife is not lawfully returned to me by January of next year, you will pay dearly.

I have returned my emissary, Lee Shau Kee, to San Francisco, and he sends me news that Ah Toy continues to live in your city, slandering the family name with her whoring. She must be returned to me in Guangzhou to complete her three year mourning period in my custody. Then I will marry her which is my right as her brother-in-law. This is not a request—it is a demand.

Ah broke away from the hideous document.

A shadow crossed Chen's face.

What were the ramifications of Tung Chao's threats? Looking back at the letter, she saw Cantonese words blending with an old but familiar vision. Tung Chao would choke her if she ever refused to bed him; she had seen Tung Chee treat his concubines the same way. Suffocation made its way from her chest up her neck, into her throat.

Yet in the midst of it all, her dragon shifted, and an illumination struck her. In Guangdong, she would have no choice but to submit to Tung Chao's hand in a brutal marriage, but here in San Francisco she could fight back. Her dragon's presence enlivened her, and she watched as it flicked its imaginary tail behind her where it lay curling down behind the tall chair, resting on the ground below.

She passed the letter back to Wong and blinked down at him. "Why did you come here? What do you want?" The seed of suspicion took root in her words and flowered in her heart.

"I could offer you some security in return for some business," he said.

She lifted her fan from the table and rested its tip against her mouth. "Business is more digestible over a good meal." She glanced at Chen. "Could you serve us that Bird's Nest soup you were preparing, followed by dumplings and crispy noodles with chicken?"

"Yes, si tau po." He slipped away toward the kitchen, unable to resist a backward glance at her.

"Wong, I know you said you could not stay for tea, but will you stay and eat with me?" Her voice was smooth but insistent.

He grinned. "I would be happy to do so. Bird's Nest Soup is one of my favorites. A small portion of course."

She glided off her chair, following behind Wong who lifted his nose in the air and sniffed to catch the fragrance of the cooking. This was a man used to having people wait on him; his bulk echoed his concept of power and control. More ripples of stomach flesh meant more means of crushing another's spirit. She had observed many men like him in Guangzhou from behind the veils while her husband conducted his porcelain factory meetings.

She had been a willing observer in the ways of the cunning. For every bite of food Wong would consume, Ah would extract a grain of information, just as she had seen Tung Chee do in his own business practice.

After reaching the shanty table, Wong pulled out his own chair and readied his chopsticks in preparation for the feast. She gave him a sidelong glance. This man's belly might expand this evening, but her pot of secret information would fill to bursting during the meal.

A few moments later, Wong made quick work of the meal laid before him—he slurped his Bird's Nest soup, masticated his rice, and chomped his crispy noodles.

Chen stood by his side, and Ah caught a half smile on his face. He plainly enjoyed preparing their food with the ample budget Ah gave him; in fact, he had learned to cook by watching the Toy family's cook in Guangzhou. On many occasions he would create special plates to set before a hungry diner. This time he hovered expectantly, a towel draped over his arm.

"Chen, it is most delicious," Ah Toy cast him her broadest smile.

He beamed. "I am glad, si tau po." With that, Chen disappeared into the kitchen area and the clatter of pots and pans resumed.

In Guangdong, Ah Toy would wait, never daring to broach a subject with a man. In Guangdong, she would stand aside, served apart from the men's table, eating alone or with the extended family's children and their mothers.

But this was San Francisco, and she would take her equal place at this table. Her dragon folded its wings back into place. Even so, Ah knew better than to interrupt a man while he was eating; thus she waited until Officer Wong pushed away from the table, patting his stomach.

After listening to his series of burps, she poured another glass of plum wine into his cup. "And . . . there was talk earlier of an offer? In return for your guarding my business?"

He lifted his wine, took a long sip, and rested the cup before him on the table. "Yes. Without Tung Chao's imports, our Cantonese community stands to lose money in the form of taxes and duty paid to our port. But if you agreed to an arrangement, this could be a good thing."

"You speak of a deal. I need details." She penned a circle on the table with an end of her chopstick.

"May I?" he asked, taking the chopstick from her hand.

"Of course," she nodded.

He pushed away the dishes on the table, and took his cup of wine, placing it to his right. On his left, he set her empty wine cup. In the middle, he drew a line with the chopstick. "Here is Guangdong." He pointed to his cup of wine. "The cup is a ship; the wine is all the women that fill the cup.

"There." He pointed to her cup. "San Francisco. Empty—all men— no Chinese women. The men in San Francisco are many, and they thirst for the women. Where are the women?" He poised the chopstick, then turned it horizontally, pointing in either direction.

She studied his table model for a moment. "In the cup . . . in Guangdong . . . you mean there are women in Guangdong who would come to San Francisco?" A lock of hair fell across her face and she wound it behind her ear.

"Exactly." He dragged his chopstick across from the full cup to the empty one. "Now, they must cross the line to get from Guangdong to San Francisco. That line must start with you in the form of an order."

"I do not clearly understand."

He gazed over at her. "Women are not schooled in such matters, so I will speak simply."

His condescending words strengthened her resolve. She leaned toward him. "I do not need simple. I need clear."

He cocked an eyebrow. "You must sign a communal order for the women's passage to San Francisco, open up a brothel to house them, and choose them when they come to auction on the wharf. There will be more women than you can pick from, but you may bid for the best ones. I am kind, so I will give you first choice at auction."

"And what do I pay for?"

"Indentured servants—in your case, women to use in your Lookee Shop, brothel, or anyway you like."

She leaned closer to him. "I need more words to understand this."

He sucked in his breath, apparently annoyed. "You pay for women to the auctioneer, you pay the tax to the Company, you pay for the bigger house, you pay tax on the income from the Lookee shop." He shook his head. "You women cannot think—your heads are full of rotten noodles."

She ignored his insult. "Will I make more money than I do now?"

He looked around the room. "Depending on the number of women you employ, you will make that times far more money than you do now. I think you are getting much gold from the miners, are you not?"

She nodded, pulling her jacket closer about her shoulders, then lifted her fan.

He continued. "These girls will sign an agreement to turn over their earnings to you in order to pay back what you paid for them at auction."

"For how long?"

"Depends on the contract you have them sign. You divide up the months and years, and that is how you figure the incremental payments they make to you."

"In the meantime, I must feed and clothe them as if I have adopted them?"

He nodded. "Well worth your trouble. After this you will be an even wealthier woman." He reached over and patted her arm. "You may go anywhere, do anything. You will have more money than any man in China, except the Emperor himself."

She flared the fan and fluttered it slightly. "And how can I be sure of your safeguard?"

"I have influence with the Kong Chow Company. I will tell them our agreement is the best plan, and they will be glad to send Tung Chao and his ships away. He causes nothing but trouble. His ships are filled with broken goods, and he refuses to repair the damage."

"And what of Lee Shau Kee? Harold Painter says he has been sent back to China, but you know he will return."

Wong shrugged. "He will be no threat without Tung Chao's influence, and besides, the story says Tung Chao has bought mines in the Placer diggings. Even if Lee Shau Kee snuck back in to work Tung Chao's diggings, he would not be interested in kidnapping a mere woman for a few coins. Does not make sense. Not when gold nuggets can give him wealth forever."

She raised her hand. "Wait a moment, Officer Wong. I know Lee Shau Kee from our younger days in Guangzhou. He must be desperate to work for Tung Chao. Even if he were up in the mines, who is to say he would strike gold? I do not believe Tung Chao would give him up so easily."

"Maybe not, but you are not listening to my offer—think carefully. This will expand your profits considerably. Would Tung Chao attempt to kidnap a wealthy woman who could buy any amount of safety she needed?" He shook his head. "I think not."

Her tone softened. "When do the ships come with these women?"

"January. You will have time between now and then to buy your brothel and make all arrangements." He stood, burped again loudly, and beamed over his multiple chins.

"I need to speak to someone first before I agree to this." She walked a tender line here and she knew it. Wong's alliance was thin as eggshell porcelain and as easily broken.

His voice tightened. "The Kong Chow Company will no longer support your interests unless I intervene. There is little time." He reached into the pocket of his silk brocade jacket and brought out a rolled paper. "I need you to sign this agreement."

She watched as he unfolded the scroll containing columns of Cantonese. "What does it say?"

"You vouch that you will to order the girls from their handler in Hong Kong, that you will come to auction and bid for the maidens. Without this paper, it will be hard for me to convince the Kong Chow Company that you are serious about receiving the girls from Hong Kong. The Company pays their passage, and you bid for the young ladies starting at the price they set."

"This all seems rushed." She looked over at Chen who frowned. Was she being forced into a decision she may regret later?

"How many girls do you want to order? They will be sending several, but I need to set a number for the Company."

She sat in stunned silence. A number? How many? As though he were ordering pairs of shoes or brooms, not people.

Wong pressed her. "I must have your answer now, not later. The Company meets tomorrow at ten, and they will be discussing Tung Chao's letter at that meeting."

"Three," she said. Why had she said that number? Was it because girls could be jealous of each other, so a group of three might be more balanced that two? She had no time to think about that now.

"I think that is a good number. Not too many to start. Women are of the lower orders and have pea brains. You will have your hands full with three." He pinched his lips together.

She took in a deep breath. "Very well. Chen, please bring me the pen and inkpot from the desk over there."

Chen scuttled over, grabbed the items, and returned. He set them on the kitchen table with slow and cautious movements.

She took the pen, dipped it into the inkpot, and waited a moment. "Where do I sign?"

Officer Wong beamed out. "I knew you would make the right decision. While holding the paper down on the table, he set his finger on a line of the scroll. "There."

As she wrote her mark on the line, she saw the day she first entered San Francisco Bay on the *Eagle*, filled with hope for a life of freedom. Now was she going to put other women into the same bondage she had escaped?

Officer Wong carefully wound the scroll and placed it into his jacket pocket, then patted it with a puffy hand. He reached for the last of the plum wine in his glass and drained the cup. He laid his chubby hand against his heart. "I am glad to see you have listened to my reason, Ah Toy. It is in your best interest." He stifled a yawn. "Now I must go."

After he gained the threshold and was about to step into the street, Wong turned. "No one must know we have talked. Other people would want the same generous deal I have given you. Do you see?"

"Hmmm. Very well." She raised her chin.

She sensed Chen's measured breathing behind her. "Do you know why you chose three girls, si tau po?"

His voice struck a deep chord that resonated through her. How well he knew her past. Her girl babies. Her pain. She nodded, her words frozen deep inside.

A few seconds later, Wong disappeared into the inky blackness of the shanty-filled streets, leaving her alone again with her thoughts. This man was clever, more than she had imagined. Or was he entrapping her in the net that men tightened around their women?

She remained for a few minutes facing the street, her back against the open door. Ah never dared set foot outside without Chen in the night, but this time, she needed to meet alone with Clark. She cast a cloak about her, pulled a gray shawl over her head, and took small steps down to Clay Street where Clark made his evening rounds. He would be passing shortly after seven at night, when the June fog was rolling over the bay, wrapping the city in a timeless hush.

The vapor dripped onto her shoulders, dampened the windowsills, and turned the dusty street to wet, sandy slush. She shivered in the darkness, yet she would not turn back. Groups of miners passed her, but they focused on themselves, not her, cloaked in the mist.

She spotted Clark at the end of the block. He was speaking to a group of miners gathered together, one raising his voice in what seemed to be an argument. That was no place for her. She hung back behind a barrel half her height, pretending to examine its label.

A young gray cat came up to her and nosed her leg. She reached down, her fingers following the outlines of its bony ribs. Its meows were desperate. "Go away," she whispered. The feline offered a low whimper, then crouched onto a trash pile next to the barrel, and Ah Toy watched the cat issue a stream of urine, scratch the mound, then look up at her. The animal's green eyes gleamed, its whiskers like strands of silver.

Poor thing. Eyes like jade. For some reason, Ah took pity on the wastrel. A mere kitten. She swept the cat into her arms where it nestled, its plaintive mews becoming a steady purr.

The crowd with Clark dispersed, and he took up whistling, swinging his nightstick as he ambled in her direction. She moved around the barrel and sidled up to him. "Mr. Clark?"

He looked down into her face, then at the cat, but then a puzzled grin crossed his features. "Do I know you? You do look familiar—."

He must be confused by her shawl.

She held up her pantaloon and revealed a lotus shoe.

"Mrs. Toy!" he said. Then, reaching out, he rubbed behind the cat's ear. "And who is this?"

"Some kitten I found—I have taken a liking to her. I think I will take her home and name her Jade." She looked up into his crystalline blue eyes. Every time she got lost in them, she was surprised as if it was their first meeting; every time she heard his voice, she lost her wits.

Had he touched her arm? There it was, that tingle again. She did not want to tear her attention away from him, but she had to. "But, what's more important than this cat, I need to talk to you."

"My dear, do you know how plum dangerous it is for you to be here—on the streets—at any hour, but even more at evening?" He reached out and placed her arm in his. "Where is Chen?"

She adjusted the cat in her arms. "I left him at the shanty. I needed to find you by myself."

"Not wise, Mrs. Toy. One of these miners could come along and fix your flint." He patted her hand where it lay on the kitten's back.

Another warm strand was building in their web, and she could not resist putting her other hand over his own. His skin was warm to the touch.

He said. "I am on duty, and I must remain here on the street, but let us have a moment together." He led her into a darkened corner at the side of a shuttered blacksmith shop and pointed out a haybale where she might sit down.

Ah perched on the straw, the cold seeping into her marrow, a kind of chill unknown in Guangzhou—this, the wintriness of the Bay in summertime. Jade seemed to sense the chill, and she snuggled into the curves of Ah's body.

Clark stood regarding her, his foot resting on the bale, and he lit up a cigar. "Now, what is so important you have to risk your health to tell me?" He puffed the tobacco to life, then blew out a stream of smoke.

After she relayed the high points of Officer Wong's visit, the straw rustled as Clark sat down next to her on the haybale. The earthy scent of horse feed mixed with smoke lingered in the damp air. His nearness kindled the dragon's fire inside of her, the intensity she had never known before with a man.

He exhaled a stream of smoke. "Hmmm. Officer Wong is always up to something." But then, his voice took on a playful air. "You know, once you make friends with a cat, you'll never be rid of her."

Ah clutched Jade within the shelter of her long sleeves. "She is so hungry. Look at her ribs. She is frightened and lonely. I might have been her."

"That may be true." His voice softened, and he drew her into the refuge of his broad chest. He lifted her face to his, and within his kiss she felt his warm tongue lace hers, softly, then throbbing, and his arms strengthened around her.

Inside her dragon fire flickered, then leaped into the air, bright flame consuming her loins, and she wanted this man. If only he could take her here, now, but something held her back.

She pressed him away in a gentle motion, resting her hand on his shoulder, then speaking in a whisper. "I did not come for this—Clark, I came to ask for advice."

He drew away, then gently wiped his lips with the back of his hand. Was that a look of sadness? He shifted and his gaze traveled from her face to the sawdust under his feet. "Is it Chen?" he asked.

Where had that question come from? "What about Chen?" Her throat went dry.

"Well, I have been wondering, but I have not been able to ask you because he is always near. Are you and he—lovers?" His nostrils flared.

She lifted her chin. "Whatever makes you think that? Chen is a servant—mostly bodyguard and cook. That is all."

"Are you certain?" He gave her a sidelong glance.

"Quite sure. He was from a poor family in Beijing who had him castrated outside the Forbidden City so that he could apply as a eunuch to the Emperor."

His mouth opened. "Castrated? Like a bull?"

"Yes. The Emperor requires it of all those who serve his concubines within the Forbidden City."

"I thought I had seen all manner of evil on my New York beat. You should have seen the shenanigans between the Dead Rabbits and Bowery Boys in the Five Points, but this . . ." His voice trailed into the dusky street.

She pulled her shawl more tightly about her. "Chen did not pass the test at the Imperial Palace. He was told his hands and feet were too small, predicting he would not be large enough to serve the Emperor. He was a disgrace, shunned by society, and so he escaped to the south, to Guangdong, hoping to hide his condition and his shame."

"What the sam hill?" Clark spoke his question into the air as if hoping to find the answer there.

She gave a shallow sigh. "It is true. My father found young Chen wandering the streets and took pity on him. Since he was harmless to women and girls, my father brought him into our family as a servant to me and my brother. He took on any roles a maid could do, bathing, dressing, fixing our hair, stitching our clothes. He helped in the kitchen. Even better, he was our bodyguard. Chen has been my loyal friend, and he will do me no harm. You may be certain."

"How can you be sure the man is trustworthy?" He set his jaw.

Clark's suspicion was strong, its force echoing in her own doubts. She went on. "He told me—even showed me—when my father hired him to be my servant. We were only thirteen years old. I would not have a man sleeping on my floor in my shanty—otherwise . . ." Her voice drifted into the street, fading into the cool rush of bay air. Somewhere the jingling bells of a coach made music in the gathering night.

Clark waited until the bell sounds died away. The space between them filled with a soft silence. Despite her good news, he studied the ground as he spoke. "I am sad for Chen—what a harsh tradition." He put his arm around her, pulling her close and whispering into her ear. "But I am happy for myself."

Fighting the urge to wrap her arms around him, she pulled away. "Now—have you forgotten the reason I have come to you?"

He gave a sigh. "Very well. About Officer Wong? Opening a new Lookee Shop?"

She nodded.

Something dark passed over his face. "I know you are doing it in exchange for the Kong Chow Company's safeguard, but—a Lookee Shop with more girls? Do you know what that entails?"

"Girls undress in front of men for gold." Her voice was firm, but she grew cold. She had to tell him about the brothel, but something held her back.

"You are right about that." He angled his head. "Frankly, I think that might endanger your new house and your own reputation. Right now, the town knows that you are a woman to 'watch, don't touch.' They speak of you with a kind of—well—reverence."

She tensed. "I know this."

"But your new girls might decide to trade their favors with the men who come to watch them. Beyond your control. Even if you do not call your new house a brothel, the men will look on your girls as prostitutes."

"I see," she said. She had not meant to talk about this so soon, but it was he who brought it up.

He went on. "There are many brothels rising in this town, some seedier than others. Every day on my rounds I am seeing more cribs opening in Little Canton." He wrinkled his nose. "Disgusting."

"Cribs? Elizabeth Dailey taught me that word, but I thought they were beds for young babies."

He shook his head. "Cribs are small rooms with barred windows facing the streets. The young girls are kept there to sleep on mats. The little wretches are fed and clothed by their master; they must give favors to a constant stream of men that line up outside their squatting." He clutched her arm. "Come with me—I will show you what I mean. A short block and a half away."

She tugged her arm away. "I do not want to see this."

"I think you will be glad you did." He shepherded her down the block and around a corner leading to a row of dirty buildings. Clumps of men were lingering outside. Flickering torches blazed outside the entrances of the first-floor cribs. Even at mid-range, through the barred windows, Ah could see the women in various stages of undress.

Bare-breasted girls looked at them through the bars, their eyes bleary, their faces tear-stained. All about the girls was a state of resignation, of despair. All about the alley was the sound of lascivious noises, grunting, deep laughter. Ah glimpsed corners in the cribs where women and men lay, the men taking their pleasures, the girls' bodies mere pale slivers of light under their heaving bodies.

Nausea rose in her gut. "Take me out of here. Now."

He hesitated. "Are you sure you have seen everything? There are other forms of degradation down there." He pointed to another line of cribs fronting the street.

"No more." She flicked open her fan and pressed it against her eyes.

He drew her close and guided her away. "I knew this would upset you, but I wanted you to know. I find these crib girls lying naked in alleyways, unconscious behind trash bins, dead in Portsmouth Plaza. Their worth, according to the Kong Chow Company, is zero. When they do not lie with men, they do not pay off their contracts. So, this work they do—this kind of hell."

"I did not know."

"Well, now you do. Guess how long these girls live?"

"Many years?"

He clucked his tongue. "Oh no. Most only live a year. I watch them die of diseases—you see, these sailors carry sickness from the outside world. Cholera, typhus, dysentery. And lots of them go insane from having sexual acts with so many men."

"They lose their minds?"

"Syphilis does that." He nodded soberly. "If you do not open a proper brothel, an illness could spread throughout your household that would threaten all of you. And—I do not want to lose you. A proper madam who takes care of her girls would make sure they are seen by the doctor regular."

They rounded the corner onto Pike Street, and she stopped. "But what should I do? I must make money. And I need the Kong Chow Company's security."

"Be vigilant when you expand your house into a brothel. Employ a small number of girls so you may protect each one. I know a new larger house with a parlor where you could expand your business. You have much money now, so you can afford to buy it.

He leaned toward her. "Bring in the girls, train them in what they must, and maybe offer the sailors fine wines and food. The girls might even dance for the men, but then tastefully do their business with them. I think the sailors would be quite eager, not only to see the beautiful Girl in Green Silk Pantaloons, but the young Celestial maidens who have arrived."

"Would I charge more in gold dust?"

"Much more, I think. And, you are becoming well-known, so you already have those sailors who make it a point to visit you when they come to port here. But—" He hesitated.

"What is it?"

"Make sure the girls know that if they are found sleeping with other men for money outside your house, they will be dismissed. Check them frequently for diseases. If you do not stay firm, your business will be ruined."

She planted a kiss on his cheek. "I am happy I agree with what you believe. This is a good idea."

After all this time in her arms, the little cat named Jade squirmed. As soon Ah and Clark reached her shanty, she set the cat down, and watched it rub against her leg.

"Clark?" She looked up into his face, his high cheekbones the only features visible in the semi-darkness.

"Yes, Mrs. Toy?" he asked. If only he would always talk to her that way, his words floating on gentle wisps of air.

She said, "Officer Wong tells me that Lee Shau Kee is no longer a threat to me, but I will ask you to continue guarding my house. And now that I will have my expanded my business, you will watch out for me and always stay close?"

"I can be by your side—that is—until January." He looked away down the street.

"Only until January?" A cold wind sliced through her.

"That is when you need to go into the shelter of the Kong Chow Company." He stared down at his hands.

"I—don't understand. *You* are my sentinel." She clutched the cat who meowed in protest.

A shadow darkened his face. "Well, everything will change for me in January, you see."

"Why?" Her lips trembled.

"I was meaning to tell you. My wife will be coming to join me on December 25th or thereabouts. She's sailing from the east around the Horn. She is a sickly woman, always has been. Her parents are getting older and they can no longer care for her. Since we married, she has been abed more than she has been upright, poor thing. And now . . ." He gazed far away down the street. Was he trying to capture something in his past, something invisible?

The walls of Pike Street pressed in around her, and her skin itched under her clothing. A dog howled on a neighboring street, and she shuddered.

Her dragon was silent.

Clark had a grim twist to his mouth.

But after a few silent moments, her dragon unleashed a torrent of thoughts. How dare Clark come to see her naked? How dare he embrace her and kiss her on the haybale? How dare he pretend to be her friend, all the time lying, letting her think she was his one and only? She bit the inside of her cheek.

Clark stepped away from her. "My wife must come while she is still strong enough to make the journey. She says I have been gone too long, and insists on coming to San Francisco." A vein pulsed in his forehead. "I am selfish. I do not want her here."

Ah regarded him in stony silence.

He waved his hand in the air. "When I came here the city police was in its infancy, but its ranks gradually filled with men like me. They came from the east with either military experience from the Mexican War, or law and order background in eastern cities like New York, Boston, or Baltimore. They tended to be seasoned men who did not shrink from dealing with populations arriving from all over the world to seize the gold."

She cocked her head to the side. "So—that still does not explain why you did not tell me about your wife, or that you even had one!"

He gave a half-hearted shrug. "Please—let me explain. Meanwhile, Susannah sent letters saying she had fallen ill, but was now residing in the care of her parents. She had consumption, but with their care she might recover and for me not to worry. I continued to send letters and money in return.

"In truth, I care for her as one might a sister or even a distant cousin. We had grown so far apart in our marriage I no longer considered her a love object"

She wanted to sneer, but she stopped herself. Was this just another filament adding to his growing web of lies? Whatever happened to the delicate web of trust they were building together?

He continued. "Yet, at the same time, I refrained from visiting dance halls or hurdy gurdy rooms where women were a lascivious spectacle. At moments I might glimpse a womanly figure on the streets of San Francisco, though in truth they were rare. At those times I wondered what they would be like in bed. So, it was during that time when I first visited your Lookee Shop."

He paused, taking a soft breath. "You were a darn sight and then—in your bare loveliness—then I saw how much I truly missed having a woman to love. In fact, I realized that Susannah had never truly loved me in return, if our union was to be called love at all. Ours was most likely a comfortable arrangement, instead of a fulfilling one. In truth, I knew she did not ever fully understand me.

"So, when I met you, naked in all your joyful beauty, I was not only entranced by your luminous skin, but also the fire in your eyes. I was attracted by your intelligence, your liveliness, your wit. You did not need me, but in time I became aware of how much I might need *you*. I found your Celestial ways strange, but I saw your delicacy. As it was, your eastern culture fascinated me, and I longed to learn more about you. Then, with the discovery of Lee Shau Kee, then Tung Chao's desire to kidnap you and take you back to China, I was angry and wanted to help you."

Ah drew back. Was he telling the truth? If so, Clark understood the constraints of a loveless marriage, and even though he and Susannah had never been in an abusive relationship, he could grasp the despair and loneliness that she might feel when trapped in a net she longed to escape. That thought hit her much as an iron ball from a slungshot might crack the skull of an unsuspecting victim.

Ah's dragon snarled. If only she could slap him, making him listen to what a fool he was to have betrayed her. He was no better than Tung Chee and all the rest she had left behind in Guangdong. At least they did not pretend to love her, then have other women.

Clark had made her think she was his alone. Even if she wanted to scream and rant, she had no rights against his legally married American wife. No matter how sickly, the woman was *his* wife. And then—if she were truly sick-to-death, was there hope of her dying?

She forced out the words. "How sad." Somehow that was all she could say. She should have known better to trust him or any man—they all used women and threw them away. She had seen more than her share of evidence at the cribs. Why had she convinced herself Clark would be any different?

But then, another softening thought rose to do battle with her dragon's ideas. After all, she knew the sense of imprisonment to an unloved spouse, and the chains that wrapped around her own heart. If she damned Clark, she would have to condemn herself. She said, "You have betrayed my trust, and for that I will not be able to forgive you. But I will remain your friend if only because of your past kindness."

"You do? You will? I wish it could be otherwise, God's truth." He brushed away a tear from the corner of his eye. "I tell you—I no longer love her."

In his words Ah Toy heard regret for a lost love, a star that once burned brightly but had long since fallen from the sky. Yet she wondered. His wife must feel the loss of him, the abandonment, so far away without the warmth of his touch, the comfort of his presence. The poor woman carried the burden of loss as well as her illness.

"Remember you have a duty." Ah's tone was firm. "Madam Ban Zhao says, 'Just as Heaven cannot be disobeyed, so the wife cannot keep away from her husband.'"

"I know this. I am sorry. I was going to tell you, but . . ." He touched her shoulder, crevices deepening around his eyes. "I love you, but I can do nothing else."

Her dragon's tail stirred a depressing stew of sticks and stones. If Clark stayed with his wife, how could he love her, too? The strands of their once tight web had slackened.

A dog cried out for the second time, and she cupped her ear, listening to its wail. "Do you hear that?"

He shrugged. "Only a mongrel."

"In Guangdong we believe that when a dog howls in the nighttime, someone is going to die." She leaned against the shanty door facing him. The cat nestled at her feet and the cool air enveloped them both.

The next morning, her arms full of bags of food from Tom's market, she elbowed her way through the crowds of white and Cantonese men on Dupont Street. She turned an ankle and dropped several oranges. "What have I done?" she cried out.

Curses! The fruit was rolling everywhere—under donkey wagons, into an alleyway, and over a pile of dung in the road. She bent down, gathering the closest oranges—now she would have to go back to the marketplace. What a waste of time.

Something caught her eye not far down the road. A group of young white toughs ambled forward in slouch hats and dirty trousers. Sure enough, they stopped, pointing at her.

Her heart thudded in her chest.

They quickened their pace toward her. "Celestial Girl," they called in a chorus, followed by whistling, jeering, and animal sounds. "Come 'ere, Miss Underdrawers, let me feel ya under dem pantaloons!"

Curses again. She stood up, settling the rest of the oranges in her basket. What was going on? What men were these? They did not speak with veneration; instead, they spoke a strange sort of English, the same she had heard on walks with Chen on the wharf. They must be the Sydney Ducks.

Oh no—one more orange rested on her foot. As she bent down to pick it up, someone's hand palmed her bottom. She jerked up. Where was he? The air was empty, close, and full of menace. Bystanders came out on their porches, some men leaning out from windows. No one offered to help. If she screamed, she was likely to draw an even larger crowd of men around her. And Clark was far away . . . and Chen, too.

In minutes the same hotblooded group encircled her, forming a human corral between her and the rest of her oranges. She knew the tactic. Young men in Guangzhou gained courage that way, ignoring law and order, gaining strength in packs.

A laugh rang out from the circle, then died away. Something changed. Step by step they advanced, and her dragon spoke caution to her. *See they wear masks, the paint marking the characters of Xiqui, Chinese opera. Look! The tall one has painted green cheeks; the short one a yellow nose; the lad with red marks around his eyes carries a threatening stick. Where is the blue? The boy with blue stripes on his face? The one who would come to the rescue on stage with goodness and peace, the salvation of the princess?* She glanced over them again—no boy with blue stripes.

The sun must have hidden behind a cloud, and the pathway turned dark, the men's faces changing from light and ruddy to dark and gray. Another look around and their colors were gone . . . her mind became a silent cavern. Had she lost her dragon, too?

She struggled to stand up high on her lotus shoes—if only she could step away and out of their path, away from the circle tightening like a noose. Forget the oranges—she needed Chen and home.

A young man sporting a red thatch of hair and a scraggly beard pushed his way forward. "Show us some of your skin, there's a good girl, and we let you go."

She had a vivid realization. The mob would try and trick her into letting down her guard.

A larger brute, his hair stiffened with dirt, added his words. "There's a pleasure, just pull down your pantalettes for us."

Their boldness made her even more determined to stand strong.

"More than that," sounded a raw voice.

"Yeah, more than that! Let us feel." The words echoed through the throng.

Not on their life—or hers, for that matter.

The air thickened with smells: chewing tobacco and day-old eggs; rotten teeth and swollen gums; the eternal odor of sweat and the salt that lay on their hair, and clothes and skin from the Bay. Life without Australian women, without the order that the female sex brought to their lives and their beds.

Their chants for skin grew louder, the smells became nauseating, and she reached inside for her inner dragon, her strength, her fire. Yet again this time her dragon lay still.

The crowd tightened around her. Her breathing came fast; she must think of something. If only Clark were making his rounds. She jumped up to peek over the human cage, but the street lay empty—she was alone. Or was she? She racked her brain . . . now what had her dragon said?

Blue for goodness, peace, salvation. No blue in sight. The men were but three feet away from her. If only—but yes—there it was. Of a sudden she knew a truth: she must be her own salvation.

Her voice rang out. "I will show skin when all men sit down."

The tall man, with a month's growth of stubbly beard, said, "What did you say, Miss Slant Eyes?"

The men's chants died out along with the question, and the tall man whipped around to the others. "She spoke, now shut yer traps. Let the lady speak."

The air collapsed into sullen silence, and she repeated. "I will show skin when all men sit down."

The men looked down into the squalor of the mud and slime, ripe with trash and refuse from the slush buckets At first, they shook their heads, and murmurs ran through their crowd. "It ain't worth it—Not me—Sit there? Nah . . ."

Then the tall man with the straggly beard bent his long legs like dried-up twigs and folded himself down onto the street. "I want to see what she got." His lips drew into a solid, determined line.

And one by one the Sydney Ducks squatted down into the mud and gush, the wet earth settling around their bottoms like a clay mold. Curious grins supplanted their savage masks, their mouths softening in a kind of reverence.

Ah moved to the middle of the enclosure and lifted her right pantaloon up to the knee. A murmur spread through the circle. She stepped from man to man so that each one could have a look. When one reached out a hand, she snapped, "No touch!" and his fingers flew back as if they had been burned.

When all had feasted at the sight of her delicious skin, she moved between two of them, aimed her lotus shoes away toward the end of the street, and set out for home. A look back revealed the group of men, seated in their circle, appearing mesmerized by their graceful vision of the Dragon King's Daughter. All she heard were the oranges jostling in her bag.

Eight

❧ A LAWLESS AIR ❧

September 1849

An afternoon's moment turned into what seemed an eternity while Ah Toy waited for Judge Almond. She settled the bag of brass filings at her feet, then looked up at the flag hanging motionless in the front of the schoolroom, and over at the high windows suspended like mirrors in the walls. The sunshine poured in, and beyond the rooftops of the privy, stables, and schoolyard, she could see the azure blue of sky.

Chen pressed a hard candy into the open palm of her right hand, and she popped it into her mouth. The syrupy sweetness flowed down her parched throat.

A visit to the court was no laughing occasion, yet until now she had tried her best to keep peace with the male customers who lined up each day outside her shanty. Chen patrolled them with his club, but the yelling, fighting and carousing was growing worse, and waves of Sydney

Ducks were appearing among her patrons. At first, she had thought of contacting the Daileys in Monterey. But they were so far away, and as Christians they might judge her for the Lookee Shop. No, she needed Judge Almond's help that day more than ever.

San Francisco possessed a lawless air: fires burned with more frequency, and at all hours she could hear the clanging of the fire bell and the ensuing rush of pump wagons across the plank streets. The city gnawed with panic, and the city fathers acted paralyzed, unable to confront the sources of the trouble.

Who would emerge to create order out of the chaos swallowing their town? The room stirred and the bailiff stepped off his chair. "All rise!" he called.

Judge Almond strode out of the adjacent room, his black robe flying around him. She heard a flow of movement around her—shuffling feet, clearing throats, and murmuring voices. He took a seat at the teacher's desk, now serving as the judge's bar.

Her pulse quickened. She ran her fingers in and out of the inkwell on the right-hand side of the student desk. Patience. Clark was working on a case of arson in which a young pioneer woman and her baby daughter had died in the fire. She would have to manage without him and stay steady.

The bailiff spoke. "In the case of Ah Toy, the witness is called. Mrs. Toy, please rise and approach the bench."

After swearing on Judge Almond's Bible, Ah perched on the stool next to him. Slouchers filled the rows of student benches; they lounged with their legs up on the tables, their cheeks swollen with plugs of chewing tobacco. Their murmurs ebbed and flowed, along with the scents of sweat, chaw, and grime. She focused on Almond to avoid the heat of men's eyes on her.

The judge peered over his glasses. "Good morning, Mrs. Toy."

She nodded a response.

Something about Almond put her at ease—was it his crinkly blue eyes, the reptilian ruddiness of his cheeks, the easy smile? Maybe he was another man in whom she could confide. Based on Clark's recent betrayal, trust was a rarity in this town ripe with murderers, rapists, and thieves.

Someone shuffled in at the back of the schoolroom. She looked out onto the sea of faces, but rays of sun from the windows clouded her view. Unexpectedly, she saw Clark slide into a student desk in the back row. Thank goodness he had come. She settled into her seat and returned the Judge's gaze. "Yes, Your Honor, about Lee Shau Kee."

The judge clucked his tongue. "I remember now. Do go on." The squeak of a door hinge intruded into the courtroom's quiet decorum. What now?

A clutch of men burst in the door, sauntering to the middle row of student desks, carrying the noxious odors and rascally air of the Sydney Ducks. Their voices rasped like nails against lead pipe.

The bailiff rose and brandished a rifle. "Order, ya ruffians!"

One of the Ducks cried out. "Whatcha gonna do, bailiff? Shoot us between the eyes?'

Her stomach churned. It was him—the man with the red thatch of hair—from the mob that accosted her on the street.

The bailiff seemed to falter, lowering his rifle.

"Men." The Judge jabbed a finger in their direction. "You are more than welcome in my courtroom as long as you are silent. Any disturbance during our proceedings and you will be ejected."

The bailiff raised his rifle again. Maybe he regained his courage.

The red thatch turned back to his mates. "Since it is all for the good of the party, silence! And take off yer hats!" "The men grumbled, then pulled off their squashed caps, an act of ornery obedience. He spoke again. "Now keep yer godawful traps shut. We want to hear our Missus Johnny."

She shuddered. "Johnny" was their derogatory slur for Cantonese people. What were they doing here? Had she gained a following of fans, much like a circus clown? She searched the crowd again for Clark—there he was, frowning at the back of the courtroom.

Appearing to ignore the men's fracas, the Judge continued his line of questioning. "So, Mrs. Toy, what brings you to court this time?"

"The men who visit me nowadays are worse behaved, Your Honor. "

"How so?"

"They yell; they fight in line outside my house. Chen, my bodyguard, patrols with his club, but they do not obey." She pointed at Chen who sat in the front row of the of the spectator's section.

The judge turned to Chen who nodded. Returning his gaze to her, Judge Almond said, "My dear Mrs. Toy, you must know that the lookee services you offer will attract just such men. You may have noticed how the city is growing, and with these many cases of arson and robbery, we do not have a means to provide you any further personal safety."

Ah Toy's mouth opened. "But—Officer Clark?"

The judge did not wait for her to finish. "I have asked the Marshal to assign Clark on special patrol, but I have no other officers who can spare the time to guard your—er—business."

"Well, there is something else I wish you to know, Judge."

"And what could that be, my dear Mrs. Toy?"

"Men—such as these—" She pointed at the Sydney Ducks forming a knot in the center of the schoolroom, their drooping hats and hardened features testifying to their quest for no good.

The judge cupped his ear. "Men like that? Those men? What are you trying to say?"

"They lookee, but they pay me in brass filings, not gold."

"What evidence do you have for the court?" His greenish cheeks flushed pink.

"The bank will no longer take my gold dust. Every time they weigh it, they tell me it is brass, not gold." She picked up a bag from the floor and poured some of its contents on the judge's desk. The brass shavings glinted against the light from the tall ornate window to their right.

The judge ran his fingers over the filings. "I see."

"It is a law broken. Thievery. They lookee, but they do not pay. Them." She pointed her finger toward the crowd.

A stream of profanity rose in response from the center of the schoolroom, the likes of which Ah Toy had seldom heard. An unkempt man in a stained gray jacket rose to his feet.

A rumble ensued. The red thatch led a chorus of men crying "Johnny Whore! Slant-Eyed Witch!" The men stood and cheered as if rooting against an opposing racehorse on a track.

She faced the men, her inner dragon huddled in a ball in her stomach, firmly wrapped in red silk. A drip-drip of sweat trickled down the back of her dress. Her mouth went dry; Chen's candy was long forgotten.

Not only did these men scoff at her, they scorned her race, her ancestors, her homeland. But America was her homeland, too. And she gritted her teeth. She had every right to be here as they did. They might have come from prisons in Australia, but she was a porcelain trader's daughter.

Her inner dragon stirred. *You must confront these men. Unless you do, you will be forever a slave.*

No, she shook her head. I can't.

You have no choice. Now turn and point your finger at the red thatch— the ugly man, the one with boils on his soul and scabs where his heart should be. Do it for yourself.

"I wish to make a statement," she said to the judge who leaned over to hear her small voice. "May I rise, Your Honor?"

"Yes, my dear." The judge wiped something from his eye.

Ah Toy stood as high as her lotus shoes would allow, as high as the extension of her full height would bear, and she raised her right hand.

The men quieted, and she pointed at the red thatch. "You are the one," she said.

That is the way. She heard her dragon's cheer, so she continued. "You trapped me on the street, you insulted my body and my dignity. And you are the one who instigates the carousing on my street. Mr. Sydney Duck, whatever your name is, you bring shame on your ancestors with your thievery and robbery. Your desire to take what does not belong to you from this town, from our people. Yes, we Cantonese are a noble people, not your gang of thieves."

The men no longer fidgeted; instead, their beady eyes widened in that same way they had on the street, in the mud, when she had said, "I will show skin when all men sit down."

Her voice rose, gaining power with each word. "You belong on a prison ship away from here. Gone. You will never be part of this great country, America. Not made of brass filings but made of gold. Hard won. Not easily gotten. Not by cheating. But by honest work. By the ways of Judge Almond and our policemen who want peace and safety for all of us." She took a breath, then continued. "I may look like Mrs. Johnny to you, but my name is Ah Toy. Let your shame follow you for all your life when you prey upon the women, the orphaned, the weak."

A lock of hair came loose from a clip and she brushed it away from her face. "Confucius teaches if a person lacks trustworthiness, what can he be good for? When a pin is missing from the yoke-bar of a large wagon, or from the collar-bar of a small wagon, how can it go?"

She turned to the judge. "San Francisco is not made of gold, the lie they teach in Guangzhou. No, this city is made of its people."

The judge nodded, then wiped something away from a corner of his eye. "You make an important point."

Again, she faced the men, "Trustworthy people make the future . . . you would tear down what good men . . . and me—good women—make. See this school?" She cast her hand to the side of the schoolroom. The crowd's gaze followed her gesture over the chalkboards; slate tablets; A B C's; blocks of McGuffey readers; and the upright piano in the corner.

"This school is where children learn to be trustworthy. You come in here—you can learn, too. And you must start by not scorning me, or my people. Everyone wants peace No one wants shame and ridicule. Do you?"

The crowd murmured a response, but whatever it was, their opinion did not matter. Instead, she took her seat beside the judge, and repinned her stray hair. Bathed in perspiration, she drew her fan out of her pouch and waved it back and forth. What would the judge say?

For the first moment after she sat down, the men fell silent. But then a cheer rose from the back of the schoolroom. Was that Clark who led the applause? Several men got to their feet and clapped. The enthusiasm grew and the ovation grew louder, followed by whistles from the crowd. Judge Almond rose, putting his hands together, in addition to the bailiff who rested his rifle on the crook of his arm and joined the show of appreciation.

Ah noticed she was the only person who remained sitting, along with Chen and the Sydney Ducks who stiffened, their arms folded in unison.

After the cheers subsided, Judge Almond spoke out. "Our good men from Australia, take note. We in the court are watching you, along with honest citizens who have their eyes on all evildoers. You risk deportation, or worse, a date with the hangman's noose, if you do not mend your ways. This lady has told you the law. Now you need to obey it. The next time I see you in my courtroom you will be under arrest. Now get out."

The bailiff raised his rifle, cocked the hammer, and pointed the muzzle directly at the Duck with the red thatch. His cheeks reddened like an overripe tomato. Clark opened the school house door, and rays of sunshine illuminated the grease-laden hair and dirt-matted jackets of the Sydney Ducks. The Australians rose in unison, and shuffled out, casting hangdog looks back at the bench.

One turned and spat on Clark who pushed him out the door, locking it firmly behind the wastrel.

The Judge spoke. "Unfortunately, there is nothing I can do about the brass filings. It is too difficult to prove which miner or Sydney Duck might have slipped them to you rather than gold. Yet, be aware, Mrs.

Toy. I have heard by a reputable source that Lee Shau Kee has returned to California, bought land in the Hangtown area, and he intends to settle there. Should he or any of the Ducks frequent your shanty or menace you in any way, I want to know about it."

Her heart thumped. "Your Honor, Harold Painter told me he had sent Lee Shau Kee back to Guangdong. He cannot be in California."

"He has been sighted in the diggings—you are aware he had invested in mining some time back?" He peered at her.

"Yes, but are you sure it is Lee Shau Kee?" She pressed a fist against her chest.

"Mrs. Toy, I practice the law in a lawless land. Who knows if it is Lee Shau Kee or his brother, cousin, or father? I only tell what is reported to me. I sure would love to get my hands on that extortionist-bastard-son-of blazes." He clenched his jaw.

"Thank you, Your Honor."

Judge Almond dipped his pen in an inkwell on the teacher's desk, wrote something on a paper, and passed it to her.

She saw an address scrawled across the paper.

He continued. "Send Chen directly to me should you face this kind of trouble again. Mayor John Geary and our city fathers must put a stop to this mayhem. And thank your Confucius for me. He is one wise man."

After she folded the paper into her pouch along with her fan, she lowered her head in the presence of Judge Almond, her trustworthy friend.

Nine

❦ SET CLOUD SAILS ❦

*L*ater that evening, Ah Toy observed the brown sausages and green and red sauces that swirled across her plate. *What on earth was that?* Never would she go alone into these restaurants for white men; such things as hash covered with gravy and slabs of pork turned her stomach. But somehow, she could bear it when as she was with Clark. So, she held her fork and regarded him across the table. She pushed the contents of her plate first into one corner, then another.

Clark filled his mouth with food, chewing and cutting, then taking a swill from the whiskey bottle beside the plate. His eating was not off-putting, but it was raw in comparison to Chen's clean style of delivering rice to his mouth with chopstick and cup.

Chen used a napkin to neaten his mouth; Clark used a napkin to wipe globs of gravy off his lower lip where the bits of gravy suspended during and after his meal.

His messiness aside, she warmed to Clark's manner. How could she stay mad at him for long? He made her laugh and think of pleasures.

Hope existed in the soft breezes that carried the mail clippers in through the Golden Gate. After leading her into quiet corners of the marketplace, he gentled a kiss on her cheek when no one saw. She forced herself to push him away. "Only friends," she said.

Another day he bought lavender oil from a French importer on the wharf, asking her forgiveness. Chen massaged her lotus feet with it. Clark brought her sprays of mint and Hawaiian coconuts. And above all, he listened to her.

Burping after his meal, Clark sat back, then refilled his tumbler from the whiskey bottle. He patted his stomach. "Some meal, eh?"

"I think so." She pretended to be joyful.

Yelling came from the restaurant's porch, and the bartender flashed outside. Sounds of a scuffle followed, and the bartender re-entered, wiping his hands on his apron. "I hate those Sydney thugs. A plague to my business."

The restaurant patrons murmured their sympathies, then focused again on their meal.

Clark nodded, lit up a fat cigar, and puffed it awake. He turned to her. "Those Ducks are the fever within the plagues that corrupt our fair city. When I first arrived, this place was calm, innocent, like waiting for a storm. Now within months after the Aussies came, we have all manner of lawlessness. A man can't go one block to another without the fear that some son of a compunction will blow his head right off. Look at how the bastards treated you. Hear tell some men are readying a hanging tree."

"What is that tree?" She pushed her plate away and rested her elbows before her on the table.

He spoke through the smoky haze. "If they can find a tall tree, stump, post, or beam, they throw a rope over it and drag a person up by the neck or his heels and hang 'em until death. A crowd usually watches— more exciting than the hurdy gurdy show."

She shuddered. "Evil. Bad luck men."

"We have our eye on those rascals. No trial—quick punishment."

"Judge Almond is there?"

He shook his head. "No—secret meeting."

She did not like the sound of that. Secret men did secret things in Guangdong. Lying things. Men, women, and children disappeared after such gatherings.

He reached across the grease-stained tablecloth and touched her hand.

She tugged her fingers away. "No, not good."

His tone softened. "No matter all that. I will stand by you, even after my wife comes to San Francisco." He swallowed. "You want my friend-ship?"

A momentary silence rose between them. Her reply came in a low, despairing voice. "Listen to me. I remember my husband making love to his concubines in the next room. First one, then the other. He would force me to watch through a curtain." Her tone hardened and her muscles stiffened. "Then he would tell me I could not make love like them. That I was not capable. That I was cold. It would be that way with you. You would be forcing me to watch you with your wife. And I would be in pain again."

He hesitated, measuring her for a moment. "My rounds include your street, so I will be passing. At least I will be somewhat nearby."

"Nearby? Not so." Her breath caught in her throat, and her dragon's wings grasped her tightly.

His voice was carefully neutral. "It is true that after she arrives, I will no longer be able to be as—close—as we are now. But I will still be checking your shanty on my beat."

She flicked open her fan and waved the cigar smoke away. "You must take care of *her* and our streets, too. But I will not watch for you as I do now. I will not have Chen make mooncakes for you. I will not serve you tea, and let you see me without my clothes. You will not kiss me at the marketplace or on the straw bale outside the stable." It took some effort, but she looked over at him.

He stretched his hand toward her, uncertainty creeping into his expression. "I am so sorry for all this. I could do nothing about it, you see."

His last statement was false, and he knew it. She fumed. "Why do you lie to me? I lived with a liar, Tung Chee. I know lying ways."

"I love you. Can you not forgive me?" He sighed heavily and stared down at his hands.

How often had she forgiven Tung Chee? Could she also give Clark the amends he was seeking? The harder she tried to ignore the truth, the more it persisted. She must say the hardest thing that would put him away from her. After swallowing a sob, she said, "Bad luck has come upon you, yet I can do nothing for you. I know you only as my friend now, nothing more." He sat staring at her across the table, his mouth partially open. There. She had said it. In return her heart gave strong, steady beats.

This time might be their last ever together. If only she could capture his face, his eyes, his tenderness. If only she had the skills of the artist who had drawn her portrait. She wanted to remember him this way. If only her dragon would stop time now the way it did when a person died as the day when her mother fled this earth and left her behind.

He took her hand. She pulled it back, but he insisted, and he enfolded it in his large palm, like a small bird nestled in a leather pocket. His gesture seemed kind and good, not one of a liar.

A scene from the past flickered in her mind. After her mother drew her last breath, Ah put her head to her mother's chest and could no longer hear the beating heart. Her dragon commanded time to stop. For many minutes, she sat listening for anything her mother might do, even if only a faint pulse or sigh. Yet none came.

Now in the same way, she and Clark must separate, and her dragon must stop time. If only she could hold her last moments with Clark. If only she could capture forever the lock of blond hair that meandered across his eyebrows, the wrinkles that deepened around his crystalline eyes, the timbre of his laughter when they shared a joke.

She wanted to sense forever his light squeeze on her upper arm when she might fall on the muddy road. She looked down at his hand holding her own. His long fingers laced through hers. What would she do without him?

His voice pierced the flow of her thoughts. "It is getting late. I will take you back to your shanty."

She debated the offer. "No. I wish to go alone."

"Then at least let me summon you a ride."

"Very well." If only she could elongate the last second next to him.

Once inside the wagon, she looked out the window, watching Clark wave goodbye at the threshold of the California Restaurant, his familiar lock of blond hair falling down across one eye. She memorized that moment and stored it next to the day when she had put her ear to her mother's lifeless body, urging her mother's heart to give one last beat, just for her—but one never came.

Weeks passed, and Ah lit incense and prepared her daily Buddhist offering of sliced apples and walnuts at the small shrine in the corner. The October winds blew in from the bay, filling her shanty with many more drafts than in September. She took a news sheet and stuffed it into a particularly large crack whose whistling sound kept her awake during the night. Chen would be back at any moment with a load of firewood meant for the kitchen stove.

She shivered, a ribbon of grief winding its way upward from her belly to her throat. Clark would be patrolling Pike Street today; he would knock at the door; she would open it a crack in her customary way. He would doff his hat, and say, "Everything all right, Mrs. Toy?" She would nod, affect a smile, and say, "Yes, thank, you, Mr. Clark." She would close the door, turn and lean her hip against it, then suppress the sob that would inevitably come.

Today's expectation weighed on her like a ship's anchor. How could she live without this man, the one who guided her through this frontier existence, a life with twists, turns, and unexpected joys? She sighed, knelt before her shrine, and immersed herself in thoughts of the Enlightened One. As if sensing her grief, Jade the cat leaped off the chair and rubbed up against her side, then lay curled there on the floor beside her.

Maybe guidance would come. She slowed her breathing and regarded the still and silent beauty of the slice of apple, its white flesh, and dark beaded core absorbing the faint light from the shanty window.

Some moments later, Chen scratched his key at the door and pushed open the latch.

She turned and saw the large burlap sack slung over his shoulder. She rose from the altar. "I thought you were going for firewood. What have you brought me today? More of those walnuts and persimmons I asked for?"

Chen eased the bag to the floor. "I did go to market. I will get firewood later." His queue meandered over his chest, and he threw it back over his shoulder. "Even though you said the post office was closed today, I went over anyway and found it open. There was a letter for you." He held it toward her.

She took the envelope and read the address that flowed across the front flap. Amidst the fancy *y's* and decorative *t's,* she noted a return address—*Dailey, Monterey City.* She fingered the envelope. She had not contacted them in the worst of recent times—should she have let them know of her dilemmas? Maybe she was wrong in failing to ask for help, or at least too stubborn.

Chen padded away into the kitchen, and she heard the scratch-scratch of drawers opening and closing.

What was in the letter? After picking up an ivory-handled knife, Ah broke open the flap and pulled out the thin vellum. A fancy scrawl marched across the horizontal lines. She held the up under the noonday light streaking in from the shanty window. Her feet ached where she stood, so she called out to Chen. "Could you please bring me a chair so I may rest my feet?"

He bobbed out of the kitchen, his apron flying, and set the chair at the dining table under the window. "There, si tau po."

She nodded and folded herself into the chair. Chen backed out of the light and into kitchen shadows.

A slash of light crossed the letter. Newsprint was always easier to read than the scribbling they called cursive handwriting. And Chen was no help. The only one who could make it easier was Clark, and she would not ask him, especially now. She set her chin. No, she would do this herself. The script lay across the page like floral work on an embroidery screen.

Rancho Pacifico
Monterey
Alta California

October 3, 1849

Dearest Ah Toy,

I have been meaning to write to you for some time, yet much has occurred to interrupt my efforts. We have finished making improvements to our property, mainly building a new barn and expanding a corral for the horses. We recently purchased a milk cow, and the boys have been helping me make butter and cheese. I now have a housemaid named Hortencia and since she speaks little English, I am learning a lot of Spanish from her. Not everyone is as eager to learn English as you.

The Reverend has been busy establishing his ministry. Here at the new church we have set up worship for those Protestants who wish to join us. We have met very interesting people, among them miners, sailors, farmers, and natives who no longer adhere to the beliefs of the

Catholic church. Several of them have come forward to receive the communion, and a few have asked for Baptism in Christ.

Stephen and George are studying their letters and numbers with me, but recently a group of male teachers has arrived to found a school, and I am pleased that when the schoolroom is prepared, they will be able to study with students their own age.

We have built a sturdy two-story house of adobe and logs, with a big stone fireplace, and the Reverend insisted we have a guest room in case of visitors to our beautiful town of Monterey. So, we would like to have you come the first week of November. We are all invited to Thomas Larkin's house for a dinner in honor of the work he is doing on the new state constitution, and we would like to bring you to meet everyone. Do not have fear: we will be by your side.

We hope that you agree to come, for there is someone named Henry Conrad, an older man that we would like you to meet. He is a British importer-exporter who grew up in Guangzhou and Hong Kong .

Please bring Chen also. He is most welcome.

Your friend in Christ,

Elizabeth Dailey

Ah folded up the letter and tucked it into her drawer. So many questions piled into her mind. Would she dare take a chance and leave Chen and the business? No, rather than leave him here, she would lock up the Lookee Shop and bring Chen along for security. Besides, she would not be with Cantonese people, so she would need his companionship. She hesitated. Would she be falsely representing herself, since people of Christian beliefs would find her lowly life shameful?

Of course the Daileys did not know she sat naked before men in exchange for gold. They would no doubt be shocked. On the other hand, she was gaining wealth and her account at the bank was growing steadily. One gold shaving followed another, and she was already becoming a rich woman. In the early days, Chen cooked chicken wings for dinner; now he had enough money to purchase beef and pork, raising eyebrows at the marketplace on Pacific Avenue. In addition, she was able to lay down some expensive Persian rugs and decorate the walls with Chinese paintings of mountain landscapes, her favorites. Soon they would expand their shanty, maybe even purchase a parlor house, escaping the shanty life for good.

She drew herself up in her chair. She must have faith that her dragon would protect her. Maybe the journey would rid her of Clark's vision; maybe she could tuck his memory into her sleeve next to her fan, and only bring it out when she wanted to, not like now when she saw his face everywhere she looked.

She stole into the kitchen. Chen was bent over, scrubbing the countertops.

He must have heard her. "Yes?" He turned, holding his cloth in mid-air.

She spoke in rapid-fire Cantonese. "Tomorrow we must prepare for a journey at the end of the month. I will make an English sign to say we are closed for one week."

"Where are we going?"

"A place called Monterey. To the Dailey house."

His eyebrows arched. "Do they have good fish there?"

"I am sure they do."

"And we will stay in a real house, not a shanty?" He fingered the edges of the cloth.

"A very nice house, at least that is what Elizabeth says."

"For one week only?" He bounced on his toes.

"Yes, Chen. For one week."

"I supposed we can leave the Lookee Shop for a short time." Chen was plainly thinking ahead. "What do we take in our suitcases?" He slapped the cloth over his shoulder and rubbed his hands together.

"This month we will plan everything. At all times you will wear your daily cheongsam, but we will be going to a formal dinner one night. A Western-style dinner. Long table, candles, porcelain plates. You know, the type the British have in Guangzhou. Violins, servants, much to eat."

He gave a nod, but his eyes darted from side to side. "Do I pack the black silk jacket you had shipped to me from Hong Kong?"

"Yes. This will be a formal occasion. I will have you take my pink and silver, along with my apricot silk to the laundry. I will wear those also." She shivered. "Now, go get firewood. I am getting cold."

"Wait, si tau po. I think you have forgotten someone."

"Who?" she asked.

He pointed at Jade who regarded them from the kitchen table where she nestled next to a bowl of oranges. "We cannot take her. How will she eat? You no longer allow her on the streets."

After a moment's pause, she said, "I will ask Mr. Tom's delivery boy to come feed her fish scraps—her favorite—from the market every day."

"In that case, I will begin to pack." He dropped his cloth on the counter, tore off his apron, and disappeared out the door.

Part Two

Way up on the Delta
Spring winds roar over the water.
How can I meet the challenge
to brave the canyon before me?

IN THE MANNER OF LI PO

One

❦ WHAT LADIES DO ❧

Monterey
November 1849

uring the first three days Ah and Chen spent at the Daileys' two-story, adobe-style ranch house, they settled into the clatter of young Freddie and James running on wood floors, the Spanish murmur of the Californio maid Hortencia, and the breakfast conversations with Reverend Dailey while Elizabeth was out tending the farm animals.

At meals, Ah navigated the use of silverware rather than chopsticks, and she sidestepped personal questions about her San Francisco life. Of course, the Daileys did not know of her status as a Lookee Girl in a notorious alley in Little Canton; of course, she would keep secret her love for John Clark.

Yet she felt no remorse about avoiding the truth; in fact, her life in Guangzhou and in San Francisco seemed far removed from the

Californio and native cultures that blended into these days in Monterey. Last night's conversation focused on the dinner at Thomas Larkin's house the following evening. They were going to spend the night there. What would everyone wear? What time would they go in the wagon? What would the weather be like?

She learned that Thomas Larkin was a famous man in California and that he continued to grieve for his little daughter Carolina who died only four years ago. The Reverend and Elizabeth had met him years ago through his father in Boston who was a Deacon.

When Ah awoke the next morning, she grinned at the scene on her daybed. Chen had set her apricot silk out that morning, along with her lotus shoes. An open satchel lay nearby. She chuckled. He might be more excited to go to the Larkins' than she was.

That morning in the breakfast room, Reverend Dailey passed her the toast plate and Hortencia poured enough coffee in her cup to swim in. Chen followed swiftly behind her, dribbling cream on top of the overflowing cup. Thankfully, he caught the excess coffee in the saucer. A warm breeze from the open window ruffled the news sheet next to his plate.

After Hortencia and Chen left for the kitchen, Ah dipped her knife into the apricot preserves, working the blade unevenly across her slice of toast. Though she had learned English table manners in Guangzhou, a must for the wife of a porcelain trader, she found western silverware awkward. Much to her chagrin, she dropped the knife and it clanged against the side of her plate.

Reverend Dailey started in his chair, put down the news sheet he had been reading, and steadied his eyes on her. He spoke in fluent Cantonese. "Are you quite prepared for Thomas Larkin's dinner tonight? Or are you a bit nervous to meet Henry Conrad?"

She met his smile, then set the knife on the table. "Chen has helped me unpack, if that is what you mean, and I have a nice qipao to wear. Hortencia has a fancy hairclip and has offered to style my hair with it tonight."

He took a sip of his coffee. "That is what ladies do, isn't it? Prepare their dress for the fancy occasion. But you also know that you will be meeting our friend Henry. I guess that is what I meant by preparation. Men do think differently than women."

She was curious, seeing the change on his face. "I hardly know what to expect about Henry Conrad, but since he is your friend, he must be a gentleman."

"He is a bit older than you—actually quite a bit older." He gave a slight grimace.

"Oh?" Maybe this meeting had been more Elizabeth's idea than his.

"I believe he is forty-five, and you are only in your early twenties, if I recall. I wonder if he is too old for you." He set down his coffee cup, securing it on the saucer.

She swept aside a wave of apprehension. "I should think he has much experience at that age. Since he lives in Guangdong, he would have knowledge of the rest of the world, in addition to this western one."

His tone warmed. "At any rate, I hope you like him. He has been a very generous friend. Though he did not attend our mission church—he is Anglican—he gave money to our school to support Elizabeth's English teaching. We are most grateful for his kindness." A crinkle appeared at the corner of his eyes.

Reverend Dailey put on his spectacles and returned to studying the farm implements for sale in the news sheet.

After a moment's silence, she said, "I wish I knew more about him, Reverend."

He set his paper down, keeping his index finger as a place mark on a want ad. "He is a likeable chap, surely. His father was a British importer from London. After he grew up in Guangzhou and Hong Kong, he went

135

to Oxford College in England, then came back to Guangdong to take control of his father's business."

"So, he speaks Cantonese?" She held still for his answer.

"Oh yes. Because he was involved in the porcelain trade, he spent a lot of time in Guangdong—that is—your province." He turned back to reading the advertisement.

Alone with her thoughts, Elizabeth munched her toast. This Henry might be someone the Daileys favored, but she would have to wait and see. No empty promises would lure her into marrying another rich and powerful man who would use her in unspeakable ways.

"One more thing," she said.

Reverend took off his spectacles and rubbed the bridge of his nose. "Yes?"

"I would like to know about his character."

He faltered for a moment, plainly gathering his thoughts. "Em—his father lived an upright life and so Henry was brought up Anglican. He was focused on running his father's business as a young man. A serious sort, I would say." He set his spectacles back on his nose and blinked.

Ah took in a breath. "Was he married before?"

"Good question. I seem to recall hearing some sad story years ago." He gazed up at the cross-beamed ceiling, plainly trying to remember.

Ah sat breathless. Were her fears premature?

He glanced at her. "All right. Now it is coming to me. Yes, that is it. But this happened long ago, mind you. He was engaged for something like five years to a British woman named Smythe—what was her first name? Elizabeth would know. I think her name was Charlotte. She was from Hong Kong. I never saw her in Guangzhou, but we did meet once at a social gathering in Hong Kong as I recall."

"So, did they marry?" She forced out each word like dropping pebbles in the water.

"Oh no." He shook his head and chewed the earpiece of his spectacles.

"What happened?" She fought against the urge to show her relief.

The Reverend lifted his spectacles and enfolded them into his cloth napkin. He rubbed the lenses thoughtfully. "In those days Henry was bent on building up his father's business. His poor father had some mishap—maybe a stroke or something. I know his father was lamed up. So, Henry had to travel all over the world to trade. Gone most of the time.

"She did not go with him?" Dare she hope for an unhappy ending to his story?

He set his spectacles back on his nose. "That would have been improper as you know. No, she stayed behind. I think one day she got tired of waiting for him and broke it off. Who knows? Maybe she met someone else."

Her uncertain thoughts mixed with shouts from the open window; the boys were rolling a hoop back and forth across the yard.

Reverend lit up his pipe and immersed himself again in reading the news sheet.

Ah forked a bit of egg into her mouth. Henry Conrad was a bachelor. Older than she. Not only would Henry have to compare favorably to John Clark, but he would also have to treat her with respect. At least she was no longer a young teenager, too naïve to question why Tung Chee paraded her on his arm, but then placed her in the shadows while he addressed his fellow businessmen.

Then no man had dared to harm her; then she was her husband's property. But here in America she had come out of the shadows; now her voice mattered. Despite the risk, no man, no matter how rich, could take that freedom away again.

Two

❧ OBSEQUIOUS ☙

After that morning's breakfast, Ah watched Chen and Hortencia clear away the dishes. He wore a frilly apron with yellow and red Mexican embroidery over his black jacket. Maybe the cook made him wear it. He seemed to enjoy the Daileys' domestic life, bustling around at Hortencia's bidding. Maybe it made him remember his life in Ah Toy's house in Guangzhou. There he was on familiar territory. It made sense that he would transfer his many abilities to life in this rough place called Monterey.

Rather than becoming more at ease like Chen, Ah grew more uncomfortable at the Daileys. Their domestic life, full of references to Bible verses, stifled her. That same feeling had happened in Guangzhou at the Daileys' mission. She focused on her English learning, sidestepping their Christian references. Funny that she missed her own shanty—there she would do and think as she pleased.

As if knowing her thoughts, Chen appeared out of the kitchen. "Do you want to go to your room? I can walk you there, si tau po."

She nodded her assent and they walked side-by-side; the whitewashed hallway was graced with open casement windows letting in the brisk autumn breezes drifting in from the nearby ocean.

"Where did you get the apron?" She held back a laugh. Never would she want him to lose face.

He patted the bright flowers on his chest. "Hortencia says I must not get grease on my shirt. She wants me to look my best in Reverend Dailey's home."

"I agree with that. Tonight we have the important dinner. Of course, you will not wear that apron, but will you wear that same shirt?"

"Hortencia says I must show it to her before I think of wearing it. Otherwise, I wear my second shirt." He glanced at the door. "Anything else, si tau po? I am needed in the kitchen."

"No, Chen. You may go." With a tug of reluctance, Ah settled alone on a hard chair before the wooden desk in her chamber. She picked up the pencil and ran her fingers over its chiseled surface.

Why was she uneasy about Chen? Was she jealous about sharing Chen with Hortencia? Ridiculous. More important matters emerged. Big thoughts. Among them, tonight's dinner party with the distinguished Henry Conrad. Would she find him disagreeable? Or a father figure?

There they were—the familiar stirrings of her dragon. *Maybe in Guangdong you would have accepted this kind of union. Maybe an arranged marriage. But now you are no longer the young teenager.* Her dragon was right. Then she was too naïve to question why Tung Chee told her always to wait in the shadows while he addressed his fellow businessmen. Then no man had dared to stare at her; then she was her husband's property. The dragon's whisper echoed in her mind. *But now you will emerge from the shadows. Now you will use your voice.*

At last she found a moment to herself. Ever since Guangzhou, a kind of peace flowed in the rhythm of finding new words in the English dictionary and writing them down with their definitions. The 1845 Webster's dictionary sat on the left side of the desk, Elizabeth's alphabetized word list to her right. She ran her hand lightly over the leather-bound book, then took a blank sheet of paper from the drawer and grasped a pencil, a gift from Elizabeth. Chen had sharpened it for her. Though lead pencils were in common use, they were hard to come by, and she cherished this one.

She chose the first word from the list. "Obsequious." Her hands flew to the dictionary, searching for the letter "O" on the side tabs, then pressed the book open. She thumbed the pages, running her fingers from top to bottom until her index finger paused on the correct word.

She pronounced the word "Ub-see-kwee-us." She copied the definition in the space next to it on the page. The first meaning read "servile complaisance." Servile? The example phrase was "an obsequious bow." She looked up the word servile: "slavishly submissive." Then back to obsequious again. The example phrase said, "Servilely compliant." So, it meant . . . *kau tau*? Someone subservient to another? How well she knew that state of being. For a moment she felt the sting of Tung Chee's kicks against her stomach.

Someone rapped at her door and pushed it open.

"Good morning." Elizabeth's crinoline skirts rustled. "I hoped I would find you here. Sorry I missed breakfast today. One of our mares foaled, and I went out to see the new colt. He is an adorable little one— all legs! The boys are intrigued since this is the first time we have had one. Lots of room to ride on our ranch, so they will have much pleasure raising him."

Ah pictured the boys riding across the golden fields surrounding the ranch.

Elizabeth continued. "I wanted you to know you may take a bath before the dinner at Thomas Larkin's this evening. I have told Hortencia to heat the water for the clawfoot tub."

A hand brushed her shoulder. Ah looked up into Elizabeth's face. "Thank you. I missed you at breakfast."

Elizabeth leaned against the desk, her full black and white plaid skirts filling the space between them. Ah noticed her friend's soft face beginning to show the wrinkles of middle age. Small brown curls mixed with gray fell onto Elizabeth's forehead and her brown hair drew into a bun atop her head. A white lace collar lay neatly against her cotton bodice. A mother of pearl inlaid cross nestled between her breasts. An aura of holiness surrounded her.

Elizabeth said, "I see by your dictionary you plan on working on your English word list today. Do you like your new pencil?"

Ah nodded. "Since I have been in your house, I've practiced many new words and phrases."

Elizabeth said, "Our home is busy, what with the boys learning their Bible verses. I fear I have not had enough time with you."

Ah felt a tug as Elizabeth leaned over and tucked a stray hair into her own bun. A sense of confinement tightened Ah's limbs. Where was the freedom she wanted here in America? Instead of letting her go, was Elizabeth pulling her back into the confines of her life in Guangdong?

Elizabeth patted the dictionary. "I am proud of you. Not only for your English, but also for your ability to start your own business in San Francisco." She shook her head. "I have been wondering, though."

"What is it you would like to know?" Ah gave Elizabeth a sideways glance and put down the pencil.

"I would like more details about what you do in this—er—business of yours. When I have asked you about it, you have changed the subject."

Ah smarted. Had she been that obvious? She should have made up a cover story about the Lookee Shop that would put Elizabeth's mind at rest. But then, how could she continue lying to such a good friend of long standing?

Silence drew a curtain between them.

Through the double-sashed open window, something clanged outside—maybe the hostler was shoeing a horse in the barn. The noise jarred her senses.

She could not ignore Elizabeth's penetrating question. If she told Elizabeth the truth, she would risk losing her friendship, but Elizabeth would see through her thin excuses.

Ah took the plunge into uncertain waters. "I—I have a business where I—we—undress before men."

Elizabeth's eyes widened and she sucked in a breath. Spots of rose mottled her cheeks. "What happens after—this—undressing?" She grimaced; Ah could tell she was expecting the worst. Luckily, that *was* the worst.

Ah fiddled with her pencil. "Nothing. We collect gold dust and the men go away."

Elizabeth pulled over a straw-backed chair and sat next to her. "I am not clear. So, the men pay to look at you in a state of—er—nakedness?" She clutched the cross between her breasts.

"Yes, that is all." Her words came thick as paste.

"They do not, um, sleep with you?" Elizabeth's lips formed a fine line.

"No. I am not a 'crib' girl. Clark showed them to me, and I am not that fallen. Only fallen a little bit." Could there be degrees of wretchedness? Maybe she was on the top rung of the ladder. She could only hope.

"Are you sure? I would not know, but I have heard that in the fallen world one mistake usually leads to another. One misstep and you will lose your very soul." She fingered her lace collar.

"I am quite sure." Ah crossed her arms, holding onto her shoulders.

Elizabeth set her jaw. "How can you be sure? This lookee business is a dangerous occupation. Why, at any moment, a desperate man could grab you, and I shudder to think what could happen next."

"Chen protects me." Her fingers stiffened around her pencil.

Elizabeth cocked her head to the side. "He is a thin bulwark, my dear."

"I have other guardians, too." Why this barrage of questions? She grew warm and the room grew close.

Elizabeth narrowed her eyes. "Such as?"

"John Clark, the policeman who guards my house every day."

Elizabeth cringed, drawing away from her. "*Pffft*. Not much against an army of men who might harm you."

She pushed back her shoulders. "Well—the Society in Little Canton, the Kong Chow Company, will watch for me as long as I pay my taxes."

Elizabeth sat; her eyes downcast. Had she disappointed her?

Ah imagined a dark veil between them.

A brown oak moth beat its wings against the open windowsill. Ah got up from her chair and approached the window. She cupped her hand, gathering the moth, then held it over the ledge, and released it out into the breeze. If only she could flutter away alongside it. She watched for a moment: the moth flew away beyond the house and disappeared among the cluster of trees. Tall branches of the Monterey cypress swayed gently back and forth in the cross breeze.

She turned back to her desk where Elizabeth sat, seeming transfixed.

Elizabeth's steady quiet unnerved her.

Despite the draft from the open window, the room grew uncomfortably warm. What had she done? Her mouth had gotten into trouble before—this was not the first time. Maybe this truth was too much for Elizabeth; maybe she and Chen needed to pack up their things and go back to San Francisco.

Three

❦ SHE WAS A HARLOT ❧

*A*t last, after an eternity of silences, Elizabeth spoke, her voice soft and low. "Let me tell you a story, my dear. Come over here where we may see each other."

She recognized the familiar missionary signs; now she faced a boring lecture. Elizabeth had often told her Jesus stories in Guangzhou, her singsong voice filled with Christian purpose.

Ah tucked the pencil behind her ear for safekeeping, then followed Elizabeth across the room. Two chairs faced each other before the unlit fireplace. Elizabeth took the seat nearest the hearth.

After Ah sank into the chair across from her, Elizabeth continued. "This one comes from the New Testament, like other Jesus stories I told you in Guangdong."

Ah found comfort in Elizabeth's reference "Yes, I remember."

Elizabeth's face softened. "One day when Jesus preached among the people, not far off a crowd of men threatened to stone a woman."

Ah clenched. "How awful. What had she done to deserve that?"

"It was said she was a harlot—probably like the crib girls you talked about." She gave Ah a pointed look.

"Oh, I see." Ah could tell where this was going. Elizabeth was lecturing her on her immorality. Her scalp prickled. And here she had come to Monterey for a rest, not a lesson. Maybe Elizabeth would be quick about it—she could only hope.

Elizabeth clasped her hands together. "The story goes on to say that after a while, Jesus broke off his preaching and confronted the men who continued to taunt the woman. They were about to attack her. She was on her knees, crying."

"Poor thing." Ah pictured herself kneeling on the ground. Tung Chee and Tung Chao were mocking her. "What did Jesus do next? He better not have picked up a stone and thrown it at the poor woman."

"Just listen, my dear. When Jesus talked to the accusers, he said, 'The one among you who is without sin should cast the first stone.'"

Ah wrinkled her nose. "Hmm. Though the saying was wise, he was taking quite a risk. If the men did not see their own sins, they might have killed her despite Jesus" She withdrew the pencil from behind her ear and nibbled its cedar wood.

"I agree, but Jesus had a way of calming people down. He was so fair and so just, they really did not want to argue with him."

"Like Confucius."

"A bit, yes. He surely was wise as Confucius."

This Christ story was more interesting than usual. Ah asked, "What happened next?"

"Jesus asked everyone to leave the area, and they did. When he was alone with the woman, he asked if she was condemned by a court of law. She said no."

"How could he tell she was not lying?" She ran her finger across the bite marks she made on the pencil.

"Jesus knew by her voice and attitude. He was very perceptive."

"He must have had great intelligence."

Elizabeth's face took on a grave expression. "But then came the most important part."

Ah brushed a pencil shaving from her lip. "What is that?"

"He did not condemn her. He told her to go and sin no more." Her eyes looked heavenward.

Ah tapped the pencil on her thigh. "That is startling. That a man would look kindly on a crib girl. Such a lowly creature."

Elizabeth let out a breath. "But it is not just a story to put away and read from time to time. Jesus' actions are an example to live by."

She nodded. "Very Confucian. In China we use his words often to regulate our lives."

"Yes, but that is not completely our western way. We follow Jesus' path in order to have eternal life."

"I am glad for you—that means you will have many lives ahead." Ah considered her Buddhist belief in reincarnation. If she lived a good life, she would be reborn in the good realms.

"So…here is my point." Elizabeth's lowered the pitch of her voice.

Ah gripped her pencil. She could pack her bag quickly if necessary.

Elizabeth continued. "My faith says I must accept you as Jesus acknowledged the woman in the story. She was called Mary Magdalen. Do you know what happened after he forgave her?"

"No, this is the first time you have ever told me the story."

"She followed him and helped him the rest of his life. She became a strong and capable woman."

"But wasn't she strong and capable all along?"

She steepled her fingers. "Of course, but her bad choices led her into sin."

"But what if that was all she could do to survive?"

Ah's question hung in the air between them. Elizabeth must have been weighing her answer.

After a moment, Elizabeth said, "Jesus forgave her without conditions as all sinners must be pardoned." Her soft words echoed in the room.

Ah glanced at the door. "Does that include me?"

"Yes, it does." Elizabeth gave her a dark look. "Not everyone, even those who call themselves Christians, believe as I do. Many would fault Jesus for forgiving Mary Magdalen. Easy to condemn but particularly hard to excuse another's wrongdoing when she is a woman."

A vision flashed through Ah's mind: the Sydney Ducks surrounded her, grinning and mocking. She set her jaw. "I know this."

Someone tapped and Hortencia's head poked around the door. "Senora, *lo siento. Usted necesitan en el granero. El bebé caballo.*"

"*Sí. Un momento*, Hortencia." Elizabeth shifted to the edge of her chair.

The maid's footsteps faded away.

"I'm needed in the barn again. The stable hand wants to see me, probably about the foal. Ah, what I want you to know is you have my forgiveness, no matter what you choose." She spoke in a quiet voice.

"Forgiveness?" Ah swallowed hard.

Elizabeth rose, her full skirts rustling over her crinolines. She crossed to Ah's chair and lifted her to her feet. She took both of Ah's hands in her own. "I love you as my daughter. I watched you grow up in the shadow of your brother, Toy Lee Lung. I knew about the way Tung Chee mistreated you. I saw you thrive learning English. Each new word seemed to give you a sense of freedom from him, something you had never had before, a window into another Western world."

Tears sprang to Ah's eyes, and Elizabeth's arms drew her close.

"I would not lose you for anything. You are a blessing to me." Elizabeth embraced her as Ah's mother should have, but never did.

Ah relaxed into the ruffled lace collar and sniffed the scent of lavender. Yet a question lingered between them. Ah pulled away. "When I meet Henry tonight, should I tell him my real occupation?"

Elizabeth's eyes grew hard as an iron bar. "No—I think that is a matter best kept between us." She took Ah's hand in hers and gave it a firm handshake.

Their secret kept for now; their secret it must stay.

Four

❦ THE WINDS ROAR ❧

Not long after Elizabeth left to revisit the foal, Ah opened the wooden box the Reverend had given to her, slid the pencil back in place, then drew a shawl about her shoulders. The clock on the wall said eleven. Restless, she peeked out the window.

Though a slight breeze ruffled the treetops, the air was clear and inviting. An amber glaze coated the grassy hills around their dwelling; green fir trees mixed with native oaks whose broad branches stretched out into the autumn landscape. At breakfast, the Reverend talked about the white sand beach not far from the ranch.

She got up from the chair and scanned the room. Where was her sunhat? It clung to the coat hook, its drawstrings meandering down to the floor. Elizabeth said she should wear the straw bonnet to protect her fair skin against the sun's rays. She planted it on her head and tied the red plaid ribbons to make a bow under her chin in the manner of San Francisco women. It wouldn't matter if the style did not go along with her silk qipao. The Daileys accepted and understood her, and parts of her outfit would blend the way oyster sauce mixed with her rice.

Ah made her way through the hallway, her hands skimming the polished oak railings. At the entryway she anticipated a struggle to open the massive door of the house. To her surprise, the door unlatched easily and swung wide open.

Beyond the front porch in the near pasture, a speckled mare flicked her tail, grazing with a black filly. A breeze blew across the dry grasses and an oak tree's branches rose and fell, so many arms waving hello. A raven perched on a pine branch and eyed her, angling its beak this way and that. Maybe it was trying to figure her out.

Chen must be out in the barn with Elizabeth and the new foal. Footsteps echoed around the corner to her left. Hortencia hustled in from the dining room and wiped her hands on a red and yellow embroidered apron. She called, "Señorita?" Her broad smile conveyed her warm, accepting manner.

Ah was drawn to Hortencia's helpful tone. "Good morning, Hortencia. I would like to find Chen so I can go to the seaside in a wagon."

"*Señorita, no comprendo. Lo siento.*" Hortencia clearly strained to understand. The brass watchchain on her chest glinted against the sun slanting in from the open doorway.

Ah pointed outside. A trickle of Spanish words filled her mind. The words *ven acá*—come here—in Spanish, sounded right. "Ven acá."

Hortencia tilted her head. Was she amazed that Ah was trying to speak Spanish? In response, she stepped to the door and pointed out the barn in the distance. "Chen–*granero.*"

Hortencia remained where she stood, her face a puzzle of noncomprehension.

Ah clenched her fists. Why was her dragon not helping her now? Spanish was even more daunting than English. Maybe it was not worth the effort to go get Chen; maybe she should go back up to her room and continue her English lesson.

Hortencia stepped forward, blinking. Her voice rose. "*Momento.*" The Californio's brown eyes melted into the wrinkles surrounding them. She pulled off her white apron and disappeared into the kitchen, then emerged wearing a maroon cloak over her black day dress.

Ah watched the housekeeper's stout form stride away toward the barn. Maybe Hortencia understood her after all, but the odds were fifty-fifty. Yet she would wait.

She shuffled into the hallway and perched on black embroidered chair with a view out the front door. A broad-chested dog of uncertain lineage meandered in the front door and flopped down in the hallway, his brown belly flat on the shaded tile.

After a few moments listening to the dog's snoring, Ah heard a crunch of footsteps approaching the front door, and she rose to get a better view.

Hortencia and Chen pointed at the front door, with Hortencia repeating "Señorita" and Chen saying "Sí", every few steps.

Chen peered into the hallway. "Si tau po?"

Ah's Cantonese words flowed across the room. "Please get a stable hand to drive us to the seaside. I wish to walk along the beach."

He grinned.

Hortencia reached out and straightened the bonnet on Ah's head. "*Aquí hay un sombrero para el sol.*"

At last she would get her wish to see Monterey Bay.

A few moments later, a lad sporting a dusty cap drew up with a pony and farm wagon, and Ah let Chen help her up to her seat alongside the driver. Chen grabbed the side handles, pulled himself up on the step, then sat next to her.

A mile or so down the weedy road, they entered an area of dunes where white and brown sand piled high into mounds. There was a crashing sound—waves—so the ocean had to be nearby.

Through a cut in the sand piles, the driver pulled up the reins, then turned to Ah and Chen. "I can go no further. The horse will get stuck in the sand. Best ya get out here. I'll wait for ya. Could use a good smoke." He pulled a cigar out of his pocket and jumped down.

A moment after, Ah stepped down into Chen's outstretched arms, allowing him to set her on her feet. He guided her arm and they descended the sandy pass onto the beach. Twin promontories curled, waves crashing on either side of the bay whose outstretched arms embraced the tides. A vision of Clark's holding her rose up, but she swept it away. No time to think of him now.

Despite the noonday sun overhead, a stiff breeze chilled her bones, and so Ah pulled her pink shawl about her. Chen was at her elbow, and he guided her across the sand, but she watched him laugh at the vibrant water ahead. "Go ahead." She waved toward the beach.

Chen skipped ahead like a child she had once seen playing on the banks of the Pearl River. A large river or a sea would make grownups lose their heads like little ones. The breeze, the sun, the blue lapping water—all created enthusiasm that blurred their ages. Chen's black queue flew behind him like a tail of a kite, his body leaning and stretching with the wind as though he and the ribbon were united.

In the distance a lone man meandered along the beach toward the rocks. He was tall and sported a faded tan. Every so often he stopped and lifted a seashell to examine. Who could he be?

She struggled to keep her sunhat on her head, but then the breeze blew it off. Held only by ribbons, it flapped against her back. But what was that? A pebble in her right shoe? She could not take another step.

After flopping down on the sand, she wrenched off her shoe; tiny grains lodged in the crevices of her toes curled onto her footbed like bent palm leaves. And when she ran her fingers over the toes, the sand pushed more deeply into the fissures. She grasped a twig that lay nearby, and dug out the worst of the grains.

Chen's shadow shielded her from the sun.

She looked up.

The wind blew his hair across his forehead. A shy grin played across his features. "What is the matter, si tau po? Please. Come down to the water. You will like it I think."

"No. I cannot walk further. The sand got between my toes." A tug of irritation burned inside her. Why could he not see her struggling?

"Take off your other shoe." His words blended with the breeze.

"Why?"

"The sand will come off…here, let me." He took a handful of dry sand and rubbed it against the sole of her exposed left foot.

"It tickles." She drew her foot back.

"Stay still. You will see what I mean."

She relaxed, though she held herself ready to pull her foot back at a moment's notice. After a second of Chen's rubbing, the sand freed itself from between her misshapen toes. "I was wrong to doubt you," she said.

He removed her other shoe and freed the sand from between those toes as well. Then, he lifted her up by her elbows, and balanced her between his outstretched arms. "Come, I will take you to the waves." After picking her up, he carried her across the beach in the gentle way a parent would carry a child. Her sunhat bounced against her back. When they reached the shoreline, he stood, breathless. "The water is cold. Prepare yourself."

Out of the corner of her eye, she saw the stranger from down the beach. He must be approaching them. She had no time for greetings; she had come to see the water. Here the light beige sand contrasted sharply with the blue green bay; there the whitecaps crowned the tips of the promontories at either end; waves crashed crazily on distant rock formations as if drunk on plum wine. She cringed but tightened her stomach muscles. *Be prepared for this.*

Easing her down in front of him, Chen put her hat back on her head, then held the backs of her arms. "Now walk a bit into the water and you will see."

"Watch those waves!" The stranger yelled in English, closing the distance between them. "They got a mighty pull."

She glanced at the stranger, his dark sandy hair blowing about, his pants rolled up to his knees; his rucksack slung across his back. The man sported long sideburns that followed the jawline midway toward his chin.

She held up her pantaloons to the knees. The waves were curling, laughing, in and out, their foam capturing, then releasing her feet, then ankles, then calves as she ventured each step into the icy water. She shivered as the water splashed, making her skin tingle.

She stayed for a moment, the tow of the water nearly pulling her off her feet, but Chen held her upright so she would not fall.

"Careful, man." The stranger said. "That undertow that can take you out quick." Though his words carried a warning, his voice was casual as if he knew her and Chen.

When the water rushed out, abandoning the bare sand, Chen pointed to a round brown knob sticking out of the water not far from shore. "Look!"

The stranger said, "I see it now." His voice rose against the waves. "It came up before, but then it disappeared." He said, "Do you see it, Miss?"

Wordless, Ah stood next to Chen who shielded his eyes from the glare and observed the sea creature. Holding the brim of her sunhat against the glare, she followed the direction of the stranger's outstretched arm.

Again, a brown knob rose above the water, and she saw two large chocolate-colored eyes, a snout like a dog's, and gray whiskers. The shiny creature rose its head above the waves and fixed a stare in her direction.

"What could it be?" She drew back. "A dog? Or fish?"

"I do not know. I do not recall seeing that in China." Chen shook his head.

"Like you, I have not seen them in China, but I have seen many along the coast of California." The stranger's words were tinged with wonder.

It was her turn to point. "Look, it is rising up again. Its back is smooth and black. Now it is diving down into the water."

Chen nodded. "It has a flipper on its tail."

She bit her lower lip. "Must be some kind of fish."

"They call them sea lions." Though the stranger's voice was light, he spoke slowly, deliberately. Was he used to foreigners?

"Sea—lions," Ah repeated.

The waves thundered against the coastline, and bits of white spray leaped up and then disappeared into the air.

"There! Another one!" Chen's cry flowed out with the foam layering the waves.

A second sea lion poked itself out of the water and looked in their direction. Ah clapped her hands. Such good luck! And then the animals vanished down into the tide.

White, gray, and speckled gulls swooped here and there over the currents where the big fish had appeared. Some gathered on the rocks, others sailed on air flows up, over, and around the promontories.

Chen tugged at her hand, and then he led her back up to a piece of driftwood. "Come sit here, si tau po."

She sat down first, then Chen's hip jostled her as he sat next to her. The stranger lingered, gazing with them at the frolicking, white-capped waves. Beyond them lay the far horizon—the China of her fears, the Guangdong of her past.

A frisson passed through her—she would never know where the bones of her little girls lay. Over which canyon had Tung Chee cast them? Where were her babies now, their tiny skeletons picked clean by vultures?

The stranger pulled the rucksack off his shoulder and drew out a small burlap bag. "I must be off. I collect shells, you see. And driftwood, too. Good for whittling." She noticed small wrinkles gathering around his hazel eyes, and the small tufts of gray hair playing at his temples. He seemed kind enough.

He ran his fingers through his wind-blown hair and rose. She looked up at him. "I am Ah, and this is Chen."

A faint smile crept across his lips. He spoke his words in Cantonese. "My name is Harry. And I wish you good fortune." The stranger wandered off, stopping from time to time, turning over mounds of seashells with a stick.

Ah startled at the Cantonese words "good fortune." Few westerners would say those words unless they had been to China where luck was prized.

After an hour in spellbound silence, the sun began to descend behind them, and Ah tugged her shawl more tightly about her shoulders. Her bonnet continued to rest against her back. The tide rose, and fingerling waves inched toward them.

Chen said, "I am getting cold." He got up, casting a long shadow on the sand.

She nodded. "The others will be wondering where we are—the Daileys and Hortencia." She gathered her hat and set it on top of her head, then retied the red plaid ribbons under her chin.

After reaching the top of the passage through the sand dunes where their wagon waited, Ah turned back toward the sparkling water, the waves surging forward, covering Chen's tracks, the tidal foam seeping over the place where they had sat a few moments before. Where was the stranger?

Far away down the beach, Harry the stranger meandered, a mere dot against the sand. If only she could capture the moment to savor this joy—if only the tide would carry out to sea her pain, her loss. Yet, like the tide, she must persevere. As Harry said, she must work toward good fortune. A question etched its way into her mind. How did Harry speak Cantonese so well? Her wonder vanished into the air, threading into the happy moments of their day.

She did not have to wait long for Chen to lift her in his arms and set her on the wagon. The driver clucked and the horse jerked to a start, then turned from the wet sand road onto the dry surface and home.

Five

❧ LIKE A PRECIOUS VASE ☙

*U*pon arrival at the Dailey house, Chen reached up into the wagon, and as customary, Ah eased into the safety of his outstretched arms. He lowered her to the ground like a precious vase. Her shadow lengthened before her on the ranch soil. Had they stayed at the beach too long?

The driver clucked the reins of his horse, and the clip-clop died way, replaced by the clucking of chickens in their pens beside the house. A black and white cow mooed in a distant pasture.

She took Chen's elbow. "I must have a bath before tonight's dinner. I am to meet Mr. Henry Conrad. I think we must hurry."

He said. "I will pour water into the basin and you may wash your feet. "

"No, Chen. Not the basin. Mrs. Dailey said I may use the clawfoot tub in the bathing room. The water is kept hot on the stove."

A half hour later, she watched Chen pour the last bucket of steaming hot water into the tub. Chen pulled her feet out of her lotus shoes and set them on the straw mat. After stepping out of her qipao, she gave the jacket and pants to him for careful folding. He had seen her naked so often in the Lookee Shop that she paid him no mind.

Chen stood up with the empty bucket, and she met his gaze. "I know what you need." He dashed out the door and returned a moment later with a long towel and a robe. "From Hortencia. For you." He left them on a chair by the door and tiptoed out, leaving the door ajar.

Someone tapped on the other side of the open door, and she reached for the towel, draped it around her body, then stood next to the clawfoot tub.

"*Señorita.*" Hortencia called out. "*Permiso?*" Without waiting for permission, Hortencia crossed the room. She stood next to Ah and grinned.

"What do you want?" Ah clutched the towel more tightly around her.

Hortencia held out a light green box with a *fleur de lis* signet stamped on top. The word *Bain* scrawled on the sides in fancy script.

At her father's porcelain company, she had seen such packaging and recognized it as French. Usually these boxes contained unusual items of high quality.

Hortencia opened the box. "*Sí?*"

Ah peered into the open box. Crystals the color of amethyst gleamed inside.

Hortencia lifted the box and Ah took a whiff of the contents. "Hmm. Lavender."

"*Un regalo de la señora.*" Hortencia sprinkled the bath salts into the water, then left the room.

Ah padded behind her, turning the key so this time the door was secured. She looked down at the lock. Who else might wander in here uninvited?

A few minutes later, Ah sank into the tub, the burning water reddening her skin. She gritted her teeth to withstand the heat, yet she let herself recline against the back of the tub while the water warmed her bones.

She stirred the lavender-scented water and made waves across her belly. Her thoughts took a dark turn. If only Clark had been with her today to see the magnificent beach. Where was he now? His wife would be arriving in San Francisco any day. She swallowed hard.

A tableau shimmered against the calm waters. She pictured Mr. and Mrs. Clark strolling down DuPont Street, arm in arm. Would Mrs. Clark close her parasol and point out a pretty pair of gloves for him to buy for her? Would she brush a kiss across his cheek the way Ah had done when they stopped at street corners? Would he carry a bag of onions home for her from the market?

Tiny knifepoints dug into her skin. His wife did not deserve him. He was meant for her. It all seemed so unfair. She slapped the water with her right hand, causing a ripple that seemed to rock her from side to side.

After the waters calmed, she plucked a bar of soap from the metal holder latched onto the side of the tub and soaped her breasts, her belly, and the hollow between her legs. Why had her body captivated Clark the first day he had come to her shanty? She looked down at the water caressing her nutbrown nipples, the pearl colored skin of her belly, and the sharp triangle of brown hair that sheltered her smooth chamber.

If only she had Clark in her arms, in this bath, to have him lower himself into her, caress her with kisses, lavish her with intimate love words. She would soap his back, run her fingers across his hips, whisper flower-words into his ear. Or would she? Her vision faded as quickly as it had appeared. Of course—it was only a waking dream. And he was not here.

She let go of the side of the tub, and her body sank to the bottom, as heavy as stone. She lifted her face up out of the water, letting her hair trail behind her in the water. She cried into the emptiness. Tears meandered down her cheeks and dissolved into the bathwater.

Brushing her tears away, she searched for her reflection in the water. The lavender crystals had turned the water a shade of purple, and she peered into the lighter shallows that revealed her small oval face. She frowned at herself: Clark would never be hers—at least not in that way. She might as well reconcile herself to the truth.

After what must have been nearly an hour, footsteps tapped on the tile floor. Hortencia returned, her cheeks the color of faded red roses. "*El tiempo passa.*" She pointed to a watch dangling on a chain around her neck.

After reaching down into the tub, Hortencia grasped Ah's left arm from under the water, and pulled it up in the air.

Was she trying to drag her out? Ah fumed—if so, this was no way to do it. She slipped down into the water and grabbed the side of the tub to pull herself away from Hortencia, then up out of the water.

She stood on unsteady legs. "Please give me the towel, Hortencia." She struggled to gain her balance, nearly fell, and leaned down to grasp the tub so she would not topple out.

"*¡Pobre niña!*" Hortencia's tone was soft and soothing. She extended the towel, and Ah covered herself with it. If only she could stop shaking.

Ah fought the panic. Bound feet meant she could not run away. She might as well have chains around them, weighing her down. When Tung Chee had tried to force her down, she had even tried to get away on her hands and knees, only to find herself held up like a feather, and carried back to his bed for more humiliating acts.

Ah sobbed her words. "I want Chen."

Hortencia's brown eyes grew large. "Señorita! Chen?"

"Yes—I mean Chen." Maybe if she repeated his name, Hortencia would understand.

The faded roses on Hortencia's cheeks burned like cinnamon candies. She said, "*Jesús me perdone.*" Turning, she fled into the hallway.

Why had Hortencia turned red? Maybe it was because she thought Chen and she were—no—it couldn't be—lovers? Ah's sobs turned to laughter at the thought.

A moment passed, then Chen appeared at the door. His Cantonese words betrayed his nervousness. "Hortencia keeps pointing to her watch. Time to dress for the Larkin's dinner."

She tightened the towel around her. "Can you walk me behind the change curtain so I may put on my dressing gown?"

"Of course, si tao po." He extended his arm and helped her across the tile floors.

Out of a corner of her eye, Ah saw Hortencia's yellow and red apron swirl behind the open door to the bathing room. A moment later, she heard a tapping sound—someone was tiptoeing away down the hall.

She could not resist a giggle. Of course. Hortencia had stayed to watch, then snuck away when there was nothing to see. The woman probably thought she and Chen were lovers. She could not be angry. Hortencia was a kindred soul, a fellow traveler in this new land, full of dust, death, and angry men.

Six

❧ AT CLOSE RANGE ❧

Late that same afternoon, a light rain shower fell, and Ah could hear its patter against the roof of their hired transport on the way to the Larkin house. This was no moment to look for privacy. The small coach creaked. Her hip bumped Chen when the vehicle strained to make it up a hill; her knees bumped Elizabeth's on the downward slide. Maybe if she looked out at the passing hills, she could avoid the nausea rising from the taint of cigar smoke that infused the blankets used for padding the coach. Why were her hands trembling? After all, this was only a meeting with the much-talked-about Henry Conrad.

After a few miles of dreary spatter, the clouds lightened, and the rain stopped. The driver entered the enclave of adobe structures, passing Californios dressed in serapes along with men and women in western wear. The men's top hats bobbed with each step, the women's long skirts swept the damp walkways. Cacti and high grasses blended with the occasional rosebush, revealing the domestic touch women gave their frontier dwellings.

After Chen helped her down, her shoes sank into sandy mud. Ah gazed up at the two-story whitewashed adobe house. It loomed large, a veranda stretching around the second floor. Tall, multi-paned windows stared out at the dusty world surrounding it.

By the looks of his property, Thomas Larkin was a successful man in these parts. In China, men surrounded themselves with grandeur to maximize their importance in the public eye. In California, Larkin did the same.

A male servant greeted them at the door and escorted them upstairs to dress for dinner. In a room filled with well-dusted children's toys, Chen helped her slide into the pink and silver qipao. She styled her up in pearl hairpins along with Hortencia's Mexican silver filigree clip. She put on her pearl and ruby earrings.

How lovely they were, dangling in the looking glass, reflecting the light from the window. She had ordered them from Hong Kong with her new money. The sight of her reflection gave her pause.

Though she had never wanted for money in Guangzhou, this sudden wealth in California carried a satisfaction. Not only did she look the part of a wealthy woman; she had earned it herself.

Chen took a step back, then sucked in a breath. "Most beautiful, si tau po." He laid a hand over his heart.

After guiding her down the stairs, he left her in front of the crackling fireplace in the drawing room. Reverend Dailey stood there, drinking a brandy. A table flanked by two tapestried chairs dominated the center of the room. A chestnut desk, some wall paintings, and a pink fainting couch lined the white walls. Someone had polished the dark wood floors to a high sheen. An even set of tall windows ensured the room was not too dark. The dying light from sunset pierced the angles of the room, sending shadows into the corners.

A young girl's portrait in a wooden frame against the wall drew her attention, and she stepped over to look at it. "Is this the Larkin's daughter?" The Reverend came over and peered with her at the painting.

She looked closely at the little girl in the white dress, her tiny shoulders bare, her left hand clutching a pale pink rose. Behind the little girl, a woman's white straw hat hung on a wall, its blue double ribbons flowing downward. The child's round face contrasted sharply with the more mature set of ringlets atop her head, framing her face. Sharp and luminous brown eyes gazed out at Ah and the world.

The Reverend murmured sadly. "Yes, it is Carolina. The Larkins lost her to typhus at three years old in '45." He tilted his head. "A good likeness it is. Such a darling she was. Luckily, they have little boy Alfred to replace her, but Thomas says Rachel is not yet recovered from the little girl's death."

Ah stared down into her empty hands. Another Carolina? Was that not the name of Henry Conrad's wife?

He pointed at the image. "Looking into Carolina's face I can't help but see the strong resemblance to Rachel. She would have grown up to be her mother's twin, I think."

"How very sorrowful to hear this," Ah said.

"Darned shame it was." Reverend's face grew sober, and he fell into silent musing.

A chill black silence surrounded them.

Not long after, a tall man of large bulk filled the doorway, his gray muttonchops catching the light. Thomas Larkin strode over to the Reverend and gave him a warm embrace. Ah joined them at the fireplace. A younger man with a short beard sauntered in and stood next to them.

Larkin beamed, his eyes reflecting the firelight. "Reverend! It is always good to be in the company of fellow Bostonians." He turned to Ah. "I welcome you to our house. Surely not as noble or ancient as those in China, but for us it is adequate."

"My pleasure, Mr. Larkin." Ah appreciated the benevolent twinkle in his eyes. "I have never been in a house like this one you call Monterey-style."

"It is the first two-story adobe house in California. Built in 1835—not much more than sand dunes here at the time. But—here—I want you to meet my good friend and fellow businessman, Sam Brannan. He is also from San Francisco."

Ah gazed up into the younger man's eyes. She wondered; did they narrow when he looked back at her? "My pleasure, Mr. Brannan."

He reached out and lifted her hand to his lips. "I am expanding my trading enterprise into Guangdong these days. Larkin here says you come from porcelain traders. Happy to know you, Mrs. Toy."

He turned back to Larkin and the Reverend. "I finally pulled my assets out of New Hope colony. Got every last gold piece I could."

"Too bad it did not succeed, Sam. The Saints worked so hard to till the land and make a go of it."

Larkin and Brannan folded their arms and faced Reverend Dailey.

The reverend asked, "New Hope? Was it a mission?"

"A Mormon farming settlement on the Stanislaus River. We started it in '46, but we ran into floods and other problems. Our community invested a lot in labor and seed, but the wheat yield was unsatisfactory." A dark look passed over Brannan's eyes. She shivered. She had seen many such clever men in Guangdong. Speculators—who knew what they were after? Fame? Power? Wealth?

She looked around for Chen, but he had gone to the kitchen and left her alone with three men. What was she to do?

The congenial Larkin turned to her, filling the awkward space. "You may not know but I have just returned from working on the Constitution for what we hope will be the new state of California."

She wrinkled her nose. "Constitution? I do not know the word."

"It is the most important document declaring the rights and purviews of all the people of the state."

She tapped her chest. "Even me? I was not born here."

Larkin chuckled softly. "Yes, Mrs. Toy, even you. Our committee spent many hours of discussion on section seventeen. I know it by heart. It says, "Foreigners who are, of who may hereafter become bona fide residents of this State, shall enjoy the same rights in respect to the possession, enjoyment, and inheritance of property, as native-born citizens.""

Sam Brannan frowned. "Easy to say, hard to do, Thomas. Such a lofty goal, but when you see the troublemakers I do from all parts of the world in San Francisco, watching them destroy life and property, you may think again about this decision."

Larkin put a hand on his shoulder. "You have always regarded humanity with less optimism than I, Sam. I think that unless we have a lofty principle in place, our citizens will not pay attention to the idea that all men are created equal."

Ah wondered. Did men include women? What would that be like? She had no idea.

Brannan tilted his head. "Though I was not at the Constitutional Convention, I do remember reading about another section that you ratified. It must have been a difficult one for the members to settle."

Ah asked, "Which one was that? I like hearing about this new constitution."

Larkin said, "Neither slavery, nor involuntary servitude, unless for the punishment of crimes, shall ever be tolerated in this State."

Reverend Dailey broke in. "Yes, it was important that our new state be founded against slavery."

Brannan stiffened, "And I also wonder how successful it will be to implement anti-slavery, anti-servitude policies when so many southerners are coming to this state. And so many people making false promises are bringing in workers from China. Maybe you will be able to talk me out of my skepticism, Thomas, but law and order in San Francisco is one of my main concerns."

Larkin frowned. "Slavery and servitude are hardly a way to make sure people obey laws. Our nation stands for liberty and our new state must also."

Brannan tapped his arm. "I fully agree with you and I believe as you do that these principles in our new constitution must abide. It is only that the Sydney Ducks are posing a real threat to our growing community in the Bay City."

Larkin nodded. "I have heard about the many fires and all the vandalism in San Francisco. All the business owners have their hands full. But let us save that discussion for another time, Sam." He turned to Ah. "You have not met my wife Rachel. She will be coming along any moment with Elizabeth. You know how women love to talk." Footsteps advanced toward them on the other side of the passage between this and the dining room.

In the meantime, three voices rose and fell, growing louder. Mrs. Dailey's high voice resounded, along with a lower, reedier male voice. Was it Henry? Ah's heart picked up a beat. Maybe he would be a friendly man.

She readied herself. Her pink lotus shoes peeked out from under her pantaloons. She held on to the fireplace mantel for balance. One side of her back grew decidedly warm.

Elizabeth Dailey approached, in mid-conversation with a tall woman whose angular cheekbones set off her thin face. Elizabeth said, "Stargazer is what we have named the new foal." Ah watched Elizabeth stride toward her, her brown ringlets bouncing against her ears.

"Here you are—." She reached for Ah's hand. "My dear, I would like you to meet our hostess, Rachel Larkin."

Rachel advanced, her eyes gleaming. She wore a jet-black silk mourning dress set off by a double layered lace collar and a black-rimmed brooch. She gave Ah an intelligent, appraising look. "Welcome to our *hacienda.* We are most honored and have heard much about you, Mrs. Toy." Her black pearl earrings dangled from her small ears.

Ah's heart skipped. What had they heard? And from whom? She returned Rachel's greeting with an uneasy smile.

Elizabeth looped an arm around Ah's shoulder and drew her close, then directed her toward the approaching gentleman. "Henry, I would like you to meet Mrs. Ah Toy." Elizabeth's brown ringlets danced up and down.

The pomade on Henry's hair glistened. "The pleasure is all mine, Mrs. Toy." Formality stiffened his words. Just like in Guangdong. British merchants often spoke with highborn manners unless they were drunk on plum wine or scotch whiskey. But wait—where had she seen him before?

Ah gave him a hesitating nod. Her backside was getting very hot and sweat gathered under her arms. She reached into her pouch, drew out her fan, then flicked it open.

Henry took a step back, studying her. He loomed tall with chestnut hair, and large brown eyes. Was he admiring the cascade of hair falling from her chignon and spilling across her left shoulder? Was he imagining the fullness of her breasts under her garment?

Though her business was to be looked at, she was ill-accustomed to a man staring at her at such close range. The room began to spin—oh no—it must be the heat—and she took a step forward and crashed into Henry's arms, sending him back at least two steps. "I am—so sorry—."

Sometime later, smelling salts pierced her senses, and she awoke to faces pressing down on her. Her sideways glance found an embroidered antimacassar, so she must be on the pink fainting couch. She first heard Elizabeth's voice. "Are you, all right? Maybe we should call for Doctor Wallace."

A headache throbbed like a hammer pounding on a wharf, yet she fought against it and tried to sit up. She planted her lotus shoes on the floor and squinted at her surroundings. Someone sat down next to her and a thigh pressed against hers. "Chen?" Stars danced across her line of sight.

"It is I, Henry, here to help you." Where had she heard that voice before? Not long ago, either. The wind, the waves, sand in her toes. . . but no—it couldn't be—yet something about him put her at ease.

"How long since you have eaten something?" It was Reverend Dailey this time.

She rubbed her eyes. "Many hours I think."

"Hortencia was supposed to have made a plate of chicken and rice for you before we left the ranch. I must speak to her about that."

She breathed a sigh. "No. It was not her fault. We—that is, Chen and I—went out to the beach. For a walk."

"Did you get your feet wet?" The Reverend's forehead wrinkled.

"Yes, I put them into the ocean."

He rolled his eyes. "No wonder you are faint. Let us take you back over to the fireplace to warm them."

If she went back over to the fireplace, she would turn into a blister and pop. She gave them a pasted-on smile. "No, I would rather eat please"

Henry leaned over, taking the lead. "As you wish. I most certainly will not force the matter. Well, we are to dine now anyway. Let me help you up and get you some food. Oh, by the way, here is your fan—you dropped it when you fainted."

"Thank you, Harry." She might as well test him right here, right now.

A red flush crept into his already tan cheeks. "Er—that is my nickname at home; you may call me Henry."

"Very well." She fought the spin in her head, took the fan, and rose. The now-familiar Henry held his arm around her shoulders, and guided her steps toward the dining room. Minutes later she faced him across a candlelit table.

Her head began to clear, and she took a moment to study him. His eyes were rounder than Clark's. They had a different expression—rather than Clark's faraway dreaminess, this man possessed a hard-edged reality. Very like the menfolk who came to do business with Tung Chee. Well-dressed, their hair pomaded into place, their collars and cuffs starched, their boots polished to a high shine. Such men in tapered black jackets sat at long tables, drinking whiskey and handling money

Amidst the patter of table conversation, she wondered. Was this man ambitious and wealthy like Sam Brannan? Though he resembled the man on the beach, in many ways he was not him. That man Harry had been carefree, full of life. This man Henry looked as staid as all the others, except for their host Thomas Larkin who sat at the end of the table, peppering his conversation with steady laughter.

In fact, Larkin dove into his roast beef with gusto, gesticulating with his fork and knife to make a point to the Reverend and Elizabeth sitting next to him.

Sam Brannan shoveled food into his mouth but did not drink wine, only water.

Water. Her mouth was dry as the sandy beach she had visited with Chen. She lifted her glass and drank deeply.

Henry unfolded his cloth napkin and spread it across his lap. "Elizabeth says you are from Guangzhou. I have been there many times and I know many of the porcelain factories." A black agate ring with an embedded diamond graced his pinkie finger. If this was Harry, why had he not worn that ring to the beach?

"Yes." A tingling dread tiptoed up her back and sat like a black crow on her shoulder. What did he already know about her? Could that prejudice him against her? And if he was the man on the beach, why did he not mention that to her right away? Was he another liar?

He unfolded his napkin and laid it on his lap. "I learned from the

Daileys that you lost your husband, Tung Chee. No wonder you do not seem sad." He shook his head. "What a cruel man. Many times we saw him thrash his workers and humiliate them before many traders."

She flinched and set down her empty water glass. "Yes, it is so." This man knew more than she thought. If only she could leave her past behind.

"And what is it you do in San Francisco? Laundress? Seamstress? Shopkeeper?" His lips parted slightly.

"Something like that." She would no more tell him the truth than walk into the waves with rocks on her back.

If the Larkins knew she was a lookee girl, they would never invite her again. What would a former U.S. Consul to Mexico, one of the most important people in California, want with her?

She piled her rice away from her black beans, speared a piece of fish with her fork, then lifted it to her mouth. By the way, where was Chen? There he stood, inside the kitchen doorway, folding tablecloths. Thank goodness he had not gone away tonight.

Reverend Dailey spoke from his end of the table. "We are very fond of our Mrs. Toy. My wife says she has great talent."

Elizabeth patted the cross hanging from her neck. "She was so willing to master English words and expressions. Easy to teach."

"I see," Henry ran a finger around the rim of his wine glass. "I can tell by her English that she is a fast learner, an eager listener."

Ah swallowed a piece of fish. Maybe this Henry would not treat her the way men did in San Francisco. There she was some sort of oddity, her exotic beauty a strange jewel for men to observe.

Meanwhile, Henry leaned back, his arm hooked into the back of the chair next to him.

Would he understand her? She wondered, but something stopped her. The soft wrinkles around his smile—was he? The puzzle remained. He couldn't be the same lively, carefree man as the wanderer she had met not long ago on the beach. And yet—.

His eyes remained fixed on hers, and she forced herself to look away. A flush of heat warmed her, and she drew back from the table. She ran her tongue across her dry lips. Her water glass was empty.

"Señorita?" the waiter asked.

"*Agua, por favor.*" She said.

"Certainly." He turned away in the midst of serving wilted spinach leaves to the various guests.

Chen's voice rang out. "I will get it." Soon after, he was by her side. Water splashed into her glass.

She tapped his forearm. "Thank you."

Rachel's cheerful voice filled the room. "Our new servant comes from Sonoma. Your Hortencia recommended him."

The young Californio beamed, thick black hair covering his forehead, a white towel slung over his arm.

Sam Brannan nodded. "Thomas, I see your house is full of delightful people. I am honored to be at your table."

She caught Brannan's eye. He flashed a beckoning smile.

"My pleasure." Thomas waved his hand, encompassing those gathered at his table. "These are many of the faces of our new state." He rose from his chair. "Now that we have an official constitution, let us toast to statehood. Let us pray California's statehood is approved by Congress come next year."

The assembly stood with their wine glasses; Thomas extended his glass and led the cheer. "To our new state of California!"

"Here, here!" Ah rose her glass along with the rest and joined the merriment.

But Thomas was not done. He said, "I give a special welcome to our guest, Mrs. Toy. Seldom do we have the honor of hosting such an interesting woman."

She said, "The Reverend and Mrs. Dailey have been very generous to me and Chen."

Heads bobbed up and down the table, then knives and forks clanged against the plates as the diners relished the rest of their meal.

When next she caught a glimpse of Henry across the table, he was lifting a salt cellar toward her. "You may need a little of this, but not too much. The beef is already quite salty." His voice resonated with kind concern.

It was then she knew. That same voice—Harry's voice—had warned her about the waves. She gave him an appraising glance. Yet this Henry was such a different man. The perfect ribbon collar, pomade stiffening his hair, the air of propriety. The stranger at the beach wore a loose jacket, his hair abandoned to the wind, his manner full of wanderlust.

"No thank you." She relaxed, considering. Not long ago, he had sat by her side contemplating magnificent Monterey Bay. Maybe he thought her an equal, the way John Clark treated her. At least for now she could imagine that.

The light grew faint in the dining room, and the servant lit an array of lanterns hanging on the walls. At the end of the meal, Thomas Larkin rose from the table. "Please join us for our evening walk."

Brannan bade his farewells, saying he had business at the wharf that evening. Before leaving, he neared Ah and said in a half-whisper, "Perhaps I will see you again in San Francisco? Our town is small; we are likely to meet someday." He gave her his calling card which she tucked into her pocket.

After Brannan's wagon disappeared, Rachel cast a warm smile to her guests. "It is our ritual, no matter the weather. Tonight, after the rains the air is mild. A light cloak should do. A bit muddy, but such a lovely constitutional. We will stay on the plank walkway around the house."

Larkin patted his stomach. "A walk will prevent dyspepsia. We must move after a hearty meal."

At times like these, Ah would ask Chen to accompany her.

But this time Henry took her side, holding a lantern. They sauntered behind the Reverend and Elizabeth. They kept pace with the Larkins who pointed out various blooming succulents and the unique veranda of their two-story house.

She glanced back. Candles were flickering in the many windows of the Larkin's house. Was that Chen on the stoop, staring after her?

The sun had already set, and darkness covered the landscape like a photographer's blanket. Ah stretched her shawl around her shoulders to block the cool air. If only she had dressed more warmly. The plank walkway rose and dipped, and she struggled to keep her balance. One misstep and she might land in the muddy loam of the street.

Henry's lantern cast an uneven light across the path. She saw him eyeing her lotus shoes. He extended his arm, and she accepted it. He tucked her arm under the crook of his elbow.

"Did you enjoy Monterey Bay this afternoon?" he asked. A glint of humor crinkled his eyes.

"The animals you called sea lions." She flashed a smile.

"I did not want to embarrass you in front of the Daileys—they might have thought it quite improper—our chance encounter on the beach."

"They might have asked a lot of questions."

"The Daileys say you are from the upper classes in Canton." Henry whispered.

"My family had much wealth going back centuries. Very traditional."

He wrinkled his forehead. "Yet Tung Chee was hardly traditional—he ran a joint stock corporation. How did your marriage get arranged?"

She shrugged. "My father told each of his children whom we were to marry, and we did not question. One day, I was betrothed. Some months later, I was married. I saw Tung Chee only once before the ceremony."

"Those are China's ancient ways. At least now you are free here in California."

She swallowed the urge to say more. Freedom was a relative thing, depending on one's gender and wealth. She took another step forward alongside him. "And you, Mr. Conrad—or Henry?"

"I usually go by Henry. May I call you Ah rather than Mrs. Toy? After the time at the beach, I already feel I know you."

"It is true that we met informally."

A crease flashed between his brows. "My dear Ah, what caused your husband's death? Is his brother Tung Chao running the company now?"

Never had anyone asked her such a dreaded question. Not Clark, not Chen, not even the officers of the Kong Chow Company. Her dragon rose up, nostrils flared, then shrank back, waiting.

She slowed her pace. Was this a trap? She did not know this man, and if he knew Tung Chao, she had no idea if Henry could be his friend. Any kind of answer would be recorded in his memory, then used against her.

She swayed, then steadied herself. They passed under an oak tree, and she reached out and set a hand on a lower branch. "I am getting tired. I want to go back."

"But we have only just begun talking. There is so much about you I would like to know." His wistful words entwined with the dry leaves surrounding them.

He had already asked enough questions. Maybe she had already said too much. "No. I must go back and rest. This has been a big night for me."

He turned back and extended his other arm in her direction. "Of course, I will take you back. If I have said anything to offend—" He inched closer.

She drew away, regarding him. "No, not at all." How easily the lie floated out of her mouth. She let him take her arm, and he guided her away from the oak onto a dry section of the road, then over a series of small humps that lay between them and the house. At last they were at the doorstep, and he released her toward Chen who took her arm.

Once she was safely across the threshold, Chen disappeared down the hallway into the kitchen, and the door clicked shut behind him.

Footsteps rang behind her and someone touched her shoulder. "Good night." A broad smile lightened Henry's features. "I would like to see you again."

"Perhaps someday." She would have to give it some thought. Especially after he had asked questions about her past. And sidestepped many revelations of his own.

"I am returning to China next week on a trading expedition, but when I come back I will find you in San Francisco."

"You will?" She pulled out her fan and snapped it open. What fueled this man's presumption? Did he consider her an easy target?

"May I know your address so I may write to you?" He leaned forward.

She stepped back. "I will be moving to a different house next year." Her fingertips outlined the open folds of her fan.

"Still in San Francisco I trust?"

"Ask Elizabeth—she will have my new address." She set the open fan against her mouth, covering it.

Though he extended his hand, she did not shake it.

Instead, she gazed up at him, then took steps toward the stairs. "Good night." Though tempted, she did not look back.

A tap sounded at her door. Whatever did Chen want now? He was already late to help her pack her things for tomorrow's journey back to the Dailey's house. He had become mates with Hortencia, now was she to lose his help to the Larkin's servant? She shuffled over and flung the door open, ready to give him a piece of her mind.

But rather than Chen, Rachel Larkin stood at the threshold, her face illuminated by the candle flickering in her hand.

"I—want to—no—I *need* to talk to you, my dear. May I come in?" Her candle's flame illuminated a porcelain doll, a hobby horse, and wooden alphabet blocks stored on a shelf.

Whatever did Rachel want? If only Ah had left this morning—then none of these meetings would never have happened. Somehow this woman's presence trapped her in a web of unwelcome threads.

She gestured to a trunk at the foot of the bed where Rachel took a seat. Ah sat in a nearby chair. Her stomach clenched. What now? This woman hardly knew her, and she was being very forward.

Rachel started the conversation without a moment's hesitation. "We know—that is, Thomas and I know—about your lookee business in San Francisco."

Hot tears sprang to Ah's eyes and she blinked. "You do?" What a rude woman this Rachel. Undoubtedly the Larkins had told Henry and maybe even the Reverend. Now what would she do?

"Thomas conducts a great deal of business in San Francisco with Sam Brannan, and when we heard your name through the Daileys, we wondered about you. Sam showed Thomas the *Alta* article about "the girl in the green silk pantaloons.""

Ah stared. "Has Henry heard about the article? The Reverend?"

"We are sure he has not since he only recently returned from China, and certainly the Daileys do not know about it."

At least Elizabeth had kept her confidence. Ah noticed her own fingers trembling. "Go on," she said, for lack of better words.

"We debated about you meeting Henry, one of our dearest friends and longtime associates. But we finally decided to go ahead when the Daileys spoke so highly of you."

"They have known me for many years, it is true. So, what made you decide to have me meet Henry? You must think me terrible for what I do."

Rachel extended a hand toward her. "I will tell you something which I rarely discuss with anyone. It has to do with my own past, one which I would rather bury." She cast a glance at the toys on the shelf.

Ah put up her palm. "No need to tell me something that pains you. I understand I may be an embarrassment—"

"No—no. That is not it at all—I want you to know something." She set the candleholder down beside her on the trunk.

"What about?" Ah rubbed her forehead. Seldom had she heard such talk of judgment as she had on this trip to Monterey. First Elizabeth's parable about Mary Magdalen and now Rachel?

"Few people know this, so I hope you will not tell anyone else." The black ribbons from her hair fluttered around her shoulders and caught the candle's light.

Ah tilted her head. A secret? She leaned in to hear more.

"When I was a young woman, I was married before to someone other than Thomas."

Ah's eyebrows rose. Now *this* was interesting.

"Back in Boston. My husband Captain Holmes was at sea for many years at a time. Without any children a sailor's wife can grow lonely, and so I was. After his being gone for three years, I received a letter to join him in Santa Barbara."

"Were you going to move there?" Ah asked.

"Perhaps, but here is the point. On the long sea voyage, I met Thomas." Rachel's eyes took on a dreamy, faraway look.

"Hmmm. He was a lively man as he is now?"

"Well—I suppose you can tell how attractive Thomas might have been in his youth—he made me laugh, he valued what I had to say, he treated me like I mattered."

A vision of Clark's face in a moment of laughter crossed Ah's mind. She had known that tender treatment and she longed for it.

Rachel lowered her voice, almost to a whisper. "In short, we fell deeply in love and me—well—I sinned with him. Not just once, but many times. Toward the end of the voyage, I was with child."

Ah absorbed the gravity of the situation. "But you were married—and on the way to meet your husband, the Captain?"

Rachel drew a heavy breath. "You cannot imagine my state of mind as I said farewell to Thomas and moved to Santa Barbara where I awaited my husband's ship. When I saw it sail into the bay and come to rest at the dock, I thought of throwing myself into the water, anything to avoid telling him the truth.

"And no matter how hard I tried to cover it with my cloak, by then, one could clearly see I was expecting a child."

Ah knew what Tung Chee would have done in her situation. "So—did your husband punish you for your infidelity?"

A silence fell. An owl hooted somewhere. Rachel's answer seemed to linger in the backchannels of her memory.

Ah sat in the dark recesses, watching Rachel's shadow on the wall. It took great courage to reveal such matters to a relative stranger. Most people covered secrets with lies the same way they whitewashed a dirty fence.

Men's voices filtered up the stairs; the men's post-dinner poker game must be breaking up, and Thomas would be wondering where Rachel was. She had little time to finish her story. But finish she must.

Ah cleared her throat, and Rachel shifted in her seat. "I waited for the ship to empty and for the captain to arrive on land. I do not know how long I stared at the ship, waiting. I was nauseated, full of fear." Rachel's eyes reflected the candle's flame.

"You must have been sick." Ah's stomach roiled at the thought of it.

"But then—the first mate came up to me. Do you know what he said?"

"No—" Ah swam in the watery brilliance of Rachel's eyes.

"My husband had died of cholera—on board ship—and had been buried at sea." She sat back, apparently filled with wonder at the situation.

"And so, you were able to be with Thomas—and your baby?" A knot formed in Ah's throat.

"Unfortunately, our baby died. You asked about punishment? That was God's vengeance for what I did." She closed her eyes.

Ah's words broke through the knot. "I lost my husband at sea. Cholera took him as well." She had trouble mouthing the truth. "And I lost three babies, too. Girls."

The owl hooted another time.

Rachel leaned toward Ah. "And so, I cannot judge you, and if we meet again, I will never mention it. You may be assured that Thomas and

179

I will not stand in the way of your possible union with Henry. You deserve happiness in this short and troubled life."

A man's voice called from outside the door. "Rachel, where are you? Time for bed."

"Just a moment, Thomas," she called. After turning back to Ah, she said, "I must go. We women must make choices that separate us from each other, but all of us deserve joy."

She took Ah's hand and pressed it. "Including you."

Ah noticed a soft swish of skirts and a drift of rose perfume before the door closed, leaving her in the sole company of the half-burned candle flickering on the trunk.

The following day was spent returning to the Daileys' house in Monterey where Ah spent her last evening. The next morning, someone tapped her shoulder, and Ah turned on her pillow. A hand pulled a strand of hair away from her face, and the morning light penetrated her eyelids, jarring her peaceful dream of floating down the Xi River, the mists rising at daybreak.

"Si tau po! Time to rise! The wagon will be here in two hours, and you have not had your morning bowl of rice." Chen shifted from one foot to another.

"All right." She let him pull aside the covers, and he took her arm, helping her sit up and steering her feet into her soft slippers. He slid out the porcelain chamber pot from under the bed and then set the privacy screen in front of her.

"Do you need my help to dress today?" He called from behind the screen.

"No, I will do it myself. I think it will be faster." She crouched and let her waters spray into the pot.

"I will be outside. Please call when you have finished."

"Yes, Chen." She wiped herself with the rag next to the bowl and glanced around the room. Light filtered through the semi-closed drapery. The dictionary, paper, and pencil continued to sit on the desk. Her undergarments and the white and gold-flowered qipao rested on the bed where Chen had set them out the previous night.

After running her fingers along the butterfly embroidery of her undergarments, she fastened the dudou around her breasts and belly, then eased on her qipao. She patted the musk in the small pocket of her dudou. The herbal scent was growing faint—time for Chen to revisit the herbal shop when they returned to Little Canton.

A few minutes later, Chen padded in, left her food on the side table, and removed the chamber pot.

She regarded her bowl of rice. The ever-thoughtful Chen had placed chicken strips across it, yet she could smell the sharp aroma of chili peppers from Hortencia's kitchen. A vision of Hortencia's giving her the bath salts crossed her mind. Only in America would she find dear Hortencia fixing Chinese food. Putting aside thoughts of eating, she stepped to the armoire. After she tugged down her valise, she called out. "Chen, please bring my clothes from the wardrobe. I am ready to pack."

"What coat will you wear today?"

"It is cold, so please lay out the long wool cloak. I will also need the scarf that Elizabeth gave me."

"The one with the blue diamond pattern?"

"Yes."

Someone tapped on the door, and Elizabeth Dailey crossed the room. Her purple hat feathers waved with each step. "I wanted to say a proper goodbye before you left for San Francisco. Reverend and I are headed to town in a separate wagon to meet our church elders. We are planning the Nativity services for Christmastide."

Ah relaxed into Elizabeth's warm embrace. "I must return to my business. When I am away, the money does not flow the way it should. And I have engaged workmen at my new house on Pike Street."

Elizabeth pulled away and gave her a searching look. "I am sure you must have quite a following for your—em—business. I will be sure to visit your new house when next I am in San Francisco." She gave Ah an uneasy smile and her hat feathers trembled.

Ah resumed tucking the edges of her garments into her valise. Someday she would tell Elizabeth the truth about her new occupation, but now was not the time.

"I have always admired the clothing you wear." Elizabeth fondled the ivory silk scarf that lay in the bottom of the valise, then she lifted a jade necklace from its silk envelope.

After holding it up against the light, she slid it back into place, tucking it into a corner of the suitcase. She turned to Ah. "You know, we think highly of Henry. He has told me he would like to see you again when he returns from his next voyage."

Ah's heart thudded. "I see." She pulled a red embroidered dudou from under a pile of clothes and edged it into the valise.

"The Reverend has told me that Henry is quite taken with you, and he intends to ask for your hand in marriage. He says you have captivated him." Elizabeth fingered the collar of a qipao that lay in the valise.

"But he knows of my previous marriage to Tung Chee and the doings of his brother Tung Chao. What of his past dealings with them? I have a hard time believing what he says is true." She folded her arms across her stomach.

Elizabeth shot her a penetrating look. "Henry is a good, god-fearing man. He knows that some men are inherently cruel. He also knows the ways of Tung Chee. Because he has lived in Canton, he understands your customs as few American men do."

"I-I do not know what to say." Something clicked in her mind.

"You do not have to say anything, my dear. He will not return for six months or more. You have time to continue your business in San Francisco. Of course, you will no longer have to work if you marry him."

"Hmmm." Ah worked to control her words. After Clark, would she be able to give herself to any man?

Elizabeth took her hand. "Think carefully about his importance in your future. He is very wealthy, and he wishes to establish a large ranch in San Jose to harvest cherries."

"A ranch?" Looking back, she remembered his kind eyes and their laughter on the beach.

Elizabeth squeezed her fingers. "The land there is very fruitful, and he says he can make much money. He will continue his importing business, but he would prefer to settle down now and raise a family."

A vision of a large Victorian house with a surrounding porch and orchard, then soft hills with running children—little girls and boys—flew in front of her and vanished.

Elizabeth pressed her hand. "You are quiet. Is he to your liking?"

"Well—I suppose—yes." After all, she had to face the fact that she was alone.

"Good. Then I shall let him know of your interest. The Reverend and I are concerned for your welfare. We want you to do well, and a match with Henry would assure you a stable future." She raised her eyebrows. "He is a cut above most men you will encounter in San Francisco."

"Thank you. I am most grateful for your consideration. You give me much to think about."

Upon leaving, Elizabeth wrapped her arms around Ah. Once again, Ah relaxed into the friendly arms. She had never known the peaceful feeling of snuggling against the warmth of a mother's chest, a mother's cheek against her own.

But then, after the horses gained the road and the wheels of the wagon spun like whirlwinds, she remembered.

Elizabeth had said, "He understands your customs as few men do."

She leaned back in her coach seat, her gaze following the grassy contours of the brown hills. He understands? If only that were true.

Part Three

The valley darkens in the moonlight
where crickets chirp
My fingers weave endless webs
Silver strands that ebb and flow

On this side of the ocean
Hearts above the mountains
We together
See no barrier
We share our thoughts and feelings

IN THE MANNER OF LI PO

One

§ A DOWNCAST GAZE §

San Francisco
January 1850

The afternoon scene at the wharf resembled a set of mah-jongg tiles thrown across a table. Ah stumbled on the plank street leading to the Washington Street pier, and Chen lifted her over a hump in the path. A clipper had arrived, and imports were being loaded onto drays, wagons, or steamboats. Bamboo and China silk were stamped in Chinese lettering on the boxes in today's shipment. According to the purser, one of those boxes was meant for her new parlor house the next day.

Among the jumble of wagons and crates, Ah stepped in silent worry. Rumors, some good, some bad, abounded in Little Canton. One concerned Lee Shau Kee, the living ghost who would not stay buried. Mr. Tom, the grocer, mentioned hearing Lee Shau Kee had returned to California, had slipped past the customs agents, and was in the Placer diggins.

Story said he was managing some holdings for Tung Chao. Her brother-in-law was tenacious: he had Lee Shau Kee try to kidnap her once; and he would not give up easily—if ever—in his quest to bring her back to China. In turn, Lee Shau Kee pledged unbounding loyalty to Tung Chao, and ultimately, to himself. That she knew as surely as the blood flowing in her veins.

She meandered by crates of furniture from England, along with barrels of hemp and sugar from Manila. Every day she witnessed a mesmerizing number of goods and services that poured into town from all over the world. Would she be able to keep up in a city that changed every day? A mixture of tent structures and wooden houses peppered the once-bare hilltops.

Chen shivered and walked briskly at her side, and she fell into musing. All this progress gave her reason to grow her current business into a parlor house, an upscale brothel. If she did not expand her business, new madams arriving daily from China and elsewhere would grind her Lookee Shop into the dust.

Money provided the only barrier between her and Lee Shau Kee. He could reach her quickly in San Francisco by taking a riverboat from Sacramento to the Bay City. The trip took a mere two days. She shuddered.

Only money would help her build her parlor house, buy security, and convince Officer Wong that Lee Shau Kee was no friend of the Kong Chow Company.

She pulled her embroidered wool cloak tightly about her shoulders. The wind blew eastward, black clouds shrouded the bay, and boats sought shelter at the many recently completed piers. No one wanted to be out in weather like this; even fishermen who ordinarily braved winter weather pulled in their nets and headed for home.

How long before the rain started to pour? Chen summoned a wagon and they made their way to Jackson Street via DuPont. Crowds of black-jacketed Chinese men thronged the gambling dens and incense shops, places to shelter from the rain. If only she could bid on the indentured servant girls and get home with Chen before the storm worsened.

The buggy driver slowed his horses, then pulled to a stop at an alleyway off Jackson Street named St. Louis Place.

Ah dropped a coin in his outstretched hand.

He cast her a wary look. "Sure, you want to go into that alley, miss? It has a mean reputation, that one." He looked down the narrow passageway, then back at her and Chen.

She said, "Yes, I am sure—some business down there."

He shook his head. "Suit yourself, Miss. Many tell of bad doin's that way. Knife fights, murders and such. Mind yerself."

Wong's letter had told her to knock at the alley's third door on the right. He called the place a "barracoon." Earlier Chen explained to her it was the barracks housing the girls to be sold into prostitution, though under the pretense of indentured servitude.

After the driver's comment, doubts crowded her thoughts. Was her idea of trading money for girls at this auction such a wise one after all? The Taiping Rebellion and ensuing famine in Guangzhou had given rise to lots of families sending young women to San Francisco. What condition would these girls be in? Would they have all their teeth?

Officer Wong's letter stated the girls went for good prices at his auction. Was expanding her Lookee Shop into a parlor house brothel a good idea? What risk was she taking? Girls could be filled with headlice and gonorrhea. Should she bring strangers like these into the happy home she shared with Chen?

Chen guided her down the filth-laden alley. She flicked open her fan and held it against her mouth, stifling the smells of urine and excrement. A Cantonese man lay snoring against a building; he was covered with a tattered blanket. Pigeons pecked at scraps of paper on the ground. Cantonese voices rose and fell, resonating from second story windows.

She pointed to the third door on the right. "This is it." A temporary

Cantonese sign marked "Auction Today." Chen guided her through the half-open door.

They made their way down a narrow hallway which opened into a large noisy room where lanterns glimmered from niches in the walls. Dampness seeped into the thinly-walled structure. Sawdust was scattered on the floor. Male onlookers crowded in, some Cantonese, some white, their coats bundled tightly around them. She studied their seemingly hungry faces: they made stiff competition.

Though her new brothel would pay taxes to the Kong Chow Company and serve their business interests, the white men at this auction had far more money and power. Many allied with one another and pooled their resources to fund more cribs and parlor houses than she alone could manage.

Officer Wong came into view. He perched stiffly on a high chair, the only furniture in the room. A straggly line of Cantonese girls shivered alongside him. Wong rubbed his temples, first on one side, then the other. His black silk cloak flowed down to the floor.

White men talked among themselves: Ah guessed some were there to place their bids; others to satisfy their curiosity about these exotic creatures.

A tall Cantonese guard in a blue cap wielded a long bamboo cane which he pounded on the floor to keep order. The girls trembled; their thin frames and gray garments gave them the look of ghosts. Ah recognized their hungry compliance—the Cantonese handlers would keep them slightly famished to make sure they did as they were told.

Officer Wong's multiple chins waggled. "You are late, Mrs. Toy. Not a good sign. Do you not see all the other bidders ready here?"

Ah cast off his remark, and Chen stepped forward with her as they faced the line of girls.

The guard presented the first young woman. Narrow-hipped and frail, she looked maybe around thirteen.

Ah shook her head. "Too young and too weak. I would not have her—she would not last among these men."

A white man murmured behind her, "The younger the better. Can't wait to bid on her."

The young girl took a half-stride forward out of line, her teeth chattering. "But I c-can count fast on the abacus. I know my f-figures. Before my uncle died, he trained me on the accounts in his restaurant."

Ah drew back. A girl who spoke out meant trouble, but maybe it was a sign this one was brave. In Guangdong, such bold action could result in a whipping. A repeated loud-mouth would earn a drowning. She pulled her fan from her sleeve and flicked it in a scooping motion. "Come closer so I can see you."

Whispers flowed behind her in the crowd of men. As the girl moved forward, her stringy black hair swung about her waist. Her hair was salvageable—Chen could wash and oil it to a sheen. What else could the girl offer?

Ah made a stirring motion with her fan. "Turn."

The girl swiveled. She had small flat feet. Unbound. She could run and walk freely.

"All the way round." Her own voice cut the air.

The girl flinched, finished her turn, and stood tall.

A small murmur rippled through the crowd of men.

After a moment, the girl crossed her arms over her chest while the hem of her gray shift billowed.

She glanced at Officer Wong. "A nice figure. Seems young, yet if she speaks the truth, I can always have her keep my accounts." She drew near, facing the girl. "Tell me your story."

"My uncle died, and my aunt threw me out onto the street in Guangzhou. I have four brothers and two sisters. Crops went bad, and no food came to market. Too many mouths to feed and no means to support me.

That is why I came to America. To work." The youngster grimaced. "I got sick on the sea voyage—"

Officer Wong broke in. "Enough, girl, now close your mouth." He flicked his hand.

"A moment please," Ah said. "What is your name?"

"Lee Lai San." Though her voice was low, her name resonated like a series of musical notes.

Ah leaned back on her platform shoes. "Write down her name."

Chen bent down and whispered. "I think this is an unwise choice. The customers will devour such a little morsel. Besides, she talks back."

She peered into his anxious eyes, then over at the slim girl who hung her head. He had a point.

Yet she knew that a parlor house girl did have to be able to stand up for herself. Besides, Ah could see herself in this child. Her dull eyes, her uncombed hair, her downcast gaze—all that had been hers, as recently as her own voyage to San Francisco. This girl named San had suffered, but now she appeared bright and willing. Ah set her lips. She must take this girl into her new parlor house.

Ah repeated. "Write down her name. I could use a good accountant."

Chen heaved a sigh. "Very well, si tau po." He penciled the girl's name in the little red-bound book alongside Ah's important notes.

San stepped back, melting into the line of girls.

"Let me see the next one."

The guard prodded another girl forward. Tall and lanky, this girl had a clear complexion and high cheekbones, yet several gaps showed between her teeth. She was missing three fingernails on each hand. Had she been tortured or abused?

Chen stepped behind the girl and whispered to the guard. What were they saying?

Ah spun around toward Officer Wong, "You think me stupid? Do you think such a young girl would appeal to the gentlemen in our new parlor house? What ever happened to her?"

Chen took his place again at her side.

The girl thrust her hands into the deep pockets of her long blue jacket. Was she trying to hide her nails?

After she absorbed the girl's angry glare, Ah shot a sideways glance toward Chen. "What do you think?"

A frown darkened his face. "The guard says she has a bad reputation. Her former master punished her by taking out her fingernails and toenails. Her teeth were knocked out in a catfight. One of many, I suspect. One can see she has been in many brothels before this."

"Oh, I see." Ah looked back at the defiant girl. All she needed was more trouble. Though the girl had reason to be angry, she could not take all the girls nor could she save them all from their unspeakable past.

She turned to Officer Wong. "Not this one. Show me another."

He waved his palm. On his cue, another girl stepped forward, her eyes rounder, her skin lighter, her nose longer than most servants in the auction. Her light brown hair was done up in a tight bun. Ah moved in closer. This girl had round, hazel eyes. What about her lineage? Maybe her blood was mixed with British. Many sailors from the opium trade in Guangzhou had left their babies behind. She was most likely one of them.

"Show me your hair." Ah aimed the tip of her fan toward the teenager.

The youngster loosened her bun with trembling fingers, and a length of hair, lighter brown than most Cantonese women, drifted over her shoulders. What a beauty. A sprinkling of freckles dusted her nose. Ah pictured her in a Manchurian red dress, catching the eye of the San Francisco merchants, bankers and politicians. Hmm. Such a maiden would bring in much gold.

She cast a look at Chen. "Your opinion?"

He edged closer to her in front of the line. "She may be excellent. I have heard no bad gossip about her from the guard."

"Girl, tell me your name" Ah tilted her head.

"Wong Sau Man. People call me Man-Man." The girl caught up her long drifts of hair, then bound the strands in a knot high atop her head. A broken ray of sun through a window caressed her high cheekbones.

"Write down her name." Ah said. This one she would take.

"Yes, si tau po." Chen's head bent over the notebook, and his pencil scratched on the page.

It would be hard to match the last girl's beauty, but Ah would try. While studying the line of maidens again, her eyes were drawn to something. The same light ray reflected off the ivory cheek of another girl second to the left at the end of the row. "Step out please," she said.

The youngster advanced out of the line. A lone tear escaped from her eye and meandered down her hollow cheekbones. She was hungry. Good sign. She would be appreciative.

Ah said, "Turn around." As she did so, Ah ran her hands over the adolescent's hips and checked the width of her waist. "Very well, now lift your skirt so I may view your legs."

The girl reddened but complied, raising her gray hem to a point below the knee.

Her legs were well formed, but thin from starvation. Yet she had muscular calves, a sign of hard work. No ankle marks, so probably she had not been kept in shackles. A promising sign.

Ah stepped closer. "Now show me your wrists and hands."

The girl extended her arms; her hands trembled.

Ah peered closely. Unmarked wrists. Long fingers, medium sized wrist bones. Good. With some food in her belly, she would be able to work the long hours of a parlor house girl. Maybe after a meal, this one would not be as hateful as the girl with the missing teeth.

Ah released the girl's hands and they fell to her sides. "Name?"

"Ma Ka Yee." Her voice trailed off into a whisper.

"Your name means happiness and elegance. Do you have any talents? Sewing? Painting?"

Yee brightened. "I can sing and play the *guqin*."

Chen sucked in a breath and leaned into Ah's ear. "She plays the seven-string instrument revealed for its graceful notes."

Ah looked at Chen. "That would be excellent entertainment in our refined parlor house." She swiveled toward Yee. "Let me hear a few notes of a song." She waited expectantly.

Yee broke into song, a sweet melody that Ah recognized from her childhood days in Guangzhou, the Pearl River flowing beside the warehouse, meandering away into the distant sky.

Ah held up her hand. "That is enough. I hear your prowess."

Yee's song faded into the crowd, and she shivered where she stood.

Ah said, "You can sing well, Ma Ka Yee. May your song and playing of the guqin bring sunshine to our house and gold to our coffers." She tapped Chen's shoulder. "Write her name down."

"Of course,." He scratched the girl's name into the notebook.

After examining other girls and finding them unsuitable, Ah made offers for the previous girls, $470 for San, $560 for Yee, and $575 for Man-Man. As was customary, all bids were made in secret, and Officer Wong chose the highest bidder.

After a few moments, Wong disappeared into a side office and closed the door behind him. The men's voices around her rose, and their talk turned to other matters such as whether to buy and sell futures in joint stock companies.

Meanwhile, Ah kept her eye on the shivering girls, framed against a tableau of leering men and cigar smoke. She remembered Tung Chee had locked her out one night during a cold spell, a punishment for talking back to him. That same cold now seeped into the marrow of her bones; after some time, she was so numb she could hardly feel her skin.

Two

❦ OF LEE SHAU KEE ❦

*A*fter a few moments, Chen closed the small red silk note-book. He pressed it into Ah's open hand. This process was taking too long. Daily business affairs were conducted in rapid fashion throughout the young city. No one had time to wait. Wasted time meant lost opportunity.

Someone gave a sharp intake of breath. What happened?

Chen scanned the edge of the crowd. His hand was tented over his forehead.

"What is it, Chen?"

"I am sure I saw Lee Shau Kee at the back of the crowd during the auction. At first, I thought my mind was tricking me, but then—" His head jerked around.

Her heart quickened. "What?"

"Now I am sure it was him. There." He pointed to the back of the crowd. "I could not miss that face." He sucked in a breath. "Such an ugly man."

She whirled in the direction of Chen's outstretched finger. "Where is he? I must call Mr. Clark."

Chen looked back again. "I do not see Lee now. Maybe he is inside this barracoon. But I think this is not a good time to report him. Besides, what if I am mistaken, and it is not him? You must finish making offers for the auction girls. Then we must return to the new parlor house."

"But—" A memory sliced across her vision. Lee Shau Kee's bag had enveloped her in the midst of the chattering tea shop. Chen was right. This was not a good time. It was a crucial time. If Lee Shau Kee were here and not bent on kidnapping her, what was his intention?

Her mind reeled with more questions. Painter said Lee had been sent back to China. Judge Almond and Wong had said he might be in Placerville, up in the mines. So, what would he be doing here at this auction? If he no longer worked for Tung Chao, then why be so friendly with Officer Wong? If he had gone back to China, how had he re-entered through the Customs House?

Why had Judge Almond not enforced an order barring Lee's reentry? A cold fire gripped her. Lee Shau Kee had returned: the mere mention of his name took her breath away.

The floor gave a sudden tilt beneath her feet.

Why should she trust what Officer Wong or anyone else said to her?

She turned back to the sad-faced girls who shivered in misery. What fate awaited them? Other men in top hats and thick coats stood behind her, waiting for results of their bids; other men would not have the delicacy she would use with these girls. The prettiest would end up in parlor houses. The less attractive would be used for menial jobs, cooking or cleaning. Those who did not learn fast would end their days in those filthy cribs.

After a moment, the office door squeaked open, and Officer Wong's bulk hovered at the threshold. "Mrs. Toy, I need to hear your offer again."

"Again?" Ah approached him, and Chen's hand steadied her elbow.

She thumbed open the red book and read him her offer for each girl.

Wong's secretary made notes. Then he and Wong disappeared again behind the closed door.

She heard murmurs on the other side of the door. Her fidgety hands would not settle; her dragon huddled in a silent ball. If Lee Shau Kee had returned from either China or the gold fields, was he here watching her?

She quick-scanned the onlookers behind her, but she saw only a sea of unfamiliar faces. If he was inside the office, was he convincing Wong not to take her bid? What would be the point of that? A snake would be eating its own tail. Her girls would make much money for her and generate taxes for the Kong Chow Company.

She stood tapping her fan on her thigh. All she could think of was that day, the bag over her head, that day she could hardly breathe. Maybe Lee Shau Kee had slithered his way into the graces of Officer Wong. Then Lee Shau Kee would coil up and strike when his prey was unprepared. Tung Chao had the means and scruples to get what he wanted through Lee Shau Kee—at any cost.

Her fan collapsed beneath her fingers.

Officer Wong approached, his body reeking of stale rice and opium smoke.

She readied for the news.

But rather than meet her on business-like terms, he yawned. Plainly this was a boring matter, too lowly for him. "Mrs. Toy," he said, "you may have Lee Lai San and Ma Ka Yee. But not Wong Sau Man. Someone else outbid you for her."

Chen's shoulder brushed hers, signaling his standing guard.

After digesting the news for a moment, Ah flicked open her fan, waving Chen away. This she would do herself.

She planted herself before Officer Wong, close enough to touch him. His small stature was surprising. Except for his visit to her shanty, she had always seen him up on his dais, looking over her.

Her voice rang out. "Who outbid me for the Man-Man girl with hazel eyes? You guaranteed me the first bid." She fluttered her fan back and forth between them.

His gaze followed the fan's arc, seeming mesmerized. He cleared his throat loudly.

She planted her feet. "I will not go away until you tell me who offered more than I did."

He leaned forward until she could see the hair in his nostrils.

She fluttered her fan, clearing away the foul odor coming from his mouth.

He said, "I have no secrets. Lee Shau Kee outbid you."

No secrets? Indeed. She snapped her fan shut. A cry burst out of her throat. "No! You will not sell such a fine work of art to that slug!"

"Yes, I would. Anyone can make a higher bid. And he outbid you."

Her Cantonese burst out like gunshots. "Haven't I been faithful, paying my taxes with all the gold shavings I can spare from my lookee business? As the first Cantonese woman in San Francisco, you know my devotion to the Kong Chow Company and its purposes. I will be expanding my business into a large parlor house. More girls will bring in more money, so more taxes for you."

Wong settled back onto his wide hips, his many chins nestling onto his chest. "The Kong Chow Company looks out for you. That you cannot deny." His eyelids lowered, hooded like a hawk's.

She shook her head. What a scoundrel. Wong was as bad as all the rest. "It is true that I have benefited from your safeguards." She stepped forward. "You have also enjoyed the revenue from my taxes. And remember all of my special offerings at festivals and banquets."

Wong's eyes narrowed, and he stood his ground. "I would like to help you, but Lee Shau Kee would desire the treasure for himself."

"Not true. Man-Man is not for his own use. Lee Shau Kee does his business with lowly dogs and other animals."

Wong lowered his eyelids. "I think—"

"No," she said.

Wong raised his eyebrows.

She knew he was not used to such contradiction from a woman, but she had to go on. "I know his intentions. Look at the girl. Her hazel eyes mean she is mixed with British. Such a fine specimen would go well in Tung Chao's stable of women back in Guangdong. If Lee Shau Kee takes her back, she will be doomed."

"One moment." Wong's bulk vanished into the office.

She cast a look down the line of remaining girls, their skin ashen, their eyes downcast. They must wish they were dead. Ah clung to Chen. Around her the cigar smoke in the room loomed dark as evening, and the rain pattered on the roof above their heads. The girls quivered under the guard's stern glare, their group miserable and cold as the grave.

She glared at the guard. "Your girls are unwell."

"Hmph." The guard held up his cane, plainly listening to the rising din of the crowd, now growing impatient.

Ah watched, considering. Maybe the guard would protect the precious cargo, for each girl would bring a pretty price in San Francisco.

She gave a quick exhale. So few women and so many men. Muscles in her neck tightened. "Chen, what is taking so long? What should I do?"

"Si tau po. You must be patient. Wait to see what you have gained, then measure that against what you have lost." His queue fell forward across his right shoulder.

"Sage advice." She nodded. Would this waiting never end? After a while, the office door creaked open, and Officer Wong waved her inside.

Within the dark confines of the office, the servant girls and the guard were stuck together like roaches on a ball of glue. The air smelled of sweat, straw, and grease. The floorboards creaked with each step that Ah took along with Chen. She glanced around the small room: no sign of Lee Shau Kee. Where else could he be?

Wong sat on a rawhide chair and sipped from a glass of plum wine. His chins wobbled as he spoke, his long stringy beard catching the light. "I have given your words much thought, Mrs. Toy. Here is my decision. Take San and Yee. I must find Lee Shau Kee and negotiate the matter of the other baggage."

Baggage. Her chest squeezed. Lee's invisible strings were meant to dangle her like a puppet. To him she was none other than *baggage* like the hazel-eyed girl named Man-Man. How easily women were captured, then bought, sold, and thrown into the bay like so much fish offal.

She said, "Wong, you are trading with dark forces that will ruin you and our city. Beware that Lee wants nothing more than to do Tung Chao's bidding. Unless you stand up to him, he will consider you weak and powerless. He will laugh behind his hand at you."

Wong gave her an implacable stare.

After taking a deep breath, she continued. "If Lee Shau Kee wins this girl, he will know he can go even further with *you* next time. And who knows? Lee Shau Kee might end up in your high chair, telling *you* what to do." She drew back—her thoughts tumbled out, becoming words that might harm her. *Oh no.* She never should have said that. There went her big mouth.

Wong's eyes narrowed, then he squinted. "You dare to speak to me the way you would treat a servant? And yet you want me to do favors for you?" He shifted his bulk. "Tread lightly, Ah Toy. You are just a woman, a mere fleabite to be scratched. You have no position here but for me. Go home. I will summon you when I have news. Now, away with your cargo."

The guard eased forward with San and Yee.

"Come with us now," Ah said.

The girls nodded. Chen put his hand on their shoulders and steered them out of the office, through the crowd of men and into the alleyway.

The girls' ribcages pressed against their flimsy garments; their thin arms were no more substantial than twigs floating in the flotsam against the dock.

Three

❧ HERS TO PROTECT ❧

After the ride home, safely inside the shanty, San and Yee huddled together on chairs facing the small candle's flame in the center of the table. They sipped from their soup bowls, the light catching tears drizzling on their cheeks. Ah sat with them in silence. No need for conversation; what was needed now was peace.

After the meal, Chen put them down on the mattresses he had prepared for them. Ah watched his face soften when covering them with blankets, tucking them in like small children.

He turned to Ah, his eyes tender. "You have saved their lives, si tau po."

She gazed up at him, then down at the girls. "That may be true, but Lee Shau Kee is back in San Francisco. Tung Chao's ghost haunts me like an unburied ancestor."

Chen nodded. "I will sleep now." He shuffled off to his mat for the night.

The girls fell into deep slumbers, their breathing soft and regular. Ah lifted up the lantern, letting the light play over their delicate features and frail limbs. San had a round face with a tiny upturned nose. Yee's face was long, her cheekbones hollowed, the results of long famine. With luck from Goddess Mazu and good food from Chen's kitchen, they would recover from their journey. She sighed. They would need all their strength in this world of men called San Francisco.

The next morning's knock at the shanty door roused Ah from a deep sleep. She heard Chen padding to the door, two voices murmuring, and the door shutting abruptly.

She stood up from her mat, holding her arms out for balance. She reached for her long robe, twisted the strings around her waist, and padded to the table where she sat, blinking sleep out of her eyes.

Chen stood in the mid-space between her and the doorway, a paper clutched in his hand.

"What does it say?" She focused her bleary eyes on him.

He broke the seal and unfolded the paper. "Wong summons you to the office of the Kong Chow Company for a meeting. He does not say anything about his decision."

"Of course not, he would be keeping it to himself. If that note were stolen from the messenger on the road, someone could be in danger."

She cast her eyes over the girls on the adjacent mats, their arms flung wide in sleep. A wave of satisfaction washed over her. They were now in her employ, and her mood brightened. She had lost her babies, but these girls would be hers to protect. That also extended to the girl named Man-Man.

If only Wong could see how much she wanted to shield Man-Man from Tung Chao's grasp. But he was a man—how could he know a woman's fear? She glanced at Chen; his eyes wide with interest. What the world needed was a thousand men like Chen, marching with an army of kind soldiers.

An hour later, she sat before Wong in his office at the Kong Chow Company, Chen in the chair by her side. Through the window, she watched a series of white and gray puffy clouds scuttling over the bay. Another rain shower was soon to arrive.

"And what offer?" Her stomach clenched.

Wong folded his hands over his stomach. "Lee Shau Kee is prepared to make a deal."

"Since the girl Man-Man is meant for Tung Chao, he will exchange the girl."

"For whom? I have paid for San and Yee."

A grin played across Wong's face. "Not for them. For *you*."

"For *me*?" Though she said the words, she scarcely absorbed their meaning.

"Then you may go back to Guangzhou in Man-Man's place."

So she had been correct about Lee Shau Kee's motives. "You cannot be serious." She laughed bitterly, then reached over and clutched Chen's hand.

"That is what he said." Wong arched his eyebrows. "Lee Shau Kee would no longer bother the Kong Chow Company."

She glanced aside at Chen. Was that a flash of terror in his expression? She faced Officer Wong, her words hardening. "I thought you were my friend. Now I cannot be sure. How could you not laugh this offer away, push Lee Shau Kee out the door?"

He shook his head. "I tried to negotiate, but Lee Shau Kee stands firm. Tung Chao is bent on this deal."

She shook her head, and her voice carried an acrimonious tone. "I would not trade my life for a trifle—that you must know. I would never agree to such a deal."

"Unfortunate." Wong licked grease from his long thumbnail.

She simmered. "However, I would make a counteroffer for Man-Man. On one condition."

"That is?" He ran his fingers back and forth across his mouth.

"It must be final on both sides." She held her breath.

He tilted his head, then gave her a thin-lipped smile. "Very well. Write down your bid and give it to me."

She gave a sigh and extended her hand. "Chen, paper and pencil."

He ripped a piece of paper from the red silk notebook and passed it to her, along with the pencil.

She wrote in Cantonese—*gold nugget worth 700 dollars.* She passed the paper to Officer Wong.

He glanced at the paper and enfolded it in his palm. His eyes took on a faraway look; his fingers moved back and forth across the surface of the note. His fingernails left small brown tracks on the paper.

Ah shrank back. Those tracks must be the remnants of stale pork drippings.

He said, "I must get a counteroffer from Lee Shau Kee and compare the two. You will be contacted." He rose and turned, his silk robe unfurling.

She let Chen guide her steps out the door, and they stayed together under the eaves of the building.

The rain pelted the street, mixing horse dung with mud. Men dashed by, aiming for the nearest doorway.

She leaned on Chen, lost in thought. After the shower passed, Ah would have Chen seek a wagon back to the shanty. She would do all she could to help this girl named Man-Man. What a ridiculous offer Lee Shau Kee had made, but now she knew two truths: Tung Chao's intentions teemed with vengeance, and he would never give up.

After a while, the rainstorm eased its hold on the city, the former heavy drops now lightly speckling the puddles in the street. Ah and Chen would not have long to wait before they could go. She thought of the word "home." In Webster's dictionary the word home had been defined as a dwelling place, but she remembered pausing as she read the second meaning: "HOME is the sacred refuge of our life."

Home was their new parlor house, the home she had bought and

GINI GROSSENBACHER

paid for with her own money. Home was their sacred refuge in America. She lifted her face to the sky, watching the raindrops fall lightly, resembling tiny diamonds, their facets catching light while they descended.

Tung Chao would never understand. She was no longer subservient, to be used, then tossed into the charnel house. She could outflank him, for her money was as good as his. No longer his wife-slave, she could never again be a servant, an underling. Yet she chewed her lip. Whether he was here in the city or not, at any time Lee Shau Kee could sail toward her from the east, floating in from Guangdong on the morning tide.

Lee Shau Kee was capable of anything—lying, cheating, kidnapping. Nothing was outside his realm. She knew the dustbins and bogs where he grew up in Guangzhou. His path to survival had included bared teeth and sharpened knives. Human life was to be used as a bargaining chip, nothing more.

Footsteps pounded inside the building behind them. Her pulse quickened, and she exchanged glances with Chen. A door hinge squeaked, and Wong's gold brocade jacket filled her view.

Wong shuffled back a step. "Still here? I thought you would be gone by now. I was hoping to find my messenger outside, but I see he would have taken shelter in the rain."

Chen said, "We were waiting for the rain to ease up."

Wong sniffed. "Well, you have saved me some trouble finding a messenger. You have outbid Lee Shau Kee—the girl is yours."

A momentary flash occurred. How had Wong gotten the counteroffer so fast? Lee Shau Kee must have been near Wong's office—maybe somewhere inside the barracoon?

She gritted her teeth, then spat out the words "Thank you."

Wong handed her a rolled paper similar to those he had given her for San and Yee. "My secretary has drafted a Bill of Sale for Man-Man, along with a sample contract. Please take it, have her sign the contract, and bring your $700 in gold nuggets back to me."

She took the paper and gripped it between her thumb and forefinger. "By the way, was Lee Shau Kee with you while we were in the office?"

Someone tugged at her sleeve. A shadow crossed Chen's face. "Si tau po, you are getting wet in the sprinkles."

She gently pushed his hand away. "No, Chen, I must know this."

Wong's voice hardened. "What does it matter, Ah Toy? You have gotten your way. Leave it at that or you may jeopardize my decision. Now let me go and bring Man-Man out to you."

"Very well." She looked up at the sky, the rain sprinkling down like the teardrops of heaven. She bowed her head and gave thanks to the Goddess Mazu, a momentary peace washing over her.

Four

❧ A STRANGE FILAMENT ☙

*T*he next morning the stepladder teetered under Chen's weight, and Ah struggled to keep it steady. She sucked in her breath. *Please do not let him fall.* From the top step, Chen drove a nail into the wooden planking above the threshold of the new Pike Street parlor house. Though Clark had first pointed it out, she had chosen the two-story wooden building for its sturdy design: a second story balcony extended out onto the street, and the tall windows let in plenty of light. It had cost her a pretty penny, but the banker had called it an "investment." After seeing her bag of gold coins, he had told her in no uncertain terms, "You can afford this, Mrs. Toy."

Cantonese men in black jackets sauntered around the ladder that jutted out in the way, The road was muddy from the recent rains. Some passing men carried bags from the marketplace; others gestured to a companion as they walked. Some loitering men lingered on street corners, smoking. One picked his teeth with a sliver of wood while he leaned against the wooden building across the street. The chatter of Cantonese voices drifted up to her like those at Guangzhou's humming wharf.

Chen's voice faltered. "Pass up the *bagua*—I get dizzy at the top of ladders." He looked down, his legs trembling.

A light mist blurred her vision, and Ah lifted her sleeve and wiped her eyes. "Wait! Let me see if the nail is centered."

"Tell me quickly before I lose my balance." His voice trembled.

She tilted her head. "Yes, that is good."

"Now! Pass me the bagua." He reached down; his palm open.

Ah Toy plunged her hand down into the silk satchel across her shoulder and pulled out the shiny disk; its surface reflected a burst of sunlight penetrating the mist. "Here—there is a hook on the back which will catch the nail if you hang it correctly. I want it to look the same way it did at my father's house."

Chen set the bagua on the nail, then straightened it. He adjusted the mirror set into an octagonal frame and rested it above the crossbeams of the threshold. The bagua gleamed in its new setting.

Ah peered up, examining the hexagram, its parallel lines of the *I Ching* etched around the central mirror. She pointed to the lines, reciting, "Heaven, Earth, Thunder, Water, Mountain, Wind, Flame, and Lake. These are the fundamentals of reality." She brushed back the strands of hair lingering around her face. "Good—*feng shui* defense from the noisy street. This will ward away all evil spirits that approach the parlor house."

"Fortune will come our way." Chen's smile faded as he took tender steps down to the ground.

She extended an arm to help him. "You have helped and I am grateful."

"No, si tau po—it is *you* who have helped me. Without you I would be over there." He pointed down the street where a man crouched under a blanket against a building. "Many Cantonese men are lost to poverty and opium. They come to San Francisco expecting golden streets, only to find them paved with lead. Their bones are shipped back to China with no story but shame for their ancestors." He gave a slight shudder.

She nodded. "Their remains will be buried in silence."

He said, "And they will be ignored on Ching Lee festival days."

She winced. The memories of ancestors were hallowed—to be forgotten was akin to never having lived at all. No one would come to clean their gravesites. A day did not pass without thoughts of her three daughters moldering at the bottom of the cliff.

A light-hearted voice from the house broke into her musings. "Good morning. I heard pounding, so I came to see." The girl named Man-Man tiptoed over the threshold and joined her in the street. Her light brown hair flowed across her shoulders. She looked down at the muddy puddles and lifted the hem of the pink silk pantaloons that Ah gave her the previous night.

"I am glad to hear you are risen from your sleep. San and Yee were up earlier, and now they are cleaning their rooms." Ah gave her an appraising glance.

"I had nightmares, deep and long, of the voyage. I thought I drowned, but I awoke to see I was on land."

"I had many such dreams after my sea journey." Ah bit her lower lip.

Man-Man gazed up at the bagua gleaming above the threshold. "Negative energy here?"

"Yes, the bagua will help us redirect it."

"I see. I have much to learn. I thought there would be nothing but positive energy in America."

Man-Man's words loosened the rope that tied Ah to the present moment. If she let them, her memories floated on the horizon like a small boat, sails aloft, subject to the wind. For a minute, she let her thoughts run free: her own first day on the wharf, the kindness of the Daileys, followed by the terrible news that her job as a servant was lost. Then her finding the shanty with Chen and establishing the "lookee" house. Clark's blue eyes were contemplating her naked body. His warm lips were kissing hers.

A ship's horn blasted down at the wharf. She had no time to linger in the wake of remembrance. "Chen, close up the ladder. We will store it inside."

Man-Man's voice rose and fell like soft waves. "Mrs. Toy, what should I wear today? In addition to this apparel, I have only one outfit, the black pajama and blue jacket. All are soiled."

"Come, we must find some silk jackets for you to wear. And are you hungry?"

"Yes, I long for rice and fish." Hunger deepened the girl's voice.

"You are outspoken. I admire that." Ah called to Chen. "Can we find such a meal in the larder?"

"I am about to order cook to fix a morning meal for all the young women in our care."

"Very good. We have a new cook, now that our parlor house is finished. And with you girls, our business is complete and ready to start." She gave Man-Man a sideways glance. "Now, we must go to my desk in the parlor. I need you to sign your bill of sale—er—your contract."

The girl swallowed hard.

Once inside the parlor, Ah pointed to the chair in front of the desk. "Please sit."

The girl eased into the chair and sat at the edge. Her gaze darted around the room.

After settling into her own chair, Ah untied the red ribbon, unrolled the paper, and secured its corners with brass paperweights. She sensed Man-Man's eyes on her; the girl's face was a speechless mask.

Ah said, "Since this is in formal Cantonese language, I will read it out loud. In the document you are referred to as Wong Sau Man, your formal name."

Man-Man nodded.

Ah cleared her throat, then began the reading.

"*An Agreement to Assist a Young Girl Named Wong Sau Man*"

"*Because she became indebted to her mistress for passage, food, & etc., and has nothing to pay, she makes her body over to the woman Ah Toy, to serve as a prostitute to make out the sum of $700. The money shall draw no interest, and Wong Sau Man shall receive no wages.*"

Man-Man stirred. "I do not get any money from you, now or ever?"

"Quite right. Let us proceed." Ah continued.

"Wong Sau Man shall serve four and a half years. On this day of agreement Wong Sau Man receives the sum of $700 in her own hands."

"But you say that I receive the money." Small red smears painted Man-Man's cheeks.

"Only a formality. I pay the money directly to the Kong Chow Company who acts as your agent."

Ah went on. *"When the time is out, Wong Sau Man may be her own master, and no man shall trouble her. If she runs away before the time is out and any expense is incurred in catching, then Wong Sau Man must pay that expense. If she conceives, she shall serve one year more."*

"Any questions so far?" Ah asked.

"I must not become pregnant?" The color in Man-Man's face faded like old wallpaper.

Ah held up her hand. "There is more about that in the next section which I will now read." She pressed her attention down to the paper. *"There are four great sicknesses against which Wong Sau Man is secured for one hundred days. The first three are namely leprosy, epilepsy, and 'stone woman,' the inability to have carnal intercourse with men. For any of these diseases, she may be returned to the Kong Chow Company within one hundred days. The last and fourth great sickness is pregnancy. Should Wong Sau Man become pregnant, she will be returned to the Kong Chow Company immediately. If Wong Sau Man should be deemed to go back to China, then she shall serve another party in San Francisco till her time is out. For a proof of this agreement this paper."*

She tapped the paper. "This is where we sign our names. Do you see?"

Man-Man rubbed her eyes, then blinked down at the paper.

X_____Ah Toy
X_____Wong Sau Man
Dated twenty-third day first month of the present year 1850.

"Understood?" Ah's voice lowered.

"I should not become sick either," Man-Man said. Her shoulders drooped.

"You are expected to stay well and be dedicated to our house and all its affairs." Ah picked up the nibbed pen, dipped it in her inkwell, and handed it to Man-Man. She held her index finger on the paper where Man-Man should sign.

After all was completed, she blew on the paper to dry the ink and called out, "Chen! Please come."

He arrived all too fast. Had he been listening outside the parlor door?

She drew the ribbon tightly around the paper roll. She opened the strongbox under the desk, took out a large gold nugget, and passed it to him. "For Officer Wong. No stopping along the way, all right?"

"Certainly, si tau po." He eased quietly out the door.

"Now, you are official. We must go upstairs, and I will show you the proper way to bathe and fix your hair." Ah wrinkled her nose. "You carry the staleness of the ship on your body."

Man-Man shrugged. "We had nowhere to wash."

"For now, you may wear one of my old silk jackets, but you are much taller than I am. I will take you to the tailor shop and they will make some qipao for you to wear. You must present an enticing figure to the men."

"The men?" The girl drew back.

"Yes, you will be expected to sleep with them each night. Much gold will go from their hands into our pockets."

Man-Man trembled. "I do not like to sleep with men."

Ah gave a sigh. "Many provincial girls do not know how to do acts with men. But you like to talk to men? You like to have them admire you?"

The girl's eyes darted left to right. "Yes—I suppose."

"In time you will learn how to sleep with men. They will show you what they want, and you do it. It is very simple really. You just learn not to think about it. Think of something happy, maybe a favorite flower."

Tears brimmed in the girl's eyes. "My uncle raped me and my sister for many years. It started when we were only ten and twelve. When I told my father, he said I should be quiet to keep peace in the family."

Though Ah was tempted to fall into the valley of Man-Man's story, she resisted. Not only was she unsure it was true, she also had more pressing matters to consider—namely the building of her new parlor house. The world around them had cruel, sharp teeth, and it would chew them into bits if they did not resist its appetite.

"Go have your breakfast in the kitchen."

"But—."

Was the girl objecting? Ah rose to her feet. "Get up now."

Man-Man stood.

Ah stared down at the girl's flat feet. A hot pang coursed through her. "Look at you. Lucky in your misery. Your feet are flat, and you will never suffer the limiting pain of bound feet like mine. You can run from abuse—run hard and fast down the street, across the wharf, up into the hills. You can live in a warm parlor house with food in your belly, unlike other girls captured and kept like animals in cages. I offer you a way to survive."

The girl stood silent, her gaze seeming vacant. Had she even heard what Ah had said? Or was she too weak to understand?

"*Pfft*." Ah shook her head. "Ungrateful."

The door clicked behind Man-Man as she left the room.

Ah sat back down, taking Jade into her lap, scratching the cat behind her ears. The girl may not appreciate her offer, but she was young. In time she would learn.

Such a youth would make a good assistant in her parlor house business. Her lighter hair, hazel eyes, and long legs would entice white men, yet her intelligence would serve the household well. She would learn to show discernment among the men, choosing how and when to keep secrets. Such a girl would be loyal if treated well, but disloyal if abused. If disloyal—well—she would be sent back to Canton on the next sail.

Ah envisioned her dragon sleeping, curled on its velvet bed: refreshing, soft sleep in the mists. It would save its energy for times she needed it. Yet now, it was satisfied. She inhaled, savoring the fragrant wood shavings of the newly laid parlor house floor.

Five

❦ DO NOT FORGET ME ❧

That same afternoon's sunlight bathed Ah's second story room. She stepped onto her balcony and stood at the railing. A mix of black-jacketed men scurried down below. Sunny days and clear nights chased away the rain, and on these clear nights a starlit canopy lit up the Bay. The upstairs breeze rustled her hair and caressed her face. What a change from her former ground-level shanty where she used to hear every outside footstep through the thin walls.

Her house. The sound of that made her pause. She planned that each of the girls would have their own spacious room on the second story of the new dwelling. Along with Chen's smaller room next to Ah's, a total of five bedrooms completed the second story plan.

Chen attended to her needs, dumping her chamber pot, laundering her clothes and helping her select the most appropriate outfit for the occasion. He made it his special duty to massage her feet at night with an oil mixed with camphor, cloves, and menthol. His gentle touch erased the cares of the day. He dusted and polished her jewelry collection, now growing larger, a sign of her wealth. But more than all that, he remained her trusted confidante, her anchor on this quaking soil.

She spotted Chen's tall form moving in the familiar mix of Cantonese men's black jackets and round-toed shoes down below. His queue flew behind his brisk steps. "Chen?" she called.

"I went to the Post Office in Portsmouth Plaza." He looked up. "Mail for you, si tau po." He held up a brown envelope.

Ah met him in the downstairs parlor. She took the letter. "Do I see a corner of the envelope peeled away? Were you spying?"

A grin played across his face. "I must admit, I was curious." Then he drew himself up straight. "But I am always by your side—evil men and evil spirits will not get past me."

"Chen it is *I* who protect *you*. We need each other in this strange country." She basked in the warmth between them.

Wonder tinged his voice. "I am most grateful for the honor." He tilted his head and smiled.

She patted his hand. "Now you must go have the new cook prepare the evening meal. Our new girls are too thin. We must fatten them. Have cook prepare the roast duck with orange sauce. Lots of fat in the gravy. I need their thin legs softer for men to rest upon."

"As you wish." He pushed his cap up on his head.

She grabbed the ivory handled knife from the side table, and opened the envelope, then sat on the edge of the settee. The scrawling letters floated across the page of white paper that bore the sheen of expensive vellum.

> *Monterey, California*
> *January 15, 1850*

Dear Mrs. Toy,
   Nary a day passes that I do not think of your lovely features. I am very lonely now in the midst of men's affairs. Unfortunately, some

large matters call me back to Canton again, yet I wish to see you before I take my leave for China. I will be on board ship in San Francisco harbor on February 13, and I would very much like to have you dine with me.

I know that San Francisco streets are rough, and I do not want to venture far from the ship. Thus, I will send a wagon to your address Elizabeth gave me, and you may meet me at the Excelsior Restaurant. Gold spoons, quite civilized. My ship's Captain told me the vegetables come from the Sandwich Islands. I shall meet you there at 1800 hours. Since you will be unable to contact me before that date, I shall wait for you for one hour at the Excelsior. Should you not appear, I will figure you have declined my invitation.

Very much looking forward to your presence.

Your humble servant,

Henry Conrad

She folded the letter and sat back on the settee. She must think. February 11th was New Year's Eve, followed by the celebrations of New Year's Day. Henry's invitation for February 13th crowded her busy schedule, yet—. This was the year of the Dog, an auspicious sign. A dog's arrival symbolized good fortune. Perhaps Henry would bring the luck she welcomed.

The soft, hovering notes of the guqin came from upstairs. She imagined Yee sitting upright on the bedroom chair, plucking the stringed instrument, her eyes closed in concentration. The girl played well; her fingers created soft, thoughtful harmonies that filled the house and drifted out onto the street below.

Ah ran her finger across the smooth paper. A series of questions leaped into her mind, in tune with the soft notes of Yee's guqin. Even though Henry might bring good fortune, how would he fit into her life her in the Bay City? Did the Daileys think he would rescue her? What was wrong with the path she was choosing for herself?

She nodded her head. Though they might see her role as madam to be degrading, this life had brought her freedom. Henry had no idea that she was now ran an upscale brothel. Elizabeth would never tell him. Nor would Rachel Larkin. Would it matter if Henry knew? What difference would that make? She was hardly a proper wife for him. Did he pursue her out of respect for the Daileys? What good was a woman with bound feet on a ranch?

Jade jumped up beside her, and she scratched her ears, but her thoughts took a different turn. In truth, the only man whom she truly needed, or even wanted, was Clark. His tender kisses, his warm embrace—those were the actions that mattered. What could Henry offer her? She was a wealthy woman now; she owned property. She held up her chin. After all, Officer Wong made deals with her.

She tapped the letter. Maybe if she'd been a young girl, Henry would make her feel remarkable, and she would pray for his offer of marriage. But at this point, she was reluctant. Even if he accepted her life in the flesh trade, she would not easily yield to a man who wanted to claim her as a prize to display.

Today she had freedom like the dancing waves and the sea dogs playing in Monterey Bay. She had liberty to tell her side of any story in court. For the first time in her life, she had both independence and control of her future. And the joyous Chinese New Year—the Year of the Dog—was soon to arrive.

A spark of apprehension took hold, and for a brief second, she saw Lee Shau Kee, the tall and skinny teenager who spent his youth on the wharves in front of her father's porcelain factory. That vision brought on a sudden recollection that rose as vividly as the day it happened.

One afternoon long ago, she and her brother Toy Lee Lung were leaving the building where Elizabeth Dailey held their English lessons.

Lee Shau Kee and some rough boys were kicking what first looked to be a ball between them, laughing. As she concentrated, the memory became clearer, and she had wondered at the time what object they were rolling around. Curious, she and her brother drew nearer and stood outside the circle of boys.

A wash of red stained the wood planking of the wharf within the boys' circle, and with each kick, a gush of blood spurted in the air. Then she saw it—ears, snout, head—all bathed in dirt-covered blood. A pig's head. The laughter was uproarious; the bloodlust palpable.

"Lee Shau Kee is a nasty boy," her brother had whispered.

She clearly remembered the way her stomach roiled, and her knees knocked together like twigs. She grabbed Toy Lee Lung's arm. "Take me home, brother—please take me home."

As the memory faded, she glanced down into Jade's green eyes, flecked with gold. The cat purred, knowing all.

February 11, 1850

On Chinese New Year's Eve, the round tables at DuPont Street Restaurant were piled high with food, the center rotating with steaming plates of chicken, beef, and fish. In addition, the servers rolled their carts out from the kitchen, platters brimming with favorites such as oysters and mollusks. The sound of chopsticks on plates mixed with men's voices. The fragrances of spiced mussels, clams, and crab filled the air. Ah glanced over at Chen who watched her protectively from the corner. If she tried to speak to him, the ambient noise would squelch her words. Normally she would cause a stir when dining here, but tonight's celebrations gave her anonymity. Men were distracted, laughing and stuffing rice-laden chopsticks into their mouths.

Crashing cymbals, part of a small parade, marched past the window. She and Chen, along with several other diners, abandoned their tables and crowded outside the restaurant. Revelers packed DuPont Street, gawking and cheering. Signs pasted on the walls of Little Canton heralded the Year of the Dog.

The crowd observed men holding sticks as they held up the long pink and red Flying Lion, which dipped and flowed with their gestures, mimicking the drives of a crouching and springing feline. Other men carried red and white banners, or lit firecrackers which alternately sprayed sparks and puffed black smoke into the air.

A sudden mix of red, yellow, and black-jacketed men crowded toward the street from all directions, their queues dangling from under their caps. Officials of the Kong Chow Company, the merchant's guild, formed a line across Dupont Street. Among them she saw Officer Wong marching east with his fellow men. And everywhere lanterns, round, oblong, or square, aimed light in various directions while firecrackers pulsed along the way.

Someone touched her arm." Nice parade, isn't it?" She looked up into Clark's blue eyes. Her heart gave a jolt. What was he doing here? What would he say?

The parade's noise was quelling, firecrackers exploding further away. Maybe before the Golden Dragon display, she could hear his news. Battling her rising pulse, she gestured him inside, and Chen followed them back to their table, his eyes wide, expectant.

Clark pulled out the chair next to hers, helped her sit down, then slid into the empty seat. "I am happy to see you, I missed you." He unfastened the buttons of his thick peacoat. "It is brisk out tonight."

"Would you like a plate?" she asked. "The food might warm you." She forced out the faltering words.

He shook his head. "No, I am on my beat, but I have time for you." His gaze would melt iron.

At another time before this, she might have welcomed those words. But this time her stomach tightened, and her heart beat against her ribs. "I have not seen you in some time. Did your wife arrive safely?"

"Only three days ago, but Officer Wong said I must not fail to see the Chinese New Year festivities, so I am here to honor him. I was surprised to see you here, but I am glad, too."

Maybe if she looked away from him, her heart would stop its thundering. She turned to a dish of shiny oysters in their shells and spooned several onto her plate. "I am glad to hear you you—and—she—are well."

She was unable to resist a sideways look. The strong, high cheekbones, the stray lock of blond hair falling over his forehead—there sat her heartbreak and her joy. She peered out toward the street. "Why is your wife not with you tonight?" She must not let him see the tears brimming under her eyelids.

He shrugged. "Susannah did not fare well on the journey; her voyage around the Horn was very hard. Mosquitoes and biting bugs made life quite unbearable. She spends most of her time abed these days. That is why you have not seen me. I have spent many days nursing her."

She blinked and nodded slowly. "I am most sorry to hear that." Though her lips spoke the words, she was hardly sorry.

Chen brought her a bowl of steaming chicken soup, and he set it down on the red tablecloth. If only Ah could dive into it and disappear. Before she had longed to see Clark, but now, to have him here, yet not be able to have him—this was unbearable. She asked, "Will you be continuing to patrol our Little Canton?"

He nodded. "Officer Wong has told me your new parlor house is open on Pike Street. He admires the work you have done. Some of the finest Celestial craftspeople have worked on the interior, he says."

Using her chopsticks, she tugged an oyster out of its shell. "I want to give my customers the feeling of a Cantonese gentleman's home, so they are warm and generous to my girls."

"And I am sure your girls will be kind and loving to them. They say you paid a pretty penny for them. Officer Wong tells me Lee Shau Kee nearly outbid you for a certain maiden."

So, gossip was being passed around about her. She set down her chopsticks. "How can you be so casual about my affairs?"

His eyes filled with uncertainty. A strange silence lingered in the space between them.

Her dragon woke and stirred, stoking the fires in her breast. "Do you not remember it was Lee Shau Kee who drew the bag over my head, threw me over his shoulder, and threatened to take me back to my brother-in-law in Guangdong? Or has that wife of yours made you erase me from your mind?"

The group of diners sharing Ah's round table stopped talking and raised their chopsticks expectantly. Were they listening in?

He glanced at the other men around the table. "Shh—no need to raise your voice."

Though she seethed, she recognized his desire for privacy. She lowered her voice to a whisper. "Do not forget me."

The lines softened around his mouth. "Now I am back on my beat, I will never be far from you." He bit his lip. "I love you."

She savored those three words slowly, turning each one over in her mind. But then—behind his words lay the prickly forest of lies.

She stroked an eyebrow. "You love me more than your wife? *Pfft!* How can that be?"

He took her hand in his. "Ever since I stood in line outside your shanty and saw you naked, I have loved you. Ever since we rescued you from the clutches of Lee Shau Kee, I have wanted you. Ever since we walked in the rain together, and sat before the candlelight, I have longed for your presence. I shall never love anyone more than you."

Was that a knife jabbing at her chest? His words penetrated her soul, that same soul torn by the losses of her daughters and the shame of her station. His words should have brought her joy, yet now they carried nothing but dark visions. For he could never be hers, not here, not anywhere.

He reached out an arm and cradled the back of her chair, pulling her closer. "Ever since that day I saw you naked, I wanted you right away, but I had to hold back because Susannah still needed me. On the day I first left New York for the gold hills, my father Josiah warned me not to abandon Susannah, that I would end up regretting such a misdeed. So, I treaded softly in this new relationship with you, dear Ah Toy."

Passion rose inside her like the hottest flame, clouding her thoughts like the smoke that masked the city's raging fires.

He clutched her hand, caressing her palm. "In a way, you captivated me in a way that no woman had ever done, and I am drawn to you. By the same token, I am afraid that furthering our love might jeopardize my strained tie with Susannah. So, there it is—duty demands I let you go."

Heat filled her, and she envisioned herself bursting with anger-flame, her body alight like a candle's wick. What a torture. She could no longer sit here so close to him without being able to touch him. She could not bear to hear one more word of these words that slashed at her heart and pierced her soul. Something compelled her to stand up, and so she did. "Good night, Mr. Clark."

He stammered. "B-but you haven't eaten anything? Stay for the last firecrackers and the Golden Dragon, the end of the parade. Have some plum wine with me. Tell me of your new house. The new girls you have hired. All of it." His blue eyes stabbed hers.

"No, not this time." She tore herself away from his warm hands, shook her head, and waved to Chen. He brought her cloak and helped her to her feet. She looked down into his blue eyes, now misty and vacant. "You know where to find me." Her tone was clipped and cold.

"But Ah, I do not understand." His voice waivered the way a breezy curtain flaps against a broken window.

"I am Mrs. Toy to you, Officer Clark." Holding back a rush of tears, she faced away, her eyes focused on the diners bent over their bowls and plates.

His face darkened. "If that is what you wish." His shoulders drooped and his tone hardened as he assumed a policeman's mask.

"Yes, that is how I want it." Her cloak swished around her, and Chen's steady arm guided her out the door, through the New Year's revels thronging with men, then up to Pike Street and home. Broken sobs gathered like lumps of coal in her throat. Her dragon stirred. *Though you must swallow coal today, you must take the force of that rage and convert it to raw energy. You must not think of him and his silk-lined words, layered with dagger tips. Your parlor house is what matters now. And your girls.*

The following morning, San, Yee, and Man-Man assembled on the settee, their brightly colored qipao contrasting with the soft outlines of their freshly-washed hair. Ah perched on an adjacent chair, facing her charges. San and Yee managed weak smiles; Man-Man flashed her a look of disdain. The aroma of fried wonton lingered in the parlor house after the morning's repast.

At last the girls were beginning to look less gaunt; Chen made sure they ate all the food he placed before them. She vowed to create girls who could please men. Each day she gave them a lesson in behavior and attitude, and though the girls were reluctant at first, they became more vocal. With their growing confidence, she hoped they could face up to the men who would demand not only sex, but also companionship.

Ah took in a breath, then spoke. "This morning I want to continue our instruction on your protocol with the gentlemen callers. Do you recall where we stopped our lesson yesterday?"

San itched her cheek thoughtfully. "I think we finished learning how to serve the men the dinner and entertainment?"

Ah held back a grin. It was hard not to like this girl's forward manner. San was quick on the abacus and helped her settle the new accounts.

Ah's voice assumed a parental tone. "Let us talk about how to entertain the gentlemen in the bedroom. There is a certain way to go about it properly. This is a parlor house, not a brothel. We need to maintain a certain decorum or elegance. Understood?"

Man-Man stared. The color drained from her freckled cheeks. "I do not understand. A man in the bedroom means pain to me."

Yee glanced at her and snapped. "You do not understand anything, do you? You must listen to Mrs. Toy."

"You have seaweed for a brain." Man-Man gave a retort, tossing her long brown hair back over her shoulder.

"Nothing like your paste-face—." Yee reddened.

Ah clapped her hands. "Girls! Remember your contracts, each of you. If you do what I am about to tell you, you will be able to pay them off."

San said. "I am ready to learn."

"At least *you* have some sense, so I will go ahead." Ah sat up higher in her chair. "After the man arrives in your room, you are to have him sit on the chair or bed and remove his boots. This is so that our expensive bedclothes are not stained with mud. You will then serve the man a brandy from the snifter on the side table. This is the preferred drink for men who visit Little Canton."

Yee interrupted, "You told us yesterday that brandy relaxes the men."

Ah nodded, "You are a fast learner."

Yee sniffed and glared at Man-Man.

Ah tapped her lotus shoe against the floor. "Let me go on."

The girls quieted, so Ah continued. "After the brandy, you are to undress the man and lay his clothes on the trunk at the foot of each bed, careful not to muss the items."

Man-Man said, "I am already nervous about this. What if the man interrupts me while I am undressing him?"

Ah said, "You must calmly insist that he be patient. Remember the bell-pull—if a man refuses to cooperate, call Chen and he will remove the customer."

Man-Man frowned. "I have never known a man to follow my directions." She gave a deep sigh.

"That may be true but let us continue. After blowing out half the candles so that the room is dimmed, you girls will undress before the man. Do it slowly, one garment at a time, in order to stimulate his appetite. Then you are to join the man in bed. Lie on your back. The man will be eager to mount you."

Man-Man burst out. "Like a horse!"

Ah waved aside her comment. "You are to close your eyes and think of wild peonies, soft velvet, and rhythmic songs that accompany the squeaking of bedsprings as the men take you, sometimes over and over."

"Now, let us practice closing our eyes, thinking of soft fields before us."

San and Yee relaxed their shoulders and closed their eyes. Man-Man's eyes snapped open and she gazed around the room.

"Man-Man." Ah's tone was firm.

The girl reluctantly obeyed, her eyelids fluttering in her attempts to keep them shut.

After a few moments, Ah continued. "If a man hurts you, you are to tell him once to stop; if he continues to hurt you, as I said before, you are to ring the bell-pull and Chen will arrive, knife in hand, and escort the man out of the parlor house."

Man-Man said, "I do not think this protocol will work. A man cannot control such an appetite in this way."

Yee rolled her eyes. "What is wrong with you?"

"Hold your tongue," San said. "We are fortunate to be in such an orderly house."

Yee said, "San is right. Mrs. Toy tells us that we will be protected. Man-Man you are a stupid girl. Such talk and you will be in the streets along with the dead dogs and crib girls."

Ah said, "Chen and I have selected the men very well. Besides, Chen has much practice escorting men away during our old lookee business. He will be careful in making sure all is well."

Chen emerged from the shadows. "You may have reason to be afraid, but Mrs. Toy wants her parlor house to succeed. You will help by following her directions."

After the lesson, the girls rose to attend to the tidying of their rooms. On their way out, Ah caught Man-Man's heated glare. Had she made a mistake taking on such a wildly gorgeous creature? Had she overreached in wanting to have only the most beautiful girls for her parlor house?

No answers came to her. She heard only the sound of the girls' fading footsteps. What was that *scree-scraw* out in the street? She opened the window and peered out. A knife-sharpener was moving blades across his whetstone in the street, and a crowd of customers had begun to form.

Six

❦ GOLD SPOONS ❧

That same evening, Chen guided Ah across the plank sidewalk and over the threshold to the Excelsior Restaurant. A white-coated waiter greeted them at the door and escorted them to the tables covered with damask cloth. What elegant surroundings. The gold-plated silverware gleamed under the flickering candelabra, and the china was decorated with small pink and green flowers.

Henry stood at a middle table adjacent to the oaken bar. His jacket was open, revealing a gold brocade waistcoat. A smile lit his face like the world at dawn. "Mrs. Toy, what a joy to see you." His voice carried across the restaurant.

Male customers at tables turned and gazed. She heard their whispering as she passed. The words "lookee girl, lookee girl," rippled across the room. Had Henry heard their voices? If so, he did not show it.

After Ah took his side, Henry turned to Chen. "I remember you, too." He extended his hand, and Chen shook it, then dropped his hands.

She unhooked her arm from under Chen's slackened elbow. She murmured in Cantonese "Eat over there, Chen, but please keep an eye on me."

"Yes, *si tau po*." He backed away, and the waiter seated him at an adjacent table.

Ah stared down at the menu. She ran her index finger down the list, stopping at *steak* and *potatoes*. "I have heard the vegetables are very fresh here."

"I mentioned that in my letter. We shall be sure to order a plateful. A drink, my dear?"

She shook her head. "Liquor in bottles makes my head spin. I prefer tea."

"Well, I will celebrate with a finger of whiskey, followed by a bottle of champagne. Perhaps you will take a sip?"

"Yes, perhaps."

After the waiter delivered their drinks, and Ah placed her order, Henry sipped his whiskey and Ah stirred her tea. Maybe the leaves in the bottom of her cup would foretell happiness with Henry, but her mind clouded with visions of Clark. Try as she might, she could not seem to wish him away.

Henry lit a clay pipe and puffed the tobacco to life. "Elizabeth Dailey says you run a thriving business, selling silk fabrics to townspeople."

"Where did she learn that?" She gave a little cough, waving the smoke away from her face.

"From Hortencia who got it from Chen." His tone was matter-of-fact. "Or is it mere kitchen gossip?"

"There is some truth to it. My business is growing." She leaned back while the waiter spread a white linen napkin across her lap. *Thank the Goddess for Chen's protective lie.* "I will have to get after him for spreading news."

Once into the main course of their meal, after chattering about the Daileys' affairs and Henry's many trips to China, he steered the conversation into a deeper path within the landscape of their relationship. He paused, his fork and knife resting in each hand over his dinner plate. "I have an important matter to discuss."

"I see." She lifted the pot, poured green tea into her empty cup, and raised it to her lips. Her hand shook slightly.

"After my next voyage, I have plans to return to my property in San Jose." She noticed he was watching her intently, his gaze fixed on hers.

"Where is San Jose?" At least she could pretend to be interested.

"South of where we are now, perhaps four hours by stage." His voice rose with obvious enthusiasm.

"And what plans would those be?" She kept her expression restrained, thoughtful.

He leaned toward her. "I wish to start a ranch. I plan to raise horses and plant a cherry orchard. A ship's captain I know bought some land there and divided it into fifty-acre parcels. Awhile back, I bought the land. I have longed dreamed of cultivating it."

She set her teacup back on the table. "You do not wish to go back and forth to China anymore?"

He shook his head. "No, I have spent the last twenty years sailing around the world, most recently working in the China trade. In fact, my desire is to settle down, marry and raise a family."

A brief shiver rippled through her. "Hmm, I see." Her fingers played with the fringe dangling from the white tablecloth.

"A family—with you." A pink tint traveled from his neck up to his cheeks.

She laid her right hand against her chest. "With me?" She gave an anxious cough.

"I know this must be overwhelming news." He held up a hand. "There is only one thing. I would ask you to wait until next year since I must wrap up my businesses in various ports of call."

Ah sat back. A vision of a large two-story house with a surrounding porch flitted across her plate. She saw herself mending a small boy's trousers before a crackling fire. A small boy with eyes like hers, but hair blond, the forelock falling across his forehead. The little boy bore an uncanny resemblance to John Clark.

Henry puffed on his pipe. "I have much wealth, my dear. I would like to make you my wife and the mother of our children. I know we are very different, but I have lived and traveled much among the people of Guangdong."

She drew her fan out of her pouch and fluttered it. "I think that would be good for us—that you know my culture. There is a major requirement, though."

"What would that be?"

"I would need to bring Chen."

"Every mistress of the house needs her personal servant. I saw many servants like him in China. It shall be as you desire"

"I would also need to think about other agreements that keeps safe my financial earnings. After all, I also have great wealth." Ah leaned back in her chair, regarding him.

"Of course." His voice was eager, yet there was something missing, something she wanted to hear that he had not said. But she could not put her finger on it. Once he returned to California for good, he would surely know about her parlor house business, unless he already knew. How would she reveal that and how would he react? Oh well, there was time to figure that out before she had to commit to him. Or was there?

At the end of their dinner together, Ah gathered her dragon's strength and allowed Henry to move his chair next to hers and pull her close to him. Her gaze followed his pipe as he rested it in the ashtray on the table.

He relaxed a hand on her arm. What should have given her a thrill gave her an opposite feeling, akin to a raw and primitive grief. A stab of guilt tightened her throat. Maybe it was something like betrayal—was she giving away part of herself in making a match with Henry? Maybe she was being ridiculous.

After all, he was offering her the ideal life, the safety and security all women dream of but can never achieve. She would return to America's version of the noble life, the world she knew growing up in her parents' wealthy household in Guangzhou.

But arguments crept into her mind. Elizabeth Dailey's knowledge about her real occupation left her ashamed. Would that doom her future with Henry? He might learn the truth about her from sailors aboard ship. Or even from a passing stranger. In truth, would she care?

"Something wrong?" He leaned over, his cold cheek brushing hers.

"No—no." She looked into his brown eyes, observing the crinkles gathering around the corners. Though lacking Clark's striking features, she might get used to Henry's wise, steady demeanor. And there was always the true Harry—from the beach—behind the mask. Maybe in time that playful side of him might emerge.

She felt the cool brush of his hand on her arm. He said, "I will always take care of you. You may rest assured. I have bankers and accountants who will settle our financial plans. I think we will be very happy together."

His sentiments fell like raindrops on smooth stones, the multi-colored pebbles that layered the pathway to her favorite temple in Guangzhou. And like the rain on those stones, the words bounced off rather than penetrating the rock. So she shifted uneasily. Though she received the message, his declarations may not belong to her.

Seven

⚜ IVORY SILK ⚜

March 1850

That evening the parlor house was aglitter with candles. Men had been pre-selected to enter. Ah had chosen three customers from her former Lookee Shop: men with all their teeth; men with clean-shaven faces; men who had taken a bath. They had been given invitation cards, in both Cantonese and English. Their evening's entertainment included dinner and a girl. It cost them much in gold which thudded into Ah's strongbox near the front door.

As in the lookee days, Chen stood at the door and frisked each man as he entered. After Ah took their gold, she handed them a glass of plum wine and pointed them toward their seats in the drawing room. They sat on lacquered chairs, among Chinese scrolls and bamboo plants. Brightly colored vases, large and small, decorated corners; gold-rimmed bowls reflected the candlelight from sconces on the walls. Tables laden with flowery plants shared space with incense burners whose smoke spiraled lazily into the air, spreading the aroma of jasmine.

San and Man-Man took delicate steps, serving the men tumblers of whiskey and cigars. Yee plucked the strings of the guqin and sang in her best deep voice while the men cleared their throats and stretched out their legs, settling into the chairs. Cigar smoke blended with incense, creating a haze like the day's early fog over the hills. The girls circulated, removing the men's shoes and massaging their feet.

After Yee's repertoire finished, the girls escorted the customers to the dining room where a long table awaited, heaping with platters of Chinese cuisine. The finest dumplings, noodles, and mounds of duck breast shimmered in the candlelight. San, Yee, and Man-Man went to each man, serving him food and *baiju*, a strong alcoholic drink. They took turns showing each man how to use chopsticks, although they had forks available in case the men became tired of the effort.

The night's revels complete, each girl took a man's hand and led him upstairs to her room. Chen made his rounds until midnight, pressing his ear to the outside of their doors.

The next morning, Ah and Chen stood at the front door to give the men their cloaks and top hats and make an appointment for a return visit. Ah wished for a regular clientele to visit her parlor house. Known customers were preferable to the wild, rowdy bunch who wandered, drunk and violent, into brothels, A known customer might have a wife at home, but he might wish to seek the companionship of a lovely Celestial woman who would not talk endlessly of sewing.

Cabbages, onions, and leeks lay in rows across the next morning's market table. Ah surveyed a mound of flies gathered on a pomegranate, next to celery gleaming in stately stalks. Prices in Cantonese lay on cards before each item for sale. She glanced sideways. Chen fondled an orange, holding it to his nose. All around her, voices buzzed—some Cantonese men lingered in blue jackets and black pants; others looked at news sheets pasted on the sides of buildings.

Someone's finger poked her shoulder. She saw a flash of ivory silk and recognized fellow madam, Li Fan. Her faded cheeks looked pasty as beige wallpaper.

"Good morning, Li Fan. How is your business?" Ah forced a smile.

"My girls demand food; if I had my way, they would starve so that I could use them more freely. Men like them gaunt and hungry." Li Fan's teeth clicked like two chopsticks striking each other.

A firm hand gripped her arm. Ah took a sideways glimpse of Chen, then she patted his hand.

He cast her a sour look.

She whispered, "It is all right. Let me speak to a fellow madam."

He withdrew a couple of feet, joining the men who were examining the billboard on the wall. Wisps of fog caught on the edges of buildings.

Li Fan's protruding front tooth gleamed. "I have heard much about you lately from Lee Shau Kee."

"Oh?" Ah cringed. "Whatever is he up to now?"

Li Fan continued. "He says that Tung Chao has given up on bringing you back to Guangzhou. He has taken a new bride of twelve years old. He crows that he was her first lover, and that she is pregnant."

"Hmmm." Ah swallowed, holding up her chin.

Li Fan leaned closer. "Tung Chao's fortune teller says the child will be a boy." Her mouth curved into an unpleasant twist.

Ah forced a tight-lipped smile. "I do not care anymore."

"Want to know what he calls you?" Li Fan's voice rose with the jab.

The butcher and the shoppers in the marketplace quieted. Were they staring at her?

"What?" Ah shuddered. Nothing could be worse than public humiliation.

"He calls you bad luck, bad girl wife. Good riddance, he says. You brought bad fortune to his house and his name."

Ah hung onto the side of the table. The celery stalks jiggled. "How come you care about my past? Your opinion means dirt to me. Your cribs are pigsties for the innocent girls you put them in—nothing but cages."

"I make much money—that brings me good fortune." A red stain oozed across Li Fan's cheeks.

Ah measured her words. "I think you do not understand Confucius. Good fortune first, then money. Your spirit is thin as a chicken leg picked clean by vultures. How can you be so nasty to other girls?"

"I escaped such a cruel fate myself. Besides, my girls feel nothing. They are happy in their opium world." She chewed on a ragged thumbnail.

Ah put up a hand. "Even worse. You work them with drugs, so they feel nothing. You reduce them to animals that men hump for cash. You make me nauseated, sick to death." Ah tried to ignore her heart's thudding in her chest. How she would love to reach out and strangle this woman.

Saliva bubbled in each corner of Li Fan's mouth. "Get away from me! You talk of your parlor house as though it was as magnificent as the Forbidden City—how can you think to call your place important? You are phony—just like me—but at least I am honest." She wagged her finger. "You—you—!" She stepped even closer. "Are wrapped in lies!"

An old man with a scar across his face backed away. The men trickled out of the market stall. No one wanted to witness a catfight unless they had taken bets on the winner.

Perspiration dampened her neck. Ah stayed silent. Her dragon held its ground, stoic, unflinching before this woman with the stained wallpaper face.

Li Fan persisted. "You are no better than me. Look at those mess of feet! You can't even walk. Pretense only. You think you are of noble blood, do you? How many lies are you telling yourself?"

"Better my lies than those you tell to those girls whom you have reduced to pieces of meat. I am sad for you. How long do they live under your care? Six months? A year? Longer than your girls, to be sure. They think they are special, but they are only meat, too. You are cruel since you do not give them opium to quell their pain." The red stains on Li Fan's bland cheeks deepened into scarlet.

Ah put her hands on her hips. "I tell them their worth every day—you have no idea what human worth is."

Li Fan stepped back, her cheeks a mosaic of crisscrossed lines. "Your girls' bones will be in the same crate as my girls' on their way back to Guangzhou. You will be penniless, and you will be asking me for money for their passage. But I will refuse." She planted her feet.

Ah had enough. One more ridiculous comment and she would smack Li Fan's red-swirled face. Her dragon hunkered down, ready to spring. *No. Do not allow Li Fan to win. Better go home, save face. Less gossip for Li Fan to report to Lee Shau Kee, and for Tung Chao to savor back home as he beds his twelve-year-old concubine.*

She absorbed the importance of her dragon's advice.

Chen's breathing quickened next to her. "Careful, si tau po. Clark is watching."

She glanced out onto the foggy street where Clark observed her and Li Fan. He took a wide-legged stance and puffed on a cigar. Sudden, sharp fingernails dug into her arm. She flinched and looked up. Li Fan's limp cheeks drooped over her like red, splotchy sails.

Ah gritted her teeth. "Go away." Maybe if she batted at her, the pest would disappear.

Li Fan grimaced. "Not before I tell you a story. A big story you must hear." Was that a hiss in her voice?

Ah took a step back away from this coiling snake. "What story?"

"One of your girls." Li Fan's shrill tone pierced the air.

The pale green webs of Ah's dragon's tail wrapped around her, the armored plates girding her. "Go on. Tell me." She drew in a breath. *Prepare.*

"Man-Man has been seen in Fong's opium den on Stockton Street, lying next to old men smoking pipe and sleeping."

Chen broke in. "Not only old but young men, too. I heard at the marketplace."

Ah whirled, facing Chen. "And you never told me?"

He shrugged, avoiding her gaze.

Her first impulse was to correct him, but she must learn more. "When was Man-Man seen at the opium den?"

Li Fan glared. "Often on many days since she came to San Francisco. Story says she was an opium eater in Guangzhou—that is why her former master cast her out." She licked her lips, plainly proud of her superior knowledge.

"Who told you this story? Lee Shau Kee? That terrific liar?"

"I will not tell you who gave me the information. But—as a fellow madam—I had to tell you. We share a sisterhood of misery." Was her face softening? Somehow kindness did not set well on her—too much lacquer on a painted chair.

Ah's jaw tightened. "I will not slither into your snake pit. You talk suffering where none exists. You make girls into opium eaters, lying in their own filth and waste, then invite men to take them against their will until they are nearly dead."

Li Fan's mouth knotted. "You lie! Who knows what you do in that new fancy house of yours. With that strange eunuch Chen over there. You are sickness—your legs shrivel and your lotus feet rot. What is worse? To say *yes* to opium in my girls or to deny it and pretend your girls are clean?" With that, Li Fan cast her ivory silk jacket about her, and stalked away down the street.

Ah glanced at the spot where Clark had stood watching her. A wisp of smoke lingered there, swirling in the fog like a dissolving memory.

Ah took a deep breath and watched Li Fan evaporate around the corner. The madam was poison, but she made a good point. If Man-Man snuck out to the opium dens, she was clever at hiding it.

As though clutched in the shadows, the shoppers waiting in the streets released their guard and flowed through the marketplace. Cantonese chatter filled the street once again. Men examined stalks of bok choy, looking for bugs or discolorations. Their coins clinked into the waiting hands of the shopkeepers.

She pondered her situation. Who would provoke Man-Man to go to the opium dens? Was Man-Man's behavior Lee Shau Kee's doing? Or did Man-Man do it herself on her own? On the other hand, did Fan tell a lie to cause trouble where there was none? If only she could put all the pieces together.

Chen whispered. "Pay Li Fan no mind, si tau po. Let us go to the fish market. Cook complains our kitchen is bare and the girls will complain."

Ah paused, reeled in her questions like fish on the end of a line, and followed Chen out of the market.

A few minutes passed. After turning the corner onto DuPont Street, footsteps tromped behind her, followed by the sound of a familiar voice. "I heard you were in an argument at the market. What was the matter?" A male voice—*his* voice—spoke English in the street.

Lost in thought, had she missed seeing Clark approaching?

He stood before her, his seven-point badge catching bits of light emerging through the noonday fog.

She said, "Nothing—it was nothing." Without warning her body ached for his touch.

Shafts of his blond hair caught a ray of sunshine breaking the fog. His brows knitted together over his blue eyes.

Chen stepped between them. "Si tau po and Li Fan were in discussion about a girl. That is all."

"A discussion? I have a hard time believing that. Li Fan starts arguments everywhere she goes," Clark said.

Clearing her head, she looked into Clark's clear eyes. After a moment's surprise, she trembled. Though a smile crossed his face, he was nearly dead to her. She must pay him little mind. Chen must not reveal her secrets—she would chastise him later.

Clark's smile faded. "Li Fan will do anything to stop anyone who stands in her way. Be careful. I have an eye on her and her cribs. They are filthy and her practices are base. Do not do business with her—stay away."

Ah drew herself up on her lotus shoes. "I do not think you understand her at all. You do not know women—you never will." She was shocked at her own bitter tone.

His eyes narrowed. "I wish only to protect your interests."

He was so near she could touch him. But she must ignore the pulsing desire in her stomach. She could not fight her acrid tone. "Interests? Foolish man. Close down the opium dens if you care about my interests. They are a plague on this city. They spring up fast, like weeds in May. Do you know how many young girls are dying in those dens?" She grabbed Chen's arm. "Walk me home. We have much to do."

"But Mrs. Toy—" Clark's voice faltered.

She stepped around him and shuffled toward Pike Street in silent fury. Hot tears dribbled down her cheeks. Clark meant the world to her, yet how far away he seemed. Why must he continue to appear, then disappear, within her life? If only fortunes had seen differently to unite them forever, instead of keeping them apart. If she could run away she would. Maybe somewhere else she could forget him.

She looked down at her bound feet, remembering. The day her mother broke her toes and turned them under, the pain, the tears, the agony of weeks and months as her feet and toes conformed to the practice. She hung onto her mother's words.

These lotus feet will make you free. You will marry a rich man because of them. They will make you every man's delight, and you will dance in their arms. The lotus flower, symbol of your femininity, a man's greatest prize.

A series of screams disturbed Ah's early morning sleep. Dawn had not begun to spread its rosy light over Little Canton. She padded to the bedroom window, and looked out. Pike Street lay empty, dark, and still. The screams sounded again. Louder this time. What was going on? She shrugged into her lily-flowered robe and gave a loud knock on Chen's door. No time to wait for him. She stumbled down the stairs, her bare feet colder with each step.

Something drew her to the parlor, so she crossed from the staircase to the parlor door and stepped into the room, her heart pounding in her ears. San and Yee stood cowering in the center of the room, a candle casting long shadows on the wall behind them.

Ah growled, chewing her words. "What are you doing here? Why the screams? You woke me from a sound sleep."

The girls were clearly startled at the sound of her voice, and they pointed, and stood aside. Ah pushed past them, took their candle, and swept the light over the scene. Before her lay a three-foot-high pile of crates marked with Cantonese lettering.

"Someone delivered crates. What are you girls upset about?" And then she saw it: enough to make her lose all of yesterday's meals, breakfast, lunch, and dinner. Nausea roiled in her gut.

"Chen!" Her own cry pierced the house, and his running footsteps sounded, followed by thumping down the stairs.

"Yes, si tau po! What is the matter?" He brushed sleep crumbs from his right eye.

"Look!" She pointed at the top of the crate. Someone had set four pears in a straight line. Each pair looked identical. Green with a yellow spot in the same place.

Chen put his hand over his mouth and spoke through his fingers. "The pears symbolize separation from the beloved. Someone wants us to suffer from loss."

San turned to Yee, "The number four."

Her voice echoed throughout the group. Ah shuddered, as did they all. In Cantonese the word for number *four* was the same as *death*. And so, the very mention of the word came to be equated with death. In Guangdong, people avoided saying the number, writing the number, or even naming floors of buildings the number four.

"Who has done this?" Chen asked.

"I not only ask who, but why?" She stood back, her index finger pressing her lower lip.

San's hands were shaking. "There is something else, si tau po."

Ah rubbed her temple. "What?" A new crisis? How she could absorb any more information? At this point the four pears were all she could think of. Yet she must be strong for these girls.

San grabbed Yee's arm. "Man-Man is not in her bed. I checked for her when I came down the stairs. I was scared . . . I heard steps, the door slam. I wondered who . . ."

Ah steeled herself. "Girls, go back to bed and lock your doors from the inside. You will be safe, and I will come get you at breakfast time. Chen, let us light the torch and open the door. We must check the street outside, then the rest of the house."

The girls shuffled up the stairs while whispering between themselves.

Chen lit a torch and pulled open the front door. He pointed to the marks on the lock. Someone had used a chisel to break in. Once outside, he held the light overhead while Ah studied the landscape of the street. The muddy surfaces near the house lay empty of wagons, horses, and men.

In the middle of horse droppings, a rat perked up, sniffed the air, then scuttled under a shanty. A ship's bell pealed in the far distance, but otherwise she saw no signs of life. Whatever the matter, Ah and Chen would have to wait until the morning light.

Turning back to the doorway, she said, "We must move the trunk against the inside of the front door so whoever it was cannot come in again." She shivered in the pre-dawn breeze.

After Chen dragged the trunk in place, securing the door, he saw her to her room. He paused at her threshold. "Si tau po?"

Ah faced him. "Yes, Chen?"

The torch cast orange and black streaks across his face. "I wonder if—" He tilted his head, a frown pulling down the corners of his mouth.

"Go ahead, Chen. If I guess correctly you are about to say you wonder if this is the black work of Li Fan. Right?"

He nodded, the light dancing around him.

"You are right to wonder, but we must wait and see. Buddha says, "Three things can not belong hidden: the sun, the moon, and the truth.""

He closed his eyes, plainly absorbing her words, then padded down the hallway. Soon after, the door to his bedroom clicked shut behind him.

A few minutes later, she lay in bed, Jade curled at her hip, the cat purring softly. Above her the ceiling turned from black to gray to white, the dawn's rays illuminating the bow window. Someone—maybe Li Fan—maybe someone else—hated her, not from afar, but up close. That someone was willing to trespass and intimidate, someone who knew her beliefs, her superstitions. Someone who worked to instill so much fear she would flee back to Guangdong, back to the prickly arms of Tung Chao.

At the mention of her brother-in-law, her mind took a sudden twist. Lee Shau Kee's hardened features rose in her mind: his tufts of black hair, the coarse lines around his eyes, his jutting chin—all testified to the menace that dogged her in the Bay City.

She drew the covers up around her neck. She had lost Clark, now *this*. The moment of success, would she have to face another battle? Did she have the strength to fight? Her thoughts took refuge in the past.

When she was a young girl in Guangzhou exploring life among the lily pads in her father's garden pond, she had wondered what love with two people would be like. She would watch two frogs mate, separate, then mate again. The male frog never struck or bit the female. As time went on, and she lost count of the many welts Tung Chee gave her, she would think of the lily pads. Why was she destined never to have the loving kindness known even to the lowliest of garden frogs?

After next morning's breakfast, Chen went to get Officer Clark. Ah had to admit he would be the only one to call—the Kong Chow Company may not to be trusted to be fair in this matter. They had stakes in all community businesses, including Li Fan's.

Who could have broken in the front door and left the death threat in her parlor? Ah fumed, pacing her hallway. Each step on her lotus shoes brought a jolt of hatred. Who would do this to her? To them? The only woman with whom she had recent words had been Li Fan; besides, Cantonese madams would never ruin each other's businesses. Or would they?

The women may share a common hatred, they may spread gossip about another, but it seemed pointless for Li Fan to avenge her this way. Ah shook her head. No matter who did such an atrocious act, the spreading news would twist like grapevines around a stake. Some gossipers may hear the truth; others may hear someone put four pears in the parlor house. People would shake their heads, pretend to be shocked, then spread the news further.

She swallowed hard, considering. Former customers might say her house was diseased, even that men died there. Each telling would carry exaggerations until her place would be empty of johns—no one would dare to visit. The indentured girls would leave her; only loyal Chen might stay until she no longer could afford to pay him. She folded down on the bottom step of her stairs, her soul withered and empty. Why was she not born a frog? Anything would be better than this current life.

After a moment, outside voices grew louder, then someone opened the front door. Clark entered first, doffing his hat, followed by Chen.

A frown smothered Clark's energetic smile. He pointed. "In there?"

She nodded, then leaned against the staircase. Chen stepped over and helped her stand up; together they watched Clark approach and open the parlor door. They followed him inside.

Clark paced the perimeter of the room, looking not only at the pile of crates and the four pears, but also behind chairs and up the fireplace chimney.

Chen said, "In our Chinese beliefs, the number four is a very bad sign of death. Pears mean separation and loss. That is why we are afraid." His chin trembled.

Clark cocked his head and raised his eyebrows. "I heard about the number four from gamblers, but I did not know about pears. Your culture has many powerful superstitions."

Chen said, "Old as centuries."

"Indeed." Clark took another stroll around the display of crates and pears, this time jotting in his notebook.

For some reason, Ah backed out of the room. She could not bear to see the sight of the pears even one more time, and their message of death to her house. She sagged on the settee in the hallway outside.

After some minutes, Clark walked toward her, followed by Chen. "May we talk?"

"Shall we sit in there?" She pointed toward the dining room. She led them to the long table. "Please, sit, you, too, Chen."

And they sat, Ah at the end, the two men on either side of her. Her thigh trembled: Clark was so close. She fought the urge to gaze up at him. Anytime she luxuriated in the sight of him, she paid with regrets afterward. For he would likely never belong to her.

Clark looked around. "Where are your girls? I wish to take their statements."

She gave a heavy sigh. "I sent them to their rooms. I wanted to talk to you before I disturbed them further."

Clark flipped open the leather-bound notebook. "Chen filled me in about the girls' discovery, but I think you might tell me of anyone you suspect." He licked the tip of a blunt pencil, and above his previous notes he wrote "Ah Toy House."

She placed her hands on the table, then laced her fingers together. "Has this ever happened before?"

He shook his head. "Never seen anything like this on my beat. Someone doesn't like you, and that person is trying to send you a message."

She leaned toward him. "What do you mean?"

"Well, I suspect they are bent on ruining your business, or at least your reputation. Whoever did this left scant evidence. No footprints, no traces. Only chisel marks at your front door." His eyes narrowed. "Be aware that whoever did this may not stop here. Do you suspect anyone? Is there anyone who wishes you harm? A dissatisfied john?"

"No one other than Lee Shau Kee whom you know worked for my brother-in-law back in Guangdong. But that was last year, and story says Tung Chao may be giving up his interest in my whereabouts."

"Giving up?" He gave her a probing look. "A jewel like you? Not likely." He shifted in his seat. "Yesterday I saw you in an argument with Li Fan. Could she possibly wish you harm?"

"There is always that possibility, but I would rather not concern you with her at this time. I do not want to stir up the dirt for fear of what she might do in revenge."

His lips parted slightly. "Hmmm. I would keep an eye out for her and have Chen let me know if she acts suspicious."

Chen said, "Do you think she would have someone do this to hurt Mrs. Toy?"

Clark shrugged. "We never know. Our Bay City varmints come in all shapes and sizes. Like I said before, we need to keep our eyes out for anything unusual. If I hear anything being said on the street, I will let you know, but most likely it will be said in Cantonese, so your ears are more valuable than mine."

After a brief interview with San and Yee, Clark gave a short bow before leaving, his smooth cheekbones reflecting the morning light appearing in the hallway. Her longing for him sprang up like a tickling fire; she stood breathless as he took halting steps out the door.

To her own surprise, tears sprang up in her eyes, and she wiped them away with her sleeve. She had lost Clark; now would she lose the parlor house, too?

Eight

❧ SOYBEAN CURD ☙

April 1850

The days passed, and when Clark found Man-Man wandering near the wharf and returned her to the house, Ah Toy continued to worry. The girl would disappear for days at a time, returning to the parlor house disheveled and disoriented. San and Yee stayed to themselves, offering their services to the male customers at the required times, tidying their rooms and washing garments in the early afternoons.

Ah noticed them avoiding Man-Man. Rather than keep her company, after midday meals the girls would vanish into the street together to go to the market. At first, male customers were drawn to Man-Man's exotic looks, her lighter colored hair and eyes, but after lying with her, they would complain she fell asleep before they could obtain the sexual favors they bought.

When Ah talked to Man-Man about it, she said she did not like the way their penis felt inside of her. She said the men's eager entry hurt her, and she was happier when they only lay next to her in the bed. Ah hoped Man-Man would get used to accepting men into her bed and her body. With time, the girl might relax, and the entry would not be as painful. Otherwise, she would be violating an element of her contract—was she a *stone-woman*?

Ah wondered privately if she should take Man-Man to the healer who would know about such matters? But no—she would not take an indentured servant to such a healer. After all, it was her contract that mattered. If the girl did not comply, she would be cast out.

Ah conferred with Chen over the matter of Man-Man's whereabouts, but other than to inspect the local opium dens, Chen had no ideas or solutions. The opium dens were dark—full of threat of kidnap or worse. There had to be a better plan. She brightened. Maybe Officer Wong would know.

Chen hired Flannery's wagon, and they traveled the streets to the office of the Kong Chow Company. Through the half-open door, Ah saw Wong hoist a mighty chopstick full of rice noodles into his mouth. Oh no—they were interrupting Wong's midday meal. His cheeks bulged, but he grabbed his chopsticks, speared some soybean curd and poked it into his mouth. With all that food, his face might pop. But no, with one gulp the mass drained into his gullet.

She clucked her tongue. His eating habits reminded her of sturgeon that fishermen fed in a makeshift aquarium on the wharf. What would she find in Officer Wong's gullet? Live eels? A school of minnows? Octopus legs?

He swallowed water from a glass, and gave her a sideways glance. "Mrs. Toy, I do not like business at mealtime. Who left the door open?" His annoyance was second only to his gluttony—he slurped his soup from the edge of the bowl, and spun his chopsticks around, gathering another conglomeration of noodles. His lips smacked; his burping filled the room.

Ah waited, her attention divided between this live Buddha eating his fill and a painting on the wall of enormous cranes lifting into the air. Though imprisoned on paper, the birds' spirits were free the way she wanted to be.

Her dragon whispered. *Not here, not now. Wong is not a person of trust.* Thus, she worked to squash the desire to blurt out her worst concerns.

Her dragon was right: she would not let Officer Wong know too much about her concerns. She would only fish for information, though he was a big catch, and her net was small.

She seized her chance. "I have a matter to discuss."

He pushed his chair back, his eyes red, his eyelids swollen. Too much plum wine the night before. "I have very little time. What is your issue?"

"My lovely Man-Man whom I bought at your auction—you must remember her beauty—she is lost to me more than once a week. She disappears into the opium dens and comes out sick and troubled. I fear for her safety and what health she may have left."

Officer Wong licked his lips. Was he remembering the last soybean curd he had savored? "I have no power to change your girl's behavior. It is your fault for keeping a disorderly house. You should keep her in a crib. Since you are lax with your rules, if she chooses to leave your house and go somewhere, there is nothing to be done. Nothing a good beating with a whip wouldn't cure." He waved his right hand.

"On your advice, I will tighten my house rules, but I am curious, Officer Wong. Do you *not* want to help me protect this girl in any way possible? After all, you have a stake in my parlor house. If I do well, you do well. I pay taxes, the money you once received from Tung Chao."

Wong rubbed his eyes with his fists. "I need my nap." His voice was softening.

"Before you go to sleep, please think about my concern. Is it not in your best interest to help me?"

He heaved a sigh. "You are your own security, Mrs. Toy."

She fought against the urge to scream. "Why do you *not* do something about the filthy cribs and opium dens that spring up in Little Canton? It gets worse—more dens, more dying—drugged people wander the streets, bump into walls, and lie next to dogs at corners."

He fondled his triple chins. His eyes rose to the ceiling. Was he seeking a complex solution, or merely thinking of a way to get rid of her?

Ah held her tongue.

A few moments passed. At last he spoke. "Cribs and opium dens thrive because they are popular, used not only by Cantonese people but other denizens of this city. I do not discourage them—they help our community make money like your business does." He reached under the table, and Ah heard two pieces of wood scratching on one another. What was he fingering under there—a secret compartment?

He extracted a large gold nugget, the size of his fist, and held it up in the mixed glow from the candle and the doorway. Even in the low light, the ore glimmered. "This kind of money, Mrs. Toy."

Her skin tingled. That size of gold nugget was worth many months running her parlor house. How many had Wong collected?

He fingered the ore sample, fondling its many fissures and crannies. Then he rapped on the table, "Leung!"

A manservant in a blue jacket and black pants strode forward from the next room.

Ah sat back, a Confucian childhood saying rising in her mouth. She said, "The scholar does not consider gold and jade to be precious treasures, but loyalty and good faith."

Wong gave her a close-lipped smile. "Confucius does not live in America." He rapped on his desk and a servant appeared. "My bed, Leung. Take me there."

His manservant pulled out his master's chair and helped Wong to his feet.

Officer Wong clutched the gold piece in his right fist, then rose and glided from the room, his body resembling a large junk, sails adrift, seeking safe harbor.

Had she not resented the power and prestige he carried, Ah would have admired the nonchalant elegance of Officer Wong. He carried himself with such finesse, with such obvious disregard for the people he served.

The next day Ah and Chen ate shrimp and rice in the silent air inside and outside the parlor house. A coal-sized lump sat in her throat, and each swallow of rice brought pain. Yet it was not the swallowing that hurt—it was the ache that Clark had not heard any news, or if so, he had not come by to see how she and Chen were faring after the threat of the four pears had passed.

Her eyes burned, and she swept a tear away with her sleeve. Putting down her chopsticks, she rose from the table. "I cannot eat."

Chen's face mirrored her own unease. "Nor can I. Si tau po, is there somewhere you wish to go this morning?"

"I must think on it. Let me dress and I will let you know."

Chen nodded. "Of course." He backed away, rice bowls in hand, toward the kitchen.

A few moments later in her curtained room upstairs, Ah fingered the silks hanging in her chifforobe. She could hardly see their colors in the dim light. She crossed to the window and drew aside the muslin curtain. The sky above the rooftops was blue—azure blue—the crisp, clear San Francisco morning one knows only in dreams.

The sun's rays warmed her face through the tall window, and she looked down at the tops of men's heads in the street. Some men carried market goods, stalks of bok choy rising from within their bags. Others stopped to consider the bagua above her front door. Though musical, their voices were faint, indistinguishable. She searched the faces down below…no John Clark. Where could he be? Her jaw clenched and she balled her fists.

Turning, she saw her silk jackets catching bits of sun and shadow from the chifforobe's open door. A teal jacket with yellow strips hung in the middle. She would wear that today.

A half an hour later, Chen met her downstairs. "Where do we go now?"

"To Officer Clark's house."

His eyes widened. "Yes, si tau po."

He tendered her down their narrow street, then delivered her into Flannery's wagon waiting at the end of the block. They meandered through the walking crowds of black-jacketed men on Dupont Street.

Nine

❧ THE DRAGON'S WHISPER ❧

Chen was the one who knocked on Clark's door. Ah's palms grew sweaty and damp. The two-story wooden house leaned to one side, like a listing ship. Such was the makeshift way of construction after the many fires, sometimes four a year, that swept through the city. The front door, its nails fighting against the hinges, scratched open on its threshold.

Clark stared down at them, his tousled hair and puffy eyelids reflecting a sleepless night. He wore a frayed blue bathrobe. "What is the matter?" He broke into a crooked grin, but then a frown replaced it.

If only she could reach out and take his face in her hands, then trace a smile back into those lips, she would. Yet much was at stake, so she averted her eyes.

Who wanted so much to ruin her business? Could it be Li Fan? Nothing appeared out of bounds for that snake. A liaison with Wong—including sexual favors—might increase the size of Li Fan's coffers. Would the woman stoop so low?

If only Ah could smash the fears that clung to her like the biting gnats on the Pearl River. After a few moments, her breathing slowed, and there it was—her dragon's presence, carrying wisdom. She considered. The darkness carried sadness and despair, the *yin* of shadow, of the feminine. Within it there was always the glimmer of *yang*, the opposite, the light. For now, she would stay comforted that within the yang she would see the truth of what had happened that night.

Ah said, "We went to see Officer Wong about Man-Man and the opium dens, and we must tell you the details."

"Of course." Clark beckoned them into the dingy sitting room and closed the door behind them. They sat on an aging settee that bowed in the middle. Light from the window filtered through cobwebs lacing the tops of windows. Cigar smoke spiraled from an ash tray sitting on the central round table covered with a dusty gingham cloth.

Ah inhaled, then coughed. She drew out her Empress of China fan, flicked it open and observed the bare-masted ships painted across its surface. Maybe by holding it against her nose and mouth, she could breathe.

After relaying the details of the talk with Wong, Ah sat back, letting her fan drift back and forth in slow, gentle moves.

"Who do you think got Man-Man to try opium?" Clark scratched the stubbles of his day-old beard.

Ah tensed. "The one person who could have enough hatred would be Li Fan. You suspected her yourself when someone left the four pears in our house, and now she may be getting more vicious."

"What makes you say that?" He leaned in closer.

"Li Fan is like the viper who finds the pulsing vein in a weak lamb. She knows Man-Man is vulnerable to this drug."

"What have you done to Man-Man—that is, to stop her?"

"I have whipped poor Man-Man and warned her of dismissal. But she continues to disappear for long periods of time and returns unable to walk straight. What will Li Fan do next? I am afraid to think."

Clark rubbed the back of his neck. "When I warned you and offered you more security, you did not seem to need my help. I can only assist you when you desire it."

Ah fluttered her fan—maybe she could clear the heated air between them.

He continued. "Li Fan is sour on you, and for good reason. You are strong and your parlor house is great shakes among the wealthiest of miners. Your girls are sweet and beautiful. Fan's cribs remain some of the filthiest in Little Canton, and her girls wander the streets, diseased and ill. It's a sin to Moses. Shameful." He wrinkled his nose.

Ah sat back, absorbing his words. He spoke the truth, and she would have to apologize to him, despite her anger and frustration. No matter that he chose his wife over her; no matter that he stayed loyal in a loveless marriage.

Though raised long ago as a pampered highborn daughter, Ah must now lower herself to this man who stole her heart, split it into pieces, then danced upon it. Her dragon's whisper filled her ears. *Humble yourself.*

She lay her fan down, then spread it out across the table. Maybe positive energy would rise from it. "I wish to apologize. I know I have been rude to you. I am showing you how much—"

His expression softened; his gaze fixed on the fan. "Yes. Go on."

"I wish to prove that Li Fan is behind Man-Man and her opium habit. I must guard my parlor house, Chen, and my girls." She emphasized each word, tapping one of the ships painted across the fan.

Clark frowned, plainly wary. "In order to do that you must have proof. Tangible evidence that she, or whoever she hired, took Man-Man to the opium house and encouraged her to go there often. If you cannot prove this, you will have no case."

She inched closer to him. "When I bring suit against Li Fan, will you talk to Judge Almond again and testify on my behalf?"

He reddened, maybe hurt that she did not trust him. "Of course. Have I not always defended your person and your business concerns?"

Each word fell on her like drops of water on a dry lakebed. *He cared for her.* She wanted time to stop—to hold the words—there—inside each minute or second they could be with each other, though the next fleeting moment would tear them apart.

Ah heard footsteps. Their moment faded the way starlight does at dawn.

A feeble voice called from the direction of the hallway. "John?"

Ah clutched her fan . . . it would be Susannah, his wife . . . she would be tall, graceful, blond hair in a chignon . . . like the white ladies smiling out at her from fashion advertisements in the broadsheets.

The door swung open. Instead of the stately mistress, a frail, bent, woman with straggly brown-gray hair stood at the threshold. Her day dress sagged like a gray sail in calm winds. Her face, though illuminated by sapphire eyes, bore the crisscrossed lines of twice-used rice paper.

Clark rose and stepped to her. "You need to stay in bed."

"No, I heard voices. I would like to meet your company." After introductions Susannah wheezed lightly, but then a deep, scurrilous cough followed, shaking her frame. Sputum bubbled on her lips, and Clark pulled a handkerchief from his pants pocket and wiped off a line of blood seeping onto her chin.

Clark settled her into the rocking chair and covered her with a quilt. He spread the covering over her shoulders, then tucked the sides around her.

Susannah surveyed her surroundings, then closed her eyes, her breathing a series of rumblings across a distant plain.

Ah knew the signs. The poor woman must be dying. She exchanged a knowing glance with Chen, then rose and stepped out into the hallway.

Clark followed her and Chen from the entryway into the street. "My wife has not long now. Doctor Johnson says her consumption eats the fabric of her lungs. Soon she will be unable to breathe, and she will go to heaven." He looked skyward, his eyes watering.

Ah lifted her hand toward him, then let it fall to her side. Clark's pain was not hers to share; instead, it belonged to a deep and lasting love for someone other than himself. The realization hit her. This man was far above any men she had known, other than Chen, her loyal servant.

Clark persisted in a loveless marriage in order to keep Susannah alive as long as possible. Not for his sake—but for her own. Ah had never met a man like that. One who cared so much for another he would sacrifice his own happiness and satisfaction in order to prolong a life.

Any jealousy, any wishes that she and Clark might find love together were tucked away into a box in her mind. These selfish thoughts paled in comparison to the shining lamp of his devotion to Susannah. *He was a good man.* Though Ah had long suspected it, now she was sure.

Ten

❦ THE STRANGE, SWEET FLOWER ❦

After Flannery's wagon delivered Ah and Chen to the parlor house, San met them on the threshold. The girl's pale face had lost its luster, and her forehead wrinkled in concern. "Man-Man is missing again. This time I think it is bad."

"What makes you think that?" Ah shuffled back a step.

San spoke in rapid Cantonese. "She has gotten very weak, and when I confronted her this morning, she said she might never return. When I asked her why, she said only smoking in the dens brought her true happiness."

"This has happened very fast." Chen's eyes widened.

San shook her head. "Man-Man said she cannot get to sleep in the parlor house. She does not like men on top of her. There in the den she can dream peaceful dreams."

"Do you know which den?" Ah asked.

"No, but I know the area of the quarter. There are many cribs and dens in that place, and she most likely goes there. She mentions the name Kuang a time or two, especially when she is in her delirium. We could try to find him. Maybe he would know."

Some force pulled Ah into the ground. What could she do? She turned to Chen, "We must not linger. If she is that sick, Man-Man may be heading toward her final days. I know the opium dens in Guangzhou. My brother said once men disappeared inside, they were changed forever, only to die when the smoke ate their brains."

Chen nodded. "I have heard of many cases. The drug takes them and drowns them in its perfume."

What kind of mindless, senseless death was that? Ah shuddered. In the past weeks she had watched the vibrant face of Man-Man turn sallow, her gaze listless, unfocused. A stone-woman was one of the three great sicknesses. What had the contract said? Ah strained to remember. Then she saw it in her mind's eye. The *"stone-woman," inability to have carnal intercourse with men.* The contract's words tore, sharp as razor cuts, across her memory.

A few hours later, dusk descended around Ah as she followed Chen through the streets of Little Canton. Amid a low hum of voices, the shopkeepers closed up their displays; they unrolled bamboo shades over the entrance to their stalls and carried baskets of fruit back into the stores for safekeeping.

Chen's footsteps slowed in front of her. "This makes five opium dens, and no one knows the name Kuang. I am hungry and tired, *si tau po.* Please, can we go home to rest?"

Seagulls landed on empty market crates, poked at stray lettuce leaves, and carried them away. Late day voices and sounds of drawers opening and closing replaced the din of midday voices and the jangle of cart horses' livery bells. Shopkeepers counted their day's bills and coins, and stuffed them into bags for the next day's bank deposit.

Chen was right. Unless they stopped now, she would be too exhausted to search the following day. She pictured him bringing her warm water and herbal medicines, wrapping her sore feet after long walks. Yet—she could make one last stop. "Chen, please. Only one more. Unless we find Man-Man, we may lose her."

He stopped, then turned back, his gaze plainly weary. "This is the last time we walk so far. You will suffer tomorrow."

"I know." Ah looked down at her lotus shoes. Her bound feet were the curse she must bear, the mountain she must overcome.

She straggled behind Chen into one last opium den tucked behind a clothing shop. They descended a flight of stairs into hellish darkness. Dampness clung to the walls. Dingy rows of bunk beds lined each room. She peered into the incense-filled haze, inhaling sweat mixed with a strange flower's perfume. After her eyes adjusted to the light, she saw men's and women's jackets, camisoles, and petticoats hung on pegs on the filthy wall.

She drew back, trembling. White women, too? This drug was no arbiter of gender, class or race—all who succumbed invited death. A rhythmic sound filled the air. Each time someone drew smoke from an opium pipe, she heard the *aahh—oohh* of inhaling, then exhaling. She waved away the smoke whirling around her head. Her eyes burned, and she blinked several times.

Chen spoke to a Cantonese man with gaunt cheeks. He turned back to Ah. "This is Kuang. We have found him at last!"

Though Ah's heart raced, she stayed at a distance, fearing what she might discover next.

Kuang struck a match and lit a candle, then passed it to Chen. He said, "I do remember Man-Man. In fact, she is a frequent customer. Follow me." He tiptoed toward a dark corner of the chamber. "Watch your step."

Ah skirted piles of men's urine-stained trousers, pairs of mismatched leather shoes, and half-eaten plates of food. She reached out for Chen's arm and found it. In the darkness he remained a shadow, his face lit only by the occasional glimmer from the wall sconces and the flash of the candle in his hand.

Kuang stopped, surveyed the customers, then pointed to the corner. Men lay about in bunks, bare-chested, bare-footed. Disturbing noises swirled around her—occasional coughs, moans, sighs, then nonsense words uttered within fitful dreams. She gave a sniff. A drift of feces. Of course, she should have known. Bodily functions were no longer controlled under the drug's influence. How deep had Man-Man tumbled into this dark well?

Chen bore the sputtering candle high above his head. "There," he said.

Ah drew closer—yes, there she was. She sucked in a breath. Man-Man's once-luxurious brown hair now lay in tangles around her recumbent form. She huddled against the wall, a beige blanket lying across her hips. Her body lay quite still—her swollen tongue emerged from between her lips. Dried saliva spun a lacy web across her open mouth.

Kuang jabbed her, but the girl made no response.

Chen rolled her over onto her back. "Here. We need more light over her." He passed the candle to Kuang who held it up higher.

Chen reached out and felt the girl's neck. He turned back and shook his head. "No pulse."

Ah took a step closer.

Man-Man's hazel eyes rested in a fixed, glassy gaze.

Ah held a sob in check. What did the girl see out of those eyes? She who had abandoned earth, its peoples, its problems. The flickering light illuminated Man-Man's cheek, indented from being pressed against the pillow. How long had she been dead? If only she had gotten here earlier, maybe she could have saved her. But this—.

An opium pipe rested beside the girl on the bed. Even within the thick sweetness of the drug, Chen plainly caught the whiff of Man-Man's decay—the pungent odor of her flesh gone stale. He groaned.

Ah watched him spread his right hand over his nose. Watching him, she experienced the dull sensation of nausea rising in her gut, so she flicked open her fan and held it up to her nose and mouth.

Kuang said, "I must summon the proprietor. This will be reported. Last time a man died, I ignored him and I got whipped."

Overcome with dizziness, Ah staggered away, skirting piles of clothing, cast-off pipes, and men snoring on the floor. She found her way outside and vomited into the street. Drawing a handkerchief from her pouch, she wiped her lips.

In a few moments, Chen tapped her elbow. "What must I do, si tau po?"

"Run for Clark. He will know what to do."

"But you are unwell. You skin is ashen."

"Go—I will be fine. Get Clark."

He sped away down the street, the sound of his swift footsteps growing faint, then dying away.

The street revolved around, and she retched. She gave in to the spasms until no food came up, only bile. Again, she wiped her mouth. She could not rid herself of the sweet aroma of death. She sniffed her sleeve. The stale perfume of decaying flesh mixed with the flowery smell of opium and incense lingered in the fabric of her qipao. However she tried, would she be able to free herself not only of the vision, but also of the greasy film clinging to her body?

She closed her eyes, reached back for the comforting surface of the clapboard wall, and leaned her hips against it. Then, bending over her knees, she absorbed the smell of horse dung and rotting garbage lying in the street. How welcomed it was—so much better that than the stench of human death.

Eleven

❧ CURIOUS LOOKS ❧

*S*oon after Chen's race to find him, Clark arrived, swinging his night stick. Ah noticed his face was drawn and severe. After a brief greeting, he and Chen disappeared inside the opium den. Night was falling, and shadows were lengthening Except for pinpricks of light from the occasional window, the street was turning into a dark passage. Inside their shanties, denizens lit their candles, then moved with them from room to room.

Out of a corner of her eye, Ah saw a sharp burst of a match flame at street level. A trio of Cantonese men observed her from under the overhang across the street. One smoked a pipe, the other two puffed fat cigars. She strained to see their faces. Were they looking at her with the usual curiosity? If only she could make out their idle chatter. The presence of a policeman might signal one of two things: an arrest or a murder. The tall man under the overhang tipped his black hat toward her, his head cocked and ready for news. He would relish being the first to know and report the latest story.

After long minutes, Chen walked backward out of the building, carrying his end of a stretcher. Clark held the other end. Man-Man's body was wrapped with a dingy sheet, dampened with brown smears. They stepped into the street.

She tiptoed up to Clark. "Where will you take her?"

The perfume of rot and opium clung to him. He said, "I will make a full report at the precinct, but I will deliver her to Officer Wong for disposal."

"Why Officer Wong, and not the police department? Do you trust him?"

"In such cases, the coroner's office defers to the Kong Chow Company—they will determine whether to bury her in San Francisco or to ship her bones to Guangdong. Officer Wong will find out where her family resides. It is an unofficial agreement with the coroner's office. I could take her to the coroner, but she would end up with Officer Wong anyway. Might as well save time."

"I see." Ah recognized the informal formalities of the town's young legal order.

"It is best for you to return to your parlor house. May I take Chen with me to Officer Wong?"

"But I want to help."

"I know you are worried, but you can do little for Man-Man now. She has gone to heaven. Best go back and comfort your girls. They will wonder where you are, and I do not want them wandering the streets looking for you and Chen."

With reluctance Ah stepped away down DuPont Street toward Pike. She could not seem to shake off her sadness. Was she responsible for Man-Man's death? Had she done or said something to cause her to become a *stone-woman*? A thoughtless comment? A command? What had she overlooked? Or worse, had one of her clients injured her? Maybe she had been too afraid to report the abuse. Had Li Fan been involved, encouraging poor Man-Man? At any rate, it was too late now—that secret had spiraled away in opium smoke.

She remembered Man-Man's trembling beauty the day she stepped forward from the line on the wharf. She shook her head. Such a pitiful end to one so young. Such an exceptional beauty, sold into slavery, lost in the world of the opium dens with no hope of redemption. Man-Man would never find her true love, never marry or raise a family. She would never hold a grandchild or kiss the cheek of an old friend. She would never grow old on this earth.

Once inside the parlor house, Ah stepped to her altar and lit a stick of incense. The tap-tap of the girls' footsteps on the floorboards above broke the silence of the room from time to time.

After she collapsed onto her knees, she invoked the Goddess Mazu. *Dear Goddess, give me the words to tell the girls about Man-Man, and yet fill them with hope that their futures will be brighter and full of grace. Though I failed Man-Man somehow, I must make their lives better so they will never seek comfort in an opium den.*

Her dragon curled in the silence, slumbering within her, its dreams luring her into deep contemplation.

After two weeks passed Ah surveyed the morning street from her open doorway. Too early for the usual peddlers and wagons that wended their way through town. Too early for passersby who strode briskly toward their markets or the wharf.

She wearied of the invisible blanket that settled around her, her dragon barely stirring these days. She had not seen Clark in the streets since Man-Man's death. Her being ached for him—even a glance of his crossing a distant street or lingering with another officer at Portsmouth Plaza would bring her joy.

Though she had wished him to be almost dead to her, she worried that she had gone too far with her wants. Life was empty and useless without him, an empty soup bowl set before a starving child.

Maybe she needed to seek a fortune teller who would examine her face and tell her about herself. She could not remember the last time she had gotten her fortune told, but she was sure it was in Guangzhou.

"Chen," she raised her voice. Maybe he could hear her from the drawing room where he was setting the morning fire.

He appeared, rubbing his hands on a rag. "Yes, si tau po. Is it about the leak?" He stared down at the rag.

"What leak?"

Chen raised his eyebrows. "The one I told you about—in the front bedroom. San says it is over the bed, and when it rains, it is bad for business. She has had to lie with her customer under the bed the last time it rained."

What would she do without Chen keeping track of the house? She said, "Oh, yes, now I remember. I am glad you reminded me. Today while I am at the fortune teller, you must get the carpenter to repair the roof. We cannot lose any business over it."

He slung the rag over his shoulder. "I will do that. Now shall I call for Flannery to take you to the fortuneteller? I know he usually waits for the market to open. I can catch him if I go now."

"Yes—he should be around the block on Spofford Street." She set her jaw.

"So, you are not going to Tien Hau Temple, but instead to the face fortune teller?"

"Yes, Chen. You are most perceptive."

"I have had a good fortune told there, si tau po."

"Let us hope that is true for me as well." For a moment, her eyes lingered on his. She drew strength from the light burning within him, the confidence he conveyed.

An hour later, Ah sat before the fortune teller. His robes draped a violet purple, his ancient face deeply grooved. Though it was morning, the heavy curtain in the room cast deep shadows across the wooden floor.

The fortune teller set his elbows on the table and he observed her over steepled fingers. "First, Ah Toy, you must tell me of your ancestry, of your parentage. I must know of your father." His voice resonated with wisdom, love, and experience. His tone was soft, his voice inviting.

After relating her Cantonese parentage, she sat across the table from him while he measured the areas of her face. He paused from time to time to check his charts and books, then continued to examine her eyebrows, forehead, length and shape of nose, size of cheeks, her lips, and chin.

After many minutes of study, the fortuneteller sat back, his black eyes glinting in the light from the lantern. "Are you ready, my little bird?"

"Yes, please tell me."

"Your face has matching eyes and eyebrows, so you will marry a handsome one. You are fortunate; not many of those I see have such even features. Many eyes droop or the eyebrows are too thin, too thick, or too wavy to be straight. Yours are evenly matched, symmetrical."

"Who will that handsome one be? And when?"

"My art tells me only what is on your face; the other details are up to the fates. And up to you—" He paused, and a shadow crept across his face. The lantern flickered.

A feeling of unease tingled in her spine. "Yes?" For an instant, words failed her.

"There is something missing now, something you must do, little bird." He drew back into the shadows, the candle lighting his hands which floated over his reference books.

Her hands trembled. "Please—tell me and I will do it."

His fingers formed a steeple. "I have told fortunes for forty years, yet I have never come upon one who possesses an inner dragon. I sense its latent fire, even when I touch your cheek and measure your lips. You contain an inner flame that can easily be bent toward evil, yet you have a generous heart that sees truth in life."

She touched her throat. "I have never told anyone about it—I knew it was there, but I did not understand."

He spoke in a quiet voice. "Little bird, you are a daughter of the Dragon King. Since you have attained wealth, you may think you have already reached enlightenment, but you are mistaken. From an early time, you have been defiled and are not a pure vessel of the Law."

She drew back. "I have been debased, yes, but that was the fault of my murderous husband."

"Perhaps the fates decreed you had to endure those trials. Without your purity, you must normally be reborn again and again, and carry out the practice of Buddhist austerities over a period of many lifetimes, in order to finally be able to obtain the enlightened life condition of Buddhahood."

Her heart sank. First, she would marry a handsome man, but now she would face multiple rebirths before she attained nirvana. That would take more eternities than she could count, more than a flock of cranes rising over the marshlands.

"What must I do, teacher?" She swept away a tear meandering down her cheek.

"Unless you continually stoke the dragon's energy, it will die. You must pay attention to its signs and signals, for the dragon is the gift of the king. Without the king's defense, you will be lost."

She shifted in her chair. "But I am discouraged and saddened. I have encountered death, I have lost a man I love, and I am very lonely."

"No matter, little bird. Summon your dragon to you. Listen for its messages. Let it carry you on his back. Your fate and its fate are one. Do not disappoint your king. Or yourself."

He rose, his purple robes reflecting the lantern's glow.

Part Four

And once again we meet
The bay breeze lifts our song
Interrupting it
Tossing it away against the clouds
And if you wonder if I regret our parting?
It is a tangle of vines
Whirling
Endless twine, the life of the heart.

IN THE MANNER OF LI PO

One

❧ THE GRASS GROWS GREEN ❧

June 1851

Ah watched another year roll away; the seventh deadly fire roared over the city, destroying three-quarters of the buildings. Sawdust mixed with mud as Mayor Geary and the city fathers busied teams of workmen to rebuild the skeletal town. Each day Ah gave thankful offerings that Goddess Mazu had spared her parlor house, but Sydney Ducks threatened to torch any new building, and the community lived in fear of another conflagration. She kept her distance from Li Fan who appeared often with her withered girls in the marketplace.

Henry would send her letters from China every six weeks, only to say he would let her know when he would return to marry her. For now, he was a forest in the background of her tapestry, not the central figure. She took comfort when the Daileys sent word every few months, along with God's blessing.

Clark continued to walk his beat, and Ah managed to shorten any meeting with him, trying to calm her quaking heart. His wife continued to linger in her illness. How much longer could the poor woman last? By all accounts, her lungs consisted of tissue paper.

Customers continued their visits to Ah's parlor house, sleeping with San or Yee under a roof well repaired, their beds clean and dry. Jade prowled the street outside, and nosed the parlor house rooms for the odd mouse. The feline seemed extra vigilant since the four pears had invaded the house.

Ah noted the many nations represented as she wrote the customers' names in her ledger—Californios, Spanish, French, Sandwich Islanders, British, French. Along with the east coast Americans, young lanky men visited with starlit eyes, fresh from the mines with gold in their pockets.

When they entered the parlor house, she continued to make certain demands. The men would stand in front of her. She would sniff them for opium, front to back, then clear the air with her fan. She pinched her nose against the traces of urine, whiskey, and tobacco that clung to their bodies. Afterwards, Chen would guide them down the hallway to the bath where they were given a good soaping and toweling off before meeting San or Yee.

The city had expanded from a few hundred in 1849 to the current population of over 25,000. These days Ah kept to the business of running the parlor house. She continued to be wary of certain men who came to the house—any drunk Australian was quickly turned away. She also made it her practice to listen outside the girls' rooms when customers were present. The normal rhythm of bed springs was of no concern; harsh sounds or exclamations and she would open the door and make sure her girls were not harmed.

Chen confiscated all gunslinger's pistols and stored them in a special room. A knife or slungshot was held and not returned until the owners had done their business and were well out the door.

Ah continued to worry. The Sydney Ducks increased their menace, robbing businesses and leaving their owners for dead. They prowled the streets, using women and children as scouts, attacking and robbing their unsuspecting victims.

To that end, Ah gave San and Yee revolvers to keep in their drawers next to the bed, and Chen had shown them how to use the weapons. Ah was clear in her instructions: at any sign of abuse, the girl was to pull on the bell chord to summon Chen. He expressed fear that he alone could not fully protect the house from the daily violence outside.

That morning, Ah practiced her English, spreading out *the Daily Alta California* across the table, pushing aside her tea pot and cup. The police were going after the Sydney Ducks again after their latest arson strike. Her headache began its familiar thrum.

"Chen!" she called.

"Yes, si tau po." He yelled from the kitchen.

"Come and tell me what you know."

"About what?" He appeared with a dishtowel flung over his right shoulder, his face wet with dishwashing steam. "If it is about the cook and dishwasher, they did not show up this morning. I do not know where they are, and I have been cleaning up the mess they left last night."

"Never mind that for the moment—there is something here in the *Alta*."

He cast a shadow over the paper from where he stood behind her, peering at the newsprint from over her shoulder.

She glanced up at him, then pointed to the paper. "See what it says here—a new militia is calling itself the Committee of Vigilance. You know anything about this?"

He shifted to the side of the table. "I heard stories, but I thought they were just rumors. Now there is much talk in the streets about this Committee. Story says it is made up of business leaders fed up with the crime in our town."

She tapped the broadsheet. "I do not blame them. They have endured so much loss of property. Every time they rebuild, the Hounds, the white-male gang of hoodlums from New York, or the Sydney Ducks, burn it down."

Reaching over the table, he placed his hand on the article, his eyes moving back and forth over the page. After a moment he said, "Remember they held a trial for two men back in February, bypassing the courts and Mayor Geary?"

She looked over at him. "Yes, I seem to remember, but the details are hazy."

"Story is that the Sydney Ducks are planning another arson sweep across the city, destroying as many buildings as possible. This time they aim to devastate everything in town—including everyone living here." His Cantonese words came slowly this time.

She bit her lower lip. "So many more people live here now—they might end up murdering more if this happens again. These Australians are vicious." She trembled. "But maybe these new Vigilantes are good."

He lifted his hand from the paper and rested it under his chin. "No, si tau po. They are taking the law into their own hands. That is not good."

"Why not? If they plan to fight against the Ducks, they would have our support."

"They will not only go against the Ducks. Rumor says they will clean up Little Canton, getting rid of all opium dens, parlor houses, and gambling. Many Cantonese businesses would be forced to close. They want to send all immigrants back to their homelands."

"Our Kong Chow Company would protect us." She scratched the back of her hand.

He gave her a glance that would melt iron. "Would it be able to stand up to forces greater than itself?"

She checked her breath. "I do not understand your suspicion." Sometimes Chen spoke with an authority he should not have.

His gaze became intense. "Word is the Vigilantes are made of people who hate anyone who is not white. Their vengeance is fueled by desire to cleanse the city of unwanted populations. They say we Cantonese take away their jobs." He clasped his hands together, whitening his knuckles.

"That is hard to believe. Our Little Canton is thriving, and I do not see the whites interfere. We mix with them, they mix with us. We do our business, they do theirs."

Chen breathed out. "That is the reason they hate us. They are angry we are taking their business away from them, in addition to the land they claim as rightfully theirs. Their anger simmers below the surface."

"What are we to do?" She hated this feeling of helplessness, of being controlled by forces larger than she was, invisible powers that held her down.

"Time will tell." He gave her a deferential nod and backed away toward the kitchen.

"I worry now that time is not enough," she said.

The next day brought a heavy rain that fell in curtains between Ah's doorstep and the mud-covered street. She dreaded going in and out in weather that made walking even more difficult, but her headache was pounding. People said a horse had drowned in the deep mud the day before—what if she slipped into it herself?

Chen summoned a wagon, and their driver Flannery stopped and let her off at her favorite herbalist on Stockton Street. After delivering her onto the plank walkway, Chen lit a cigar and took up guard outside the herbalist.

A soft bell chimed as she pushed open the door. A man in a deep brown Mandarin jacket stood at the far end of the counter.

She reached out and shook his hand. "Please—something for a headache."

After releasing her hand, the herbalist motioned her to sit on a stool while he stood before more than fifty drawers containing various herbs and ancient Chinese medicines. "Tell me your symptoms."

She closed her red umbrella; the rainwater slipped off and dripped onto the plank floor. Her temples pulsated. An iron band seemed to enclose the back of her skull, adding weight when she moved her head.

The doorbell rang again, and two men took their places behind her in a makeshift line.

She bent toward the herbalist and lowered her voice. "I have frequent throbbing in my skull—back here." She palmed the crown of her head. "Sometimes the hurt expands around my head, like a harness holding a horse's bit. When I have troubles, the band grows tighter."

He nodded. "Your head is the confluence of yang, closely connected with all your other body parts. Your organs are connected through the flow of *qi* through the meridians or the collection of acupuncture points. Would you like me to try my needles with you today? We could go to my room back there. Many of my patients tell me they have great relief from acupuncture." He gestured to a hallway, a yellow silk curtain creating a divider between rooms.

She shook her head. "No, I have tried acupuncture, but all I want today is some herbs to quell the pain."

"Very well. Let me see your tongue," He bent across the counter, his eyebrows knitted together.

She opened her mouth and stuck it out. After a few seconds of lifting, poking and tapping her tongue, he drummed his fingertips on the counter. "As I expected. It is purple. "

"What color should it be?" she asked.

"The healthy tongue is pink. Tell me, daughter—how long have you had these headaches?"

"They started in Guangzhou when my husband would hit me."

He frowned. "Where did he strike you?"

"He would cuff me about the head when he said I disobeyed him. Once he took a big stick and beat me about the head. I could not remember anything more, and I was dizzy for a long time after that."

He tilted his head. "I am sorry to hear about your bad fortune in the past life. I believe you have a headache that is the result of those injuries— it will persist, especially in times of great worry."

A surge of gratitude flowed within her, and for a moment she forgot her headache. He seemed to understand in a way no one else did. "What can you do for me?" She blinked away the blurriness.

He gave a half-nod. "I can put together a prescription that will activate your blood and help your *qi* flow more smoothly." He thus busied himself, opening and shutting various drawers, filling small green envelopes with dried herbs. Each of his movements gave her hope— maybe soon he could take away her pain.

Meanwhile, two Cantonese men waiting in line behind her were engaged in conversation, and during the interim, she caught their words. She turned her head slightly, enough to gauge the speakers, then to eavesdrop.

The squat man with a long mustache spoke first. "They say it is to be at midnight. Jenkins will be eating his last dinner tonight."

"What are they hanging him for?" The tall man next to him picked a side tooth with his fingernail.

The other fondled his mustache. "Stole a safe from an office. Supposed to be full of money."

"That deserves a hanging. Seems a bit harsh." He licked his lips.

"Law says it is grand larceny, a hanging crime."

"How do you know?" He squinted, plainly skeptical. Vigilante gossip provided entertainment to the town; most of the time the rumors were unfounded.

"Officer Clark." The squat man drew himself up, plainly proud of his superior knowledge.

"Why would you believe him? He is merely a policeman. They know nothing."

"Not anymore. He is now in the special patrol of the Vigilante Committee."

"Since when?"

The squat man sniffed. "He told me as of yesterday. He even showed me his enrollment badge. Looks official."

"News to me, hmmm . . . So, it is tonight? Where?" His voice lowered, and Ah strained to hear the answer.

"Plaza. Word is they'll hang him from the flagpole in the center of the Plaza or somewhere they can find a beam."

The other man clucked his tongue. "Hmmm. Serves him right for what he did."

She tensed. A Vigilante hanging. Such an event would draw crowds. Clark would be there—would she have a chance to see him? She must tell Chen. For a moment she thought she detected her dragon stirring, but no—she must have been mistaken.

A voice broke into her thoughts.

"Mrs. Toy, here is your remedy." The herbalist gathered the envelopes, folded them in a page of notes, and passed them across the counter to her. "You must unblock your orifices and invigorate your blood. Take this mixture of Chinese safflower, red peony root, and musk with green onion stalk. You will find that it will activate your *yang qi*, promote your blood flow, and regulate your spleen."

"Very well," she said. Even the sound of his precise directions gave her some relief.

He tapped a small green bottle. "Here is some yellow rice wine and fresh ginger to mix with it." After he deposited the lot in a sack covered with Chinese calligraphy, he smiled. "May good fortune and good health abide with you, Mrs. Toy."

She gathered the sack and lifted her umbrella. "How often do I take the medicines?"

"Follow the administrations on this paper. You should start to feel better in a day or two. Come back if you need more medicines." His eyes crinkled.

She handed him a gold coin.

He bit it, then dropped it into the till.

Ah turned and elbowed past the two Cantonese men in line behind her. She gave a silent prayer. *Thank you Goddess Mazu for two things—*

first for the gifts of medicines for my headaches—second for letting me hear about the hanging and Clark's name again today. I miss him so. It has been so long, I thought you had forgotten my love for him.

With that she flashed open her umbrella and stepped onto the planks facing the muddy street, the bag of medicines swinging on her arm. Chen brightened at her appearance. "Can you hail Flannery's wagon?" she asked, pointing at two drivers and their wagons resting their horses at the end of Kearny Street. Chen called Flannery's name, and one driver clucked his mule toward her.

"Where to? Swinney's dyin' o' boredom." Flannery driver leaned down, his tattered hat covering one eye. The mule eyed her with interest.

"Pike Street," Chen said.

"Take the long way—that way Swinney can stretch her legs," Ah said. Once on board the wagon, she rested the bag of herbal remedies on her lap—they must work so she could attend the hanging that night.

Two

❧ A STRANGE QUIET ☙

That evening's moon illuminated the ordinarily black streets, a rare sight since Ah rarely peeked from behind the night curtains at her parlor house. The only other light shining on the streets was from the occasional saloon, torches carried by a gaggle of men, or a lantern carried by a night watchman. The *clop-clop* of Swinney pulling their wagon echoed up and down the dim and vacant muddy lanes as they wended their way toward the Plaza.

An eerie calm clutched the streets, as if some unholy act were about to take place. In Guangzhou, the town was always deathly quiet before the mobs emerged to satisfy their bloodlust at a scene of execution. Her father took her as a child to witness the quartering of a thief—he said it was to teach her to follow the righteous path. She could still see the long, stringy white tubes pulled out of the screaming accused. Blood everywhere. The scene haunted her dreams for years. Yet something compelled her to go witness this scene of rough justice. Maybe it was the hope that with this hanging, the town's chaos would end. Maybe this hanging would change their hateful talk about Little Canton.

Next to her Chen cleared his throat, and her ideas took another path.

No matter she was no longer in Guangzhou—no matter she was in San Francisco—savagery rose in the human breast whenever it had the chance. And where were the townspeople at this hour? She speculated, fingering the tip of her fan. The few women in the town would be nestling in their beds or comforting their babes in arms.

Cantonese men would stay in their quarters, away from these benders of law and order. Sydney Ducks would be lurking about with their thieves, planning their pickpocketing moves as the crowds converged. The Californios would stay away, long since experienced in the cruel, haphazard attacks from the Sydney Ducks who preyed on the unsuspecting edges of a crowd.

With a jolt, their wagon reached the edge of the Plaza. Swinney the mule halted before a line of rough-dressed men bearing rifles. One stepped forward. "Go no further." The Vigilante's face bore a frown like a theater mask—his eyes were fierce and penetrating.

Flannery turned, holding Swinney's reins tightly against the oncoming crowd. "I canna go no further, lads."

"I am not sure this is a good idea." Chen's eyes darted around at the growing mob.

"Perhaps not, but we must go on. Besides, Officer Clark is here, and he will guard us." If only her belief was as firm as her voice.

"If you say so." Yet Chen shook his head, plainly skeptical. After planting his feet on the ground, he reached up and pulled Ah down from the wagon. She felt him wrapping her woolen cloak around her. His hands were strong but gentle. "You should pull the hood over your head, si tau po. Men will recognize you."

She anchored a hand on her hip. "Why are you worried that someone will recognize me here? Look—these men are busy waiting for *that*—they are not interested in me." She pointed across the Plaza toward a crowd of men amassing around the south end of an old adobe building.

The lights from within the building pierced the darkness of the Plaza, and dozens of men approached from Kearny, Clay and Dupont Streets. Many in the throng shouldered rifles that glinted under the torches they carried.

For once, the summer's night fog abandoned the city, and she held her head back: a canopy of brilliant stars blinked overhead. The moonlight silvered the open landscape, tinting the edges of buildings, sides of faces, and raised bayonets in the Plaza. Around her and Chen, male voices hummed insistently, so many angry bees whose hives had been disturbed.

Within a few minutes, the mob doubled in size, and the voices grew louder. "We want justice! Law and order! Hang him now!" The throngs raised the chant, slowly at first, then at a faster pace, accompanied by the stamping of feet and thumping of rifle butts on the ground. The occasional sound of gunfire broke into the chorus.

Ah's senses pulsated: the mob fused into one beating heart whose blood ran with not only vengeance, but also trepidation. What had these men to fear? Her father had told her about such rebellions in China. They were going against the very laws they believed in, yet they were bent on breaking those laws in the name of order. According to her father's stories, this would end badly.

Pushed to the middle of the crowd, she stood straight as a toothpick, held upright by the crush of a hundred men. A hand touched the back of her shoulder. What was that? She glanced behind her.

Chen loomed tall and straight. "I am right here. Do not be worried."

She sighed into her bound feet, and let out a breath. Something caught her attention. Was that a spark or flame? She glanced to her right. A man in the crowd puffed on a cigar, and the smoke formed sweet, choke-inducing haze above the heads in the crowd. With sudden force, a ripple of shouts swept through the crowd.

"What is happening?" She turned back to Chen.

"Look over there!" He pointed toward someone who stood on sandbank in front of the Rassette House on the Plaza.

From her view, the man looked small, but he had his hands on his hips, appearing to wait for the crowd to calm. Something about the man looked familiar. "Who is he?" she asked.

Chen's whisper penetrated the hood of her cloak. "Sam Brannan."

"The same Sam Brannan we met at the Larkin house in Monterey?"

"He owns the store and he is a member of the Vigilance Committee."

"How do you know all of this? They do not tell their stories to Cantonese men."

"In the tea shop I learn everything." His high cheekbones reflected the torchlights flaming in the crowd.

Ah understood the swift communication common to her people, so she gazed again at the man Chen called Brannan. That same man had sat at the dinner table that night at the Larkin House. She struggled to see through and over the tops of the man-crowd, but Brannan was shouting out something, and gradually, the voices quelled. Rather than their formerly venomous pitch, the tone shifted to cautious excitement.

And where was Clark? If only she could find him in the crowd. She drew herself up as tall as she could on her lotus shoes, but soon gave up trying. Her small stature was no match for the human forest.

Brannan's words soared into the crowd like so many heated arrows. "I have been charged by the Committee of Vigilance with telling you that the accused, John Jenkins, has been fairly tried, found guilty, and has been sentenced to death within the hour. Do the people approve the action of the Committee?"

A fierce roar rose from the depths of the crowd, like thunder rumbling in thick rainclouds. Although a few "nays" were shouted, the rolling cadence of "hang him" quashed the dissenters.

Jerked back by the motion of the throng, Ah lost her footing. She tumbled against a tall bearded man next to her, and her hood came off, revealing her hair which fell in a cascade around her shoulders.

"What is this? Celestial girl?" The whites of his eyes glinted like eggshells in the silvery light.

No time to grab Chen. Where was her dragon now? Yet as she glared at the man beside her, she noticed something familiar about him. He wasn't—couldn't be—Harold Painter from that day on the wharf so long ago. She rarely forgot a face, probably out of self-defense.

Though Painter was not what she would call a good man, he had been on the side of the law in San Francisco, such as it was. At least he was not a Sydney Duck. Maybe he would know where Clark was tonight.

"Mr. Painter?" She tapped his arm.

He looked startled at the sound of his own name. "How do ya know me?"

Chen pressed up against Ah's back, and she relaxed, knowing she had security—at last. Almost as good as her dragon's.

She fluttered her fan to move the rank air which clung to Painter's clothing. "I am Ah Toy." She was forced to raise her voice to almost a shout in the roaring crowd.

Painter bent down toward her; his pock-marked face lit by the torches around them. "I remember now…some gorgeous eyes you got…we talked on the wharf that day. You were looking for someone. Say, did you ever find him?" He removed his squash cap and scratched his balding head.

"You must have forgotten—Lee Shau Kee—you said you had deport-ed him."

His thin smile revealed a line of ragged teeth. "Oh yeah, a real pleas-ure that one. Sneaky devil."

"So, he is back—he cannot be kept out of San Francisco?"

"*Pfft*. Can't seem to keep him out—hear tell he comes in secret ways under the very noses of the Customs men. Here tell he is in town doing the hell's work." His look shifted, plainly worried he had divulged too much to her. "But I've been deporting many scoundrels since then. And—em—now—" He paused, tapping his Vigilante badge.

"I see you have joined the new—er—law force?" What else would she call this strange new lawless band, the Vigilante militia?

He bounced on the edges of his toes. "I'm aboard all ships to turn away incoming migrants from our shores. 'Smatter of fact, that woulda been you some year or two ago, eh, almond eyes?" He resembled a shark who smelled the scent of blood in the water.

She could not tear her gaze away from Painter's glee at telling of his newfound responsibility.

"Won't be long now." His voice took on a sinister tone.

She stepped closer. "What do you mean?"

"Us Vigilantes, we means to clean this town of all these undesirous populations—such as yourself, no offense. Mr. Coleman and the Vigilance Committee don't take kindly to gambling and pimping in our town. So—won't be long now, gorgeous."

His threat was unmistakable. No matter how she considered it, the words 'won't be long now' meant that plans were imminent to go after non-whites in this town. How long before other nooses went up? How long before she would witness a Cantonese man being hanged?

She cringed, growing silent, moving away from this Harold Painter. He was no better than the thugs he planned to murder. Vengeance never solved problems—it only made them worse. But his truth gave her pause—she imagined the four pears lined up on the crates in her parlor. She blinked to clear that night's image from her mind and heart.

Not long after, a shout burst from the crowd, and Ah saw a rope catch a gleam of torchlight from the old adobe building. She jumped high enough to see a noose looping over a high beam jutting out of the structure. A loud *aaahh* floated through the crowd, followed by a drum signaling a processional dividing the crowd.

Ah swung to her left in time to see the Vigilante guard. They held fixed bayonets in a column four across. Jenkins, the prisoner in chains, shuffled in the middle of the column. Two guards held him upright.

The crowd surged, and a group of toughs streamed toward the column, but they were held back by Vigilante guards and sympathizers within the crowd. Ah shook her head. If they were trying to rescue Jenkins, they had slight chance of succeeding, since they looked as weak as fennel seeds at the bottom of a bowl of chicken dumplings.

From her spot in the crowd, Ah could see that Jenkins was not a small man; to be sure, his girth was double that of Chen. Jenkins could even be several inches taller. The crowd relaxed after the procession passed, and not long after, another *aaaahhh* soared through the crowd.

For once she could see what was happening, since once the noose was fixed on Jenkins' neck, the guards pulled the rope and the giant's body jerked upward.

Sam Brannan boomed to the crowd. "Every lover of liberty and good order lay hold of the rope!"

The crowd cried out its approval, a bellowed *hooray* she had only heard once before at the execution in Guangzhou. Ah felt a tightness grip her chest. Bloodlust spoke now as it had then, and this bay hamlet lost its innocence forever.

Three

❧ SNARLING DOGS ❧

After all the choking spasms ended, Jenkins face contorted in a hellacious grin that stayed fixed on the crowd even after he expired. Men continued to raise their fists, hurling curses and epithets at the dead man who had wreaked havoc on so many lives in San Francisco. Ah tried to blink away the vision of the prisoner's smirk, but it lingered every time she closed her eyes.

Justice was served, yet why was the crowd so excited? They snarled, dogs scrounging for bits of a deer carcass, bloody and torn. Any such lust posed danger since it could easily turn on itself—neighbor could accuse neighbor, with this monkey court secretly disposing of the enemies that would oppose its aims. A strange dread pooled in her throat, weakening her resolve.

A few moments later, Ah saw a flash of black serge, a torch held aloft, and the smile she would recognize anywhere. John Clark beamed down at her.

For a moment she lost all sense of time and place as she scanned his features, the face she loved. But then, she caught her breath.

A crease appeared between his eyes. "You did not send Chen for me?"

Her words stumbled out. "*Emmm*—the crowds—and all this—" She fluttered her fan toward the throngs that continued to stir. Were they waiting for someone else to hang? Her nerves jangled.

Clark's voice rang out. "I am glad to see you, but this is some danger, eh?" He turned to Chen. "Let us have a moment."

Chen drew back. "I shall remain here."

"All right," he nodded. Clark's hand held hers, and he guided her over toward the edge of the Plaza. She fought against the tingle of his fingers. On their way, the crowd of men tipped their hats to him.

Once free of the crowd, his hand lingered on her shoulder. "Such a long time. You look so very—well. Where have you been?"

At last her dragon flared, though its flames were faint. She said, "You know very well where I have been . . . why have you not come to our street on patrol?"

He splayed a hand against his upper chest. "I have been occupied with matters at the wharf—the Vigilante movement is sound, and I agree with their support of us policemen. That is why I agreed leave the city police to join their ranks."

Her chin trembled. "Does this not conflict with the City of San Francisco's government? I know both are against the Sydney Ducks, but it seems a risky move for you. Are the Vigilantes outside the law?" She tapped the closed fan against the back of her hand.

"My dear Ah, you are misinformed. We *are* the law now. The city government is not applying law and order in this town—*we* are."

"But I have heard they are against us Cantonese and wish to deport us." Her stomach clenched as she imagined herself with Chen, crowded onto the *Eagle*, flags flying toward Hong Kong.

He hesitated. "Well—em—that is a part of their beliefs, but not the part I ascribe to."

Heat roiled in her belly. "How can you follow one belief, not another, and still call yourself a member of the Committee? Are you not riding a horse with two heads, one facing the side of the law, the other facing anarchy? Are you not putting yourself in danger? Master Confucius says, 'Men stay alive through straightforward conduct. When the crooked stay alive, it is simply a matter of escaping through luck.'"

He rubbed his lips. "It is well worth the risk. The law is run amuck in our town. We suppressed the Hounds, but now the darn Ducks are out of control. Do you know what people say every time they murder someone or rob a store?"

"What?"

"'The Ducks are cackling in the pond.' They make a laughing stock of Mayor Geary and all of the branches who have sworn to serve and protect the citizens of our town." His mouth twisted grimly.

She crossed her arms. "So, you think that by hanging these Australians, you will make the town safer?"

"An eye for an eye, or so the saying goes." He planted his feet in a wide stance, his expression steady.

She caught a glimpse of the waiting Chen out of the corner of her eye. Thanks to Chen for always being there. Her focus shifted back to Clark's strong form, so solid as he stood in front of her. He represented security, not only to her but also to their town. But then, why was he not as faithful to her as Chen was? He told her he loved her—once.

How could she escape the urge to lace her arms through his, to pull him close, to tell him she would never let him go? The crowd began to disperse; wagons with spectators drew away from the edge of the Plaza, headed for home. The only way to avoid the pain he caused was to put city blocks between herself and him. She lifted her closed fan in the air, then called, "Chen, please get us Flannery and the wagon."

He nodded and paced away toward the fringe of the crowd.

Clark said, "Wait, Chen! And Ah, I need to tell you about something very important—listen carefully."

The urgency in his voice immobilized her, and she shut her fan.

Chen turned and came back to them.

"Go on," Ah said.

Clark's voice lowered to a murmur. "I am privy to the Committee hearings, so I learn about their plans. Lately Sam Brannan and William Coleman, the heads of the Vigilantes, have been talking about the Celestials in San Francisco."

"Complaints?" She cringed.

"Many citizens want to cleanse the town of prostitution and gambling." His gentle voice hardened.

"Cleanse?" Her fingers trembled, so she tucked them along with her fan into her deep pockets. "The city fathers enjoy the services of prostitution and gambling in Little Canton. I do not understand how the Committee would object."

"To be blunt, yesterday I heard the Committee say your name. Some high-falutin' john made a complaint about your bawdy house."

She stiffened. "What sort of complaint?"

"No specifics—none that I could catch—something about Man-Man's death."

"Who was the john? This is the first I have heard about it. Why was I not told?" She crossed her arms.

"Hush—keep your voice low. This crowd has ears. The Vigilantes are a confidential society, and all proceedings and decisions are top secret. When they surprise the accused, they mete out swift and brutal justice. Like *that*." He pointed to Jenkins' body, still dangling at the end of the rope.

Ah's teeth chattered, not from the night air, but from the thought that someone hated her so much they would dispose of her like fish offal into the bay.

After a futile series of tosses and turns in her bed at the parlor house, once more she stared at the early light creeping across her bedroom ceiling. She could not relax, let alone slumber. Jade snuggled against her side. She ran her fingers over the cat's soft ears. Who had reported her to the Vigilante Committee? And better yet, who wanted so much to ruin her business? Could it be Li Fan? Was it only a coincidence that the complaint followed the day after she spoke to Officer Wong?

A sour taste rose in her mouth. Nothing appeared out of bounds for Li Fan. A liaison with Wong—including sexual favors—might increase the size of her coffers. Would she stoop so low as to deal with the Vigilantes? Did she influence one of her own johns, currying favors with him in return for a false report about Ah Toy?

If only Ah could still the fears that clung to her like the biting gnats on the Pearl River. After a few moments, her breathing slowed, and there it was—her dragon's presence, carrying wisdom. She considered. The darkness carried sadness and despair, the *yin* of shadow, of the feminine. Within it there was always the glimmer of *yang*, the opposite, the light. For now, she would stay comforted that within the yang she would see the truth of what had happened tonight.

Would Clark come tomorrow to comfort her? When would Henry Conrad return, and what would she say to him? She must go to Officer Wong about these matters. She plumped her pillow under her head, sensing the soft plates of her dragon's tail curling around her. Jade's soft form huddled against her within the shadows.

The next afternoon, Officer Wong sat behind his desk, his multiple chins spilling over his collar, his eyes looking past Ah who sat across from him. On the wall, the red silk tapestry with gold lettering shifted with the slight breeze from the open window. What was taking so long for him to answer her question about who left the four pears and might have complained about her to the Vigilantes? Was he dreaming of pork dumplings?

The man needed waking up. "Wong!" She heard her own strident tone.

He blinked, apparently returning to the present world. "As to the matter of who has threatened your house—I have no information about that. Er—I was trying to remember what the rumors say about you . . . so many reports come to the office. We discard most of them as idle story." He sucked a bit of scum from his third fingernail. "Li Fan was here yesterday . . ." His voice drifted off and his eyes again took up the faraway look.

"Li Fan?" Her curiosity stirred. That woman seemed to be everywhere with trouble. And was she there to service Wong's needs?

"The very same." While regarding her, he licked his lips, plainly savoring the contents of his fingernail. Could he be remembering the taste of Li Fan's skin?

If only she could tear the truth out of Wong. "So, what did she say?" Her former shreds of respect swirled in a whirlpool of disgust.

He tilted his head. "Hmmm—she heard some blather by way of a wealthy Cantonese miner. One with connections to your family. Of course, many from Guangdong are connected to such an influential man as your brother-in-law."

None other than Lee Shau Kee must be at Tung Chao's sad business again, pretending to be a member of her family, but she sat back for a second, holding her thoughts inside where her dragon could shelter them. "So . . . what was the complaint?"

"That you run what they call a 'bawdy house'—I think in their language it means a house of prostitution. They study your house since the death of Man-Man. They have you under suspicion and hold you responsible for her death. They say maybe you even caused it." His faced stiffened.

Her dragon rustled. So much was at stake. The threat of the four pears appeared again, but in a different form, and even more deadly. She rose—tears blurred her vision—no one must see her crying, especially

Officer Wong who would give her up instantly. Most likely he knew about the four pears. Most likely he knew who the culprit was.

She gave a sigh. Life in Guangdong taught her the value of a woman's life—to Wong, she was worth less than the scum under his fingernail—food bits not even worth licking as an after-meal delight.

His chair creaked and he shifted his bulk. Was he making a renewed attempt to help?

He said, "Daughter, you are upset by this news."

"I fear for my own safety and that of my girls."

"Rightly so. Should this story reach the Vigilantes, they will not hesitate to arrest you. Then you will be in mortal danger. These men will take your girls, confiscate your property, even spend all of your money."

She quieted. His words sounded final. She could lose the girls, even her parlor house, but her hard-earned money ensured her well-being, her future—how could such wolves take everything? She swallowed a sob.

He went on. "And Chen? What use would they have for a eunuch? They might string him up for deviant behavior. and try to deport you back to Guangdong. They are blocking non-white men when they disembark from their ships. They have already been sending those they perceive as criminals back to their homelands—*you* could be next."

She swallowed a hard knot. The situation was heading from bad to worse. Each word raised a vision in her mind—Chen was twisting from the beam, his queue dangling over his back, his shoulder blades bent and broken like chicken wings. Next, she saw herself naked under Tung Chee husband who raped and whipped her at the same time. This must not happen again—*ever.*

She leveled her gaze at Wong. "What can we do to stop them?"

He shook his head. "Nothing right now. Mayor Geary has told the Kong Chow Company that he is powerless. The Vigilantes are well-organized, well-armed, and they have money. He told us to lay low and handle our disturbances in Little Canton by ourselves. Any crime that gets the attention of the Vigilance will be our undoing and yours."

"So…how can I not be noticed?"

"Stay in Little Canton—avoid all public gatherings where these men are apt to meet." His eyebrows drew together. "Otherwise we might be fishing you out of Washerwoman's Lagoon."

She rose and gathered her jacket and fan. "Thank you, Officer Wong."

He resumed a faraway look. Maybe it was time for luncheon—or Li Fan.

She stepped into the street, dislodging a seagull strutting in front of her. Disturbed, it rose into an arc, gaining the height of the rooftops, then soaring on the wind currents out toward the Bay. Her gaze followed its flight over the rooftops onto the far horizon.

Wong had warned her to stay in bounds. But how she longed to be that gull—such freedom it must have. So gawky and awkward on land where it strutted from side to side with webbed feet. But in the air, it rivaled the grace and beauty of a hawk, its wings outstretched, its snowy gray and white feathers harmonizing with the clouds and fog of its own canvas.

Next morning Chen swept ashes away from the front stoop, then went about polishing the brass door knocker. Workmen pounded nails, replacing the burned siding of the parlor house. Neighbors stood across the street, smoked clay pipes, and watched the carpenter. She sat on a bench in the hallway, lost in thought. In a recent letter, Elizabeth Daily had continued to stress her language skills. She had said . . . *Read widely in the news, my dear. It will give you good practice for vocabulary. Do you remember how I taught you in Guangzhou? Say the unfamiliar words aloud—sound them out by syllables, using the method I taught you. Persist. I wish you well.*

Elizabeth was right. Words were power and she would continue to study them. Ah shuffled to the kitchen table. Within minutes, she spread out The *Daily San Francisco Herald*, smoothing the thin paper with her fingertips. Next to the paper, she set her English-Cantonese dictionary.

She brushed away a speck of egg and a bit of plum sauce that had sprinkled on the page. The headline of one article drew her attention, so remembering Mrs. Dailey's training, she looked up all the unfamiliar words in her dictionary—*dislodged, tarp, affixed, gruesome*. Above those words, she printed the Cantonese word, then she read the English word aloud to herself. She then read the article, line by line as Mrs. Dailey had suggested.

BODY RECOVERED IN THE BAY.

On Monday last, a fisherman off the shoals at Tonquin point spotted what looked like a white shirt clinging to a rock. Curious, the man pulled up his nets and headed toward it. Once there, he took a pole and dislodged what he thought was a white tarp—rather, to his horror, it was the remains of a human body. Though missing a right arm and right leg, the Vigilante badge was yet affixed to the remnants of a torn jacket clinging to the body. The man's throat had been cut. Thus, the fisherman took the body on board, then brought it in to harbor where The Vigilante Committee took charge of the body. The Committee identified it as one Harold Painter, former San Francisco police detective, enrolled in the Committee of Vigilance. A search for murder suspects is underway. Anyone with knowledge of this gruesome crime should contact The Committee of Vigilance at its headquarters in Sam Brannan's building.

What did this mean? Her heart raced; her head whirled. She took a gulp of tea from her cup, considering the news. Who would want to kill Harold Painter? Since the Vigilantes employed him to block immigrants from entering San Francisco, as well as deporting undesirables, then Painter could have made some powerful enemies. She needed to talk this out with someone.

"Chen!" She jammed her feet into her lotus shoes. When she reached the front door, she saw him sweeping the broom from one end of their stoop to the other, sending billows of dust into the street where they choked ungrateful passersby. Waving away the dirt, she said, "I need to speak to you."

Chen swiveled, broom in hand.

The dust settled, revealing a passing Cantonese man who gave her a sidelong look, so she pulled Chen's arm. "Come—inside—it is important." She closed the front door, aware that the same Cantonese man continued to linger outside. Story traveled like lightning bugs from house to house in Little Canton. A simple quarrel or a scattershot of lies could feed the gossip mongers for days.

Chen rested his broom against the hall table. "What? Such a hurry to find me. Something wrong?"

She took a deep breath before speaking. "I need your help—I cannot figure this out alone. Come—to the parlor."

After settling Chen on the black lacquer settee, Ah closed the door and perched on the edge of a chair. Jade leaped up on her lap and rubbed her head against the underside of her chin. She reached up and stroked the cat's fur. "The newspapers report that Harold Painter was found dead, probably murdered."

His brown eyes watered. "I am always sorry to hear of a bad luck death, si tau po. What must I make of this?" He rubbed the side of his temple.

"Something about this death bothers me. Painter was sending immigrants back to their homelands, taking their fortunes, splitting up their families."

"I remember him telling you this the night of the Vigilante hanging."

"Exactly. In Chapter Two the Master Confucius instructs, "See a person's means. Observe his motives. Examine that in which he rests. How can a person conceal his character?"

"What is meant?"

"I think the Master teaches us that Painter could not conceal his hatred for the people he was sending away. When doing evil on the wharf as a police detective, he thought he could hide his cruel nature."

"I follow . . . so you say. Do you mean that when he joined the Vigilance Committee who wanted to send more immigrants away, he could not conceal his own evil?" Chen tilted his head.

"I believe so. And there is one immigrant who would have much to revenge—."

"Who might that be, si tau po?"

"Lee Shau Kee."

He paled, then got up, his hands shaking. "I-I must finish my chores outside. Remember, today I accompany cook to market. We have to buy for tomorrow night's dinner party."

She frowned. "But you are not worried—about the Vigilantes?"

He shook his head. "No—they are after larger fish. They will be looking for someone who murdered Harold Painter, someone with much more to avenge than you can imagine."

"I hope you are right." She drew a breath and set her jaw.

Chen picked up his broom and padded out the door into the hallway. She heard the scratch-scratch of his broom against the front door stoop where he resumed his sweeping.

Ah noticed a slice of sun casting a beam through the window, its light illuminating a white chrysanthemum in a vase. Rather than pushing Jade off her lap, she remained in contemplation.

Though the white flower shone in brilliance, the green leaves underneath lay in complete shade. Then she heard her dragon's whisper, first faint, then growing stronger with each word. *Remember the yin and yang—your white flower now rests in pure light, yet pure darkness is bound to emerge with equal strength.* She held Jade to her breast, the cat's purr reverberating, a soft rumble against her chest.

Four

❧ SILK WORMS SILENTLY SPIN ❧

July 1851

A month passed without incident, but that morning Ah Toy found herself sitting cross-legged on a straw pallet in an icy, small-windowed room of what might be a warehouse. A curtain spread across a makeshift door of two by fours put up in a hurry. Her arms ached where the Vigilante militia had grabbed her in the shadows the previous night, yanking her from the cradle of sleep. Chen had cried and held her back, but the militia had pushed him down and beat him with sticks. San and Yee had screamed, clinging to Chen where he lay on the floor.

She massaged her lotus feet and stretched out on the pallet, drawing her muddy cloak over her body. Never mind the mud—at least the cloak protected her from drafts. But why were her feet so cold?

The straw smelled stale; the faint scratching of what must be rats came from a corner of the room. This place was dusky as a tomb. She closed her eyes and in the gloom her dragon spoke. *Be brave, warrior. Stay away from fear. Draw your magic sword. You will prevail.*

With each breath, she drew in her dragon's words like a heady potion to calm her wild impulse to scream. And a sudden realization emerged— her dragon spoke mainly when she was in dire circumstances. The why's of that remained hidden, but maybe the Dragon King's Daughter became stronger and her dragon spoke only when necessary as she emerged through her many trials. She sank deep into that strange and puzzling deliberation.

The day passed in gray silence, her only companions the street noises outside the building: the clip-clop of horses' hooves; an occasional shout; the chuffs from steam whistles; the occasional clanking of machinery. She chewed her lip. Chen could not visit her—he must be in fear for his life. At the very least, he would lock and shutter the parlor house doors, then stay inside with San and Yee. She felt a grin spread across her face. It would be a good chance for him to do some cleaning and mopping of floors. San could keep up with the accounts.

Then what of her customers? A lull such as this would mean a drop in business. Hmm . . . even more reason to think that her enemies had given a false report to police, exaggerating the activities of the parlor house, painting her as an evil influence on the city while at the same time doing the same or even worse under their own roofs. Li Fan. It had to be her—again. Wouldn't the foul woman ever tire of torturing her? Each passing day led her to a strong conclusion: Li Fan had left the four pears, led Man-Man to the opium den, and maybe even reported Ah to the Vigilantes. And no doubt Officer Wong was complicit, at least knowledgeable of Li Fan's doings. Who could she trust in this web of lies?

She needed a person of great influence, someone outside the city to help her—whose authority could reach far and wide, and either lift her away and out of San Francisco or protect her within it. Henry Conrad. She sat with his name for several minutes. The longer she considered him, the more she was convinced she needed to contact him in Guangzhou. Though she had little hope he would receive her missive in time to help her now, maybe writing to him would ease these dark thoughts peppering her imagination.

Pen and paper? She looked around the bleak cell. Nothing to write with. No sticks or implements for self-harm or escape in here.

Maybe she could convince the jailer to help. She began a series of hard knocks on the makeshift cell door. She pounded with her fists at first. No one came. Again and again she rapped. No one came. First the palm of one hand, then the other. Her knuckles stung, each contact with the wooden door a punishment. No one came.

Exhausted, she lay back down on her pallet, her throat parched. At least she could keep her mind off her growling stomach by composing such a letter in her head.

She imagined herself at her black lacquered desk in the parlor house, her English dictionary next to her, composing the message. In her mind, she jotted the note, praying the Goddess Mazu would correct her English errors.

Staccato footsteps rang out from what might have been a hallway. Doors were opening and shutting out there. The blend of sepia and gray shadows surrounding her made anything hard to see. Someone jangled the door open, maybe he was holding chains and keys.

A red-bearded fellow wearing a sailor's cap and long navy jacket appeared. "Miss?"

She sat up. "I have been trying to get your help with my knocking. Did you not hear me?"

He lifted an eyebrow and cocked his head. "I heard you, Miss, but we are occupied—a lot going on at the moment."

"What is the noise about?" At least she could squeeze some information from him.

The red beard took a step inside her makeshift cell. "Other prisoners. The Committee has been making more arrests." He turned to leave. Any hope of conversation faded fast.

She said, "Wait, please—I am thirsty and hungry. May I have some water, sir?"

He leaned back into the room and grunted, scratching the tufts of his woolly beard. "See what I can do fer ya."

"Oh, and a pen and paper to write a letter?" She flashed her most winning smile.

A tinge of pink rose on the cheeks under his beard. "I don't get paid to do this, ya know." He shook his head, pivoted on his heel, then clomped away down the hall.

After a couple of minutes, he returned with a tattered envelope. A half-sheet of paper, crumpled like dried skin, kept company with a dull-tipped pencil in his fingers. He held the paper out to her. "Here, Miss—all I could muster—but we don't deliver no China mail." He gave her a pained expression.

She took it in hand. "It will be written in English to a business owner in Canton." She fought the urge to spit at him.

"Uh—well in that case." He grunted, stepping away toward the door.

She held up a hand. "What is the date please?"

He glanced up at the ceiling for a moment, then down at her. "Hear tell it's July the twelfth." Then he disappeared out the door, turning the lock behind him.

Gripping the pencil in her right hand, she scrawled the English letters across the page. Without her dictionary, she could only hope the words made sense. There was little room to write, so she kept to the main point.

July 12, 1851

Mr. Henry Conrad
Conrad Imports, Ltd.
Guangzhou, Guangdong, China

Dear Henry,

The Vigilance Committee has arrested me on the charges of keeping a bawdy house. Please come and help me. Afraid for my life.

Ah Toy

She sat back, rereading her cryptic message. Another set of footsteps, this one lighter, shuffled outside her cell. The red-bearded guard swung open her cell door, and Clark stepped inside, holding a cup. The guard locked him inside and hurried away.

Ah regarded him through blurry eyes. A familiar throb rose inside of her, followed by the urge to weep in his presence. If only things were different—if only he were hers alone.

Clark passed a dirty tin cup full of brown water down to her, then sat next to her on the pallet.

She took a sip of water: it was silty but at least the moisture would help her dry throat.

After a moment, Clark took the cup from her hands and set it on the floor next to him. His large hands took her face and held it gently. Her hair tumbled from the clasp on the crown of her head, and she sensed the silky black strands lining her face. He twined his fingers through her hair, then drew away, regarding her. His lips formed a half-moon of sorrow, and she wanted to weep for him as well as for herself.

"What have they done?" He pulled her closer, and her soft curves melded into the contours of his body. "I can't believe the Committee will stoop so low as to level attacks on such a good woman. Your only harm is to provide pleasure to the men of San Francisco, politicians and Committee members among them." His breath cooled her face, and she lingered there with him, the only other sounds coming from outside the building. Horses clomped, blackbirds cawed, and a peddler cried, "Fresh bread! 50 cents a loaf!"

After a few moments, she drew away from him. "I have to finish addressing a letter to my friend Henry." Her voice was soft, but a hardness lined her words.

She sensed him watching as she printed English letters out on the creased envelope, crossing out the occasional misspelled word. A few moments passed; the silence lay thick between them. Was Clark wondering why she was writing to another man? If only he would tell her how much he loved her, how much she meant.

The pallet creaked under his greatcoat. "You smell of jasmine and gardenia." He breathed her in, much as an opium eater inhales drug from his pipe.

After he watched her sign the letter and address the envelope, he cleared his throat and moved away from her on the pallet. Maybe he tried to quell an instinct to shelter her in his arms and kiss away her fear.

She held the letter in her hand. "What brought you here today?" she asked. "Surely you are risking a lot to be here."

He pulled out a notepad from his jacket pocket and licked the tip of his pencil to moisten the lead. "When I learned you were arrested, I requested this hearing. I did not want you kept here for long—and they are known to leave prisoners for weeks without trial."

"A hearing? A trial? I do not even know why I am arrested. No one told me the reason. They simply put me in this cell and left me alone."

He bit his lip. "The Committee of Vigilance believes you are a suspect in the murder of Harold Painter."

"What?"

"A witness says he saw you talking to Painter the night of the Jenkins hanging."

A hard sob rose in her throat. "Ridiculous. I only exchanged a few words with him."

Clark's eyebrows drew together. "That must have been before I saw you and Chen that evening."

"Yes, it was—."

"How did you know Mr. Painter?"

"He was the contact I met after leaving the ship from Hong Kong. He arranged the position with a Mr. Brown, who unfortunately—died."

"So, you have known him for some time?" His voice was strained.

"Yet I rarely see him."

"You are not close friends?" He pressed his lips together.

She wagged a finger at him. "He is a member of the Vigilance Committee, bent on getting rid of immigrants. I would not want to see him."

He thumbed his ear. "But why did you even talk to him that evening?"

"When I first saw him, I thought he might know where you were in the crowd."

"I see. So, what did you discuss with him?"

She clenched her jaw and lowered her voice. "Before I do that, I will tell you who put me here."

He leaned in closer. "Who is that?"

"Li Fan. She hates me and wishes me nothing but ill. She and Lee Shau Kee would like to destroy me, to send me back to Guangdong into the arms of my brother-in-law whose brother nearly killed me and murdered my three daughters. She must have stirred this up." She stared down at the letter in her lap.

"What is your evidence of that?"

She bit her lip. "I have no proof. And no one will stand up to her. I think Officer Wong may even be in league with her. Yet I do not know."

He filled in the date at the top of his notebook. "I think we will keep those suspicions to the side for now. I do not want to stir up trouble in Little Canton. My task right now is simply to write down the circumstances of your arrest. Please tell me what you and Painter talked about."

"He told me how proud he was of getting rid of immigrants, and that he was particularly anxious to find Lee Shau Kee. I remember his exact words: 'Can't seem to keep him out—hear tell he comes in secret ways under the very noses of the Customs officials. Here tell he is in town doing the hell's work.'"

"How did he seem when he said those words to you about Lee Shau Kee?"

"Frustrated, upset."

"Did he act fearful?"

"No, just angry I would say. He was bent on catching Lee Shau Kee once and for all."

While she narrated the former night's incident, he covered two pages with script. "Let me read back to you what you reported. After repeating her words, he said. "A moment while I write a short summary."

Her breathing came easier now—in-out-in-out, river water flowing across pebbles on the hottest summer day. Between them passed a rhythm, a momentum, and his script streamed word-by-word across the page in harmony with her breathing.

During the early hours of the evening, members of the Vigilance Committee militia knocked on the suspect's door. Taking her from a deep sleep, the men grabbed her by the waist, and. dragged her out in front of her employees San, Yee, and Chen. When Chen objected, they told him to shut up. However, they did allow him to place a cloak about her person before they led her off to jail. Since Chen manifested belligerence, militia members restrained him with a beating, then issued him a warning that if he did not desist, he would also be arrested in the name of the Committee of Vigilance of San Francisco.

He lifted his pencil, regarding her. She swept away a chain of tears that streamed down her face.

Did he remember his lips on her cheek, their embrace, the shadows enveloping them? If only he would take her in his arms right now and kiss away the dark thoughts.

After he read back the summary of her statements about Painter, he waited. "Do you have questions for me?"

She inched away from him on the pallet. "I am surprised at your asking."

"Why?"

She struggled to control her breaking voice. "Because we know how this ends. Once a person is in Vigilance custody, they are either hanged or deported. My skin color is yellow; my homeland is China; and there are many out there who wish me gone from here."

"Is there anyone you wish me to contact on your behalf?"

"I wish to send this letter to Henry Conrad." She took his hand and pressed the letter inside his palm.

He opened his hand, looking at the address. "Who is this man?"

"A friend of mine—an importer. He has great influence and says he wishes me to consider a union with him."

He scratched his jaw. "I doubt this letter will get to him in time to help you here."

"I want to send the letter anyway." She wound a lock of her hair around her fingers.

"When you say union, does that mean marriage?" For an instant, a wistfulness filled his expression.

"Perhaps."

If silence were like a rock, a boulder wedged between them.

It was she who broke their hush. After all, she could not have him, so why did he seem so shocked that she would find interest in another man? "I need to send this letter."

"Are you sure you want to?"

"Of course, I am sure. Please see to it that it is mailed right away. I do not know how long before I will be—"

He reached out and patted her arm. "I will be happy to mail this for you, but rest assured, I will do everything I can to see you are well cared for."

A cold shiver passed through her. "And what about Chen . . . and the girls? I worry for them. They do not know the news, and the guards said I am to have no visitors. I am surprised they let you in."

"They have to—I am part of the militia."

"So, what will you do for me? Can you talk to the Committee?"

She heard shuffling footsteps, followed by the door creaking, keys clanking, and in walked the guard with a heel of bread. "Time is up, Clark." Her chest tightened and the faint light in the cell grew even dimmer.

Clark said, "But I am not yet finished with the accused."

The guard snickered. "Yeah . . . right. They all say that with the likes of the fallen women. Men are never finished with them tarts—girls like this will lie with anyone."

She held her tongue. Although she bristled, words would only make the situation worse.

Clark rose to his feet, and he reached down and pulled her to her feet. His hands had grown wintry to the touch. She guessed that the dampness of the cell had infiltrated his insides; even his bones would ache from the air in this cell. He took off his greatcoat and passed it to her. "Take it for warmth," he said.

She nodded and set it on top of her cloak.

"Now, I said." The guard prodded.

Clark said, "I will come again in a couple days. I will see Chen and get your change of clothes and your special food."

"What should I do?" Her false bravado was crumbling.

He sighed. "You will have to trust me. The Committee will consider your case in two days, so when I come next, it will be to assist you in your hearing. I will speak on your behalf."

The door clanged shut behind him, and she was alone. The guard fastened the bolts outside, and footsteps were heard no more.

Trust him. The murky tomb pulled in its walls, surrounding her with its shroud. She nibbled on the stale bread and sipped on her water, relishing each drop as it lingered on her parched tongue.

Crazy imaginings filled her head. If only she could fly away, find a slit in the wall, ease through, and travel unrecognized through the streets. She would go to the Dailey house, disguise herself as their washerwoman, laundress, anything—a fate worse than death was at least a fate.

Here she could not be sure if she had a fate waiting for her at all. The worst fortune was that of an immigrant whose adoptive country, the America she now loved, would either imprison her, drop her at the end of a noose, or foist her back into the deadly embrace of her home country. At that point, the noose might be a most appealing alternative.

Five

⟨ THE BODY IN QUESTION ⟩

When they came for her two days later, she was in a deep slumber. Their hands pulled on her arms, their movements rough and jerking. A voice rose out of nowhere. "Come, Mrs. Toy. You have been summoned to the hearing."

She blinked away dry tears. "What time is it? I have no sense of it, since it is so dark in here."

Shadows obscured their faces, but she recognized the red beard among them. Him she could trust—he brought her bread and water every day. He had even told her to call him Red. Yesterday he came an extra time to check on her. She ran her tongue over her chapped lips, and when they wrenched her to her feet, her bones ached. She was dizzy, weak and hungry.

They tried at first to march her out, but she could not walk on bare lotus feet, her toes curled under like a fist. "I cannot walk without my shoes. Where are they?"

After a moment searching the cell, Red found them in a corner, and put them in her hands. "Here they are." He turned to the other two men

311

whose faces lurked in shadow. "Wait a minute. She must put on her shoes."

The man closest to her said, "Come on, lookee girl. We ain't got all day."

Ah winced, jamming her feet into her shoes. Pain radiated up her calves like twisted strands of licorice. Sweat broke out on her forehead.

A gruff voice sounded from the other of the men. "Eh...favors for the tart now, do ya? Drag the bitch if she canna walk."

The other mumbled, "Yeah . . . what good is she anyway, just a used piece of trash. I say hang her up and be done with it."

"Hold on there . . ." Red's voice broke into their stream of hateful words.

The gruff voice answered his challenge. "Whatsa matter, Red? Thought you believed in the Committee's causes."

"She's got some rights."

"Nah . . . she ain't got no rights . . . this is our country, not hers."

"Send her back where she come from." The other man rasped.

"Heh! Then she can go back and make more babies who want to come here? Nah! I say kill her and be done with her."

If she were not involved and had overhead their conversation, Ah might think they were talking about an animal, or a horse, or even a piece of machinery. But surely not her—a person, a woman with thoughts, ideas, and aspirations. Her dragon's voice sounded . . . this moment, her darkest. *Be still. Now is not the time for arguments. You will have your chance.*

Red took her arm and led her out the door and down the hallway. They passed through an open door leading into a great room. Shelves lined the walls, replete with boxes whose labels were marked dry goods and implements sold at Mr. Brannan's store. Crates were stacked against the walls whose high windows arched, overlooking the noisy street.

Traffic must be bustling before midday dinner. She looked down on the top of a green awning over the sidewalk below. A few white women in bonnets, day dresses, and shawls walked in and out of the shops down there, market baskets dangling from their arms.

Miners passed in the usual dusty canvas overalls. One saw her at the window and elbowed another. They paused, looking up at her. Aiming her steps toward the center of the room, she observed the long oak table that served as the gathering place. Men in dark suits and ribbon ties sat in rigid expectation, their collars upright with starch, their hair slicked with pomade.

After introductions—Mr. Sam Brannan—Mr. William Coleman— Officer John Clark—Mr. Timothy Hart—and other militiamen whose names she could not catch—took their places at the table. Since she had not been handcuffed—what kind of flight risk was a woman who could not walk?—she set her hands on the table.

A secretary sat to the right of Mr. Brannan, his pen and inkpot lined up in preparation, his hand anchoring sheaves of paper. He looked at her, plainly recognizing her from their night at the Larkins, and his stern features softened.

After a glance around the table, watching the rest of the men glaring at her with cold indifference, her heart sank. So, this was how it would end? This could not be. Yet it was. She blocked the current of her thoughts—she must pay attention to their words. Even if it meant the end of her, at least she could watch the drama unfold like a spectator at the theater.

Mr. Brannan spoke first. "You have been brought before the Committee, Mrs. Toy, for charges relating to the keeping of a bawdy house, and for depraved indifference regarding the death of one Man-Man, an indentured servant in your care. Mr. Coleman will be questioning you today."

"What? Mr. Clark said I had been arrested as a suspect in the murder of Harold Painter?" She fixed her eyes on Mr. Brannan whose cheeks reddened noticeably.

313

"We have dropped those charges, since after Mr. Clark's investigation and declaration that you were in mere conversation with Mr. Painter, you are no longer a suspect." It was Coleman who spoke, his voice dripping with nonchalance. "Do you keep one such bawdy house on Pike Street?"

"Yes, but it is called a parlor house."

"And do you exchange money from customers in exchange for sexual favors at your Pike Street residence?"

"We entertain our gentlemen—"

He interrupted. "Simply answer yes or no, Mrs. Toy."

"Well, yes." She gave a downward gaze. This was humiliating.

"Are you aware that you are corrupting the moral standards of our city?"

"I do not understand." She felt more naked than when she had been a lookee girl.

He waved his hand dismissively. "Of course, you would not know the meaning of moral standards."

The gruff-voiced Timothy Hart interrupted. "She ain't got none, Your Honor Brannan."

The company around the table broke into laughter—all except Clark and Brannan who sat in stony silence. At least *they* were on her side.

Mr. Brannan pounded his gavel, then pointed at Hart. "Remove him from the room, "

"But I'm part of the Committee." Hart's words were heavy with sarcasm.

Brannan gripped the gavel. "We may be issuing rough justice, Mister, but we aim for justice all the same. Mr. Clark, take him out."

Out of the corner of her eye, Ah noted the scuffle as Clark struggled against Mr. Hart's protests, then lifted him out of his chair and pushed him out of the door.

Red went over, locked the door, and stood next to it for a moment while Clark sat down again, plainly trying to catch his breath.

Mr. Brannan said, "Thank you, Clark and Red." He peered down the table. "Now, Mr. Coleman, you may proceed."

After many questions, most of which related to Man-Man's death and her disposal thereafter, John Clark rose.

"I would like to give testimony as to the character and contributions of Mrs. Toy to our city."

Mr. Brannan nodded. "You may proceed. Mr. Coleman, you may ask the questions. Recorder, make sure to get this down."

The secretary nodded; his pen poised.

Josh, a slouch-hatted militiaman said, "I got somethin' to say."

Brannan looked over at the interloper. "Hold your fire. Let William finish the questioning."

Mr. Coleman cleared his throat. "How long have you known the accused?"

Clark glanced up at the ceiling, then back at Coleman. "Hmmm. Since 1849, pretty sure."

"And in what ways have you known the accused?"

He paused. "Served as her patrolman since around that time. San Francisco Police under Mayor Geary."

Coleman cast him a sharp glance. "Were you ever a paying customer of Mrs. Toy?"

Ah's heart beat against her ribs. *Please, Clark, tell the truth.* If they caught him in a lie, he might be hanged alongside her.

"Yes, but only a lookee customer. Never had relations with Mrs. Toy."

Coleman's cheeks reddened, an even deeper scarlet than before. "Are you quite sure, Mr. Clark?"

"Lands sakes, absolutely." He gave a strained smile.

"So—in what—other ways did you know the defendant?"

"I have assisted Mrs. Toy in such matters as a material threat to her parlor house which I suspect was perpetrated upon her by a fellow madam, Li Fan."

Coleman continued to press. "Was Li Fan ever arrested?"

"No sir."

"And why not?"

315

Clark gave a knowing look. "I have it on unofficial authority Li Fan was the lover of one of the high-ranking members of the Kong Chow Company, and he paid off the judge."

"I see. We have encountered several such cases such as these involving our immigrant communities, which is why our Vigilance Committee is now handling judicial affairs in our corrupted city."

"Here, here," Josh called from his place at the end of the table.

At this point, Mr. Brannan intervened. "It is apparent to this Committee that a turf war was in play between two Celestial madams in San Francisco. The Kong Chow Company ordinarily handled such a case. But the matter at hand is about the nature and character of Mrs. Toy. Mr. Coleman, please direct your questioning along those lines."

"Very well. "Coleman shifted in his chair. "Mr. Clark, how were you made aware of the death of one Man-Man, this woman's servant and prostitute, from an opium overdose at the house of one named Kuang?"

"I was summoned to the opium den, and Kuang said the girl was dead. I found her with an opium pipe, the smell of opium in her nose and on her person. After having seen many such victims of that sort of poisoning, I concluded that she died from overdose."

The secretary slid a paper across the table, and Coleman paused. He lifted the paper, scanning it for a moment. "And I see by these court records that her death was duly recorded and reported to the police and the city coroner. How was her body disposed?"

"As is usual custom in Little Canton, the Kong Chow Company sent the body back to China for burial. I contacted Officer Wong whose men took the body without question."

"Was there any sign of foul play?" The lines deepened around Coleman's eyes.

Clark shook his head. "No, sir. Her death looked very natural, a result of a powerful lot of drug, and I had nothing unusual to report. Her body bore no marks or evidence of a struggle."

"So, you had no reason at the time to suspect Ah Toy in the matter of Man-Man's death?"

"No, in fact in the ensuing days, Mrs. Toy explained that Man-Man would slip away from the parlor house on many occasions without warning, and they would have to go and search her whereabouts. Man-Man was fond of the opium, sir."

Coleman continued. "Now at this time, Mr. Clark, I would like you to tell us why you believe Mrs. Toy should be cleared of all morals charges relating to her parlor house. Take your time, but be thorough. The penalty for keeping a bawdy house is severe."

Ah cast a glance around the room. Silence reigned and all heads were turned, focused on John Clark.

Six

◀ AN UNBROKEN STREAM ▶

*F*or some time, Clark related his friendship with Ah Toy, their many conversations, and his understanding of her circumstances relating to the servants she employed and the way she ran the parlor house. He even attested to her participation in the town's celebrations of California's statehood in the year 1850.

He produced and circulated a newspaper description of her Cantonese food booth that was decorated with an American flag. "See, gentlemen, this extraordinary woman has adopted her new country with enthusiasm, supporting its laws, and paying her taxes to the Celestial community who collects them. In addition, she keeps an orderly house, services the needs of our male population and is an upstanding citizen."

Coleman snarled. "But what about the indentured servants she has? What are their rights?"

Josh emitted a growl. "Yeah, how can such a woman be as great as you claim? She can't walk and she can't read or write English. Let her go back where she belongs with the rest of them heathen."

Her dragon stirred. "No, gentlemen, you are wrong." Ah teetered to her feet.

The guard named Red went to her side, then a hand rested under her elbow.

Josh burst out. "Sit down, lookee girl. You ain't got nuthin' for this Committee."

Coleman exchanged glances with Sam Brannan who then spoke. "Let her say her peace, Josh. The Committee would like to hear from the defendant."

Ah lifted her chin. "Yes, I do have something to say."

Josh frowned, pushed back his chair, and crossed his arms over his belly.

Her strength gathered now, and her words poured out in an unbroken stream. "I would like to tell you first that I know how to read and write English, and I can also speak it. I learned to speak by imitating the British people in Guangzhou who did business with my father in his porcelain factory. I was brought up as nobility, and I would follow my brother to his English missionary school where I learned my early words and writing from Mrs. Dailey.

"I have to use the Chinese-English dictionary sometimes, but I am learning more words all the time, and I even read the news sheets like the *Alta California*."

The men rested against the backs of their chairs. Mr. Coleman appeared stunned, and he sat rubbing his chin back and forth. No one spoke.

She continued. "I escaped from a cruel fate in China, a husband who beat me and murdered my three daughters when they were mere infants. I did employ indentured servants, but I had them sign a contract so they could earn their freedom, telling them that I bought them out of bondage. After they worked off what they owed, they could leave my house anytime they wished. Now, you know that Man-Man went the way of drugs, and that I was helpless to change her situation. But San and Yee have remained faithful to me."

Mr. Coleman's face reddened. "But they are prostitutes."

"Yes, they are, but I keep a clean house. I service some Cantonese men as well as white, especially those who otherwise would have to bring over their wives, so I am actually keeping down the immigrant population." She stopped for a moment, checking herself. Had she stepped too far out on a fragile limb? Was she speaking against her own kind?

Coleman eyed her, chewing his pencil.

She could not resist adding another statement. "And I make sure the healer checks the girls regularly."

Coleman shuffled some papers. "What about that man Chen? Reports say he is a strange one—that he prefers men to women."

"Chen is what you call a eunuch. When he was only a child in China, he was changed so that he could no longer desire women or men for that matter. He was altered like a horse, and it was not his fault."

"Distasteful, heathen practice." Brannan went pale.

She went on. "It was the custom to employ a eunuch in the houses of nobility so that the daughters would be safe from the servants. Chen has cared for me and been by my side since we were very young. He is only three years older than I am—more than a friend, to me he is a brother."

Coleman paused. "I see. Now tell me, Mrs. Toy. Given your hateful practices and disgusting associates, why should we not deport you and send you back to Canton?"

"First, you would send me to certain bondage at my brother-in-law's hands once I arrive in Guangdong. Then, you would be removing me, a good citizen, from the community of San Francisco. Not many Cantonese women are here now, though they are beginning to arrive. And without the services I provide, more Cantonese men would be bringing wives to our town. So, there would be even more immigrants."

She found herself rising along with the tempo of words, and for once her lotus feet gave her no pain. "In order for our town to build a thriving community with all nations, we need services from all sides. San Francisco–Pike Street—my home where I am befriended and happy. I have a future here, and I honor San Francisco. I will defend our laws and keep the peace in my community.

"I have no debts and I have only one enemy, Li Fan, who tries to hurt my business from sunup to sundown. It is she you should be seeking. Look to the fox who hides in the underbrush rather than capturing the deer who frolics in plain sight. She is the fox you must seek, along with Lee Shau Kee, her benefactor, who is rumored to have many gold mines in the high country. Why destroy my life when I have done nothing to destroy yours?" She dropped, dizzy and spent, into her chair.

Coleman's voice assumed an orderly, paternal tone. "Thank you for your testimony, Mrs. Toy. We will take all of today's proceedings into consideration." He waved to the guard. "Red, you may escort the lady back into her cell." Then he called to Clark. "Officer, remain here for further inquiries."

"Thank you for your testimony, Mrs. Toy." Sam Brannan appeared contrite. Was he remembering their dinner together at the Larkin House?

Coleman threw her a benign smile, much like throwing a bone to a hungry dog. "You will hear our verdict tomorrow."

As Ah stepped toward the door, she took a momentary glance out the high window. A seagull perched on a roof across the street, the breeze ruffling his feathers. If only he could come in, swoop her up, and carry her up to Telegraph Hill, the highest peak. There she would be wrapped in blessings.

After Ah's sleepless night in this dark chamber, any sound was welcome. By now, she found the *scritch-scratch* of rats quite comforting—unlike her they were free to go in and out the holes they burrowed. She had watched them on the wharf in Guangzhou. Large and fearless, some were the size of small dogs. Once she seen a rat reach up and snatch a child's rice cake.

Her insides gnawed at her—even stale bread would be a feast. Footsteps gathered momentum, then the familiar chain and locks jangled, followed by Red's beard illuminated by a lantern.

"Time to hear the verdict," he said.

"But I am hungry and thirsty." She pulled the mixed blanket of her cloak and Clark's jacket around her. It had been hours since her last meal, and her stomach complained most of the night.

Red's face hovered over her. His lantern sputtered. "You can eat later. The Committee has little time to wait."

Her legs, ankles and the bottoms of her fee throbbed from yesterday's hearing. "My feet are quite swollen."

Red bent down. "Here, I have seen how you can hardly walk. Let me—" He lifted her up, and she put her arms around his neck while he set her on her feet.

He smelled of whiskey and tobacco, same as most inhabitants. But she did catch something different—mixed with the usual scent was a hint of rosewater and lavender. Had he worn something special just for her? Or was that the perfume his wife wore when she kissed him goodbye that morning?

He balanced her lightly like a carton of eggs, his keys clinking in his pocket, his lantern swinging on the other arm.

After Red deposited her on a chair in the meeting room, she glanced around the table. This time, she saw Mr. Coleman, Mr. Brannan, and John Clark. Red took his post at the hallway door. Through the tall windows she saw the day was overcast, and three candles crackled, splaying light around the room.

Today she noticed something new. John Clark sported dark circles under his eyes. Was that a bit of gray mixed with the blond in his sideburns? Maybe worry was transforming him.

Mr. Brannan's stern voice broke into her thoughts. "Mrs. Toy, we have reached a verdict in the matter we discussed yesterday, and we find that although your behavior is at times disturbing, we find no grounds for a capital hanging. Mr. Clark has vouched for your keeping an orderly bawdy house and—er—the clean maintenance of your soiled doves, such as they are.

"Upon Mr. Clark's advice, we will be looking into the matter of Li Fan's keeping of her house of ill-repute, and her practice of telling malicious tales about you and others in Little Canton. She is the type of Celestial we may wish to deport." He narrowed his eyes, directing his gaze at her.

She scanned his face, remembering his kind ways at the Larkin House dinner. Dare she hope? Did he believe her suspicions about Li Fan's malicious acts?

He went on. "However—any further complaints about you from someone other than Li Fan and we will meet again, under much less favorable circumstances. You have been arrested and duly warned by the Committee of Vigilance. We will have our eyes on you and your house. Understood?"

"Yes, Mr. Brannan" She bowed her head, then tightened her lips to repress the smile she longed to give him.

Red pulled out her chair and she stood, but faltered, holding on to the side of the table. Her head began its old pounding. Dizzy, she watched the room fade, but then she heard someone push out a chair and walk over toward her. She heard Red's voice say, "Clark, you may wish to carry her out and make sure she has some grub. She had nothing to eat since last night."

Clark whispered into her left ear. "Do you have anything left in the cell? Any clothes?"

She shook her head, then reached up and settled her cheek into the stiff collar against his neck.

He gathered her into his arms and carried her out and down the stairs. Everything around her was gray, outlines of shapes fading into dull white.

After Red whistled a wagon toward them, Clark lifted her inside and took a seat next to her.

Red called out. "Take good care of her, Clark. She is some pumpkins sure." He clucked his tongue and gave a quick salute.

"Indeed, she is." Clark said. He rapped his knuckles on the door of the wagon. "To Pike Street," he said, his voice sharp. The driver maneuvered his horse away from the warehouse toward Kearny Street in the direction of Little Canton.

She clutched his arm. Would Chen have pork dumplings and hot tea on the table this morning? After that and a bath, maybe she could wash away the bad fortune that clung to her like flies on a dead mule.

Seven

❧ UNDER THE BAGUA ❧

Ah held on to Clark as he gentled her out of the wagon, lifted her under the bagua, then across the threshold of the Pike Street parlor house. She reached up her left hand, smoothing a wisp of her own hair. Normally her glossy hair lay soft and clean against her head; today oily strands stuck to her cheek. *Pfft*—she was dirty as a field toad in midsummer.

Clark set her on her feet, and she winced. "I can't stand on them." He settled a chair under her, and between them, he and Clark carried her and the chair to the table. She crumpled over, too exhausted to cry.

Just then the day's glorious sunshine broke out of the dark corners of the sky and burst through the windows, illuminating the breakfast Chen had set before them. Though Chen had no time to make pork dumplings, instead he served shrimp, rice, and her favorite dish of snow peas.

Her eyes were grainy, and when she looked out at Chen, his usual steady face appeared as a double image. She blinked the dust away and willed herself to see only one view of her beloved friend. "Thank you for seeing after the girls while I was gone."

He nodded. "My pleasure, si tau po. After your arrest, Officer Wong visited us, telling us to stay in the locked house."

She turned to Clark. "Why did they not arrest Chen?"

"All arrests are made known to me, since I am part of the militia. When Chen's name was mentioned, I assured the Committee that Chen was a manservant, not responsible for the running of the house."

She clasped her hands together. "I am most grateful."

Looking over at Chen, she asked, "Did anything occur here that I should know about?"

"I had to clean off the eggs that people were throwing at our house during your time away."

"Who were the culprits?"

"Some men who want us gone."

Clark shook his head. "More work by the Sydney Ducks, most likely. Now Jenkins was made to die, they'll double up their efforts to harass our citizens."

"Story says more Ducks will hang." Chen frowned.

She said, "One more question—I sent a letter asking for Henry Conrad's help with the Vigilantes. He has influential friends, such as Thomas Larkin, who might have intervened on my behalf. Did the Committee receive any word from him?"

"No, I am afraid not. Either he refrained from getting involved, or his possible letter did not arrive in time to help you."

Ah surmised. Maybe Henry was reluctant to compromise his status and future business dealings by involvement with the Vigilantes. On the wrong side of their law, he could risk his own interests.

But then, of course, he would not have gotten her letter in time. It would have taken weeks to arrive in Guangdong by ship. Why had she even bothered to send it? Did something inside her yearn for his connection? That piece of the puzzle was missing.

She yawned and shook her head. She was no match for this place. Maybe she should give up, go away, or surrender. But where would she go? What would she do? Wait a moment—she should be basking in Clark's presence, his smiles, his nearness. But instead, she lay her head down on the kitchen table and fell fast asleep.

After she knew not how long, Ah woke up and sat in a stupor. Chen cleared the dishes away, and Clark remained at the table, jotting in a small official notebook he carried. Though she had little energy to enjoy his company, she did express her thanks to him.

"I only wish—" she said. The unspoken became a veil hanging between them.

After a pause, Clark took her hand. "We share the same desires. What is important now is that you are safe." He drew a breath. "Yet, I have other matters of late that have taken my heart away."

"Please tell me. You have not yet mentioned your wife's health. Her consumption."

He stared up at the ceiling for a moment, then took her hands in his. "Some time after you saw her, she improved, and we were hopeful that she would be fully healed. She was no longer coughing up blood, and the doctor said we might have some extra time."

"Extra?"

"Yes, the doctor told us the disease must run a course, and there are many turns along the way. Sometimes patients recover for a long period of time before getting worse again."

"Such a shame that she has this horrible disease."

"She comes from a consumptive family in New York City. She lost both a brother and sister to the disease. The doctor said some families have a run of it through the generations. A tragedy, but all too common."

She fought against the demon that would have her dance with joy at the news. And so, she thought of some way to help—what could her culture provide this woman, to ease the misery, to prepare her for the next life to come after she shed her current body?

Into the stillness between them, through the veil between her and Clark, her dragon spoke. *Your Chinese healer will know. Remember he pointed you to the room where he does acupuncture. And can you still see the drawers with his medicines? Though consumption may be too far gone, go to this healer and ask for his help. Do not delay.*

Two days afterward, Ah felt the warm, penetrating rays of the summer sun on her back. Flannery's wagon jerked to a stop, and she stepped down, Chen at her arm. A sign next to the door read "Healer" in Chinese calligraphy, sparking in gold and black lettering, and the chime once again signaled their entry.

The healer's assistant greeted her at the door with a handshake "They are in the acupuncture room. You may wait in the hallway outside."

Without speaking, Ah and Chen crept into the hallway, and through the open door she spied Susannah Clark lying on a table, the healer setting needles into various points of her ears. Where was Clark? She scanned the room.

He perched on the chair, kneading his hat like a loaf of bread, his wide eyes focused on the healer and his wife. How foreign this would be to Clark. He probably never had seen any Chinese medicines or procedure like this before.

Ah backed away from the doorway, and Chen pointed to a settee in the hall where they sat. She felt quite small in the face of Susannah's illness; suddenly she knew the way forward included her showing love to Clark in another way. Her dragon stirred and she heard its whisper. *You will endure this trial by giving love to Susannah. That will illuminate your path.*

A few moments passed in silence. Chen stirred. "Why does Clark look so scared?"

"He fears for her life, and he does not understand our Cantonese healers."

"Oh, I see." His feature softened.

"Our British traders knew our healing ways back in Guangzhou, and they used them. But here in America, not many whites understand their purpose."

Chen gave her a sidelong glance. "I suppose he does not want to lose her."

"Yes, did you notice—her skin is gray and limp against her body."

"I have seen that skin on one who is dying." He pressed his lips together.

"We must give Clark hope, though I fear there is little chance for her." With those words, she retreated into the shadow world where death romped, crushing the heart.

Eight

❦ HIS HEAVY WEIGHT ❧

After dinner that evening Chen took Ah to Clark's house. She patted the small bottle of potion inside the silk pouch at her waist. The evening's fog cast gray shadows along the walls of the street. Though she had put on an extra layered wrap, she trembled in the cool air. At the doorway she could see one candle glimmering in an upstairs window.

Chen knocked, then pushed his queue back over his shoulder.

Clark opened the door and spoke a somber hello into the air. His eyelids appeared heavy. Was it from grief or lack of sleep?

"How is Mrs. Susannah?" Chen asked.

Clark suppressed a yawn. "Her breathing is worse—she had a bloody spasm this afternoon. I'm afraid—." He turned and whispered something into the ether of the hallway.

Ah stepped forward. "Let us come in. Please show Chen where to boil hot water for herbal compresses and wash cloths."

"What are you planning to do?" He gave her a probing gaze.

"We are here to help you with *her* now."

His chin trembled. "The acupuncture may have helped, but she is failing now."

She reached out a hand and encircled his arm. "It was something to try, yet it may be too late. At least you tried to help." She felt his heavy weight leaning against her, and for the first time it was she who held him up, she whose arms encircled his waist.

After a few moments, she poked him gently. "Show Chen where your kitchen is so he may prepare warm wraps to ease her sufferings."

Clark breathed in; his eyes vacant. "Follow me, Chen."

"And her bedroom?" she asked.

"Down there." He pointed along the dim hallway.

After listening to their fading footsteps, Ah pushed open the bedroom door. There lay Susannah in the gloom; she was tucked deep into the large feather bed. Even though Ah had seen the woman earlier in the day, Susannah's physical changes were profound.

Her once glossy chestnut hair now lay in a mouse-brown spider's web against the pillow. Her round, petite face, once animated with smiles, now sank, lines crisscrossing her cheeks. She clutched her Bible, and each breath racked her chest like a curse. Ah absorbed the reality—Susannah was drowning in the liquid of her own lungs.

The woman opened her eyes, and her gaze flitted around the room. "Who, are you?" A dreadful wheeze trailed behind her words, then a *click-clack* as if many marbles jumbled in her chest.

Ah placed her hand on the woman's forehead. A sheen of hot sweat stuck to her palm. She whispered into Susannah's ear. "Your husband John—I am a friend—here to help you."

Chen arrived with the cool herbal compresses, along with a tumbler of green liquid. He extended his hand with the packs, and Ah placed them on Susannah's forehead. Meanwhile, Chen passed her the tumbler, and Ah set it against Susannah's lips. "Can you drink this?"

Someone's footsteps came closer. "Whatever are you doing?" Clark's voice made her jump, and some of the liquid splattered on Susannah's white nightgown.

Setting aside his question, Ah held the tumbler upright with her right hand, mopping up the spill with her left. Susannah's cough persisted, each time more racking.

She spoke over Susannah's rumbling. "Chen, do you know the name for this medicine in English?"

"The British in Guangdong call it Sweet Wormwood. Our Chinese healers use it for all sorts of fevers and coughing."

"Where did you get it?" Clark wrinkled his nose as if smelling something unpleasant.

She held the tumbler loosely in her hand. "From the same healer who treated Susannah with acupuncture. It may not cure her since her disease is well advanced, but he said it would not hurt her."

A breath caught in his chest. "I do not think we need to bother with your remedies at this late hour. See? She is making to die. Her passing will be a mercy—the end of her suffering. Besides, I have a feeling."

Ah looked up into his red-rimmed eyes. "What is that?"

"There is a right smart chance she will leave us soon and go to God." Clark's voice sounded firm, yet it wavered.

"None of us controls the hour of our destiny." Ah continued laying out the compresses, but she tucked the tumbler back into her jacket pocket, patting it. Someone else might need it someday.

Hours passed into the night. Clark fell asleep on the fainting couch. Chen lit lanterns and candles. The tables surrounding Susannah's bed resembled an altar for a midnight church service. Though Susannah labored to breathe, the illness destroyed her, and she fell at last into a terrible sleep, her tormented breathing like metal claws scraping pine boards. *Scrah-scrah, scrah-scrah.*

Ah continued applying her compresses, but she drew back now and then when Susannah thrashed about during her wrestling matches with death.

Chen kept his vigil next to Ah, assisting her when they needed to change the toweling around Susannah where she had exhaled and coughed up blood and sputum.

After one particularly violent interval, when Susannah choked, then expelled a stream of mucus-laden blood, Chen whispered, "Do you not fear you may catch the disease?"

Ah glanced up at him. "I have not thought of fear until now. I pray for my Goddess Mazu to protect me."

"Do you think she could protect me, too?"

"I have already asked her for your safety. Our Heavenly Goddess guides all sailors home from the sea. Susannah's voyage is near its end. The Empress Mazu will meet her when she reaches the shores and will guide her transformation into the next life."

"The Goddess is hope, salvation, and reconciliation." Chen's voice filled with reverence.

Ah peered into his eyes, noticing his black pupils reflecting the candle's flames. She said, "Susannah is well protected, and she will pass into her new being. Now we must pray for the Goddess to guide Clark on his new passage. It is he who will bear the sorrows of her loss and the loneliness he must face."

Chen patted her arm. "But si tau po, are you not glad that he will be alone? For yourself?"

She chose her words deliberately. "The Goddess teaches acceptance. A surrender to what cannot be changed. It is true that I longed for him in past moments and mourned him, but the illuminations have shown me that he cannot be mine until fate and fortune decrees it so. And that day may never come."

"So, what must we do?"

"Help him through his grief, and ask the Goddess for her continued intervention."

Chen blinked, his eyes brimming with tears.

Ah glanced at the clock on the mantel. Four o'clock. Chen huddled in a chair, his soft breathing in and out, in and out. Clark sat at the edge of the bed, holding Susannah's hand.

In the past hours, Susannah had traveled from the world of battling death into the passage of soft release, whereby her body had let go its spirit.

"She now floats with clouds." Ah whispered. "Her suffering here is at an end."

"And mine is just beginning." Clark muttered into the darkness. He covered Susannah's face with his hand, his fingers closing her eyelids. He leaned over and kissed his wife's cheek.

"Yet through this passage you will learn who you really are." Ah fought against the urge to put her arms around his shoulders, to pull him close, to kiss away his tears.

His voice was low. "I loved her, you know. Sure, we had our failings, but she was a faithful wife."

"And she will always remain that for you."

"Do you think I will see her again in heaven?" His eyes glimmered like distant stars.

Her words flowed across their divide. "Such goodness will surround you in heaven and in earth. You will see her in every cloud—every rainbow. Your memories will shine forever, and no one can erase them."

He turned and patted her hand.

She rose and crept over to Chen. "We must go home. The girls will worry at this late hour. We must go sleep before tomorrow's dawn."

He brushed his fingers against his right eye, yawned, and got up. "What is the time?"

"Four o'clock."

"And Susannah?" Chen lifted an eyebrow.

"She is well on her way, the Goddess by her side."

Chen glanced at the Clark's bowed head, then whispered into her ear. "Will the Goddess protect him too?"

"She will guide him through his path of reconciliation, yet he must face his loss alone as we all must. This I know."

She paused at the doorway, Chen at her side.

Clark had lifted his head and sat transfixed, beholding Susannah's face. He must be etching her into his memory, along with the mosaic of moments shared in their life together.

Her chest tightened. If only he were thinking of her, rather than Susannah. Shaking her head, she swept the dark thought into a dark corner of her mind and covered it with a silk cloth.

Into the silent space between them, her dragon whispered. *You have shown your goodness, child. Let that lead you to happiness.*

She muttered to herself. "I have no choice—I must believe in that."

Nine

❦ HANDS WORK THREADS ❦

August 1851

Nearly a month went by, each day blanketed within the gray fog of summer. Each day Ah fought against the urge to go visit John Clark. He no longer walked the precinct where she would see him, stopping to chat with peddlers on their rounds or rousing the occasional miner who passed out on the street.

He no longer cast his long shadow down Pike Street where from behind a curtain, Ah would peek at his profile as he passed; even if he was not hers, at least he was nearby.

Though she worried that the Vigilante warning could impact her parlor house business, Chen reported that men continued to come to see and lie with the exotic San and Yee. Story spread that Ah's parlor house and girls were the finest in the city.

That morning after her meal of *siu mai* with shrimp and rice, Ah could no longer resist the impulse—she must go with Chen and talk to

Mr. Clark. Even if he was grieving, maybe she could give him some small comfort.

After she and Chen got down from the wagon, she asked the driver Flannery to wait for her. "I should not be long," she said.

"Aye, lass," he said, tipping his hat with his whip.

Once at Clarks' house, she lifted the lion door knocker, and let it pound against the brass plate, sending a clattering ricochet of noise along the street. She exchanged glances with Chen. No one came to the door. Again, she raised the knocker; again, it fell; once again, it clanked.

Footsteps echoed toward them along the plank walkway. Ah glanced around Chen at a woman clutching her market basket, a little boy in short pants holding her arm.

"Looking for the Clarks?" The woman's bonnet lay neatly on her head, purple ribbons tied under her chin.

"Yes, why do you ask?" Ah pressed her trembling lips together.

"Haven't you heard?" The woman's white-gloved hand rose to her mouth.

"What?" Ah strained to hear.

The little boy fidgeted at her side. "Not now, Johnny. Let me talk to these good people. We'll stop at Mr. Rutherford's chocolate shop if you are good."

The little one gave a dreamy smile and calmed a bit.

The woman leaned in. "His wife died, and now he is taking her body back to New York for burial. Told my husband and me that he does not know how long he will be gone."

"When did he leave?" Ah rubbed the back of her neck, her pulsed quickening.

"This morning. Ship leaves before noon—Pacific Wharf."

Ah bounced on the tips of her lotus shoes. "Do you know the name of the ship?"

"Can't recollect. Wrote it down. Come into the house. Name's Quigley, Johanna. I live right over here." She pointed two houses down the street. "I can find it for you."

Ah drew back, considering the offer. "No—no."

Chen said, "But *si tau po*—"

"Better not waste precious time." She said her goodbyes, stepped over to the wagon, and Flannery helped her up to gain her seat. Chen drew himself up next to her.

Johanna Quigley called up to her, "Do you wish to leave a message for him, Ma'am?"

"No but thank you." Ah tapped her fan against the back of Flannery's seat. He turned toward her, his red sideburns catching the sunlight. "Where to now, lass?"

She eyed his coat, frayed around the edges. "To the wharf. Please hurry, Flannery—but wait!" She fished a bag of gold dust from a deep pocket of her coat and held it up.

Flannery's green eyes sparkled. "That's a smart chance of money." As he cracked the whip over the Swinney the mule, the wagon lurched forward, and Ah clung both Chen and the side of the frame. As Swinney veered around the corner, she glanced behind. The mule's hooves were throwing up mud in the wagon's wake.

Johanna Quigley and child ducked out of the wagon's path, the little boy barely visible behind the woman's billowing plaid skirts.

Ah wrapped a shawl tightly about herself on the windy route to the wharf; yet her underarms dampened under her silk qipao. Her palms sweaty, she picked at the wooden tip of her fan. Her skin went cold, then hot. Lights from the beginnings of a migraine flashed inside her head, and she rubbed her temples.

After ten minutes weaving around wagons of full of produce, men pushing hand carts, and Californios in serapes crossing in front of them, Flannery brought the mule to a stop at the Pacific Wharf.

Sailors bustled up and down the long gangplank; they conveyed wooden barrels and leather bags on red-handled trolleys. She breathed the mix of sea salt and steam exhaust, along with the strong fishy odor common to wharves.

Near the gate onto the wharf marked "No Entry," she spied Clark's tall form in line behind two roughshod miners who kicked their rucksacks along as the line progressed toward the gangway. The clipper ship said *SS California*. Though small compared to other US Mail steamships now bringing gold rushers up from Panama to the mines, this ship loomed large above the dock, its three masts furled, its sailors climbing up and down the rigging. A towboat was securing the lines in order to pull the ship out into the bay.

Flags flew in the breeze, and for a moment she forgot herself, lost in the excitement, the thrill of watching people on a journey across the ocean as she once had done.

Three sharp horn blasts burst from the ship. Clark would board within minutes. Her throat tightened. It was not a matter of *if*, but *when* she must get through the gate.

However, she tried, she could not seem to break through the wall of men who stood between her and Clark. At first the engines issued a low thrum but now they made a steady rumble. Sailors moved rapidly, passengers edged along the railings, looking down at the wharf. Numerous ropes tied the ship to her moorings and dockworkers scurried to unhook all ties.

How could she make Clark notice her, a tiny speck of pepper hidden in a shaker? She turned to Chen. "Please—there—do you see him?"

"Yes, what should I do?"

"Call out 'John Clark' as loud as you can, like shots from a mighty cannon. If he does not hear you, call again."

"But—I doubt—"

She dug her fingernails into his forearm. "Do it for me, Chen, please, do it for me."

Chen drew in a deep breath and called "John Clark!" with the force of his lungs.

Clark continued forward, his line moving like water nearing the edge of the rapids.

She elbowed Chen, hard this time.

"Clark!"

No answer. In fact, the engines were accelerating, the former growl now a thunder.

Another elbowing. Another call.

At last Clark turned and waved. Was that a smile on his face? She breathed a prayer. *Oh, Goddess Mazu, let the crowd part so I may go to him.*

Chen must have seen an opening in the line, because he tugged her arm and nearly dragged her through smothering coats, kicking legs, carpetbags, steamer trunks, and cursing men.

Meanwhile, Clark must have had someone keep his place in line, since he met them where the line parted, then led them to the side.

"I am most grateful to see you, Ah, and of course you, Chen."

Chen tapped her arm. "You have little time, si tau po." He stepped away and looked down the wharf. Deferential. Allowing them their screen of privacy.

Clark's smile was gentle. "I do not know what to say, other than fare-well."

"How long will you be gone?"

His brow furrowed. "I must take Susannah back to her family in New York. Many arrangements to take care of. Many gatherings. I do not know." He pointed to a second gangway where dockworkers were loading trunks and baggage. A lone pine coffin, covered with a white cloth and an embossed red and white cross, lay apart. *She* was in that box.

"But won't she—"

"No—the coffin is lead-lined. Susannah is quite safe, as well as the passengers. I made sure the funeral parlor gave her what is called the royal coffin."

The line was moving—Ah stepped along by his side. Then sudden fear stabbed her like a ceremonial knife. "You will return to San Francisco—to us?"

"Right now, I cannot think beyond today. Someday, perhaps, I will return. Yet my plans will not be firm until I see this through."

She reached up, cast her arms around his chest, and drew him to her. His body held her loosely, then tightened around her, and she felt her breasts, her waist, her thighs melt into his form. One body, one breath.

Another horn blast broke into their embrace. She let him pull away, sorrow drawing lines across his face.

"Come back." If only her words would nestle in his soul, wrap around him like a protective shield, and guard him from all harm.

Then another voice called his name, deep and forceful. "Clark, John!"

She gazed up at the gangway. The purser held a passenger list; he tipped his hat back and looked down with obvious annoyance at Clark's belongings. "Come forward, sir, or I shall cancel your name from the list." He huffed. "Can't you see how many passengers are behind you?"

Clark swiveled and called out. "A moment, man." He turned back to her. "I cannot promise."

"Come back." Her words flowed into the air.

Chen stepped to her side, his hand gentle on her shoulder. Was he trying to shelter her from another slice of pain?

"At least please write to me?"

Clark leaned away, resettling his hat on his head. "Maybe. I do not know. I am sorry, truly I am."

With that, Ah stepped back, and the tide of humans streamed around her, then up the gangplank and onto the deck. She had no other choice but to let him go. How could she force him to stay? She turned to Chen. "Must I?" A forbidden tear slipped down her cheek, and she brushed it quickly away.

"I think it is what he wants, si tau po." He palmed her shoulder one more time.

341

Ah watched the passenger lines diminish, the baggage disappear into the ship, the lines cast off, and the ship ease away from the pier. Men populated the deck, peering down at her and other well-wishers down on the dock.

She squinted. Where was Clark? After a moment, he appeared among that throng of men, then waved down at her and Chen. She fluttered her fan, and caught a sidelong glimpse of Chen, his face upturned, his queue draped forward over his chest. His hand waved farewell.

The water curled over the wake as the SS *California* headed out toward the Golden Gate Straits and the Pacific Ocean. The central smokestack belched white steam into the air. The sails unfurled and soon the ship was an undulating black line against the blue of the Pacific sky. There, beyond the horizon, was China. Long after the SS *California* had disappeared, Ah lingered alone on the wharf, picturing her infant daughters as she had nursed them at home in Guangzhou. An ocean of time separated her from the babies she had lost.

Now a continent would stand between her and the man whose love she desired. She murmured into the breeze as images of her girl babies darted and danced on the waves. Every woman must count her losses. Clark's leaving carried a bigger price for her than she could have imagined. The shadows were deepening, the sun simmering low in the eastern sky as she steered her own ship into the dark waves of the future.

Chen's voice broke into her waking dreams. "It is getting late. Mr. Flannery says Swinney is hungry and he must get home to his wife for dinner." He stretched out his hands. "I have brought your shawl—remember you left it in the wagon."

"Oh, did I? I didn't even notice."

The next afternoon, Ah held onto the right side of Flannery's wagon seat, Chen bumping her hip with each sway. She watched Swinney the mule labor up the path on the southern flank of Telegraph Hill, then jerk to a stop at a fork in the road.

No amount of Flannery's poking, prodding or whipping could get the animal one foot further. Flannery turned back, his face windburned and chapped. "That's as far as Swinney can go."

Ah heard the words, yet she was not willing to let the mule win the day. Above her on the crest of the hill, the American flag flapped in the breeze next to a tall mast with semaphore's patterned signal flags.

The flag's positions showed which ships were arriving in the Bay and if they needed help. Visible from anywhere in the city, the semaphore's flags told which ships were leaving and entering the harbor.

She turned around on her seat—to the right, the city lay behind her, wooden buildings cheek-by-jowl, laid out in a grid, to the left, wharves stretching their fingers into the bay. Some white tents were sprinkled on the lower reaches of the hill.

Men drove cattle along the street below. People scuttled everywhere, ants crossing streets and disappearing into buildings. Swinney snuffled, then emitted an *eeeee-aaaaaa*.

Ah turned to Chen. "Can you take me to the top? I have never been up there, and I wish to see the view. They tell me I can see toward China."

He blanched as if he had just tasted a sour lemon. "It is very far . . . look at the twists in the path to the top. I think it would take us more than an hour before we reach it." He pointed to the western flank. "There is another pathway, but even more steep."

She tapped Flannery's back with her fan. "Could you unhitch Swinney? I could ride her, and Chen could lead on foot?"

Chen's eyes widened. "I could?"

Flannery gave a belly laugh. "Surely you canna be serious, lass. If ye fell off Swinney, ye might break a leg. And she can be durned stubborn, that one."

Chen broke in. "You don't know how willful my si tau po can be."

343

Flannery looked up the hill, then back at her. "Why do you wanna go up there, lass?" A gust of wind caught his hat and he fought to hold it against his head.

Ah lifted her chin. "They say you can see to China from there. I wish to see it."

Flannery chuckled, then rubbed his stubbly beard. "I surely doubt that."

"Have you ever tried?" Chen added.

"Well . . . no." He caressed Swinney's flank.

Ah persisted. "So . . . how do you know? I want to see for myself. It is worth it to me."

"I don't know about yer takin' Swinney. 'Twould depend on whether you make it worth me while." His grin revealed a missing canine tooth.

"After all this time you have given us rides?" Ah tapped her sleeve. "Plenty of gold shavings in here."

"In that case—." Flannery winked.

Ah reached out toward Chen and he lifted her up from the wagon and down onto the grass.

After a few moments of unhitching and unbuckling Swinney from the wagon, Flannery threw a small native blanket over the mule's back. The animal turned back, her eyes plainly wary.

Chen drew back. "Will she bite?"

"Only if she hasn't had her treats." Flannery passed him a burlap bag.

"Smells of fish." Chen fondled the bag, his mouth turned down into a half moon.

Flannery shrugged. "She's fond of fish offal. We get plenty of it from the nets down at Long Wharf."

Ah said, "I've never heard of a mule who likes fish."

"She ain't no ordinary mule."

"When do I give this to her?" Chen pressed a hand to his nose.

"Dole it out bit by bit when she balks." Flannery coughed, stifling a chuckle.

Ten

❦ KEEP IT IN PLACE ❦

After nearly an hour of struggle, stops, and smelly fish feeds, Swinney complied with Chen's Cantonese demand, and they reached the crest of Telegraph Hill. Sure enough, Ah spied the small telegraph office next to the tall pole containing the semaphore. The largest American flag she had ever seen swept back and forth in the breeze. Thirty-one stars glided across the blue background.

After Chen helped her down off Swinney's back, she stepped over to the edge of the hill where it broke off into a steep cliff.

"Watch out!" Chen's voice rang out, competing with the gigantic flag flapping against its rope on the pole above the telegraph office.

Ah peered down at the tops of rooftops and white tents moored on the hillside below. Dozens of men drifted along the narrow beach below. She gazed out at the northern hills across the water, then in at the bay, busy with double and triple-masted ships, flags of many nations, their decks peopled with slouch-hatted men. They were young; they were seeking gold.

She looked to her right onto the series of wharves that jutted into the bay, a population of ships changing the pristine waters into a graveyard of buoys and abandoned vessels. Chen had told her that even the captains were ditching their ships in the rush for the gold hills named Placer, Amador, and Calaveras.

She remembered that day on the wharf—her set of unknowns, the Daileys, the lurching of the ship as it set into the wharf. The melon rolling into the bay. Yet despite all her struggles, she knew a sense of love for this place—its population brown, pink, gold, red—from all over the world they came.

She looked to her left, over the Golden Gate Straits and out to China. Sure enough, story said land anchored there on the far Pacific. All she could see was the vast expanse of ocean blue, dotted with thin shreds of white cloud. Better that China stayed over there, out of sight. She remembered the world map Mrs. Dailey had shown her. The continents did not travel—people did.

She made a frame with her hands. The blue, white-capped waters fit inside the painting. *Goddess Mazu please keep the continent in place—just there. Let the Zhujiang Delta hold it in place. Let its porcelain factories, laborers, and merchants weigh it down. The winding, throbbing streets, its peoples jostling one another. Leave it there. My babies' bones rest at the bottom of their cliff such as this one. Grant them peace.*

She looked down at her tiny stumped feet and the dry grass beneath them. This was now her land, the land of gold. Not the ore of miners laboring with pickaxes, pans and shovels, but the gold of freedom. The same joy she had known on the shore at Monterey now enveloped her. The pure love of this place. No matter she was not accepted for her skin; no matter she was cast in a lower position than men.

This California gave her a place, a power she had never known before. In China she would live in silence, in the darkness of subservience, protected only by her dragon. Here in San Francisco she would keep her dragon close, but she would use her own voice.

Time passed. Had it been an hour or two? The sun hovered low on the western horizon.

"Are you finished, *si tau po?*" Chen's voice brushed the silence around her.

She gave a reluctant breath. "Yes, Chen. Let us go home."

After Chen pulled Swinney's harness and helped Ah onto the mule's back, the animal nickered, seeming to know she was returning to Flannery. Swinney jounced down the hill, Ah's teeth chattering. After Flannery grabbed the mule's halter at the bottom, Ah swung off into his arms.

Flannery set her on her feet. She caught a whiff of tobacco on his breath.

Chen joined them, his chest heaving.

"How was the view?" Flannery asked, gazing down into her eyes.

She took a moment to catch her breath. "I could not see China, but I learned many things. Now I want to go home—this home, my San Francisco."

"Aye, but few people consider this a city to call home. Most want to pass through to gold diggins. Sometimes it feels more like an express station than a town. You must miss your China very much. I surely miss me Ireland." He offered a deep sigh.

She held out her arms. "Guangdong was my homeland." She made an arc sweeping over the bay. "But this Bay is my home."

A week passed in the normal succession of events. Chen would fix breakfast, the girls would prepare for their evening meetings with men, many of whom had become regular customers. Sailors were the exception: they came and went with some frequency, although steam ship captains working for the Pacific Mail visited the girls in a predictable pattern of certain days of the week.

A patch of wallpaper tore off in the hallway upstairs, and Chen was repairing it with a bucket of flour-water paste. Ah sat with the abacus and sheets of accounting spread before her on the dining room table.

The window facing the street was ajar, and noises of passing horses, people walking, and newsboys filled the air. A breeze stirred the fern plant Chen had placed in the center of the table.

Jade mewed, her tail swishing.

Chen came in and sat, careful to hold the bucket of paste on his lap. He looked over at Jade. "I think she wishes to go out."

Ah nodded, "Go ahead." She turned back to her work.

She heard Chen's chair creak, followed by more mewing. "Come on, Jade."

The *mews* grew fainter, followed by the murmurs of Chen's encouraging the cat, the opening of the front door, the *scree-scraw* of its rusty hinges.

A few minutes passed. Ah focused on her accounts, rubbing her stiff neck. Chen had spent too much money repairing the roof after the spring rains. She would have to talk to him about that. And the girls deserved new beds. How would she squeeze that out of the present income? Wait a minute—what was she worried about? She had plenty of money tucked away in the bank.

Voices came from the hallway. Who could that be? Why hadn't Chen sent them away? He knew she was busy. *Grrr . . .* for a moment, she fought the urge to get up and slam the door to protect her peace.

The voices grew louder—Chen's and—who was that?

She turned and caught a glimpse of Chen leading Henry Conrad into the room. The moment caught and spun her like a wild orchid in the breeze.

"Mr. Henry Conrad," Chen announced, plainly controlling his excitement. "Oh—and Jade did not want to go out."

"Thank you," she said.

Chen nodded and shut the door of the study.

Henry gave a half-bow. He spoke in fluent Cantonese. "I am most honored to see you, Mrs. Toy." Jade rubbed against his leg, and he stepped sideways to avoid her.

She gave a nod in turn, sweeping away a lock of hair that fell over her cheek. "I am happy to see you, too, Henry." She pointed to the settee. "Please sit. I am happy you are back from Guangdong. Did you come because of my letter?"

He brushed away a piece of dust from his sleeve. "I did receive a letter from you, but unfortunately my affairs delayed my return. Besides, by the time I got the letter, your date had long passed, so I figured your situation was long resolved."

"Then I will fill you in," she said. "It concerned my arrest and subsequent hearing before the Committee of Vigilance. Your friend Sam Brannan was one of the men in charge." She eased her fan from her sleeve and clasped it in her lap.

"I trust that everything turned out right for you. I would think Sam Brannan would extend mercy toward you, a friend of the Larkin family." He gave her a tight-lipped smile.

"They held me in the filthiest of conditions." She shuddered.

The lines deepened around his large, intelligent eyes. "I am sure it was not a pleasant ordeal for you. I will let Thomas Larkin know about it in case you have trouble with the Committee again. I am surprised to hear they had time for your case; the newspapers say they have their hands full with the Hounds and the Ducks."

She flicked open her fan. "How long will you be here this time?"

He removed his silk top hat, placing it beside him on the settee. Jade jumped up, nosing the hat.

She swept her hand. "A new style?"

He nodded. "All the rage in Hong Kong. Prince Albert is wearing such a hat in London, so all the British traders are sporting it." He lifted it, the black silk reflecting shapes and shadows. Jade sat on her haunches regarding him.

Ah said, "San Francisco gentlemen are still sporting stovepipes—it will take a while for London fashions to arrive, although British trading ships are bringing new fancy goods each day."

He raised his eyebrows. "Soon, I suspect you shall see them on every gentleman of quality."

Chinaware clattered in the hallway. The door swung open. Chen appeared with a tray bearing two cups and a pot of tea. Fresh-baked almond cookies rested on a plate. He set the offerings on the table between her and Henry.

She set her hand on the tray. "I will pour, Chen."

Jade mewed and rubbed against Chen's leg. "I believe Jade is hungry." He bent and lifted Jade into his arms, and the cat rubbed her head under his chin.

"Is there food for her in the larder?"

"Yes, si tau po. Plenty of fish heads I've been saving." He bowed, turned, and closed the study door.

Henry blanched. Something was making him uncomfortable. What was it?

She poured the tea into a blue and white cup, then passed it to him. "Would you like a cookie?"

"No, I have breakfasted."

She poured for herself, then sipped. An awkward silence covered them like a thin layer of tissue. She nibbled the edge of an almond cookie. Her sideways glance caught silhouettes of two Cantonese men as they passed outside, bits of their musical conversation wafting in through the window.

At last Henry spoke. "I am not here on an idle visit."

"Oh?" Her pulse picked up a beat.

"In fact, I have given you much thought this time away in Guangdong."

"And I have thought of you as well." The window's light played across his face.

He swallowed his tea, put his cup on the tray, then folded his hands in his lap. "I have done very well in Guangzhou. My porcelain factories are earning quadruple what they did in 1849, since the China clippers deliver the orders to America in such speedy fashion. I am free to settle down in San Jose on my cherry ranch and my business will continue to grow." He puffed out his chest, a smile spreading across his lips.

"You must be happy to experience success." If only she did not feel like a wooden doll, but she could not seem to soften the tension in her neck.

"It is for that reason I have come at this time." Was that a flush creeping into Henry's tan cheeks?

She held her breath. Something brushed her check—her dragon's wing?

"I will be able to see you more often now." Despite the formality, she could hear the excitement in his words.

"Will you be here in San Francisco?"

"I will be coming for supplies and tools in order to set up my orchard. I want you to see the land I have bought." He drew pictures in the air. "I have thirty acres of rolling hills, the air is clean and pure, the trees and bushes grow with little help. My foreman tells me the orchard saplings show promise. I am working on new plans for a house there."

"I am happy for you. Good fortune has found you, Mr. Conrad. You have received many blessings."

"Yes, I am indeed fortunate." His lips parted slightly. "Yet there is one blessing I have to receive."

She waited, listening to the *clop* of foot traffic and the *fffff—ffff* of the breeze swishing the curtains. Or was it her dragon's breath that had moved the air?

He cleared his throat, breaking the harmony. "I would like you to consider a union with me—later when I have all the affairs settled and the home built. Of course, you would no longer have to work—like *this*." He lifted his top lip—was that a sneer? How much about her parlor house did he figure out? He took his top hat, set it on his lap, and fondled the ribbon around the brim.

She said, "I cannot think about that right now. I have many affairs to manage here, and I am responsible for Chen and the girls in my care."

"I have already considered that. Perhaps you might consider my offer further, especially since I would be willing to bring Chen with us to San Jose."

"Ah yes, I remember." She waited for more.

"Chen would take on a management role. He speaks Cantonese and I still need a translator to manage my porcelain affairs reported to me from Guangdong. He may handle that while I work on the orchard business."

"Oh—" She bit her lower lip. His offer sounded kind. "Yet I have San and Yee. I would not abandon them."

He brightened. "I have also considered that. I will also need household help, and the girls would fit that role. Housemaids, overseers. The estate is vast, and the tasks are plenty. Though they would work for our estate, they would enjoy freedom that they never would have had in Guangdong—or here. That I know."

She opened her fan and gently slid it over her left cheek.

His hands stiffened around the brim of his hat. "I would like a definite answer soon."

"I find your offer most honorable. I will need time to consider it."

"I will not accept a hasty decision. Please take time to think on it more fully. I will take care of you and your household as a loving husband. I want to have you by my side for the rest of my life. Soon I will return with a more complete proposal." His words sounded crisp as dried straw.

She paused, regarding him. Were these the manners of someone who would love her?

She pondered, a vision of his land and orchards hovering in the space between them. Yet it was the unsaid that troubled her. Should she tell him of her parlor house business? That this, her fine house, was a lowly brothel disguised as a fancy residence? That the girls in her employ were indentured servants, contracted to be prostitutes? Or did he already know? The unanswered questions hung like a tapestry before them. Was she a coward for not bringing up the subject?

She fondled the handle of her fan. "When will you be back?" she asked.

"Soon when my affairs allow me to come. More than that I cannot say." His voice was gentle, his manner kind. She noted his broad forehead, the way he wore his hair down to his collar, swept to the side with a part. He may not be Clark, but he was a fashionable man, comfortable among groups of all sorts, whether they were laborers, bankers, or community leaders.

After he left, she returned to the abacus and her accounts spread across her desk. She took measure of the situation. What was stopping her from embracing this man's offer? Henry Conrad might promise her wealth, salvation, and a full life.

He was the sort who stayed away from gambling halls, loose women and such like, preferring to take a brandy at a club in the company of men who played chess.

Some might say he was stuffy. She would say he was safe.

Yet her puzzle was missing a piece.

Part Five

The autumn moon sails its bright ship in the sky
Leaves rustle in the road
The crows caw on the rooftops
Startled, surprised at the turn of the day
And the waves of sorrow
I think of you—do you know my mind?
When will we meet again?

IN THE MANNER OF LI PO

One

❦ WINTER MOON SAILS ❦

December 1851

*I*n between rainy days, December drew its paintbrush across the sky above San Francisco, daubing azure blue next to the clouds reflected in the whitecapped waters below. The dry grasses and bare oak trees gleamed on the hillsides surrounding the bay, and the breezes blew cold, clean and fresh. Chen's hands grasped hers while he helped her down from the wagon. "Would you like me to go with you?"

"No, I want to read this alone." She drew an envelope from her woolen sleeve and held it up.

"Mind yer steps, lass." Flannery's voice came from his perch.

She glanced up at him. "I only need time to read the letter. Please wait."

Swinney grunted, and Flannery leaped off the wagon. A fishy odor clung to the bag in his hand. Chen stood by Flannery's side, then cast her a glance, plainly concerned that Ah might trip or fall.

She limped to a boulder and settled on its crown where the rock indented, making a natural cradle. She absorbed the momentary sensation of warm sun on her face and hands, then tightened her western-style shawl around her.

After so many visits to the post office with no news from Clark, this moment was worth a celebration, even if small. She wanted to savor it, so she held the envelope against her breast, hearing the paper crackle, rubbing its smooth surface against her skin. What had been kind appreciation for Clark now became strong yearning. His absence formed a chasm that nothing else could fill.

She slipped her fingers under the clasp of the envelope and pulled it open, then lifted the letter out. Clark's handwriting sprawled across the page, and she imagined his hefty frame lolling across a bed.

She ran her tongue across her lips. What was his latest news?

New York
October 15, 1851

My dear Ah,

I wish I had happier news to convey, but at this time I have only to report that I was successful interring Susannah in the burial plot I found for her at Tarrytown on the Hudson.

Her family plot was full, and her family members were not helpful to me. I think they had some resentments that Susannah had joined me in San Francisco. Her father manufactures lineaments, and I think he always wanted me to join his company in order to provide a stable income for his daughter.

Thus, her kin greeted me with little enthusiasm, and I was forced to pay for her burial with my own money. I have no regrets about this, since I am now at peace that Susannah is with the Lord and is well cared for by the angels in heaven.

Ah looked skyward, watching the wide-winged seagulls floating on the air currents. At last Susannah's bones would rest with her people. Clark had done the right thing by his wife. What else did he have to say? She looked back down at the letter, her hands trembling slightly.

> *Susannah's family held a series of wakes and church services to mourn her passing. I was quite exhausted from all the gatherings, so at the internment I was taken with the ague and dyspepsia, and I felt quite disagreeable.*
>
> *Now I am in the process of disposing of what little property she held on her own. She lived a quiet yet simple life with her parents after I left for San Francisco, so there is little to disperse. I am compelled to stay here awhile to honor her memory and the thoughts of our past life together.*

Poor man, he was taken with exhaustion. No wonder after the trauma of burying his wife. She continued to read.

> *I am not sure I will come back to San Francisco now, or if ever. I have a friend at the New York Police Department, and he has invited me to apply to the 19th precinct as a beat cop. I am considering this.*

She squinted down at the letter. Had she failed to read the last lines correctly? Her hands held the vellum, then smoothed it flat across her lap. Then she lifted the paper up, scrutinizing it again. Surely, she had not understood his English—or was it his scrawling handwriting?

> *Not sure . . . if ever . . . has invited me to apply . . . am considering this.*
>
> *Thus, I remain*
> *Your most humble servant*
> *John Clark*

359

Tears pricked her eyes; she gazed through their film at the dry grasses below her feet. The boulder that once had cradled her became hard and confining. *Not sure.* Had he gone into the grave along with Susannah? *If ever.* Would his be another set of bones to mourn, along with her baby daughters? *Thus, I remain.* A chasm loomed deep and dark . . . Clark's eyes looked up at her through the sockets of a skeleton that lay below. *Your most humble servant.* Then, carried on a strong breeze, her dragon's wings enfolded her, held her in a cocoon, and she breathed in and out, in and out.

The face fortune teller's purple robes glinted against the candle's glow that evening. "What brings you here again, little bird? The last time we spoke of your sadness and discouragement. We spoke of your stoking the dragon's fire, allowing its energy to lift you up and guide you through and over obstacles." He cocked his head to one side and sat back in his chair.

Ah said, "I have lost my way, and I have come for you to help me find the road."

"Very well. Let us begin," He leaned over the table, tracing his fingers on pathways along her forehead and down the lines of her nose. His hands circulated over her cheeks, around her lips, and toward her chin. He drew back. His face was a mask of immutability, reminding her of calm waters of the Pearl River as it flowed away toward the Delta and the South China Sea.

She took long breaths, waiting.

He tilted his head. "Your cheeks flame, your skin stretches. Your mouth purses in a straight line. Your jaw muscles clench. I sense your deep anger. This could become madness without control."

She clutched the fan in her sleeve. What more had he seen?

He sat back, tucking his hands together on his lap. His former scrutiny folded into a frown. "I fear you may have lost your way, little bird." The candle sputtered next to him.

She glanced at the spiraling flame, her realizations rising to the surface. She must tell him the truth. He knew her as no one else did.

Thus, she poured out the story of Clark, her heartbreak, her longing and frustration. The story of Susannah's death and his fading away. Clark seemed to trail his wife into the chasm of death. Her visions told her that his bones would lie entwined with those of her babies.

She dabbed again at her burning eyes. "What if Clark decides to stay in New York?"

The wise man leaned toward her, arms crossed, elbows resting on the yellowing pages of his texts. "Little bird, you fear loneliness itself, not life without Clark. Consider those around you—your companion Chen, the girls who work for you in your parlor house. Who would you rather be without—a man who prefers to wallow in his own grief and stay far from you, or your friends and helpmates who stay by your side each day and who will always be there?"

She flushed. "I do love my friends and the girls are a great help in running my business—but—"

The fortune teller's expression was a mask of calm. "When you face away from the present, and you inhabit a house of dreams, you are turning from the peace and harmony your dragon extends to you."

"I am not living in dreams."

"I must speak as your father would now, and you must listen." His gentle voice grew stern.

She squeezed her eyes shut. He was right.

The wise man continued. "You are stubborn. Each time you fail to hear or sense your dragon's presence, you have retreated into willful selfishness."

"It is true that I want certain things. But what is wrong with wanting love that I never had before?"

"The harder you strive for love, the less it will come to you."

She grew warm, her wrath simmering beneath the surface like the geysers in Zhongshan she had visited with her father.

"I see you are angry, but your rage is with yourself, not with me. In order to combat this passion, gird yourself with the armor of a warrior princess. Yet choose your skirmishes wisely. Do not go to battle with those who wish you well—Clark, Chen, San, Yee . . . even Li Fan . . . these are not the sources of your misery."

Hot tears spilled down her cheeks, and she wiped them away. "If they are not the source, what is?" She pressed the palm of her right hand to her forehead.

He pointed to his head. "Your imaginings—up here—they are the wild horses you must control." He swept his hand in a half circle. "Otherwise, they will run you off the cliff into the Bay."

She shook her head. "I have not told you my whole story."

"Then, go on please. But first, let us go to my small garden—such stories are better told in nature." He rose, then extended his arm, guiding her steps outside.

Once in the courtyard, Ah gazed up at the stars and puffs of cloud that tiptoed across the sky. The light from red and yellow lanterns etched slices of light and shadow across the tiled floors.

A stone Buddha sat on a makeshift pile of boards next to a small maple tree struggling for life in a pot. Lanterns beamed golden slivers onto the rocks tucked into the garden.

The fortune teller settled her into one of the mismatched straight-back chairs that faced a table in the center.

"It is time to tell me what ails you, little bird. Do proceed." The shafts of light caught and deepened the wrinkles carved in his cheeks.

She aimed her voice toward him, over the clacking of mahjongg tiles from an open window. "Henry Conrad has made me a proposal." She gazed away from him into the center of the courtyard. Her eyes traced the Buddha's form, his elongated ears, his tranquil form settling into a pile of stones which functioned as an altar. Offerings of fresh orange slices and cracked walnuts lay around him.

"I am listening. Tell your story." His voice softened.

Moments trickled away while Ah allowed the details of Henry's offer to come forth like raindrops, one upon the other. "And I am much bewildered, teacher. I would no longer be in control of my fate with Henry . . . or would I? Should I take his offer for security, or must I wait on shifting ground like earthquakes moving the ground under our feet?"

After she finished, the fortune teller smoothed the sleeves of his robes, first the left, then the right. The shadows of Chinese men moved back and forth through the window of an adjacent room.

"My daughter, lift your spirit to the Buddha. Draw your magic sword—take on the masculine—discover your precious jewel. Then, offer it to Buddha—only then will you attain enlightenment."

"But I want my questions answered now. That is why I have come to you."

He tilted his head. "You must endure these trials, solve these questions, and make these choices with strength. Your words speak fear and dependence. You fear the unknown but remember this—when the moon fades at dawn, it sheds the day before it. The next day dawns on the undiscovered, which is never shown to anyone until that day's sunrise. Then with each moment the truth reveals itself."

"So, what must I do?" She spoke through a shroud of angry tears.

He patted her hand. "Step out into the world and its presence. Savor your intelligence and your strength. Only you can decide whether Henry Conrad is a good choice for you, or you stay alone until the mystery of Clark's feelings for you is revealed."

His robes rustled, and he rose. "Do not go yet. Stay and linger in your meditations. Search for your precious jewel." He pointed to his heart. "Your solution lies in here."

She put her hand over her heart, her breath coming and going in soft waves. She pressed her fingers into her soft breast, feeling her heartbeat: steady, rhythmic, and pure.

Late the next morning Ah was in the kitchen stealing a taste of Chen's fresh dumplings. She savored the moment alone, San and Yee having gone out looking for new silks to wear. At noon, the thundering of the door knocker filled the house. "Chen! Where are you?" The knocking persisted. After a minute's searching, she gave up and opened the door herself.

Elizabeth Dailey and Hortencia faced her on the doorstep. If the fortune teller had told her to appreciate the unknown, this was certainly a surprise.

"Come in," Ah said. "I had no idea you might be in San Francisco."

Elizabeth bent low in a curtsy, and Hortencia dipped up and down. Elizabaeth said, "We would have sent word, but Reverend Dailey had urgent business with the pastor at Old First Church. So here we are."

"*¿Que es eso?*" Hortencia pointed to the bagua above the door.

Elizabeth said, "She wants to know what that is."

Ah said, "In Cantonese it is called bagua. It wards away evil and protects our house in all directions."

Hortencia bit her lip and made the sign of the cross as she entered the house. "*Dios me protege.*" She lifted her skirts above her ankles and stepped across the threshold ahead of her mistress.

Elizabeth followed Hortencia inside. "Do not take offense. Hortencia is asking her God to protect her. She does not know your beliefs and your ways. She means no harm."

Ah recognized Hortencia's frightened aspect in this braid of many cultures that was San Francisco. "I understand. Many Californios are afraid of our Chinese customs."

After settling her guests on the lacquered settee in the drawing room, Ah relaxed back against the cushion of her chair. Jade purred, rubbed against her leg, and jumped up on her lap. The cat turned around, casting a suspicious eye at the guests.

"You have a beautiful cat." Elizabeth said.

"Jade is my friend." Ah scratched the animal's silky, fur-trimmed ears.

"Does she bite?" Hortencia drew her rosary beads from her skirt pocket and clutched them tightly in her right hand.

"No, she is loving. Would you like to hold her?"

Hortencia looked up from her rosary.

Elizabeth nodded. "Try it. You might enjoy petting her."

"*Si . . . por un momento.*" The maid's eyes crinkled upward.

Ah lifted Jade up and with Elizabeth's help, she settled Jade into Hortencia's arms. The cat nestled in the woman's lap and tucked her head under Hortencia's elbow. Her mewing softened into a deep, rhythmic purr.

Hortencia grinned. "*Ella es hermosa.*" She relaxed her grip on her rosary beads and they tumbled across the cat's back. Jade continued her purring.

Ah said, "I would offer tea, but Chen has gone out."

Elizabeth nodded. "It is no circumstance. Henry Conrad sent me your address. I asked for directions to your house at several places in Little Canton. The men acted suspicious, protective. Finally, the vegetable seller told me where you were, and *what* you were—in broken English, of course." Her smile dissolved into a thin, brittle line.

An awkward moment passed. A wagon rattled outside. A passing vendor shouted in Cantonese "Fresh oysters!"

Ah drew her magic sword. Her first instinct was to scream at her old friend, tell her all she had gone through to survive in this country that bucked her at every turn. Her second thought was to throw her and Hortencia out on the street, rejecting all the bigotry and hypocrisy their religious beliefs represented. But . . . then she would lose the love and companionship of her first teacher of English, the only white woman capable of understanding her Cantonese past and her American present. She sheathed her sword, her dragon's claws patting it into place.

She drew herself upright in her chair. "I have been very successful at this trade, and I am kind and good to my girls, San and Yee. I have even gone to court to prove it, and they allow me to stay in business. It was you who told me that Jesus forgave Mary Magdalen, remember?"

Hortencia thumbed the crucifix on her rosary, patting Jade from time to time.

Elizabeth leaned toward her. "I did tell you about Jesus' power of forgiveness, and in my faith, you have broken God's commandments. Many of them. I fear for your eternal salvation."

Jade pulled up her head and squinted over at Elizabeth.

"Yet your faith is not my own." Ah said. "You have known that since the early days in Guangzhou when you came to my father's warehouse and we sat on crates where you spread out the English books and taught the words to me."

A light appeared in Elizabeth's eyes. "Yes, I remember those days with fondness. You were such an eager learner."

"Do you remember when you tried to teach me the letter "L" and I kept saying "R" instead?"

"We did laugh about that . . . you were so very dear . . . at ten years old you were very sharp and quick. Your father was very proud. He even said if you were a boy he would have put you in charge of the porcelain export business when you grew up. Your mother, of course, did not agree."

Ah's stomach tightened at the mention of her mother. "She was the one who insisted on the arranged marriage with Tung Chee."

Elizabeth frowned. "I was afraid he would not treat you well."

Ah said, "I never expected to marry a man who would murder his own children."

Hortencia's mouth opened and her eyebrows raised.

Elizabeth bit her lower lip. "If only I could have guarded you from all that."

"Without your help, we would never have escaped from Guangzhou." Ah placed a hand on her own chest, letting it ride up and down with her own breathing.

Elizabeth reached across and patted Ah's hand. "Who knows what would have happened to you there?" Her eyes watered.

Ah said, "I would have been killed along with Tung Chee, and Chen along with us. I overheard Tung Chao discussing the poison with his concubine. He knew we were on the way to San Francisco to start a new porcelain factory here. He wanted to kill us before we could escape. I knew we had little time to get away the night you helped us find passage on the brig *Eagle*."

"I never fully understood Tung Chao's desire to kill his brother. Was it only to take over the porcelain factory?"

Ah nodded. "That was part of the reason. But Tung Chao wished to take me for his wife. I heard him tell Tung Chee on many occasions that he did not deserve me, that Tung Chao would have made me a better husband."

Elizabeth drew back. "A better husband? In what way?"

Ah shook her head. "Trust me, there was no love in Tung Chao's heart. Only rivalry. He cared as much for me as a lizard cares for the cricket he consumes."

"Pure rivalry?"

"Yes, I was part of the baggage he would rightfully inherit upon his brother's death."

Elizabeth looked around the room, then over at Hortencia who continued to listen, her eyes wide as the moon at lunar festivals. "At least your Chinese luck had a hand in getting away from all that. It just happened that we had a ship readied for our new mission in Monterey. Otherwise . . . " She breathed deeply, then said, "But that is not the reason for my visit. Of course, I wanted to come and wish you well, but Henry has told me of his intentions to marry you and to bring your household to San Jose."

"I am glad that he told you."

Elizabeth leaned toward her. "I think the highest of Henry. He is a good and honest man and would make a kind and generous husband for you."

Ah's chest tightened. "I feel that I do not love him, though I find him very likeable."

Elizabeth shrugged. "What good is love? Few women marry for it. It is a girlish fantasy, my dear."

"Did you not marry for love? What about you and the Reverend?"

Hortencia cocked her head, listening. Maybe she had never heard this story.

"My family had been poor ever since my father lost his shares in a joint stock company. They arranged all the husbands for their four daughters. The Reverend was an agreeable sort, so I considered myself fortunate. He did not seem prone to drink or womanizing. Bent on a Christly path which my family encouraged me to pursue."

"So . . . you did not know him before the wedding? I never asked you this in Guangzhou. Since you were western, I must have assumed you were free to choose your husband."

Elizabeth shook her head. "No, I did not know my husband . . . at least not very well. We were always chaperoned until the wedding night when we were finally alone, wedded in Christ's eyes."

Ah clasped her hands together. "Did you learn to love him?"

"Hmmm. I learned to like him and appreciate him with time." She gave a heavy, thoughtful sigh. "If you want me to say we were in love like the popular romances, the answer is no. But we have been together nigh on twenty years and have raised our children. We learned to depend on each other, and of course we had our faith."

Jade jumped off Hortencia's lap. The cat sat on the floor and licked her paws. In the interim, Hortencia broke her silence. "I knew my husband, too. But my family also had to approve the match. I liked him. *Amor?* I think I loved him when he died."

Ah glanced at Hortencia. "I have heard that some women grow to love their husbands. That would never have happened to me and Tung Chee." She shook her head. "Cruelty stifles love."

Elizabeth fingered the blue strings of her bonnet. "Despite your sinful ways, I think Henry would bring you out of this degraded life."

Ah startled—Sinful? Degraded? "What makes you say that, Elizabeth?"

Her teacher shook her head. "Think about what you are doing to your girls. And Chen. Henry is offering you a freedom, a life without sin. You would be a wealthy woman, and Chen will be well cared for. Your girls would be healthy, not having to suffer the pawing of strange men."

Ah considered her words in silence. Elizabeth did speak some truth.

She continued. "Weigh Henry's offer with care. This life of yours has no redemption. A man at Tom's market told me you had been arrested already. Next time what might the Vigilantes do? We have heard of their vicious tactics down in Monterey. I shudder to think what could happen to you here." Her lips pressed together.

"I know you wish the best for me. Let me take time to consider it." Ah gazed out the window, watching the silhouettes of passing men.

"Very well. I do hope you will make the best decision." Elizabeth opened the watch dangling on the chain across her breast. She glanced at it, then said, "We must go. Our ship goes back to Monterey at 2 o'clock. Long Wharf. Can you summon a wagon for us?"

A half an hour later, Ah raised her hand against the billowing dust of the departing hack. She had much to think about. Many paths were crossing this way and that. Yet she had something else she must do, and she had little time.

That afternoon Ah spread the writing paper out on her desk, and lifted her pen, then dipped it in the inkwell. Chen returned, and the smell of something frying in the kitchen permeated the house. San and Yee's footsteps could be heard on the floor above her. Jade perched on the front windowsill, her eyes narrowed into slits.

Ah set her pen to paper.

Dear Clark,

Thank you for your recent post. I am sad at the news you may be taking a job at the New York Police Department. Why will you stay in New York when you are so much needed here? You defend so many of us who are not native to this country. Our city needs you. Please come and make us whole again.

She chewed her bottom lip until it hurt. Should she tell him how much she grieved his parting? She did battle within herself. Her yin yielded to the darker impulses, the wave, the risk of saying way too much. And yet she must tell him her news. What did she have to lose? She took a deep breath, then surrendered, allowing more words to flow onto the page.

I am writing to tell you that in a fortnight I will be engaged to Henry Conrad who has asked that I marry him and move my house to join him in San Jose. I wanted to let you know this so that you would not send your letter to the wrong address. You may continue to write to me in San Francisco, but I will forward you my new address when I am in San Jose. I have decided that Chen, San, and Yee will accompany me to our new surroundings.

I am hoping that you will be in San Francisco soon. Thank you for your friendship at all times.

Most Cordial Regards,

Ah Toy

She blotted the wet ink, opened the envelope, and wrote his address on it. After folding and inserting the letter, she wet her fingers and ran it across the glue, then sealed it with a wax stamp.

"Chen!"

Chen's footsteps rattled across the hallway and into the parlor. "Si tau po?"

She passed the letter up to him. "Please mail this."

He gazed down at the envelope. "Mr. Clark?"

"Never you mind, I would like it to go out today."

He loosened the strings of his apron, then pulled it off over his head.

"I shall put the bok choy aside. If I leave now, this will go out on the mail steamer at four o'clock."

"Thank you."

He lingered by her chair. "Si tau po?"

"Yes?"

"I am glad for this. We miss him."

She cocked her head. "Yes, we do, Chen." She glanced over at Jade who sat napping in the sunshine. "Yes, we do."

Two

❦ THAT NEVER ENDS ❦

March 1852

Two frosty months passed before that day when Ah sat with Chen before Officer Wong. Large pieces of cloth were stuck into chinks in the Kong Chow Company walls to keep out the cold winds. She held her cloak tightly around her, suppressing the constant chattering of her teeth.

Wong angled his head, observing her. "Thank you for answering my request for a meeting. It has been some time. We used to talk more often." His jowls were thinning. Had he lost weight? His chins were missing their usual bulk; instead, they merely hung in flat layers on his collarbone. He fingered a ragged paper on his desk.

Ah said, "It has been awhile, but we have been very occupied here in Little Canton." She gazed up at the painting, the wall of enormous cranes lifting into the air. A slash and tear in the canvas had split the flock in half; shreds of canvas hung down, some of the cranes were veering down for a crash landing. "Whatever happened to your art-work?"

Officer Wong frowned. "Sydney Ducks are at work. Again, they have been writing on walls and breaking windows in order to frighten us. This happened last night. They snuck in during the night. Several books and records were strewn on the floor. I found this." He held up the paper on his desk. Scrawled in red lettering were the words, "Get Out, Celestials! Go Home!"

Ah exchanged glances with Chen, then shook her head. "They are the reason for the Vigilantes. Making it hard on all of us."

Wong set the ragged paper back on to the desk, his fingers trembling.

"Why did you ask me here?" An ache rose in the back of her throat.

"I have credible word that Lee Shau Kee has returned to San Francisco from the gold fields."

She cast a glance at Chen who narrowed his eyes. Was Officer Wong playing her? Was he still friends with Li Fan? She must tread carefully. She set a hand on his desk. "Surely this is not anything different. He has been in the city before, hasn't he? He did appear when we bid for San and Yee at the barracoon. Then he gave us no trouble."

"This time is different."

"I do not understand."

"He has lost all of his money in gambling."

She exchanged glances with Chen. "That has happened to many men in the gold fields."

He shook his head. "Lee Shau Kee is not an ordinary man. Word says he gambled away all his considerable wealth. He lost his home and many mines. He now carries bad fortune. He has come to many of us in Little Canton, asking for our help and money, but no one will do business with him. He is desperate."

"Need I be worried? So much time has passed I have long forgotten about him and his idle threats."

Officer Wong rose. "Please, Chen, wait outside. Your mistress and I have something to discuss."

Chen shot her a knowing look, then she heard the door close behind her.

Wong resumed his seat and leaned toward her, his bulk resting on the desk. He touched his right index finger to his lip. "Shh—. Many among us would like to know what they should not know."

She lowered her voice. "What is going on?"

"Story says Tung Chao is making demands again. The Kong Chow Company has received a letter. Your brother-in-law is requiring that we arrange for Lee Shau Kee to gather you and take you back to China."

Steady waves gripped her, first soft, then medium, then heavy. She grasped the arms of her chair.

"Though I have forbidden Lee Shau Kee, he aims to take possession of you no matter the consequences."

She clasped her knees together. "Have you contacted the police?"

"You mean the Vigilantes? You must be joking. They are merely waiting for another fracas where you are involved so they may arrest and deport you." His eyes took on a dark cast. "The wire on which you stand is very thin, Mrs. Toy. I would not contact the police. It would make matters worse for you."

She nodded. "I am thankful you have told me this, Officer Wong."

"You must be careful. Stay with Chen at all times. Do not go out at night. Lock your doors; do not let in anyone you do not recognize." His eyebrows drew together.

"Ridiculous—I will be a prisoner in my own house." Her stomach churned.

Officer Wong leaned toward her. "You are in great danger, Ah Toy. Better a prisoner than a corpse."

"I am afraid." She covered her face with her hands.

"And well you should be." She heard his clothing swish. He must be getting up. "I shall send news as I hear it."

Ah uncovered her face and rose to her feet. "I wish you many blessings."

Wong cocked his head. "I wish you safety."

Chen met her on the other side of the door. On their way out, she turned to him, whispering. "I have something important to tell you."

Chen gave her an even smile. "I already know."

"How?" She asked.

"A houseboy cultivates good hearing over time." He tapped his right ear. "The key is in the knowing, not necessarily in the acting upon such knowledge."

"Most wise," she said.

Flannery prodded Swinney on their ride home, and the mule turned and eyed Ah from time to time. Did the sweet animal know her situation? She leaned against Chen's muscled arm, clutching the seat as they swung around bumpy corners.

Her past kidnapping bobbed to the surface like a cork that had been submerged in a pond. The bag over her head, the darkness, the rough hands. No fear was equal to being taken away without consent. The helplessness, the upside-down universe, the suffocating taint of burlap in her nostrils.

Try as she might, she could not forget Lee Shau Kee's cruel, calloused hands closing around her arms and legs as he upended her. His rough mitts contrasted with Tung Chee's delicate, almost womanly hands and slim fingers, the long fingernail his weapon. Those men used their arms and legs as tentacles to devour, extinguish, and punish.

Tung Chee's cruelty lay in his dalliances with others, the courtesans who populated his chambers. What about that day when his favorite concubine had disappeared? No one ever knew what happened to her, but then one day gossip circulated that she had fallen in love with one of the servants, and that Tung Chee had strangled her. Mere gossip, of course. No one ever found anything, and no one dared report anything. The girl was a mere concubine; her life held no value.

No one would ever look for her, even in the depths of the well where he might have tossed her, or even better, deep in the ground, lost among the willow-laced forests behind the house. For Tung Chee, a woman's life was expendable, the peelings of a fruit he had long since devoured. Once soured, the fruit was no longer worth saving.

Ah and Chen rounded the corner onto Portsmouth Plaza. The Vigilante militia were marching that day with fixed bayonets. They must be training. How safe the city must feel, yet she did not. No amount of gunpowder or secret committee meetings could protect her now. Funny—could the present promise more danger than the past? Hard to believe.

Three

❧ A HALO OF DIAMONDS ☙

*T*he next afternoon on DuPont Street, the morning's rain shower had passed, leaving the streets soggy and rutted. Chen held Ah's elbow and guided her around mudpuddles. They entered Mr. Tom's fruit and vegetable shop, winding through the crowd of men who fanned out along the aisles. The men would often sneak a random grape or a strawberry at the peak of ripeness. Rows of tomatoes and cucumbers lay side by side in tempting fashion, but this time she and Chen selected oranges and blackberries.

"Those look delicious," she said.

"Just in from the valley," Mr. Tom said.

She dropped some gold shavings into his hands while Chen observed.

Mr. Tom leaned toward her, lingering a moment to chat. "Heard the story, Toy?"

Chen drew near, ever cautious.

"What about?" Ah watched Mr. Tom's son fold the fruit into some brown paper.

Mr. Tom said, "Officer Clark is to come back—next week. I heard it from the herbalist on DuPont Street who got it from the night watch-man." He batted a fly buzzing about his head, then handed her the package.

She fingered the paper. "Good news. Many in Little Canton will be glad of it." She wasn't sure if "many" included herself, but she would appear agreeable.

Tom wiped his hands on a rag. "He protects our streets, and many times interferes when we Chinese are robbed. Some non-Chinese men who come in and pick fruit do not pay—they are always a problem."

"We have missed such safeguards, I know." She bit her lower lip. She had missed more than Clark's protection, and only Chen might guess how much.

"Good day, Ah Toy." Mr. Tom turned away and worked his abacus.

Folding the fruit into his satchel, Chen turned to her, his face etched with puzzle lines.

She gazed up at him. "What is it?"

"I do not understand, si tau po. You did not say you were happy to hear of Clark's return. I thought you would find much joy at hearing the news."

"I am pleased—it is only that Clark did not write me about his re-turn." She turned away from him. Maybe if she looked at a stand of lychee nuts, Chen would not notice her tears. She ran her fingers over the tops of the nuts. Why had Clark not notified her? In fact, his not writing at all ripped at her heart. Did he not think she cared?

She feared the worst—what happened to the kind, gentle policeman who guided her arm and laughed with her in the sun? Was he no longer even to be her friend?

Chen led the way onto the street. *Guard your inner fire.* Had Chen said that? She gave him a sideways glance: he walked beside her, holding the package of fruit in his hand. It was not Chen but her dragon who had spoken.

She breathed in deeply, and peered up at the shoddy second-story balconies of Little Canton. Men stood up there, smoking. Other men in black pants and queues bustled around her. Never had she felt so solitary, so confined in this world without many women.

Yet this restraint was nothing compared to Tung Chee's captivity. He would sit on her chest to punish her, sit on her until she nearly blacked out, allowing her to awaken so that he could then pummel her black and blue. His face would redden, sweat bubbling up at his hairline, as he slapped and shook her, then swung his fists until she no longer felt the blows.

Guard your inner fire. She heard it again. Lifting her chin to the air, she knew her dragon's presence. Then...*hold fast.* A sudden breeze moved some litter mixed with leaves against the side of a haberdashery. Men relieved themselves there: the pungent odor of urine blended with whiskey in this town of many lands. She pulled her fan from her sleeve, waving it against the fumes.

Why should she trust Clark after all these disappointments? If he was returning—and she was not at all sure he was—what good was he to her? If he disregarded her and treated her as another silly woman in his way, she would draw her magic sword. He could no longer hurt her. Chen ambled a few steps ahead of her as they rounded the corner onto Pike Street.

Something twisted her ankle. She stopped for a moment, easing her lotus shoe out of the muddy crack where its heel stuck in the road. Maybe she was being too hasty. Clark could do something for her. She resumed her tiny steps. If Officer Wong was right, at least he could protect her against Lee Shau Kee.

A single ragweed pushed up through a crack between the foundation and the mud of the street. Sometimes one friend could make a difference like that one weed did to brighten the road. She trembled. If Lee Shau Kee were bent on taking her back to China, she would need not just one friend, but an army to protect her.

379

A week later, the afternoon wind off the Bay mussed Ah's hair, and she tucked a stray lock behind her ear. Henry Conrad directed Flannery to drive south from the wharf into a sandy glen. Clouds drifted like shreds of cotton overhead. She watched as he rapped his walking stick against the side of the wagon.

Flannery drew Swinney to the side of the lane and jumped down onto the sandy patch. He stood there, holding the reins. "How long, sir?" Flannery asked. He fingered an unlit cigar.

"At least a few minutes, my man." Henry said.

"Do I have time to feed Swinney her oats?" Flannery looked toward the mule.

"I should think so." Henry said.

Flannery pulled a bag from the wagon and looped the strings over Swinney's head. The mule could be heard chomping her oats. After lighting his cigar, Flannery busied himself with his animal, checking Swinney's harness and reins.

Once assured they had some privacy in the wagon, Henry turned to Ah and opened his coat. He pulled a small red and gold box from the inner pocket. "Something for you." He set the box on her lap.

She gazed at it, her mouth slightly open. What could it be? After tugging at the small wooden latch which disengaged the lid, she opened the box. Nestled inside was a green silk bag with a black braid drawstring. She held the bag in her palm.

"You brought me something from Guangzhou?"

"I had it crafted especially for you on my last visit. Go on, open it."

She loosened the drawstring at the top of the bag, and its content tumbled out onto her lap. Shredded clouds sailed overhead, and though the light was not brilliant, a ring captured the sun's weak rays. She lifted the jewel up, then held it in front of her, turning it around to catch the light.

The apple green jade ring was set in a halo of diamonds. The brilliants reflected the colors blue, yellow, and red in the sunlight; the jade emerged like a mossy pond edge into the translucent green of a bamboo forest.

She stared, unabashed. "It is beautiful. I have seen many such rings in China, and this is lovely."

"Put it on, my dear. Or better, let me." He slid the ring onto the finger of her left hand. It wobbled slightly. "Your finger is too thin. I was afraid of that."

"No matter. I can take it to Mr. Lee. His jewelry shop helped San and Yee when they received jewelry gifts from their customers."

"San and Yee? Your doves?" Were his eyes narrowing? He moved closer to her on the seat. She sensed her own small frame next to his larger bulk. So now she had her answer. He knew the truth about her parlor house. Once again, the unsaid haunted her, so she chose her words carefully.

"Though the girls were bought at auction, I treat them kindly. After all, my husband Tung Chee treated me as a slave once."

"I see. That is all in the past. What matters now is our future." He patted her hand. "I insist you wear this ring until our wedding day. Then I will give you an even bigger jewel to celebrate our life together forever."

He leaned over and kissed her. His lips were soft and moist. Maybe she would learn to feel something when he kissed her. For now, his touch merely reassured her. He caressed her cheek with the back of his hand.

He sat back, then raised his hands as if framing her portrait. "You are more exquisite than any jewel I could give you. I have been dreaming of you ever since we first met, and my thoughts are filled with our life together. Of the children we can have together. Our happy life in San Jose."

She forced a smile. "A pleasant dream."

His drew her close. "Will you marry me?"

"Yes," she said. If only she had a place to run, to hide, to think the matter over. But now this was the best option. "Yes," she said, this time more firmly.

His gaze was probing. "Do you love me?"

Oh, Goddess Mazu, what should she say? If she told the truth, it would bring them each bad luck. So, she would give him part of the truth, then paint over the untruth.

She touched his hand. "I love you in my own way." She leaned back. At least he would be satisfied—besides, she had only told a half-lie.

He clutched her hand and gave a long sigh. "Then let us set the date, two weeks from Saturday. I will ask Reverend Dailey to preside. Now I am the happiest man alive!" He pulled her to her feet, jostling the wagon and hugging her tightly.

Four

❧ TWO CRANES ❧

April 1852

That month Ah gave the cook two weeks off to go see his relatives in Monterey. Chen gladly took over the preparation of cuisine. At times like these, he plainly enjoyed running the kitchen as in the old shanty days.

San and Yee were safe upstairs, performing their nightly duties with the men who had hired them.

Not long past nine, Ah perched on a stool in the kitchen.

Chen plunged his arms deep into a hot, soapy tub of water. "I am not happy at your news, si tau po."

"Why not?" She leaned against the kitchen table, her feet aching after the long day. Why was he being so ungrateful?

"I am not sad for myself. "He wiped a mixture of steam and sweat from his brow and settled his dripping hand back in the water.

"What is it then? Do you not want to leave Little Canton, and find a peaceful life in San Jose?"

"It is not that. I agree that San Jose would be a safe harbor for all of us, San and Yee also, but I do not think you are being honest with yourself."

"How could you say that?" She clenched her jaw. Chen had some nerve.

He slapped the towel on the sideboard and stood with his hands on his hips. "I have been with you since we were eight years old. I waited on you at your father's house, I brought you herbal wraps when you were sick with coughs. I went with you as your servant for Tung Chee."

"Of course. You do not have to tell me that. We have faced much of life together. I will need your help as we close our parlor house and set ourselves up in San Jose. Henry says the house will be ready for us next month."

Chen shook his head, lifted a plate from the hot water, and dried it with the towel. "It all seems very sudden." His tone was cool.

"It may be rapid to you, but I think we will not see another chance like this come our way." If only he could see the better life Henry promised them.

"So when will you tell San and Yee? What will they say? Maybe they will not want to go." His voice was low and troubled.

"All right, Chen. I detect disapproval in your voice. Come sit at the table here. Tell me what is on your mind."

She settled down in the wooden chair, while he perched on the edge of the kitchen stool.

His face flushed. Was it dishwashing steam or anger that fueled his warmth? "You are not being honest with yourself."

"How is that?" Now it was her turn to feel warm. She cleared beads of sweat from her forehead with the back of her hand.

He shrugged his shoulders. "Because you really love Clark."

"You know this?"

"Of course. I have watched you together . . . you are like two cranes performing the mating dance. You hop about, then walk away from each other; then hop about again. Yet those of us around you see the passion between you—we can sense the sparks of your fire. You only wish to be two cranes side by side, symbols of a happily married life."

She flinched. Though she had never tried to hide her feelings for Clark, had they been that obvious to others?

Chen continued. "Our Confucius counsels, 'Wheresoever you go, go with all your heart. Not to do so is to deny yourself the happiness you deserve.'" He drew back, regarding her.

She waved away his words. "I do not see this truth that you speak. You think you see some passion between me and Clark, but you are much mistaken. It is merely the fire of friendship."

Chen hunched his shoulders, then slipped off the stool and returned to washing dishes. "You are the mistress of your own fate, si tau po. As you wish."

"I am glad you understand. By the way, I have told Henry that we will need a large kitchen for you in San Jose."

"And a large garden to grow my vegetables?"

"Yes."

"Then I will be satisfied." He flashed her a jubilant smile.

She sat reveling in their shared contentment. A soap bubble floated up from the dishwashing basin over Chen's head. She watched the bubble's path: it lingered overhead, then popped in the air.

Not long afterward, Ah set two large white chrysanthemum offerings before the statue of Buddha on her altar, bowed, then sat on her haunches in reflection and prayer. She murmured the following.

I worship the Buddha with these flowers;
May this virtue be helpful for my emancipation;
Just as these flowers fade,
Our body will undergo decay.

She remained in contemplation. Life was short. Each decision adjusted the sail of her sampan. Chen's words beat a drum in her head. *Because you really love Clark.* She struck a match, lit a stick of incense, nestled it among the flowers, then inhaled its perfume. A thin trail of smoke rose, spiraling into the air, an unpleasant truth entwined within.

By accepting Henry, she would have to live apart from Little Canton; that would take her even farther from the China where her children's bones lay. Would she have to adopt American ways? Abandon her way of dressing? Wear their clothes? Eat their food? Suffer their disdain?

Chen would have to help her into the long day dresses she had seen on Elizabeth and Hortencia. She would not be able to wear Western-style shoes; her feet were mere wedges. If she wore lotus shoes, she would look a laughing-stock.

A tableau floated in front of her, showing Henry's face. At first his aspect was painted in light, his smile brilliant and loving. Yet as his image lingered, his cheeks retreated into shadow, a smirk darkening his lips. In this scorn lay the mirror image of Tung Chee's jeer as he held her face down, covering her head with a pillow night after night while raping her. Was she imagining the worst?

Troubling thoughts pulsated through a vein in her mind. Would her life with Henry return her to the lowly subservience she had experienced with Tung Chee? She trembled. What if his mockery became a daily occurrence?

Yet she supposed that she would adapt. After all, the wedding date was set. If only she could recognize and accept what was best for her future.

Five

❧ A KNOCK AT THE DOOR ❧

Ah's next week passed without incident, the affairs of the parlor house humming in usual fashion. Again, she sat on the kitchen stool, watching Chen prepare the evening meal. Despite his crying whenever he chopped onions, she knew the simple act gave him solace. Chopping required no decision-making; it gave him freedom from the endless choices he must make in order to protect her and the girls.

Though somebody knocked at the front door, he continued to chop. The distant banging grew louder.

"Chen, should you answer the door?"

"No. Too early for visitors; maybe if I continue my chopping they will go away."

But the pounding at the door continued unabated.

"Who could it be?" Ah lowered her voice. "Remember, I do not want to see anyone. My head pains me today, and I need to rest."

Chen huffed, put down the knife, and wiped his eyes with a towel. He directed his words toward the door. "How persistent do you have to be?" He muttered his harshest Cantonese. "Why can you not leave us alone at this hour?"

Still grumbling, he stalked out the kitchen toward the front door. Ah followed him, lingering behind in the shadowy hallway.

He was half way through the third sentence, "How can you think—?" He swung open the door, slapping the towel over his shoulder, preparing to give a full-throated insult to the visitor.

Instead of the usual walnut peddler or knife sharpener, John Clark stared down at him.

Ah drew back into the shadows of the dark hallway. Her breath stopped in her throat.

Chen stood wordless; his face was lit by the sun beaming through the doorway.

Why did he not greet Clark? Was it the tears from chopping onions that had clouded Chen's vision? Or maybe he had not had enough sleep the night before?

"Chen, do you not recognize me? Surely, I have not been gone that long." Clark removed his top hat, revealing his crown of thick blond hair.

Ah drew back further. Even if she could talk to him, what would she say, now that she was promised to Henry?

At last Chen seemed to find his voice. "Mr. Clark, please step inside." He waved Clark into the hallway, then forward to the sitting room.

After a couple of minutes passed, Ah tiptoed forward from the shade and peeked through a crack in the hallway door. She could see the men clearly in the room beyond, sure that her viewing angle was hidden from them.

Clark cast a glance toward the middle of the room, that same spot where the four pears had appeared previously. Maybe he was remembering that night so long ago.

She pushed the hair out of her face, if only to get a better look at him. She clutched a fold of her silk jacket.

After settling on the couch, he gazed over at Chen. "You are looking well."

Chen nodded. "I often do." He sat across from Clark on the wing-back chair, the one non-Asian furnishing in the room.

She grinned. Chen broke Ah Toy's parlor house rules—servants must never sit with the guests. Maybe he hoped the imprint of his rear end would disappear from the upholstery before she found him there.

"Where is Ah Toy?" Clark looked toward the door.

Heat radiated through her chest at his mention of her own name.

Chen inhaled, obviously preparing his words. "Out shopping with San and Yee."

Ah held a hand over her mouth to cover a smile. Chen was a good and fast liar when he needed to be.

Clark fondled his hat brim. "Tell me which shop, and I shall go find her."

Chen clenched his teeth. "I think that is not a good idea," he said.

Clark frowned. "Forever why not?"

Chen fell silent. His mind would be meandering between Cantonese and English words, a territory which both emboldened and challenged him. "Hmmmm," he said.

Clark's face reddened. "Chen, are you hiding something? Out with it, my man. Why would it not be a good idea?" He looked up at the ceiling, then let out a heavy sigh.

Silence reigned between the men. Chen hesitated once again.

Ah peered through the crack in the door. Chen was probably wondering if he should tell Clark the truth—or not. She watched him gaze at Clark whose lips pressed flat.

Then Chen broke Ah Toy's rules for servants—again. The poor man could not help himself. "I will face great trouble from my mistress for telling you this. You can never tell her how you learned this information."

Clark leaned forward, sliding his chair closer. "Of course, Chen, your secret is safe with me."

"She is to be married. She is out shopping for a wedding garment. Then for flowers."

Clark blinked rapidly. Was he trying not to show his surprise?

She held her breath for a moment. A debate raged inside of her: if she went to Clark, here and now, as she was sorely tempted, her risk was great. After his wife's loss, Clark had already drifted away from her to New York. How could such a man be trusted?

Clark stiffened; his knuckles white around the rim of his hat. "She is going to wed?"

"Next week to Henry Conrad." Chen's words dropped like the weight of boulders on her back. He made it sound so final.

Clark frowned. "She wrote that she was to wed the importer, but I am flabbergasted she is going ahead with it. She hardly knows him. Why ever would she marry *him*?"

Ah put her hands over her lips to keep from crying out. Why *would* she marry Henry Conrad?

Chen wasted no time answering. "You never asked her yourself."

Clark cleared his throat. "Well, I never thought about that, I guess . . . ."

Ah let her breath out softly. Poor devil, the man was an idiot. If he did not ask her to marry him, then he did not deserve her. Though Henry was more of a companion than a lover, he had promised her a ranch, a great house, and space for all her household. *And*—he had given her an apple jade ring. *That* was why she was marrying him. At least that was good enough reason for now.

Chen shifted in his chair. "You do not seek the beauty in your life, do you? You are the fish who lies so deeply in your own mossy pond that you cannot see light from above."

Ah bit her thumb. *Oh no*—had Chen said too much?

Clark faded into the wallpaper of his own life, his hands limp, the top hat sliding to the floor at his feet. He bent down and retrieved the hat. "You may be right, though I hate to hear it from anyone. No offense to you, Chen."

To her amazement, Chen risked again, slinging out his words like dice. "Of course, I am right. My mistress loves only you—she marries

Henry for security. While you have been gone, the Vigilantes tightened their grip, and all of us feel their threat."

"So, I have come too late? She is already spoken for?" Clark looked a sorry mess.

Ah cringed. Why had her dragon gone silent the moment she needed its counsel?

Chen said, "Can you not see? Has lichen grown over the whites of your eyes? Are you blind and deaf?"

Whatever was Chen thinking? How would Clark react?

"I-I was burying my wife." Clark's words trickled like dish water down a drain.

Chen said, "While you were busying yourself with the dead, you were killing the living."

Clark squinted at Chen as if he were examining tiny print on a news sheet. "I do love her, but in truth, I never saw that...I guess I thought she would always wait for me. How could I have missed it?"

Chen's voice softened. "I do not know. I am sure my mistress will not see you as she prepares to be a bride, but I know she would be pleased if you came to the wedding."

"Yes, of course, I will come to wish her well and see her off. I only wish her happiness."

Clark's gaze drifted off . . . his mind must be lurking in the dark realms.

Once again, she fought the urge to go to him—in mere steps, she would be at his side, in his embrace, in the sunlight of his face. But she could not—after all this.

Chen held his tongue. Ah was just as glad. After all, these were not his affairs. Or were they?

After seeing Clark out the door, Chen returned to his chopping in the kitchen where Ah rejoined him. She watched him hold the knife over a rather large yellow onion, lift the blade, then bring it down, splitting the onion in half. He reached for another onion and continued the process.

She stretched out her arms on the table, mesmerized by his motions. Poor Clark was like the onion. Without her at his side, he might be severed from the love that would make him whole again. But then— what was she left with? Would Henry Conrad be enough? She looked at the curling, discarded onion skins below Chen's table on the floor. Was that to be her future life?

She shook her head, then continued watching Chen dice the onions. He wiped his eyes from time to time. She wondered. Were his tears for himself, for her, or for Clark?

She wiped away her own tear, but this was not the onion's fault. Her longing brought up a searing truth: Clark's passion made war with Henry's security, but though passion would flame and flare, security would win her. Hard work and diligence had taught her that lesson. What good was love on an empty stomach? And so she watched Chen's deft hand cradling the knife. Even though she wanted Clark with all her heart, he may not be the best for her.

Late that afternoon Ah tried on her wedding dress. Her small breasts barely filled out the tight-fitting bodice. American women must be much larger, at least that is what the dry goods man had said. He only had two in stock, since there were few women in San Francisco. But he believed in being ready at all times for the possible bride to come along. He said more dresses would arrive next month on the Pacific Mail steamer.

But she had no time to wait, since her wedding was only days away. The eggshell satin dress looked different now as she wore it in the soft daylight of her bedroom, and the hem dragged badly on the floor. The lace overdress was quite full, and she swept it from side to side, listening to the *swish-swish*.

San sat on a corner chair, her black braid falling across her breast. Did fear or novelty keep the girl silent? It was certainly not the first time either of them had seen a wedding dress, after all. In Guangzhou they had seen a British bride and groom from time to time, going and coming from the Presbyterian church, their landau gleaming, horses frothing.

A knock sounded on the door, then Chen peered into the room. His squinting features filled the mirror in front of her. "Yes?" Ah asked.

He stood for a moment, apparently trying to compose his thoughts. He must be startled to see her in western dress. His eyes widened at the mountain of lace hanging in layers about the skirt.

"I have a wedding present for you." He extended a thickly padded red silk bag toward her.

"Thank you. She took the bag from him and set it on the bed. "I am trying on my dress. What do you think?"

He tilted his head. "Be careful, si tau po. This skirt is going to balloon out into the air if you aren't careful. Without my help, a gust of wind might blow you out to the Bay. I also think the top is too big. Maybe a few pins would make it smaller."

San rose up from her chair. "I have the pins the dry goodsman gave me." She held a box out toward him." Do you know how to measure and fit the dress for si tau po?"

Chen gave an authoritative sniff. He had spent much time in Guangzhou watching Ah Toy's personal tailor at work. Alongside the tailor, he learned to measure and make many garments from scratch. "May I, si tau po?" Chen pointed toward the bodice of the dress.

"Certainly, go ahead," Ah said.

With deft fingers, Chen folded the material where it gapped and sagged, first above, then below her breasts. He turned to San. "There is some blue chalk and straight pins in the kitchen drawer, next to where I keep the knives. Go get it. I will use it in my measuring."

San stepped out; meanwhile, Chen folded, then crimped the satin, first around the bodice, then the back where matching cloth-covered buttons lined up in a vertical row.

San returned with chalk and pins, and Chen repeated his steps, marking excess material with blue chalk. Afterwards Ah went behind a curtain and removed the dress. In a moment she reappeared in her yellow silk robe, carrying the dress.

San brought it to Chen and he examined the parts where he would alter the garment. He said, "Before I go to work on your dress, I want you to open my gift." His eyes filled with a kind of mist.

Ah patted the mattress next to her. "Come, sit next to me while I open it."

Chen complied, settling onto the mattress. He brushed his knuckles across his right eye, perhaps to clear a tear gathering there.

Ah untied the silk ribbons and tugged open the bag. "Oh, it is a fan." She extracted the large gold fan and let it fall open, its spread showing a dragon playing across a field of poppies.

A grin lingered on his lips. "It is different, and I ordered the design from Hong Kong especially for you."

"The tips are very sharp!" She pulled her index finger away and sucked a bit of blood from a small cut.

"It is not meant to hurt you, si tau po, but to protect you."

She fell silent, seeking comfort in his moist eyes.

"Clark and I have always been there to guard you, but now—with your new husband—I fear there will be times when you will be alone. And you must have a weapon."

She closed the fan, holding it upright between her palms.

San watched, nodding slightly.

Chen leaned in closer. "You see the long blades? Now it is like a cutting knife. Very sharp. It can even cut through wood." He made a sawing motion with his hand.

"Sharp enough for onions." She settled the bladed fan across her lap.

San gazed at its reflection. "I have seen many of those knife fans in Guangzhou."

Chen said, "Keep it in this strong bag. It is small enough for your pouch. A secret between you and your fan. You may use it like a regular fan any time, but in case of trouble—"

For the first time she absorbed the full impact of his unstated warning. This fan showed the truth about what she was going to do. A marriage with Henry was filled with the unknown. She clutched the fan in its bag.

After sitting in silence for a moment, he stood. "I must finish with your wedding dress." He lifted the gown, let it fall over his arms, and disappeared into his room.

"What would I do without Chen?" Ah sat on her bed, her yellow robe pooling around her in shimmering folds.

San gave a warm smile. "We all value Chen, si tau po. He is welcome as rain on parched soil."

Ah nodded, her thoughts turning and returning to their escape from Guangzhou. The midnight wagon. She held onto her seat, sandwiched between Chen and Tung Chee. She could still feel the jostling of the wagon whose horses plunged ahead on the shadowy road. She could still see Tung Chee's face, his jaws set firmly. Chen's hand tapped hers, and his encouraging words echoed in her mind . . . *a few more miles and we will reach the Daileys'—they are waiting for us to board the ship. We will make it to our new life. Do not fear.*

Six

⟨ THROUGH THE ONE OPEN DOOR ⟩

On the first of May, her wedding day dawned clear, a day when San Francisco's emerald green hills embraced the white-lapped waters of the Bay. Ah could not resist going to the window to watch Chen and the girls leave for the church. San and Yee had festooned Flannery's wagon with white roses and yellow ribbons. The girls stood next to Flannery who sported a suit and top hat, his gold-red beard gleaming. He called up to her. "Hey Lass, see me special attire?"

She giggled, something she rarely ever did.

At ten that morning, Chen was scheduled to leap off Flannery's wagon and help the girls find their places at the pews inside the church. The day before, during a practice run, the wagon sank into the muddy drifts before the Old First Church on Sacramento Street, causing a ruckus among passersby. She had never heard such swearing from a man in her life, except for dockworkers loading cargo on ships in Guangzhou.

Passersby gawked, some offering to help.

Ah called out the window. "Mr. Flannery! Did you ever get the mud off your wagon?"

Flannery tapped Swinney with his whip. As the wheels inched forward, he yelled up to her. "Took me a few prayers and a lot of rags, but she's gleamin' today. Look at Swinney." He jumped down and touched her mane. A thread of white and yellow ribbons decorated her reins. Swinney's mane burst with sprays of purple lupine and orange poppies tucked into her braid. As though seeking Ah's approval, the mule snorted and tossed her head in the air.

San laughed and clapped her hands together.

"You look very well, Mr. Flannery," Ah said.

"Glad you approve, me darlin'. I'll be back shortly to take ye to the church."

Chen looked up at Ah and gave her a slight wave, then helped San and Yee as they swung up into the wagon. She heard him call out to the driver. "Flannery, please help Ah Toy up there when you come back to get her.

"I will not be there, and I am afraid she will fall. Such deep mud . . . especially in front of Old First. She must not get her wedding dress dirty."

"Why aren't ye stayin' back to be escortin' her, Mr. Chen?" Flannery frowned.

"She does not want anyone to help her." Chen brushed a fleck of dirt from his black jacket, specially ordered from Hong Kong. "When she makes up her mind—." He flushed.

It was true. She could do this herself. After all, it was her wedding day.

Flannery carried on the banter. "Aye, she's a stubborn lass, I can assure ye. But I'll help her up into the wagon. She'll be the sight of San Francisco for this fine day's weddin'." He touched his whip to his hat, and Swinney drew the wagon down the road.

Ah stayed there, leaning out the window, watching Flannery guide Swinney as they turned the corner at the end of the block. The wagon parted a crowd of black-jacketed men, then it swerved into a right-hand turn.

After reaching down to the bed, she lifted up her western wedding dress, its eggshell satin reflecting the light. This was no qipao. What would she look like as a bride?

She grinned. Even though she might be the sight of the town, Chen could not dissuade her from wearing western garb on this, her most special of days. She opened the lid of a shoebox next to the dress on the bed. She fingered the tissue paper wrapped around the sparkling off-white lotus shoes from Guangzhou. They were satin, appliquéd with sprays of pink roses.

If only her mother could see her wear them, the same mother who had broken Ah's feet when she was only five years old. She pulled the shoes from the box. "See, mother," she said. "Of course, I cannot change what you did to me that day, but I can change the direction of my life. All you said to me that day was false. It is only when I left Guangdong that I began to discover the truth. Your lies split me that day. My feet are the evidence of that."

An hour later, Flannery and Swinney safely delivered her to Old First. She looked up at the structure, not knowing whether to laugh or cry. What had happened to the church? Old First had seen better months; since the earthquakes and ravages of fire, parts of the structure consisted of little more than a lean-to. Inside, a canvas was slung up where stained-glass windows once gleamed. Occasional breezes whistled into the church from outside.

Though Chen said he much preferred a Buddhist temple, Christ was a wise man worthy of respect, so Ah was content to be married there. She remembered the details from yesterday's practice. Elizabeth would be waiting for her inside at the altar, next to Reverend Dailey and the two boys.

Elizabeth, of course, had made sure that Ah and Henry had the proper ritual, helping Ah select the music and yesterday showing her how to step down the aisle. Reverend Dailey had cleared the way with the church elders, convincing them that through this marriage to Henry, Ah would be ripe for conversion. Thus, they allowed her inside.

Flannery tied Swinney to a hitching post, guided Ah through the door of the church and across the vestibule, then deposited her near the center door. His face softened as he gazed down at her. "Yer not to be seen until it's time. Bad luck, ye see. But ye can always spy through the open door—like *this*." He held his cap against his chest, his belly protruding while he stuck his head around the open door. Though finely dressed, he reeked of horse manure and whiskey, and she wrinkled her nose.

On his direction, she took up her position in the vestibule, peering through the one open door. Her heart was thumping rapidly. She had a clear view of the altar from there, in addition to the surrounding pews.

"I'll have yer wagon ready after the ceremony," Flannery patted her arm like a kindly father. Afterwards, he clomped into the church and slid into a left middle pew.

From her place at the back of the church, she struggled to identify those sitting in the pews. A thrum of low chatter filled the space.

Wasn't that Elizabeth, Hortencia, and the Daileys' two sons, sitting erect in the right-hand pews? Since Henry had no family, they filled the groom's side of the church.

Candles sputtered on the altar. That sharp flower smell must be someone's cologne. A haze rode down on sunrays streaming from the high windows.

Who was sitting for her on the left side of the church? She squinted. There was the back of San's green Manchurian dress, a pink peony set into her upswept hair. Next to her rested the taller Yee, her hair flowing onto her shoulders in long black strands. No one else sat with them. Wait a moment—where was Chen?

She looked around, her hands sweating. Oh, there he was, bending and sneaking past the bowed heads of worshipers apparently trying to pray. Were their eyes following him as he slunk around the back of the pews? She couldn't help but smile. Trembling, he took the side aisle, then slid into the pew.

His backside met the wooden planking of the pew, and he gazed over at San and Yee who greeted him with faint nods. He relaxed into the bench. At last he was no longer a moving target for the observer. She chuckled. He must have been watching her enter the vestibule, ready to catch her if she fell.

Henry stood to the left of Reverend Dailey. His hair shone with pomade; his ribboned collar stood straight. From time to time, Henry and Dailey exchanged glances. A melodeon attempted a version of "How Great Thou Art" in an off-key middle C. At times, a gust of wind would blow in from the west window, flapping the canvas and causing the altar cloths to rise like sails.

Reverend Dailey frowned, lifted a brick from the floor, then went back to the altar and put the brick on top of the cloth so it would not blow away. Elizabeth, the witness for Ah Toy, rose from the pew and took her place to the right of the Reverend. From time to time, she drew her woolen shawl close about her shoulders.

Moments passed in an eternal succession of heartbeats. Elizabeth told her it would seem like ages. Better to wait, she had said. That way the bride's appearance would be a surprise.

Where was Clark? Had he not come to see her as he had promised Chen? She scanned the pews again—she would know him anywhere. She pressed her lips tightly.

The churchgoers fidgeted and Ah sensed their communal impatience. She took a momentary glance at Chen who occupied himself by staring around at the nooks and crannies of the church. A ladder rested behind the altar, leaning against a side wall.

She guessed his thoughts: he was making a mental list of items to buy for that night's dinner party. The table had been set in the dining room. San and Yee had laid out the finest silver and China plates. The candles had burned low. Soon Chen would have to visit the dry goods store to replenish them.

The Reverend Dailey raised his hand. She took a deep breath. *It was time.* Slowly, carefully, she made her way from the back of the church onto the wooden floorboards of the aisle. Once but a whisper, her feet now tapped loudly as she gained confidence, each tiny step following one after another, toward life with Henry Conrad.

Something stirred the air behind her. The melodeon was playing, the audience was whispering . . . maybe it was Clark . . . but then . . . what was that frown on Chen's face? A crude chill encased her. Something was terribly wrong. Screams and shouts surrounded her. A familiar large burlap bag was being thrown over her, shrouding her in an embryonic nightmare, her wedding march ending in a dark black womb.

Seven

❧ THE TIGHT GAG ❧

Ah woke to the scratch of burlap on her face and the taste of dust on her lips. Porcelain dust. She would recognize it anywhere. A tight cloth gag stretched between her teeth, making it hard to swallow. Her head pounded. Had she been drugged? Her hands were bound, but her legs were free. She stuck her elbows and legs out as far as she could. Her elbows knocked against wood on either side of her. Her feet met wood through the burlap.

When she attempted to sit up, her head hit a hard surface. Was she in some sort of coffin? Tiny bits of light penetrated the bag, so she must be in something more like a crate than a solid wooden box. She was rocked from side to side, and when she heard the persistent creaking of wood against water, she knew. She was on board a ship; was she heading toward China? She cringed. How far out to sea?

Her thoughts cleared now. Where could she be? Not in a cabin, but rather in an open area where the light played from many directions. Maybe the cargo hold? If Lee Shau Kee kidnapped her and planned to make a quick exit with her at Hong Kong harbor, he might put her near a staircase to make a quick getaway. A cargo hold would be filled with crew, and they might be suspicious.

She remembered the brig *Eagle*. On that trading vessel, her cabin faced inward onto a closed, broad-beamed deck. A companionway separated the cabins from the other side where some crates were stacked near the staircase.

From her time on the wharf at her father's porcelain factory, she had gone aboard many clipper ships that had such configurations. If that was where she was, she might be able to hear activity above deck through a staircase leading up to the upper deck. If she were secreted in the cargo hold below the waterline, her luck would run out fast, for no one would find her there.

A dull ache threaded its way up her spine and her head drummed painfully. Her throat was dry and parched behind the tight gag in her mouth. How long had she been a prisoner? A series of scenes, followed by blanks, played in her head. The earliest thing she remembered . . . she strained to recollect . . . a rush of footsteps behind her in the church, then . . . *thunk* on her head. Nothing else was clear.

Lee Shau Kee had pulled off the burlap bag. Where had she been when he had done that? The white clapboard walls of the cabin flashed, along with the recessed bed whose alcove featured a privacy curtain. When he had raised the bag, she scratched, bit, and gouged him. He lifted a loose board and aimed it for her head. He must have hit her hard. How much time had she been unconscious? Obviously, enough time for him to put her here in this makeshift coffin.

A jarring thought occurred. He had already knocked her out twice now to keep her quiet. Was he growing tired of this struggle? Would he be rough with her next time? Would there be a next time?

Someone padded around on the deck where she lay. She stifled her irregular breathing. A jostling motion shifted her from side to side. No one else but Lee Shau Kee would be interested in her crate. He must be lifting her box, maybe rearranging it. Whack! A shower of dust permeated her burlap bag. She suppressed a cough.

What was going on? Maybe Lee Shau Kee was trying to move, then cover, her crate with heavier boxes in order to hide it. Could he hear the thudding of her heart? Something slid past, then another layer of dirt filtered into her resting place. *Do not sneeze.*

The steps faded away, and she lay back in her dusty cocoon. How long did he plan to leave her there? She would not survive the journey of several weeks in such a space. Would he feed her? What about letting her out to relieve herself? She already stank of urine. Surely, he would free her at some point—she was valuable to him.

If only she could get to the first mate or the captain. China clippers did not trade in human cargo—too much risk from the port authorities at either end of the line.

A trader's mission was to make fast money by clipping over the oceans, exchanging cargo, then speeding away again. Clippers were renowned for their sailing speed. A charge of kidnapping and an ensuing investigation caused delays up and down the line. Not good for business.

She stretched her fingers, now almost numb. Her wrists were bound together behind her back—with what? She felt a cord dangling from one wrist. How thick was the rope? By the feel she figured the line to be about the width of a laundry cord. Bracing her elbows against the side of the crate to steady her arms, she moved her hands from left to right along the rope, following the back of her waistline. The work was doubly hard with her arms tied behind her. *Curses!* Why could she not see?

Finally—her pouch lay against her right hip. No doubt Lee Shau Kee had slung her over his shoulder, drugged her, then slotted her inside the sack before making fast to the ship. No time to search her for a pouch or weapon. Besides, he would be unfamiliar with all the layers of petticoats inside a western wedding dress. After she woke in the cabin, he struggled to grip her through the slippery lace and satin.

Though she had not wanted to wear an American dress to her wedding, maybe it had helped her after all. As she fingered her pouch, she traced the outline of her fan. What had Chen said? *You see, it is like a cutting knife, very sharp.*

For many minutes, she worked her fingers to untie the satin strings of her pouch. Water slapped the outer hull of the ship; smells of caulking, oil, and tobacco wafted around her in whiffs, then in waves. She took a rest, her arms strained, her elbows knotted with fatigue.

When she was able, she relocated her pouch, then eased open the strings holding the thick material that formed the opening. Like spider legs, her fingers crept into the bag and found the fan. Slowly they went—any sharp movements might lead to sharp cuts. She might bleed to death, and no one would find her there until China. She gave a choked laugh. Some present she would make for Tung Chao.

With more delicate probing, she worked to draw the fan out through the opening of her pouch. Why would it not come out? No matter how hard she pulled, she could not work the string open wide enough to extract the fan.

Her arms were heavy, her fingers stiff from strain. Time to give up. Another thought consumed her—if Lee Shau Kee were to return, he would find her with the fan-knife, and she would lose it altogether. But wait a minute. If she had the knife in hand, she could lie in wait for him.

With that in mind, she gave the fan one last jerk. The mouth of the pouch gave way, and she was able to pull the pouch down around the fan-knife and slide the weapon out.

Once the fan lay fully in the palm of her right hand, she was tempted to run both sets of fingers across its razor-sharp indentations and protrusions. Wait. Any mishandling and she might cut herself. And then she heard the lost voice of her dragon. *My daughter, this is a mighty weapon. Now, use it to save yourself.* She had her dragon's approval—now if only she also had its ferocity.

Within fifteen minutes, the steady rocking changed its rhythm to more of an up-and-down movement. Maybe the ship had stopped in the water, though she could not be sure. On the deck above, a series of sharp whistles pierced the air. From her previous China voyage, she remembered a whistle would sound, followed by a shouted order. Sure enough, someone called an order through what sounded like a trumpet. Some words were muffled, but she thought she heard, "There . . . go! Cast . . . mooring lines across! Greetings from *The Oregon!*"

Their ship must be lining up parallel to another vessel. She recalled seeing *The Oregon* at times on the wharf. It was a US mail steamship that went back and forth to Panama. Why would that ship be lining up with this one? To take on a late passenger? To add cargo? That would be highly unusual.

The jagged, up-and-down movements of the waves racked her stomach. *Do not throw up—not here, not now.* They must be nearing the Golden Gate passage out of San Francisco Bay She remembered seeing those straits from the top of Telegraph Hill.

Ships would struggle with the angular movements of the winds and the cross-waves, worrying any but the most experienced captain. Any farther out and they would be swept to sea or founder on the rocky points.

After the crew's muffled cries across the bow, there was a new noise on the weather deck of the ship. What was it? Maybe rope ladders were being unfolded. New jumbles, new footfalls. Someone was coming on board.

An authoritative voice rang out. It must be the captain. Though barely audible, she strained to hear the blunted words. "Lads, yer welcome to . . . *The Surprise.* . . be warned. . . twenty minutes . . . straits . . . treacherous . . . tides running fast . . . sound three bells." A gust of wind caused the beams to shudder, and she strained to hear the rest of what he might say.

"Be back on yer own ship, *The Oregon,* or we . . . cast off . . . you onboard our ship . . . all the way to Hong Kong."

Again, she wondered. Where was she being held? Maybe among the cargo on the second deck. Why was she able to hear what was said above on the weather deck? Maybe Lee Shau Kee had set her in a corner with some boxes and crates by a stairwell leading up to the upper deck. She tensed, gripping her fan. Since her dragon had gone silent, Goddess Mazu would have to guide her now.

Not long after *The Oregon's* arrival alongside *The Surprise*, Ah continued to lie on her side. She gripped her fan and began working the knife back and forth against the burlap bag where it lay behind her. If only she could slash a hole in it. Though the burlap was stiff, the knife was sharp, and one-by-one the threads gave way. Why was it taking so long? At first, she could poke her fingers through the opening, then her entire fist. She continued to slash, and at one point, she missed and cut her index finger instead. She flinched. Never mind the pain, so little time.

A jarring thought occurred—if Lee Shau Kee returned, she would be in real trouble. If he saw her efforts to get out of the bag, what would he do?

With all her might, she rolled around inside the burlap sack, trying to work the material around so that she could see through the slash she had made. She grew thirsty and breathed in jagged huffs. The burlap scraped the surface of her skin.

At last, after many tries, she located the slash she made. Peering through, she saw the one-inch slats of the crate that formed her prison. Through a slim opening between two slats, she spied a nearby crate. "Porcelain" was burned in both English and Cantonese on its side. The light out there was faint and shadowy, likely coming from lanterns.

She could see nothing above her. The surface was slatted; no light filtered through as it did on the sides. If she guessed correctly, Lee Shau Kee placed heavy boxes on top of hers.

She stretched her head around as far as she could, looking in all directions through the hole in the burlap. "Tea" was stamped on another nearby crate. What was in there? Only straw? Then it must be empty.

Now, how to get out. Maybe she could cut her way out of the whole bag. Then she could use the knife to weaken a wooden slat. But first she needed to free her hands. She held the knife perpendicular to the rope on her wrists, then angled it downward. That proved more difficult a bargain. Without being able to see, she might slit her own wrists with the sharp blade.

Despite that, she sawed through the series of button knots that tightened the rope at her wrists. Lee Shau Kee had doubled the lines, and each line was knotted in many places. After many tries, she lay back. How would she ever find the strength to go on?

Within the soft shroud of darkness, cut by tiny shafts of light, she heard the still small voice of her dragon.

What matters is not the success or failure of your quest. You are the Dragon King's Daughter, but you have not yet attained enlightenment. Many more obstacles await you. Now you must fight on.

Had she fallen asleep? Had her dragon really spoken? Maybe her dragon was right. Maybe she had failed to free her wrists, but she could not give up the struggle.

But getting out of the crate was another matter. If she were to begin sawing the wood slats with the fan-knife, the *ee—aw* sound would draw attention to herself. Sure, it might attract help, but the wrong kind. What if Lee Shau Kee were to find her bag was cut? He could take her knife or use it against her. He might stuff her inside several bags, burying her so deeply she would never have a chance of escape.

A faint voice whispered in her ear. *Stay still.* Her dragon had not abandoned her.

A series of voices and footsteps traveled downward from the weather deck into the hold. People must be coming down the staircase onto the deck where she lay hidden. Their mumblings could now be distinguished as words.

The first voice carried a commanding tone. It must be the captain. "I demand to know what you are about, sir."

A tenor voice rang out. Maybe the first mate. "This is a most inopportune moment to meet. Do ye not know we are at the front of a gathering storm?"

Clark's familiar voice filled the air. "We seek the whereabouts of a passenger 'Gnim, Iak,' traveling with a woman he claims to be his wife."

His voice jolted her core. She must signal him. If only she could call out, but the gag muffled her sound. She tried rocking from side to side in order to make noise, in addition to kicking her feet. Nothing moved. Lee Shau Kee had put so much weight on top of her, she was immobilized. After several tries, she quieted. She had to hear what they were saying.

"Why do you seek—?" The captain's question drifted in the muffled air.

Clark said, "We believe he kidnapped a woman and may seek to harm her."

The captain's voice rose again, this time closer. "I see. My capable first mate will handle the matter. I must see to the helmsman, for these waters are called 'the graveyard' for good reason. I will give you little time for the search. I have a schedule to keep."

Boots tromped in her direction, then stopped a distance away. More than two sets of footsteps. Could Chen be with Clark? Her muscles tightened.

The first mate's voice echoed. "The few guest cabins we have are on this deck, sharing space with the cargo."

"Come on, I am over here!" She pounded her feet against the crate. "Why can you not hear me?" Her stomach knotted.

"Two crew quarters house passengers on this voyage." That might be the voice of the first mate leading the party. "The roster is inside this journal. Just let me get it out of my satchel. I see now. Down there. Portside at the stern."

"What else is down there?" Clark asked.

"Me! I am here!" Her cries gurgled into the cotton fabric of the gag.

"Some cargo that is waiting to go into the hold. We had to leave on schedule, so we plan to put it down there once we are at sea."

The ship was rocking heavily, side to side. Someone rapped on the door of what must be a cabin.

Chen might be clenching his fists on one side of the door. Lee Shau Kee could be on the other side.

A door creaked opened. The first mate's words blended with those of a new voice.

The first mate said, "Is this your man?" Who was he talking to?

Clark said. "No. Sorry to disturb you, sir."

They must be talking to someone in the cabin.

The first mate said. "There was a mix-up in the cabin numbers. I apologize, sir."

The new voice huffed in an Englishman's accent. "Quite all right."

A door latched shut.

Ah gave a sigh. Not Lee Shau Kee. So, her guess was right—he would be hiding. But where?

The group strolled in what must be her direction. If only she could push her feet upward against the top of the crate and pound them. Hard as she tried, nothing would move. Were they stepping closer? She stopped; her feet fixed on the underside of the crate.

Clark said, "Look—down there—an open door."

She sweated profusely. Was it possible that he was so close to her yet so far away? Sudden tears burned her eyes. What if he were never to find her, even though he could have crossed the companionway, reached out, and touched her crate?

The first mate said, "One moment lest we disturb another passenger." He must be thumbing pages of his roster. "This cabin is booked—ah, here it is: *Last Name: Gnim, First Name: Iak, traveling with wife—*"

She lay blinking in the darkness. So that is what Lee Shau Kee had told the shipping agent when he booked their passage. How strange and disquieting.

What must be a cabin door squeaked open.

Chen said, "Clark, you are blocking my view."

A warmth spread throughout her body. *Chen.* Thank the Goddess. At least if she were to die or go back to China, she would have heard his voice one last time.

Clark said, "Look there—a Chinese man's black jacket, hat, and shoes."

"Ah has been here. I smell her scent of lavender," Chen said. "What is in that canvas bag in the corner? What is that bitter smell? Must be urine."

"You got me there. Check the contents." Clark's voice was breaking.

Silence ensued. Clark or Chen must be untying the roped end of the bag.

"Look!" Clark said. "Ah's green Manchurian silk jacket and matching pants. I have seen this on her so many times." His voice shredded. Was he in despair?

The first mate mumbled something, but she could not tell what it was.

Chen said, "What have they done to her? But wait—there is something else in the bag."

"Oh no." Clark's voice trailed away.

"Let me see—her favorite shoes, the white with pink roses."

She flinched. Her wedding shoes. "Over here!" Ah pounded her feet again and rocked side to side, but no sounds would come. But then—a wary thought possessed her—if she did make noise, Lee Shau Kee could ambush the two men. Where the devil was he?

Clark said, "Land sakes, my friend. We must investigate this."

Chen growled. "How can you be so matter of fact when we may have lost her? I will hatchet the skull of whoever did this."

Clark counseled Chen with an uncharacteristic Asian wisdom. "In my years patrolling Little Canton, I have learned much. The more I rush to judgment, the worse the outcome. Let us take each fact as we find it, then make our conclusions later." He paused, maybe tapping his arm. "Please, I need your calm."

"I will try, but—" Chen's snarl buried the rest of his sentence.

"Where else could these passengers be?" Clark asked.

"All passengers are confined to quarters until we are at sea. Nevertheless, they could be anywhere." The first mate's voice dropped off, and Ah imagined him gazing around the deck.

"What is over there in the corner next to the staircase?" Clark asked. "Storage? Freight?"

The mate said, "Either empty crates, or those with seconds returning to Guangdong. No passengers."

Chen said, "Take us there."

Ah cried out into her gag. "Over here, but be careful, friends. Lee Shau Kee could be nearby."

The mate's voice held firm. "No one goes there except the crew. Captain's orders."

Clark said, "This should convince you otherwise." Was Clark tapping his Vigilante badge?

The first mate's voice was somber. "Only the captain has the mandate. Besides, your insignia does not move me. You do not have authority over maritime law."

Clark said, "So who does?"

The mate snarled. "Only the captain."

Ah dove into her thoughts. On the Guangdong wharf, a first mate could be bought easily. Lee Shau Kee could have purchased their good graces. Some banknotes and gold nuggets would cover any language gaps that may have existed.

Ah swallowed hard against her gag. She was at the mercy of worse than thugs—that is, if they had not already snuffed out her future. And around them, nothing but shark-infested waters. Was that sweat dripping down her spine? She shifted where she lay. What could she do?

Breaking the pause, Clark spat out the words, "Find-the-captain-now." She pictured him, fingering the revolver snug in its holster at his hip, then lifting it steadily, aiming it toward the first mate.

Meanwhile the waves must be mounting, causing the ship to roll; any minute the men could lose their footing. The first mate could reach out for Clark's gun, or worse, Clark could hit the side of the hull and the gun could go off in any direction. No doubt Chen would stiffen and lurch with the tides.

The first mate must be biding his time. If he waited long enough, the captain would order the third bell on *The Surprise,* and they would lose their chance.

Clark did not speak.

Ah groaned. Why was Clark wavering now instead of going forward? Was he afraid of what he might find? She gave a silent appeal. Clark— act, do not hesitate! And what about Chen? He had the responsibility to push Clark into action.

At last she heard Chen's words rise into the dim pause. "A man who is really brave must act. Clark, take heed. This man must obey."

A click resonated up and down the companionway. She knew that sound. Clark had pulled back the hammer and cocked the revolver.

A multitude of steps trickled away from her, back toward the ladder leading up to the deck, then stopped. She pictured the men standing at the foot of the staircase.

The mate grumbled. "I'll do as you say this time, just because you have a gun on me. But this shall be reported." She heard his footfalls going up the ladder.

Another voice, faint this time. She could not make out the words.

Maybe the first mate was speaking to someone on the deck above. After a short pause, the first mate's words rang clear. "Get the captain. Now."

"But—" A voice argued.

The mate rumbled. "Now, on the double."

"Aye." The faint voice squawked.

The first bell pealed.

For Ah, the seconds passed in an endless flow. Inside her, the tug of despair went to war against the desire for freedom. Yet what was a moment's liberation versus permanent safety in a world without that mongrel Lee Shau Kee? Each side presented itself in turn, an endless cycle of light-then-darkness.

Not long after, the same footsteps shimmied down the stepladder. The first mate must be rejoining Clark and Chen in the companionway.

The first mate rasped. "I have spoken to the captain. He wants to know: what authority do you have to command this ship?"

Clark said, "The Committee of Vigilance, San Francisco. You are not out of our waters yet. If you do not cooperate, your ship will return to our shores, and you will face the secret tribunal."

Was Clark stretching the truth? Or maybe Clark realized he had few seconds to save her? For the first time, she saw a different quality in the man who broke her heart. Clark's conviviality, his likeable demeanor, transformed into steely armor. At last he showed his bravery.

Clark continued, his voice deepening. "Take us through your cargo bay here in the hold. Lead us into the darkest corners. We are looking for your missing passengers."

Silence ensued. The waves crisscrossed the hull of the ship, the beams whining like children.

Clark bore down. "I won't hesitate to shoot you here where you stand. You are blocking justice, sir."

Another hesitation. This first mate had some nerve.

Then a profane thought came to her. Was the first mate mired in some ungodly corruption? Tung Chao might own this ship. Should Clark make a false move, the crew could swarm down, capture him and Chen, and either throw them over, or take them back to Tung Chao for his savage justice. The first mate knew that the longer they waited, the more likely *The Oregon* would abandon them, and they would be off to China.

Clark's voice sailed into the air. "Hold him, Chen"

Ah gripped her fan, gathering all the energy she had. If Lee Shau Kee were to reach in and grab her, she would be ready.

At last the first mate spoke, maybe to a nearby deckhand. "Very well. Bring the lantern."

For the next few moments, Ah heard nothing save the water slapping against the sides of the hold, at times crashing, as the ship tossed up and down in the eternal rocking of the Bay straits. Instead of the shuffling footsteps of several men, she heard creeping sounds. It had to be Lee Shau Kee.

Then she noticed a faint odor outside the crate. Perfume suffused with urine. That lavender perfume, the French bath salts from Elizabeth Dailey. *Urine*…she wrinkled her nose. She had been a captive and would urinate—someone was holding her clothes—maybe Lee Shau Kee—but how did he get her clothes? Had he gotten the upper hand? Where was Clark? Chen? She trembled. Lee Shau kee was here—now.

Someone was tossing what sounded like ropes, cables and chains nearby. Maybe some rigging was piled up. Whatever was Lee Shau Kee doing? Outlandish thoughts flooded her mind. He might be preparing a rope and cable in order to sneak her above deck and drop her over the side into the water. A shiver took hold of her. Though she had wanted to die many times in the hands of Tung Chee, America continued to beckon. She wanted to live—here—now.

Then she heard someone pushing what might be boxes off the top of her crate. Someone ripped at the nails that locked the cover. *She was now in big trouble.* Lee Shau Kee would know she had tried to escape. She lay back inside her slashed bag, with one hand closing the hole she had cut, the other gripping her fan-knife. The wood gave way, followed by a rush of air. At last the cover was off.

Someone's hands were reaching into the crate, ranging on top of her burlap sack, over her head, arms, and torso. And when he flattened the material against her head, he was tracing the features of forehead, eyes, nose. Was it Lee Shau Kee? Did he think she was dead?

She held her breath, one-two-three-four . . . if she exhaled, she must do it very slowly so the bag would not puff out under his fingers. *Lie very still.* She tightened her hold on the burlap and the grip on the fan. When she had the chance, she would pierce him with the knife any way she could. Even if she had her hands tied behind her back, she could at least stab him.

Sets of footsteps were pounding in her direction on the planking.

"Chen," Clark was calling.

The voice attached to the fingers on her bag said, "Over here." Though the voice was muffled, she knew it was Chen's. His soft tone radiated around her.

Relief came in waves. "Chen?" she asked, her gagged voice no more than a whisper.

A light glinted overhead through the burlap bag. "Yes, I am here, si tau po."

Someone pulled the burlap bag off her head. Clark's blond hair glimmered in the flow of light.

"Ah, I knew you would be here." Clark took a sharp breath. "Look at that gash—that bastard hit her on the head."

Relief filled her like the shores at high tide, but the gag imprisoned her voice.

Clark helped her sit up. "We need to get you out of here—I'll give you the story later. Chen, can you hold the lantern steady while I lift her?"

As he picked her up and stood her on her feet, something clattered to the deck.

"What was that?" Clark said.

"The fan-knife I gave her." Chen said. His voice trembled. "What has he done to our darling girl?"

"Her hair is a tangle. Oh, mercy." Clark gave a near-sob. He untied her gag and gently tugged it from her mouth.

She swallowed hard; dry spittle mixed with cloth fibers muted her voice. "Lee Shau Kee—it was Lee Shau Kee." She took a deep gulp of air.

Through half-open lids, she saw Chen pull the burlap bag down to her waist. She shivered; her skin was naked against the prickling cold air. She could feel Chen's ear at her chest. "Her breathing comes fast."

"But look, pick up that fan-knife and cut her hands loose." Tenderness layered Clark's request; he clutched her to his side.

She heard the swish of Chen's jacket, followed by the press of his fingers against the backs of her wrists. With up and down movements, he worked the fan-knife against the rope and freed her. She looked first over at Chen, then up at Clark. Tears brimmed in his eyes.

"She is sweaty, but the air is so cold. Let us wrap her up and get her out of here." Clark leaned in and brushed his lips against her cheek. "I am so glad you are alive." His voice broke like breakers against a shoal.

She sensed his fingers folding the burlap back up around her shoulders. Why was it her thoughts came fast, but they would not become words?

Clark said, "Here, Chen, take the gun. Keep my Colt on these sailors, but march them to the top deck."

Chen grunted his reply, then motioned the men toward the stairwell. Chen held the gun against the two sailors. "Go in front of me. In China we have little mercy for murderers."

Clark lifted her into his arms. "Finally, we found you."

"How did you know? You said you would tell me the story." She looked into his eyes, hollow in the darkness.

"Chen smelled the scent of lavender and urine on your clothing in the cabin. He searched in and around this area, and this crate had the same scent, so he guessed you might be inside of it."

"I suspected as much, but I am glad that was the same truth as I imagined."

He sniffed her neck, then smiled. "There is a scent of lavender about you, even now."

"So glad it was Chen who found me, but where is Lee Shau Kee?" Ah collapsed against his chest.

"He is on this ship somewhere." Clark followed the men, carrying her up to the ladder and onto the weather deck.

The second bell pierced the air.

Outside a stiff breeze sharpened its tips against her face, a painful reminder that all was not resolved. Clark set Ah down onto a makeshift cot created from a bundle of sail. He took off his long peacoat, then draped it around her shoulders. He leaned her into a sitting position against the wall of the stock house which faced midships on the deck.

The sea air awakened her now, and she observed an unsettling scene. The skies had darkened to deep charcoal with flecks of white as clouds chased the storm. A crack of thunder sounded, followed by a flash of lightning over Telegraph Hill.

"Where in the hell is Lee Shau Kee?" Clark's questioning curse shot into the air, carrying his frustrations.

Ah gained strength with each gulp of fresh air.

Clark breathed out. "It will only be minutes until the third bell, until we must leave the ship and lose Lee Shau Kee."

Chen said, "We must find him. Where is he—I will shoot him myself!"

The first mate said, "I had no idea he would do this."

Ah managed a crooked smile. What a liar. Of course, he knew.

Chen ignited like a flint's spark. "The greatest wickedness comes from men like you who see nothing, though torture goes on under their thumbnails."

The first mate shrugged. "He seemed legitimate when he registered for passage. He said this woman was his wife, too frail to walk far."

Chen said, "Find him, or I will tear your guts from your belly and feed them to the dogs. We do that to evil men in China."

Ah gave a faint smile. The first mate had better watch out—Chen was a man of his word.

After a grimace, the mate led the way back down the ladder and Chen followed. Around the hatch, a gaggle of sailors kept watch, exchanging sour glances. The deck tossed, the westerly winds growing wilder.

Someone tapped her shoulder and she looked up at Clark's tall body swaying with the motion of the ship. His voice pierced the winds. "In a few minutes I will take you to *The Surprise*." He pointed at the gangway, and when Ah turned her head, she saw the clipper ship tendered there, the other ship's crew watching them with upturned faces.

Clark stepped over to the staircase, and his voice rose and fell with the waves. "Chen, you must come! It is too dangerous to wait any longer."

"What is he finding down there?" Ah asked. Someone burst up out of the staircase. "What was that?"

A black line zigged then zagged against the tossing deck of the clipper ship—a figure shimmied up the ratline of the mainmast.

A sliver of panic sliced into her and she gasped. "Lee Shau Kee."

Then another flash out of the stairwell—lightning flared behind Chen. He took off after the figure in black.

Lee Shau Kee continued his climb. He reached and scrambled his way up each rope, rising ever higher toward the crow's nest.

Ah gazed upwards, her mouth falling open. The mainmast must be eighty feet or more.

"Chen, go after him! There he is!" Clark shouted.

Chen jumped onto the ratlines, following Lee Shau Kee's upward track. The revolver glinted against Chen's belt.

Ah's mind filled with prayers. *Goddess Mazu, give him strength to do this.*

Chen climbed at least sixty feet up the mast, where the wind had no choice but to whistle in his ears and make hash of his sleek black queue.

He extended his right arm, then grabbed onto Lee Shau Kee's left leg. He pulled down at Lee Shau Kee who kicked hard against his grip.

Something happened. Chen's right arm dropped away from Lee Shau Kee. Chen appeared dazed, looking down at his fingers. Lee Shau Kee scampered up even higher.

"Chen must be hurt," Clark said. "Looks like something's amiss with his arm."

Ah absorbed the scene. Even if his right arm were injured, Chen would need to hold onto the ratline in order to prevent Lee Shau Kee from scuttling down. Drifts of fog were settling through the yardarms. The glaze of Lee Shau Kee's form hovered above Chen.

At least Chen was still holding on to a line with his left arm, but then Lee Shau Kee pulled himself three feet farther up the ratline; lightning flashed—at least it looked like lightning—then Chen grabbed his chest.

Clark asked, "What happened? Has he been shot?"

Chen looked down; his left foot tangled in a web of rope.

Clark called to Chen. "Get out your gun—aim and shoot, man!"

Chen snatched the gun from his waistband, felt for the revolver's trigger, and aimed the gun at Lee Shau Kee. The ship lurched, and the revolver discharged, its kick throwing Chen backwards. He sailed downward.

Luckily, the sudden jerk left his feet in a tangle of rope, and he hung awkwardly, dangerously off the ratlines, like some jungle boy whose foot was snagged in a mass of thick vines. He reached out his left hand and held on to the lines, maybe trying to ease the pain of the rope strangling his left ankle.

Clark said, "I can't tell if Chen hit him, can you?"

Ah shook her head, dizzy from looking up. "I see no blood yet on his jacket."

High up on the mast near the crow's nest, Lee Shau Kee leveled a gun toward Chen, his target swinging below him.

She squeezed her eyes shut, then a gun fired into the wind whistling above her. She could not help but blink at the ratlines and the mast.

Chen continued to dangle, his body going limp. If he had been shot, he might have fainted or already be dead. But now, where was Lee Shau Kee?

The scoundrel hung by one arm from a vertical rope suspended from the yardarm of the main mast seventy feet above them. Ah could not see his facial expression, but each toss of the ship caused him to lose an inch of his grip.

Each time he tried to hoist his other hand onto the rope, he lost another inch of line, and he dropped, losing his grasp. He kicked and flailed against the air, but it was no use.

The crew and the captain stared upward, their mouths gaping. What was that movement?

Lee Shau Kee was falling. His lithe, slim body, small as an arrow, plunged onto the weather deck of *The Surprise*. A loud crash reverberated through the ship's planking, followed by a shudder, then a moan.

Eight

❧ FOREVER HIS LEGACY ❧

A moment of silence punctuated the rush of the wind and the roar of the blue-green waves, their whitecaps smashing the ship in all directions. In these moments Ah realized the impact of sudden death. In these moments no one could speak. But she also knew that Chen was alive. After dedicating himself to her security, he had saved her life today. That was a debt she could not repay.

The crew unraveled Chen from the ratlines, and they placed him on a stretcher. He lay there, limp and pale.

Clark knelt by his side and covered his body with a serge blanket.

The captain glanced furtively at his pocket watch, then at the skies.

"How is our poor Chen?" Ah poured out her question.

Clark nodded over at her. "Strong pulse."

The captain pulled his greatcoat about him, his face an iron mask. "Makes no difference to me. I want all of you off my ship. What a delay you have caused my company."

She swallowed hard, watching the crew stuff Lee Shau Kee's lifeless remains into a canvas bag. Not long ago, he had jammed her into a burlap bag and left her to suffer in that crate belowdecks. How fitting he would lie moldering in this bag at the bottom of San Francisco Bay. His bones would never return to China for a family burial with his ancestors. Disgrace would forever be his legacy.

The first mate came forward. "Captain, would you like to say some words over the lad?"

"Not on your hide. That bastard ruined my schedule. Let the sharks have him."

The sailors hoisted the body bag over the side. It tumbled into the water with a resounding splash. The same crewmen carried Chen to the side and lowered him down a rope ladder onto a launch where *The Oregon's* crew met him and took him aboard ship.

Clark came to Ah's side and helped her to her feet. "No more bells."

She looked into his blue crystalline eyes, rimmed with black circles. "I am ready to go home now."

"No wonder." Clark lifted Ah into his arms.

She clung to him, her arms around his neck, savoring the sweet tobacco and whiskey scent layering his beard. Dare she tell him the word "home" meant the warmth of his embrace? That would have to wait. Waves were tipping both ships and making each step a trial. With lurching steps, he carried her across the plank onto *The Oregon.*

In his surgery below decks, the ship's doctor examined Ah, gave her sips of water, and wrapped her in an oversized sailor's nightshirt. Her dark hair slung over her shoulder; her teeth would not stop chattering. The doctor placed a dressing on her headwound, then tied a thin towel under her neck to hold the bandage in place.

A dull ache thrummed with each pump of blood in her head. Right now, all she wanted was to go to Clark. She half-sat against the pillow, her palm held up, preparing to swat away the cup in the doctor's hand.

He stepped back. "Only a dose of laudanum."

"I do not need it. I have seen that bad drug. Let me get up."

"Suit yourself, but you are in rather bad shape, my dear." The doctor helped her slide her legs over the side of the cot and guided her arm while she tried to stand.

Her legs trembled like India rubber, and the doctor's cabin spun around once. She felt for the edge of the cot and sat down.

The doctor hovered, pushing back the hair curling over his forehead. "I think it is best if you wait and gather some strength. I do not know why the Celestials do this foot operation on their women. Cripples them." He extended a tin box. "Here, nibble on this hard tack."

She took the horrid cracker, then gummed it. Enough to make her gag. That sore throat again.

"More water to wash it down?" he offered.

She accepted the chipped porcelain cup from him. "Where is Clark?"

"Officer Clark, the Vigilante? He must be with another passenger in the other medicine bay. We had someone else with a wound." The doctor swabbed her forehead with a cool cloth.

"Who was that?" she asked.

"A Celestial. All I know."

"My poor friend Chen. I know he hurt his arm. Was he shot? Can he even walk?"

"Do not concern yourself with that, young lady. Now you must rest. You have been through a mountain of trouble." Though his glance was fatherly, she caught a hint of condescension.

In better days she would bristle, then probe him for more information. But this was not a better day. Too exhausted to ask more questions, she lay back on the cot, staring at the lantern swinging from side to side on a crossbeam. Chen. If only she had the strength to get up and go to his side. Patience.

For the next hour, *The Oregon* chuffed its return to the Washington Street Wharf. Clark lifted Ah from her cot, set a blanket around her shoulders, and carried her above decks. They stopped at the gangway where Clark set her on her feet. Ah gazed down through bleary eyes at the crowd of men in top hats gathered on the dock.

The *Alta California* news reporter Harold Snow and his illustrator, Joe Ludding, emerged from the throng. Snow was talking to a shipping agent, and Ludding was sketching something she could not make out.

Chen limped over and joined Ah and Clark. His left hand was bandaged, and his arm was in a sling. He appeared drawn and pale in the gray light.

She whispered to Chen, "I was so worried."

He patted his chest. "Lee Shau Kee's bullet grazed me, but Doc says it is only a surface wound. As for my arm, Doc says the wrist is broken, nothing more. Doc says I got an ankle sprain, and I must keep a poultice on it when we get home."

"Home. I want to be there, too." She shivered under the blanket; all she wanted was her bed and Jade. Maybe San and Yee could put herbal compresses on her head to stop the pain.

The crowd stilled, some men in jackets, some in top hats, others with satchels. Snow and Ludding stared at her intently. What did they want from her?

A carriage drawn by a smart bay horse pulled up at the wharf. Henry Conrad leaped out and joined the party on the dock. Lines on his face telegraphed rage and disgust. "I received a note from the shipping agent who said Ah Toy had arrived at the Washington Street Wharf." He stepped toward her. "What enterprise have you been on?"

She shriveled a little at the disappointment in his voice. As hard as she tried to speak, the words stuck in her throat. At the very least, he should offer to take her back home. After all, they were nearly man and wife. Whatever was wrong with him?

Clark bristled. "She was the victim of a heinous plot to take her back to China."

She clung to Clark's shoulder, burying her face in his peacoat.

Henry's voice pierced the air. "So there I am at the church, waiting to take my wedding vows with this—this hussy, when someone she obviously knows—probably one of her johns, comes up behind and kidnaps her. B'gads, do you think I regret the trust I placed in her? You damned well better believe it!"

Clark's muscles tightened. "Her husband's family sent someone to take her back to marry her brother-in-law. He had been threatening this for some time, man. I have served Mrs. Toy as her policeman for some years now, and I know she is afraid for her life."

"You believe what she says?" Henry spat out the words like bitter seeds. "Most likely she made a deal with a man, and it went sour. She is but a sister of misery."

Clark said, "I saw what happened. And it is not the first time she has been kidnapped."

"You'll not convince me that she did not plan this escapade. I was a fool to believe Elizabeth Dailey's words, that Ah Toy would make me a good wife." He sneered. "I should have known better, that someone this beautiful would be so bad."

"Ah Toy would make a good wife for any man lucky enough to have her." Clark's arm tightened around her shoulders.

"*Pfft.* Let me see her hand. The left one." Whatever was Henry talking about? His tone carried an edge of disgust.

Chen took halting steps forward, his right arm in a sling. "I will free it."

Ah felt his free hand easing her left arm out of the blanket, then gentling her hand in his open left palm.

Conrad pointed a bony finger at her hand. "That. I want that."

Whatever was he talking about?

"Do not touch her. I will do it." Chen spoke firmly.

Her head pounded. Then she sensed a painful tug on her ring finger. *What were they doing?* She gave a sideways glance. Chen was edging the jade ring over her knuckle, and off her finger.

"Give me that ring. I have much to tell Elizabeth Dailey." Henry bit off his words and spat them toward her

Clark lowered his brow. "Tell Elizabeth this news—Ah was kidnapped. She could have died during this ordeal."

"Once again, this was a matter of her own making. That I am sure." Henry stroked his throat and grimaced.

While clinging to Clark, Ah turned her head toward Henry. "Take your ring. You make a mockery."

He fingered the ring. "But I blame Elizabeth and the Reverend most of all. They misled me into thinking *you*—a soiled dove—could be reformed." A sneer curled his upper lip.

There it was again—his scowl. She had been right. Why did she not trust her own judgment? His was the voice of a cad and a scoundrel, so much like Tung Chao.

Clark snapped a reply. "She is not the soiled one—you are."

Chen stepped in. "Wealth is desired by everyone. But wealth alone does not make a good and honest man."

Henry tore a velvet box from his coat pocket and jerked it open. A ring with a large gold nugget gleamed in the sunshine. "This was to be our wedding ring. No more. I will send it where it belongs, along with the jade ring and all of her lies."

Ah leveled her eyes on his. "Keep your wedding ring. I will never marry you."

A murmur went through the crowd. Even a skillful miner would have to seek long and hard to find such a large gold piece.

Harold Snow elbowed his way forward toward her, Joe Ludding at his heels. "Care to answer some questions, Miss Toy? Must have been some rescue!"

Clark brushed him away. "Later, Snow."

"Just a word, please—." Before Snow could finish his sentence, Joe Ludding pointed toward the water's edge. "Look there!"

Henry stepped to the edge of the dock and hurled the box with the rings into the water. He looked directly at Ah. "Now the tides can wear them down into flecks of sand."

She followed the arc as the box flew into the air, then dropped into the water. Bubbles rose up in the center of the point where the box landed, wide circles flaring around it. Within seconds, the slip-slap of the outgoing tide erased all signs of the deed.

The bystanders babbled among themselves. Harold Snow was filling his notepad with words. Joe Ludding made a sketch showing a man tossing a nugget into the bay. A straw-hatted man sucking a toothpick pulled the onlookers into a tight circle of conversation. Harold Snow and Joe Ludding would get another story on the front page of *The Alta*.

Ah shook her head. *Good for them.* Better those rings end up in the belly of a shark than on her hand in another loveless marriage.

Nine

❦ THE WHITE MARK ❦

Three days later, Ah lay on the fainting couch in her parlor house. Her muscles ached, especially those in her chest and upper arms. After pushing back her sleeves, she saw the state of her swollen wrists. The bruises were still there, the former purple marks now fading into green. She eyed her ring finger, a white mark the only reminder that Henry's jade ring had once been there. Strangely, rather than loss, she felt relief and peace.

She rose to a sitting position. "Come, Jade, let me scratch you behind the ears." The cat mewed softly, and she reached out her hands and caressed the animal's soft fur. She could only guess at the time of day. Her familiar scrolls glimmered on the walls, and her brass Buddha sat in tranquility on the side table.

The sounds of San Francisco spoke to her through the open window. Outside she heard the calls of vegetable vendors, and the clank of machinery. Cantonese voices filtered in through the open window. No doubt they were arguing some point or another or sharing the latest story. She relaxed back onto the couch. It must be noon or later.

The door hinges squeaked, followed by footsteps on the floorboards. With a limping gait, Chen ushered Clark into the room.

A warm glow permeated her being. *He* had come to see her.

Chen's arm was still in a sling. He said, "Make it brief, Mr. Clark. She is very weak and remembers but a few things. The doctor says that will go away in time, but she must rest for now." The door clicked, and she heard the rustle of what must have been the removal of a topcoat, followed by a hat being set on the side table.

Clark's tall form came into view, hovering over her. "May I?" He patted an area next to her on the couch that Jade had vacated.

The cat mewed a greeting from her place on Ah's lap. When Ah pushed her off onto the floor, the creature hissed, sounding like a cross between a teapot's whistle and nails against a chalkboard.

"She is the loudest cat I have heard in these parts." He shook his head.

"Pay her no mind." Ah laughed. "She always does that—jealousy, I think."

A grin enlivened his face. "She has a right to envy. She is guarding her precious treasure—*you*."

What was different about his voice? It was softer. Where was the hard grief, the bitter echo of loss after Susannah's death?

"Please sit down. Are you here on an official visit from the Vigilantes?" Ah imposed an iron control on herself.

"No, I am here on an unofficial visit. I did bring you today's copy of *The Alta California*. Front page article about our rescue and Henry throwing the rings." He set the paper on a side table.

"I am not sure I like my private life to be known to others." She frowned, drawing back.

"But the other business I come about is most urgent." He reached out and grasped her left hand. His touch was nearly unbearable in its tenderness.

Trembling, she laced her fingers through his, drawing him closer. "I am done with urgent business, the last bit of excitement nearly killed me."

"The business I speak of is—of the mind. And hopefully, of the heart." His intense look sent a tremor through her.

"It may be that my head—" She fingered the area on her temple that was beginning to scab. "I mean it may be my mind does not work well now. I do not understand."

Clark unlaced his hand, sat down on the couch, and inched closer toward her until his hip rested next to hers. "I have been mistaken."

His thigh pressed against hers and she trembled. "In what way? You knew I was to marry Henry." A hot ache rose in her throat.

"That was my mistake. You see, I thought that after Susannah died, I could move on, stay in New York, and start a new life. I wanted you so much. Do you remember the day we first met when I paid to see your naked body?" His voice took on a huskier tone; his gaze flickered over her face.

"Yes, I do recall. But you stayed with Susannah, you were a faithful husband." She hesitated a moment, watching him in profile.

"Yes, I did. I believe in duty. So much that I thought I needed to preserve her memory forever as her widower. But when I got your letter, I knew I made a mistake. When you said you would marry Henry, I thought I would lose you forever." He leaned down and whispered, his breath warming her ear.

She inhaled sharply at his contact, but a question lingered. "Why did you act surprised when Chen told you I loved you still?"

"You knew about that?" Red patches appeared on his cheeks.

"Yes, I watched you and Chen from behind the door that day." If only she could ignore the strange aching in her limbs.

"Oh, you did?" Clark shrugged, looking down at the floor. "I figured it was too late, that you had already decided. Why did you not answer my letter, tell me how much you loved me?"

"I guess I would not be able to live another day if you rejected me." If only she could stop the pulse pounding in her ears.

"Oh, mercy. I was so blind . . . I did not realize . . . ." His voice cracked.

"And why did you not come to see me at my wedding?" She tilted her head toward him.

He shook his head vehemently. "I came. I slipped into the back pew when you were starting down the aisle. It is true, I almost did not come. You do not realize the extent of my grief. A funny thing, this kind of sorrow mixed with guilt. You think it is over after a time when a loved one—in my case, Susannah—dies. But it comes back when a new loss shows up."

"I understand. Many events bring up the deaths of my baby daughters."

"I came back for you because I realized I could not live one more day without you. Then, when Chen told me you were to marry Henry, I grew so numb. All I wanted to do was sleep, to crawl into a hole. I know it makes no sense to you, but there it is."

She nodded. "It does make sense to me. I have also gone numb when I think of my daughters' bones on the lonely cliffside. But another thing confuses me. Why did you never write back to tell me that you were caught in sorrow? I would have waited for you."

He lowered his head between his hands for a moment, then looked into her eyes.

"I was a coward. Funny—I have cornered men with knives, fought gun battles, even rescued drowning men in the Bay. But I was afraid then that if I asked you would say no."

"Are you afraid now?" Her heart hammered foolishly.

He shook his head. "No, actually I am not."

"So...go ahead."

Her took her hand, enfolding it in his. "Ah Toy, will you be my wife?"

A moment passed. The curtains swished at the open window. A songbird trilled its melody from a neighboring rooftop.

"Yes, John Clark, I will marry you." The words made their way effortlessly into the air between them.

He brushed his lips across hers where they lingered. His touch took away the pain in her head, opened the dark spaces of the yin, replacing them with light and openness to the world. In return, her fingers explored the nooks and crannies of his face, and she kissed his nose, his lips, his cheeks, letting her lips savor the landscape she thought would never be hers.

Despite her aching body, the bruises painted on her back and shoulders, she clutched him to her, taking his spirit into hers where they could find the peaceful whole, the place of complete acceptance and love.

She felt the force of his body against hers, the gentle rhythm of his mouth opening hers as he kissed her, running his fingers over her eyes, mouth, and into the dark splendor of her long, black hair. He eased her down next to him and his hands explored the hollows of her back.

A warming shiver coursed through her, and she traced the outline of his lips with her index finger. "I do not understand something. It is about Lee Shau Kee."

"Tell me." He held her fingertips in the palm of his hand.

"Why did he go up the mast and make himself such a target? Anyone could have shot him."

He buried his face in her hair. "My guess is that after Chen flushed him out of the hold, he had nowhere else to go but up there, maybe in the hopes that he could outclimb even the best sailor."

"Maybe he was wishing to die."

He nodded. "It is true—if he slipped, he would have surely killed himself, if not by falling on the deck, at least by landing in the water. In those wild straits, no one could be saved. The sharks would get him first."

"Maybe he knew he was doomed whether or not he went back to China."

"How is that?"

"If he stayed on the clipper and went back, Tung Chao would not forgive his losing me. If he stayed in San Francisco, the Vigilantes would mostly likely try and hang him."

"I certainly would have arrested him." He hooked himself onto an elbow for a moment and gazed down into her upturned face. "Just tell me one thing."

"Yes?"

"What happened after Lee Shau Kee took you from the church and put you on the ship? Did you give that bastard a good fight?"

"When he threw me on the bed in the cabin, and took me out of the burlap bag, I fought back hard. Whatever I could do to defend myself. He had to take a wooden board to hit me over the head in order to quiet me. I saw him lift it, and I knew he was aiming for my head. I reached up, but he swatted my hands away and that was when the world went black. The next time I woke up was in the crate on the ship."

"So, you fought like a cat." He gave her a knowing grin.

She shook her head. "No, I fought like the Dragon King's Daughter."

A gleam sparkled in his eyes. "That's the answer I wanted to hear."

She nestled into his arms, savoring another deep kiss, carrying the past into the present.

Not long after, Chen knocked at the door, then entered. Normally his stride was forceful; today he grimaced with each step.

Ah withdrew from Clark's arms, but he remained seated by her side.

Chen startled. "I am sorry to interrupt."

In seconds, Jade jumped onto her lap to fill the empty space where Clark had been. The cat purred loudly, plainly delighted to have her mistress back.

Chen grinned. "We have a visitor."

Clark rose, smoothed his jacket, and took a seat on a side chair.

"Who is it?" Ah said.

A woman's voice came from the hallway, the door swung open, and Li Fan appeared. Long dangling gold earrings swung as she sidled into the room.

Ah saw Chen turn to watch. Li Fan would catch anyone's attention.

Li Fan's black Manchurian gown with white egrets sparkled against the light from the window; her ebony hair shone in a fashionably twisted bun at the back of her head. Despite not being invited, she perched on a lacquered chair.

Ah said, "After what you have done, you have nerve coming here." She gazed over at Chen's plainly worried expression. Clark stiffened at her side. Li Fan's cruelty was legendary. She could be dangerous, especially now that Ah was recovering.

"Too bad Chen let you in. If only he could wind up his mistakes like string on a ball." Ah gave Chen a pointed look and he stared at the floor.

"I insisted. It is not Chen's doing." Li Fan lifted a bottle out of her satchel. "I have brought champagne." She turned to Chen. "Get some glasses. I have a story to tell. I also want your San and Yee to be present."

Ah said, "This had better be fast, otherwise we will pour your dirty champagne in the street."

A dark shadow crossed Clark's face.

Chen set glasses out on the table. Clark went up the stairs for San and Yee, returning in a few moments with the girls. Back in the sitting room, Clark uncorked the champagne, and Chen poured a fizzing sample into each glass.

"Let us make a toast." Li Fan raised her glass. "To the death of Lee Shau Kee."

She went the rounds clinking glasses, first with Ah, then Chen, followed by Clark, San, and Yee.

"Very fizzy," Ah said.

Chen drank a sip but made a face.

"You do not like it? It is French after all." Li Fan's eyebrows arched.

Ah wrinkled her nose. "No, I find the taste sour. I will never get used to western drinks."

"There is something I do not understand, Miss Li." Clark put his glass on the table. "Why would you toast Lee Shau Kee's death? Word is you had thrown your lot in with him—and by association, with Tung Chao."

Li Fan's red lips folded into a frown. "How little you know of our Chinese culture. You only make judgments based on the slight amount you observe."

He shrugged. "That may be true, but humans everywhere know good and evil when they see it."

A knock sounded on the outer door. Who could it be? Chen limped out, then re-entered with Officer Wong in tow.

"No need to stand up." Officer Wong beamed over his many chins. "I heard of your kidnapping and I wish to verify that you are of sound health, daughter." He stepped toward Ah and gave her an affectionate pat on the shoulder. Then he turned. "Li Fan? I am much amused to see you here."

"I have come to tell my story." Her long earrings glittered.

He rubbed his chin. "I would not, if I were you, child. There are some stories that belong within certain walls, not spread beyond them."

Li Fan raised her champagne glass toward him. "Yet some secrets are meant to be revealed."

Ah said, "Li Fan, you have raised my curiosity. Why have you come here? What story? Secrets? And why the champagne? Certainly, in the past you would have drunk champagne to celebrate my death, not my resurrection." She marveled at the word *resurrection*, one of Mrs. Dailey's favorites.

Li Fan said, "I did not expect you to follow me, Officer Wong. But you are not the only one in this room who knows my secrets." She glanced from person to person.

Ah watched as each person shifted uncomfortably under her gaze. The woman had a strange power, to be sure.

Her voice rang out. "I am here to make amends for leaving the four pears in your parlor that night many months ago. I know you suspected me, but I did not act alone. Lee Shau Kee held me to it."

Ah waved her hand. "I am weary of conflict. Even the sound of his name nauseates me."

Li Fan said, "I hope you know how overjoyed I am that he is dead—that worm, that snail, the putrefaction of my life."

"I do not understand. I never knew you were one of *his*."

"Lee Shau Kee held me in bondage. One misstep and I would go to his master in Guangzhou, one Tung Chao, who would use me as a concubine."

"You knew all along that Tung Chao was my husband's brother?"

"We all had your story—the way Tung Chee treated you. And how Tung Chao wanted you back in China." Li Fan tipped back her head and let the champagne fill her mouth, then swallowed it down. "I would like to say I am sorry to have been trouble for you. I would like us to be friends."

Clark said, "To hell with your champagne and your amends. You need to go now."

Li Fan's cheeks reddened. "Mrs. Toy may think differently."

Ah said, "I have three questions for you. After you left the four pears, did you lead Man-Man to the opium den?"

"Of course I left the pears. I hated you then. But I meant to make you mad—that is all. And yes—I took Man-Man there, but only the first time. How was I to know she would like it so much?" Li Fan swayed in her chair. Was she getting drunk?

Clark leaned forward. "I will arrest you. The Vigilantes will be interested in your story of mayhem and murder."

Ah put out her hand. "No—let me speak. The scoundrel Lee Shau Kee is now food for the sharks. He belongs with the old world and its evils." She waved her hand. "Just look around you. We are building a new city here in San Francisco. Since we have arrived, businesses are sprouting up everywhere. Though we have earthquakes and fires, the city endures. Rainstorms and floods will not deter us."

She turned away from Li Fan and scanned the others. "We do not all look alike, but we get along. All the more reason we should accept Li

Fan's apology. She comes from Guangdong, my home. Even more she carries our traditions which may otherwise disappear in this great feast called America."

"Aye," Clark said. "You have a point. If I report her to the Vigilante Committee, they may return for you. Remember you have already been arrested. And they have little mercy."

San and Yee whispered to each other.

Ah said, "I would like to hear what you are saying."

San said, "We think it wise to accept Li Fan's amends. It will bring good fortune to our merciful house."

Officer Wong said, "That is the best justice we can hope for."

Ah said, "I agree." She raised her glass. "I make a toast to Li Fan and to our peaceful future."

Chen broke in, "*Gom bui*, cheers!"

Jade rested on Ah's lap. When all the glasses clinked in unison, the cat kneaded her front paws and blinked her eyes.

An hour later, all the guests departed. Chen, San and Yee wandered out of the room and up the stairs. Jade followed Chen, her tail waving in the air like a question mark.

Clark took his former place, cradling Ah on the couch. He pulled her close.

Ah inhaled the mixture of sweet tobacco and whiskey that so endeared him to her.

"I have a question for you." He tilted his head, his blue eyes flashing. Small red circles formed on his cheeks.

She rested her head against his broad chest, listening to his heartbeat. "What sort of question?" she asked.

"Do you remember when we finally knew that Lee Shau Kee was dead on *The Surprise*? I turned to you and said, 'No more bells.'"

Ah bit her lower lip. "Yes, I do remember that."

His cheeks flamed red. "I wanted to say, 'No more bells until our wedding day.'"

"Why didn't you say it then?"

"I was afraid after all you had been through."

"You? The courageous man who saved my life?"

He grimaced, and his lip trembled for a moment. "A brave woman like you can make a coward of a man like me."

"Nonsense. Are you saying we will have bells at our wedding?"

"Yes, I suppose I am."

"Well then, I suppose we will." She grinned, reached up, and kissed his lips with all the fire she could muster. Then she pulled him closer, nuzzling his cheek. "Now I have a question for you. I think you are holding a secret. Why this sudden change in Li Fan? Why this sudden urge to confess?"

Clark eyed her. "I suppose it will do little harm to tell you now." He sighed. "If you must know, Li Fan murdered Harold Painter."

She shook her head, but a twinge in her shoulder pulled her back against his chest. "I never would have guessed. Something tells me he deserved what he got. Am I right?"

"As my future bride, I must trust you will not tell anyone else."

Ah nodded. "You must tell me what happened."

"Well, this here Painter sent two of Li Fan's prize soiled doves back to China after calling them immigrants, which infuriated her. So, she had men throw him in the bay. When our Vigilante militia rescued Painter in the water, we revived him. As I was wrapping him into a blanket, he whispered, 'Li Fan. I know she—' Then he had terrible shivers, and he made to die."

"I still don't understand." Ah scanned Clark's face.

He winked. "You see, after Painter died, I went and made a deal with Li Fan. If she turned into a confidential informant, I would not turn her over to the Vigilantes for certain death. She had guaranteed security.

That way, I was free to pursue Lee Shau Kee. Unfortunately, he found you before I got a chance to settle his hash."

"You are too clever for words, my love."

"What did you call me?"

"My love."

"Say that again." His fingers outlined her breasts, then fingered open the top buttons of her qipao.

She opened her mouth to reply, only to find her words melting into Clark's warm lips.

Epilogue

❧ ONE YEAR LATER ☙

From the crest of Telegraph Hill, the sun rose above the surface of the earth, its yellow fingers caressing the hilltops enfolding San Francisco Bay. The sun's burst of reds, oranges, and blues sailed above a black line of clouds. Above her, the sky extended a pale blue canopy, with further thin streaks of mist painted overhead.

Ah scanned the panorama from left to right. Where were the familiar junks and sampans cutting into the water with their red sails? None in sight. Only clusters of abandoned ships, rocking at anchor.

As the sun rose further, the Bay's calm waters formed a soft palette of blues and grays that ebbed and flowed around the many wharves stretching into flat points on the water's surface. This tranquility would not last. As soon as the tides and winds shifted, the Bay would transform into a white-capped tapestry of blues, grays, and browns.

Bare-masted ships clustered around the wharves, and a steamship chuffed away from a dock, its stack decanting a thin line of smoke. Black pinpoints moved up and down the wharves, people reduced to mere insects from this distance.

She sensed her dragon flick its tail, then nestle around her on the rock where she perched. She gazed back and waved at Clark, Chen, and Flannery who waited for her at the bottom of the hill. They had argued over her riding up the hill alone on Swinney, but she had insisted, and they had finally given in.

Swinney glanced at her, lingering by her side. The mule nuzzled some tufts of grass, then leaned over expectantly, awaiting further orders.

Ah regarded her stomach, now spreading in the middle months of pregnancy. Inside grew a small round melon that fluttered like a butterfly.

She fingered the gold wedding band around her left hand, then lent her prayer to the wind.

Thank you, Goddess Mazu. You teach us to bring together the good and bad, the wealth and poverty, the sickness and health of our lives. You sing us toward the union of male and female, yin and yang. In your hands, we travel on the sampan, our bodies and spirits encountering kindness and cruelty, sunrise and sunset.

A seagull landed on a nearby rock and angled his head inquisitively toward her.

Thank you, Goddess, for showing me the light of truth when it mattered the most. And stay with me to guide my new son or daughter to be born in this, my new land, America.

The signal flags flapped above her. And the sun continued its ascent over the earth.

Finale

❦

FOREVER ONE

The journey ended; the storms now calmed
The hillsides burst with yellow mustard, purple lupine and orange poppies
The fish leap from tidal pools
And the clipper ships unfurl their sails, catching the wind
I lie with you at last my love
I brush the hair from your eye
And dab kisses on your glowing cheek
At last those clouds, dark and threatening,
Have gone
And we—so long separated—are now forever one.

IN THE MANNER OF LI PO

Afterword

This fictional story of Ah Toy is based on the historical person who appears in accounts from the era. My aim is to amplify several topics in the novel: the position of Chinese immigrant women in Victorian America, the foundation of California's 19th century sex trade, and the role of the Chinese in the development of America's cultural fabric. Ah Toy's story may be found in the *City of the Golden Fifties* by Pauline Jacobson (1941). I have taken liberties with Ah Toy's parlor house scenes; in actuality there would be far less entertainment provided to the customer and considerably less comfort to the prostitute.

On San Francisco: Having been a former resident of San Francisco, and having worked near Chinatown and Market Street, I had long wished to write novels about the Victorian era. I revisited the Mission Dolores, Chinatown, Waverly Place, and Portsmouth Square (formerly known as Portsmouth Plaza). Sadly, many buildings have changed since the 1908 earthquake, yet one can still trace the routes of earlier days. Indeed, a visit to Chinatown today differs in tone but not the spirit of 1850s.

Although I used numerous references to create this book, here are a few for those who want to find out more about some of the topics mentioned. On San Francisco's Chinatown (Little Canton) and its surrounds: I made visits to The Chinese Historical Society of America Museum, situated in the heart of San Francisco's Chinatown. Located in the historic Julia Morgan-designed Chinese YWCA building, the Museum introduces the rich history of the Chinese American experience. I am thankful to Palma J. You, Gallery Coordinator, who provided me with advice and resources. The Chinese Historical Society bookstore is an endless source of author inspiration. On their recommendation, I received authorial advice from Jeffrey L. Staley, Ph.D., author of *Gum Moon: A Novel of San Francisco Chinatown*, (2018).

Among the many resources, I consulted was *A History of the Chinese in California, A Syllabus*, Chinn and Choy, editors, (1984). I read *Chinese San Francisco:1850-1943 – A Trans-Pacific Community* by Yong Chen (2000); *The Chinese Looking Glass* by Dennis Bloodworth, (1967).

San Francisco's Chinatown: A Revised Edition (Images of America) by Judy Yung and Chinese Historical Society of America (2016); *Unbound Voices: A Documentary History of Chinese Women in San Francisco* by Judy Yung (1999); *Unbound Feet: A Social History of Chinese Women in San Francisco: 1st (first) Edition* by Judy Yung (1994).

On the life aboard, and construction of, clipper ships, I consulted *Rough Passage* by Robin Lloyd (2013), and *The American-Built Clipper Ship 1850-1856* by William J. Crothers (2000).

On prostitution in America: *Daughters of Joy, Sisters of Misery* by Anne M. Butler (1987); *Upstairs Girls: Prostitution in the American West* by Michael Rutter (2005); *Their Sisters' Keepers* by Marilyn Wood Hill (1993);*Confidence Men and Painted Women: A Study of Middle-Class Culture in America, 1830-1870* by Karen Halttunen (1982); *The Madams of San Francisco* by Curt Gentry (1964). On 1850s fashion: *Victorian and Edwardian Fashions from "La Mode Illustree"* by Joanne Olian, editor (19980; *Historic Dress in America:1607-1870* by Elisabeth McClellan (1904); *Victorian and Edwardian Fashion: A Photographic Survey*, Alison Gernsheim 1981.

For historic 1850s San Francisco: I relied on *The Fantastic City* by Amelia Ransome Neville (1932); *The Annals of San Francisco* by Soule, Gihon and Nisbet, (1855, 1999); *San Francisco 1846-1856: From Hamlet to City* by Roger W. Lotchin (1997); *The Barbary Coast*, Herbert Asbury (1947);

Acknowledgments

Here I wish to thank my fellow author, Cheryl Stapp, for her excellent historical editing and advice about the life and times in Gold Rush San Francisco. My content editor, Michael Mohr, provided meticulous attention to detail and unflagging support to various drafts. My copyeditor/proofreader, Danita Moon, assisted in the final manuscript formation.

I also wish to thank Palma J. You, Gallery Coordinator of the Chinese Historical Society for providing me additional resources and direction. In addition, a special thanks to author and China scholar, Jeffrey L. Staley, Ph.D., whose insight assisted my research.

This novel's foundation was created with the assistance from the members of Elk Grove Writers and Artists community. Early inspiration came from Zoe Keithley, my writing mentor. Various manuscript versions were heard and developed with the assistance of the following writing partners: Rick Davis, Lisa Dornback, Judy Vaughan, Kathleen Torian Taylor, Lorna Norisse, Dee Bright, Margaret Duarte, Dorothy Rice, Amanda Williams, Carolyn Radmanovich, Elaine Faber, Sharon Darrow, Liz Abess, Michael Richard, Judy Pierce, and Susan Harrison.

A shout-out goes to Kim Edwards, President of California Writers Club, Sacramento branch, for always believing in me.

Fellow Historical Novel Society member authors Mark Weideranders, Kathy Boyd Fellure, Erika Mailman, and Gina Mulligan provided much support and encouragement along the path to publication.

A special thanks to Parris Afton Bonds, co-founder of Romance Writers of America. Her attention and inspiration has kept me on the upward path toward fully believing in myself.

Many thanks go to friends Beth Leonard Schatz and Carole Stone. Additional appreciation goes to fellow authors Anara Guard, Marilyn Reynolds, and Ian Wilson who have maintained an active interest in my writing journey and have greatly supported my efforts.

Fellow Historical Writers of America member, author Holly Maddux has provided much collegial support along the way.

Fellow author Virginia Simpson has given invaluable support on marketing and promotion.

You are all precious to me.

About the Author

Multiple award-winning novelist and historian Gini Grossenbacher is one of California's respected and sought-after creative writing coaches and educators. Her debut novel, *Madam of My Heart*, won the Independent Publisher (IPPY) 2018 Silver Medal for historical fiction. The book was a finalist in the 2018 American Fiction Awards for Historical Fiction; it won an honorable mention at the 2018 San Francisco Book Festival for General Fiction; and it was runner-up in the 2017 Hollywood Book Festival.

Gini is a prominent literacy activist who developed an award-winning and innovative curriculum for the teaching of literature and the language arts in San Juan and Elk Grove School Districts in Northern California. She is a sought-after speaker and literary critic who has appeared in print, online interviews, blogs, workshops, and broadcast media on the subject of critical writing techniques and the joys of historical fiction.

In 2013 she founded Elk Grove Writers and Artists in Northern California, where she provides community writing courses, writing coaching, editing services, and manuscript critique groups.

Gini has a B.A. cum laude in English from Oregon's Lewis & Clark College, where she studied with poet laureate William Stafford. She has done postgraduate work in European history and Italian literature in ancient Perugia and has a master's degree in educational leadership from La Verne University, Los Angeles. She has also completed post-graduate course work in copyediting from UC San Diego Extension.

Gini is also a lifelong forensic historian with a special hands-on interest in the recovery of women's narratives too often neglected in the stories nations and great cities tell about their origins. She has done in-place literary and historical research across five continents and wandered back alleys and elegant high streets from Bangkok and Kyoto to Singapore and Hong Kong, from Mexico City and Martinique to Caracas, from London and Paris to Rome and the medieval hills and historic towns where Francis and Clare of Assisi reinvented European monasticism.

Madam in Silk is Gini's second novel, the prequel to *The American Madams* series. She is currently at work on her next novel, *Madam in Lace*, Volume 2 in *The American Madams* series. To learn more or request Gini as a speaker, go to www.ginigrossenbacher.com, or contact her publicist, Cristina Deptula, authorslargeandsmall@gmail.com.

Author's Note

The inspiration from Ah Toy was born from reading about the first Chinese woman in San Francisco who became a madam there.

Since the records of her early life are sketchy or non-existent, some legends indicate she arrived in San Francisco alone, and some indicate she left a husband back in China. Since she came from Guangzhou, known at the time for its porcelain trade, I created her persona as from a trading family. All accounts agree that she had bound feet, and I concluded her family had money and status in China. In addition, all accounts agree that she either ran a lookee house or a house of prostitution. She managed to defend herself and her interests in court many times, which led me to conclude she must have had a more than passable level of English.

In order to smooth the narrative, I imagined that though women were not necessarily allowed to learn languages in Canton at the time, that perhaps the missionaries, such as the Daileys, would have instructed her in their school. Many accounts state that the miners had epithets for her, among them "The Girl in Apricot Silk" and "The Girl in the Green Silk Pantaloons." All accounts comment on her striking beauty and her forceful defense of her interests. In addition, they mention that she became quite wealthy in her position. Furthermore, some stories mention that she did meet and marry John Clark, the policeman, that she did return to Guangdong, and later she married a Henry Conrad and lived in San Jose.

Though I employed the outline of Ah Toy's life experiences to craft this story, her actions in the novel remain completely fictional. The historical figures such as Thomas and Rachel Larkin, Sam Brannan, and William Coleman are used fictitiously, but the activities of the Sydney Ducks and the Committee of Vigilance are based on actual events. I could find no record of Ah Toy having been arrested by the Committee, but it stands to reason that she might have met up with their members. The Vigilante hanging in Portsmouth Plaza is based on accounts from the time period.

The San Francisco and Monterey scenes are based on historical research: consultations with historians, historical images, and on-site research rounded out the background.

Curious readers should check out more on American Madams and other little-known women of American history who gave much of themselves to advance the rights and causes we often take for granted.

TURN THE PAGE FOR A PREVIEW OF

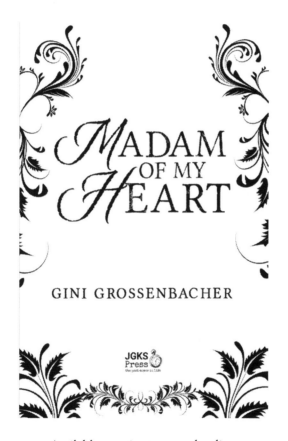

MADAM
OF MY
HEART

GINI GROSSENBACHER

JGKS
Press

Available now in stores and online

One

AS THOUGH DREAMING

New Orleans, Louisiana
May 1850

An orange twilight faded into night on the wharf, casting deep shadows into the room. Brianna sipped warm water from a flask and nibbled on stale crackers from her landlady, Madame Goulet. Night shouts floated into the boardinghouse through the open window as stevedores unloaded cargo from the last ships to arrive. A gangplank smacked on the pier, followed by the calls of sailors as they tied giant ropes and chains to the dock. Drunken laughter rose from the boardwalk, and faint strains of banjo music plunked in the distance. What was going on out there?

She peeked over the windowsill at the wharf. As the harbor quieted and stars brightened, fear tugged, and then twisted her throat. A lone stevedore coiled a rope, and then grabbed his jacket from a post and strode away toward town. The path was clear—it had to be—no time to waste. The window latch scraped shut between her thumb and forefinger. She lifted the carpetbag and found it heavier than she had expected, its precious contents nestled inside. A small key on a string glinted on the dark-red-stained bedsheets. She looped it around her neck; its weight lodged between her milk-laden breasts.

Her pulse throbbed in her ears as she crept downstairs, out of the building, and across the street to the pier. No one must see her. Mud splashed her shoes. On the quay, she explored piles of cast-off rigging. A weight—any weight—would keep the bag from floating back up to the surface. A block and tackle rested next to a gangplank from a merchant ship. If only it weren't so heavy in her arms.

Brianna cast her legs over the side of the pier. Careful not to tear this skirt, her one and only. Was that a bump down at the end of the pier? She hunched down, her palms sweaty. It must be a boat at its moorings. Luckily, no one else lingered about. The bag unlatched easily, and she lifted the package, then settled the wood pieces underneath it. They'd weigh it down.

Time to let it go. She dropped the satchel into the water. A small splash sent ripples across the black river. The bag submerged, but my God, it was floating right back up to the surface, its maroon flowers dripping.

"No, for God's sake!" The carpetbag was bobbing out on the seaward tide—not what she'd planned at all. She grabbed a stevedore's pole lying nearby. Kneeling down on the planks, she fished the bag out of the water. What if a drunken sailor were to see her? Or worse, the night watch? She set her teeth. No turning back now. She had to do this now, this way—no other choice.

Brianna made her way farther down the long pier, dragging the damp bag, rummaging in the darkness for a lead weight. She stumbled over a heavy link of iron chain left by a dockhand inside the shelter of a giant shipping crate. A bit of luck. Would she have the strength to hoist it? Luckily, the chain yielded. Courage. Stooping, she placed the chain under the package in the carpetbag. The links clanked as she moved the bag and pulled together the leather straps.

Brianna's temples pounded in the humid air. She dangled the key from the string between her teeth and sat on the edge of the dock. Her throat constricted like a winding sheet. This time, her plan had to work.

The bag lingered for a moment on the surface, but then the Father of Waters swallowed up her secret. Bubbles surfaced at the point where the cargo descended. Finally, the tension started to melt. Her carpetbag pursued a silent pathway downward to the bottom, its final resting place the illustrious Port of New Orleans.

Meanwhile, Nancy De Salle tiptoed from Skipper Seymour's cot to the ceramic washbowl. His snoring rocked the vessel. Her eyes shifted to the porthole facing the wharf. What was that movement? She squinted. None other than a young woman on the pier, alone. Whatever was she doing? Nancy wet her fingers and rubbed them against the glass, then peered into the darkness. Backlit by the stars, the girl was outlined in silver. Sure enough. The waif placed a red pouch on the water and watched it disappear into the deep. So fascinating. Next, the poor girl sat cross-legged on the dock, her eyes closed. Nancy breathed a sigh, wiping her dirty fingers against the soiled towel on the rack. How well she knew that story.

Discussion Questions

1. When Ah Toy is a child, she has bound feet which she must overcome in order to survive in America. Did you have any childhood experiences that you had to overcome in order to be the person you are today? What did those experiences teach you?

2. Once in San Francisco, Ah Toy decides to open a Lookee House since she feels she has no other options for employment. Why does she believe that? Can you think of another solution to her problem?

3. Describe John Clark's view of women early in the novel. How does his treatment of women compare with Henry Conrad's? How does the society of their time contribute to that view? How does John Clark's vantage point shift by the end of the book?

4. Ah Toy relies not only on her dragon's counsel, but also Chen, John Clark, and the Daileys throughout the book. Would you say her reliance on others was acceptable, or should she have been more self-reliant? How does her voice and confidence emerge through the novel?

5. Throughout the book, Ah Toy struggles to free herself from physical and emotional bondage at the hands of men. Given her place in history, how is her servitude of San, Yee, and Man-Man both hypocritical and understandable?

6. Ah Toy discovers Man-Man's addiction to opium too late to help her. Do you think San and Yee had a role in covering up Man-Man's attraction to the drug? What might have led Man-Man to start using drugs in the first place? Have you ever watched another person self-destruct or make unwise personal choices? Have you ever felt powerless to help them?

7. According to History.net, the California Gold Rush was the largest mass migration in American history, since it caused 300,000 people to migrate to California from all parts of the world. What lasting impact do you think this mix of cultures and backgrounds had on American society? What evidence of that do you see in California or your own state today?

8. Ah Toy follows Confucian principles, citing them in the novel. She mentions, "Master Confucius says, 'Men stay alive through straightforward conduct. When the crooked stay alive, it is simply a matter of escaping through luck.'" How do the characters in the story stay alive through straightforward conduct, despite their changing times? What other characters escape through luck? What are some examples that illustrate this principle in our own time in history?

9. In what ways are Ah Toy and John Clark able to heal from the trauma of the past at the end of the novel? In what ways have you, or others you know, healed from life's pitfalls?

10. Ah Toy makes frequent observations of, and visits to, Telegraph Hill "where she will be wrapped in blessings." How does her desire to view the world in regard to Telegraph Hill change throughout the novel? How does her final scene on the Hill foreshadow the adventures that await her and John Clark after the final pages?